The Complete Season One

Ryan Casey

ryancaseybooks.com

Copyright © 2013 by Ryan Casey.

All rights reserved. No part of this publication may be reproduced, distributed or transmitted in any form or by any means, including photocopying, recording, or other electronic or mechanical methods, without the prior written permission of the publisher, except in the case of brief quotations embodied in critical reviews and certain other noncommercial uses permitted by copyright law.

Publisher's Note: This is a work of fiction. Names, characters, places, and incidents are a product o f the author's imagination. Locales and public names are sometimes used for atmospheric purposes. Any resemblance to actual people, living or dead, or to businesses, companies, events, institutions, or locales is completely coincidental.

Dead Days/Ryan Casey. -- 1st ed.
ISBN-13: 978-1497405332
ISBN-10: 1497405335

AUTHOR'S NOTE

There are a lot of zombie stories out there nowadays.

Thanks to the rise of AMC's *The Walking Dead*, zombies are hot right now. Very hot. But what is it about *The Walking Dead* that makes the show so appealing? What sets it aside from multitude of zombie movies and books? The answer lies, I believe, in the characters.

Dead Days is also a character tale. With each of the six episodes that make up the first season, I asked myself what I would do were I in the situations the characters find themselves in? Would I have it in me to make the tough decisions? Although the work is far from autobiographical — the protagonist is way too heroic for me — I think that through studying the emotions and behaviour of humans, we can learn a lot about survival in this hypothetical apocalypse.

Dead Days is a story. It's an adventure. While it strives for some level of gritty realism, it is entertainment. Within each eighteen to twenty-two thousand word episode, there is a story. There are twists. There are turns. There will be blood and there will be tears. Nobody is safe.

Dead Days is the six-part serial adventure I've always wanted to write, inspired by some of my favourite TV shows. I hope you stick around to see how this goes down.

Enjoy the ride,
Ryan Casey.

DEAD DAYS: SEASON ONE

Episode One

Chapter One

'WHEN YOU HEAR THEM COMING, YOU know it's already too late to do anything about them.'

To this day, those words formed the best piece of advice Riley Jameson had received about dealing with the creatures. The shuffling of hundreds of decaying feet against the warm tarmac of the roads. The pitiful groans, like a choir of dead angels, restless and never-ending. But the worst sound of all, worse than anything one of those creatures made — a scream. A human scream from somebody not quite as fortunate as him. At first, Riley felt a sense of pity in the bottom of his stomach when he heard those cries. A woman, perhaps holding her toddler, cradling him in her arms as the creatures surrounded her. Or a teenager, spotty and twitchy, jeans caught around the mangled remains of a car, surrounded; his inevitable fate staring him in the face with bloody greyed-out eyes.

But after a few incidents, it wasn't a sense of pity he felt for the victims. When surviving in this new world, pity was hopeless. Pity diminished. In the place of pity, a sense of frustration.

Screams attracted attention. And once the creatures' attention was attracted, they didn't back down. Instead of thinking, 'how far away is that poor woman and her toddler? I'd love to try and save her,' the thoughts changed to, 'I hope to God that woman is far enough away from us, and I hope to God they finish her off and shut her up as soon as possible.'

Such was life in the Dead Days.

Riley lit a cigarette with his shaking hand and stared at the wreckage of the building in front of him. His heart pounded. Flames swallowed the front of the building. Screams and cries surrounded him, blurring in the corner of his eyes.

"Riley, we have to go, mate. You have to snap out of this. I'm sorry."

He recognised the voice, but it floated in through one ear and out of the other as he inhaled the smoke of the cigarette. A buzz enveloped him. A calmness that he hadn't felt in days. Weeks, even.

"Have you got that fucker out of his trance yet?" Another voice, further away. More screaming. More sobbing.

A hand rested on his shoulder. "Mate, I'm being honest with you here. There's nothing left of it. It's no use. I'm so sorry, but we're going to have to go."

A windowpane crumbled to the ground. A child cried behind him. The smoke disappeared into the night sky, from his cigarette, from the building. How had it ended up this way? After everything they'd worked for — everything they'd struggled so hard for — why did it have to come to this?

"Oh, fuck. Fuck, fuck, fuck." Another voice. "Bottom of the street. We've gotta go. We've really gotta go."

To Riley's right, at the bottom of the street, he could just about make out their shuffling in the glow of the flames. Their groans growing closer. Like ants, all of them headed in one direction — their direction.

'When you hear them coming, you know it's already too late to do anything about them.'

He dropped his cigarette to the floor and turned to the rest of the group. The ones left of them, anyway. The way they stared at him. The way their eyes scanned him, wide and desperate. A longing for him to join them. A longing for his company. How things had changed.

"Are you coming?"

Riley took a deep breath. The warmth of the burning building stung his skin as if standing too close to a bonfire. And the groans. The feet. Ten. Maybe twenty.

He had no choice, not really. It was run or stand still. And when you stood still, you were torn to pieces.

He nodded and he walked.

'When you hear them coming, you know it's already too late to do anything about them.'

Perhaps the person who had given him that advice was right about that. But one thing that they were wrong about was their declaration that they'd outlive the rest of the group.

They ran into the night, away from the approaching creatures and the burning glow of the building, into the darkness, into whatever else the Dead Days had in store for them.

Chapter Two

THE PHONES CHIMED THROUGH THE WAITING area. He squeezed his tingling hands against one another and tried to cover the patch of spilt coffee on his groin. On a clear white shirt, it would've been messy but manageable. A brown stain on a shirt was clearly food or drink. Shrugged off as an accident.

A colourless patch on the trouser groin was generally viewed as a different sort of accident.

He looked out through the window at the city centre. Rain plummeted down on crowds of day-time benefit snatchers, who still wore their tight legging bottoms and flesh-revealing hoodies despite the onset of autumn. At the end of the road, a large van sped down the street, swerving into a roadside puddle and covering an innocent passer-by in a wave of water. The drenched man stumbled and cursed at the driver, who sped off into the distance.

The door creaked. His heart thumped as he snapped out of

his daydream. Out of the windowless office, Jennifer emerged. Shiny dark hair. Beautiful soft skin.

He slipped his hand further over his groin, just to make sure the patch was still hidden.

"How'd it go, babe?" he asked.

Jennifer, who had walked past him without even acknowledging him, frowned, and stepped back, as if she was a DVD rewinding herself. Her ass wobbled as she did. *Tighter grip of the trousers. Don't want any* real *accidents to happen...*

"Babe?"

He shrugged. "Just, y'know. A nice friendly thing to call a respectable lady like yourself. Right?"

Jennifer furrowed her eyebrow further. "Don't you have a special lady in your life already, Riley? How would she feel if she found out you were calling co-workers 'babe', hmm?"

"Now, come on," Riley said. "No need to bring her into it."

A smile flickered across Jennifer's face. "Probably not the best thing to call a 'respectable lady' right in the middle of redeployment interviews either, hmm?"

"I'm just being friendly!" Riley laughed. "Seriously. How'd it go?"

"Riley Jameson?"

Riley and Jennifer looked over at the door to the office where the interviews were being held. The same bald man who had let everybody else in stood there. Overgrown freckles stretched over his crinkly head. Circular glasses rested on his arched, hairy nose.

"Yes?" Riley stumbled to his feet and loosened his collar. "Yes. Ready."

The bald man smiled and nodded. He caught a glance of Riley's groin, then disappeared back into the office.

Riley tensed his fists. *Remember what the online course said — deep breaths in through the nostrils, hold for four seconds, release. Breathe, hold, release.* He closed his eyes and walked towards the door.

"Good luck, 'babe'." Jennifer winked as he gripped the

handle of the office door.

"Thanks. But I act on knowledge and commitment, not on luck."

"Hmm." Jennifer started to walk away. "Knowledge and commitment are good. Pissing yourself isn't. You might want to cover that stain up if you want to keep your job. He's quite the ruthless chap. Laters."

She shuffled down the corridor and past the main offices as Riley's cheeks tingled. So much for fucking deep breathing exercises.

He didn't have chance to register the commotion on the television news bulletin as he entered the office.

The interviewer thumbed through a bunch of papers in front of him. It turned out his name was Graham Large. At the beginning of the interview, Riley made an ill-fated joke about how he was "rather small for a Large man". Mr. Large simply stared on from behind his round glasses and asked if Riley needed a few moments to compose himself.

Nobody had spoken for some time. Riley gripped his thighs and waited. The clock ticked through silence, every second stretching out like a number of minutes. Graham tapped his knuckles against the table, flicking through Riley's résumé with his other hand. Every now and then, he made a clicking sound with his throat, which made Riley grit his teeth and cringe.

"Well, everything *looks* okay."

Riley blinked as Graham caught him off guard, and sat back in his chair. "Ye—Yes? Okay. That's good. Isn't it?"

Graham stuck out his bottom lip and moved his head from side to side. "Yes. It's a very solid résumé. You've been responsible for a great number of well-received articles in the music world. Classical to… to R N B, or whatever it's called."

"R & B," Riley interrupted.

Graham shrugged. "Like I said." He turned the page and

ran his finger down it. "It's clear your editor here at Lancashire News thinks the world of you, too."

"Mr. Devitts is a wonderful man," Riley said. "Without him, I'm not sure I'd have got this opportunity. Not that I'm saying I'm not good enough to work on the paper. I am good enough. More than good enough. It's just..." He coughed and stopped talking.

Graham stared at Riley. "Okay. Well, like I say, everything looks good your end. You're a top music 'journo', you write good pieces, and you've got a talent with the old keyboard." He twiddled his fingertips against his desk, imitating typing.

A weight floated from Riley's shoulders. Six months of redeployment interviews. After the spending cuts required the culling of dead weight, it became much harder to hold down a job in journalism, especially media based. He knew a few people from the nationals who had lost their jobs. The landscape was becoming trickier to crack. The rise of blogs — everybody being a journalist — was a more serious challenge to traditional music journalism than anybody liked to admit.

"And you're the only 'muso' here." Graham nodded at Riley, searching for approval.

"Absolutely. I not only offer a unique take on a wide range of music, I offer the *only* take on music in the North West England area."

"Precisely." Graham closed the papers and rested his hands against the table. He leaned back into his chair and glanced at the door.

Riley shuffled in his chair. The silence returned to the room. The ticking of the clock. Did he say something? Or did he just leave? He'd saved his job, right?

"So..." Riley started.

"So the problem is I just don't think there's much room for a music journalist at the Lancashire News anymore."

Riley's mouth opened. He felt the weight come crumbling back down on his shoulders again as Graham stared on at him, poker-faced as ever. "Right. Because..."

"Because... Well, the blogs. The internet and all that. Demand. I don't think there's room anymore."

"Right." Heat worked its way up through Riley's chest. "And that's despite, y'know, being a top music journalist."

Graham nodded. "Right."

"And yeah. Despite you acknowledging I'm respected here."

Graham continued to nod.

Riley puffed out a breath of air and slumped back in his chair. Six years of working in this place. Six years of doing what he loved, and earning a living wage for it. Six years, all disappearing in a puff of smoke. All because of some arrogant toss who didn't even know the meaning of R&B.

"Is there anything I can say to... y'know? Change your mind?"

Graham shook his head. "I don't think so, Mr. Jameson. We'll be in touch."

Riley stepped to his feet. Shook Graham's limp hand and walked out of the office and down the corridor. The chatter went on. Phones continued to ring. Car horns erupted outside the window. The office buzzed around Riley as he walked towards the exit door. Six years of doing what he loved, gone.

Somebody called his name behind him. Probably Jennifer. Probably ready to gloat. He pulled open the stairway door and climbed down the steps.

Had he been totally focused, he would've noticed the small group of journalists gathered around the office television, hands covering their mouths, as the commotion excelled.

He held the phone to his ear as he walked down the high street. Mothers gripped their children's hands and rushed in and out of shops. Cars queued in the middle of the high street, honking at one another. The sirens of a police car sounded somewhere in the distance. "Preston's daily robbery," as Ted would put it. He'd have to let him know about the outcome of his interview, and what it meant for the flat. Paying rent was enough of a strain on its own, but supporting a jobless layabout who spent all day sat on his arse watching American TV marathons was almost impossible.

And now he was one of those jobless layabouts, just like Ted. Ted would have to take a bit of responsibility and stop sponging off others. Riley would have to move out. Move back in with her, if she'd have him.

"Don't you have a special lady in your life already?"

Cheeky bitch.

"Hello?"

"Er, hey, Grandma. Are you...?"

"Oh, Riley! You okay, kid? How'd it go?"

Riley tensed his jaw. He couldn't worry her, not after Grandpa's death. Not so soon afterwards, anyway. "Yeah. Yeah, it was okay."

"Okay? Well it was either good or it wasn't. Did you keep your job or what?"

"I..." A woman barged past Riley, running in the opposite direction. She almost knocked his phone out of his hand. "Watch where you're going!"

"You what, kid?"

"Not you, Grandma. Just somebody in the street. It..." Up ahead, more people ran towards him. Was there some sort of fun run on today or something? "Is something going on in town?"

"Always something going on in town these days. Anyway, the job — did you get it?"

Riley stared at the street ahead. Some of the running people rushed inside shops, slamming the doors shut as more runners smacked against the windows. "Yeah. I did. Grandma, have you checked the news?"

"Oh, of course you did! Oh, I'm so proud, Riley. Knew you'd get the job. Me and Bernice always love reading all your music stuff. Oh, you know who would be proud of you? Grandpa. He'd be so proud."

Riley saw his block of flats emerging a few hundred yards ahead. More and more people rushed past, shouting and looking over their shoulders. That expression on their faces. It wasn't a look of exertion from a mere fun run. It was a look of fear. Of panic.

"I'll have to treat you. Have to get my friends round and all celebrate."

"Don't be silly, Grandma." Riley keyed in the code for the gate of his block of flats. The high street was completely empty of people now. Cars were lined up at the opposite end of town, queueing to get on the bridge that led out of Preston and towards the surrounding areas.

"Well, if I don't treat you, who will? That imaginary girlfriend of yours? The fat housemate? No — I'll treat you. I'll —"

The gate closed behind Riley. "Seriously, Grandma. Have you checked the news today?"

There was a pause on the line as Riley walked through the courtyard and towards the parking area. The main elevator had broken recently, so there was no option but to take the stairs, accessed through the parking area.

"Grandma?"

He walked into the darkness of the parking area. Usually, it was packed with cars. The Milners. The Watsons. The four or five cars belonging to town workers who slipped them a few quid for daily access to a parking spot.

They were all gone, except for a white Fiat Punto, right in front of the stairway door.

"Speaking of news, I did see something on the news this morning. Some riots in town. But everywhere's rioting these days, aren't they? Joan said she had to hit a boy with her brolly when she was in Manchester. Tried to steal her purse, he did."

Riley approached the Fiat Punto. There was something stretched across the white paint of its exterior. A light flickered intermittently above. An unfinished attempt at a paint job. Deep, dark red paint. Strange. The car belonged to Andy, who always defended the beauty of the white car. Must've finally seen sense.

It was as he got closer to the car that he realised it wasn't a paint job at all.

Blood dripped down from the bottom of the car boot. It echoed through the parking area as it hit the ground and pooled onto the cold concrete.

Riley gulped. What sort of shit had gone down here? "Grandma, when were these riots? And did... Was anyone seriously hurt?"

"Oh, I don't know. Probably. Anyway, Riley, I have to go. Somebody's at the door. Probably one of those salesmen. Always coming at this time. Get round soon. I'll get the neighbours over and we'll celebrate with some cake." The phone cut to silence.

Riley continued to move around the car. In the flickering of the light, he could see smaller patches of blood leaving the main pool at the boot of the car. Almost as if they were in a pattern.

Footsteps.

When he moved around the side of the car, his phone dropped from his hand.

It took a moment for his eyes to process the scene. Bloody handprints were spread across the side of the white Punto. The door was slightly ajar.

And on the floor, at the end of the trail of footprints, Andy's body. Chunks of his neck were missing. His bloodshot eyes stared up at the ceiling in fear, completely lifeless. His chest had been torn completely open, his ribcage on display. Intestines and innards were spread out on top of him.

Riley turned away and heaved. *Fuck*. He'd have to tell Ted. Tell Ted and call the police. Something bad had happened here. *Fuck*. They couldn't stay here. Not after this. Not after—

Something groaned somewhere behind him.

He frowned. The groan came from the side of the Punto. Maybe there was still somebody in the car. Maybe there had been an attempted double murder and one of them had survived.

He looked at the Punto again as the groaning continued, low and raspy, and he realised that there was no second survivor after all.

The groaning was coming from Andy's butchered dead body.

Chapter Three

RILEY TENSED HIS FISTS. HE STAGGERED forward, then backwards again. He couldn't quite interpret what he saw. Andy was dead — had to be dead. The way his ribs protruded out of his flesh. His intestines stretched across the floor in front of him, laced with small tears. The blood on the car door, drip, drip, dripping to the floor. He was dead. He couldn't possibly be alive.

And yet, he let out another groan. Arched his neck upright. His eyes were as glassy as they were when Riley arrived, but it was as if he was trying to see something. Trying to see Riley.

"Andy." Riley shook. He had to help him. He must've been hurt in the riots. That's what it had to be. Clinging onto his last fragment of life. He had to help him, somehow.

Riley grabbed his phone with his shaky hand and tried to open up the contacts list. His screen had cracked on collision with the floor. A white line ran through the usual interactive display. *Fuck*. Another repair he'd have to pay out for.

Andy continued to groan. His bitten down fingernails dug into the concrete beside him. Riley could see his was tensing every muscle in his upper body. Blood dribbled out from his mouth and down his chin.

"Andy, you can't... You have to stay still." *Shit*. What did he do? What did anybody do with a man who should be dead groaning and struggling on the floor?

Riley crouched down and moved his hand towards Andy's head. He had to try something. Arch his neck upright, or whatever they'd taught him in that Health and Safety lecture a few years back.

As he reached for his neck, Andy growled and snapped his teeth at Riley's wrist.

Riley yanked his arm away and stumbled back. There were teeth marks in his blazer material. *Fuck*. He'd have to get that checked when he got back to the flat. Yes — get back to the flat. That's what he needed to do. Borrow Ted's phone and get some help.

Andy continued to gnash his teeth. He was almost arched upright now. The guts. The blood. None of it even seemed real anymore. It was like a waxwork in Madame Tussauds. A bad dream that he still hadn't quite adjusted to.

Riley stood up and started to stagger to the stairway door at the side of the Punto. As he did, Andy stretched up, still clicking his teeth against one another.

But Riley didn't notice the teeth for long, as Andy's upper body tore itself free from his legs.

Andy's innards slid free of his lower body as he moved onto his stomach. He dragged himself with his hands, his fingers bleeding from digging into the ground. He groaned and groaned as, slowly, he started to get closer to Riley.

"Fuck. Fuck, fuck, fuck." Riley turned from Andy and grabbed the handle of the stairway door. Andy continued to groan behind him. A dead man in two halves. A dead man alive. This wasn't real.

This was the stuff he read about in books. Things he

watched and cheered on in films and television shows. This wasn't real. It couldn't be real.

He opened the door into the darkness of the stairway and slammed it shut behind him. Andy continued to groan. He could still hear him as he dragged his body against the floor, getting closer and closer.

Riley rushed up the stairway without looking back. He thought he heard moans crying out from the walls. The dust that covered the tiny window at the top of the first set of stairs had the print of a hand pressed against it.

The bloody handprint.

Andy's dead body pulling itself in two.

No. There was a logical explanation for it all. Andy couldn't have been dead. And when he'd snapped his teeth at Riley, he was just having a seizure, or something.

The shuffling against the floor. The tapping against the stairway door.

Three floors to go. Two floors to go… *Keep calm. Deep breaths in and deep breaths out.*

When he reached his floor, he yanked his keys out of his pocket and rushed towards his flat. The door was on the left of a long, dusty corridor. Mould grew on the walls beside the bathroom at the bottom. There were six flats on each floor. All the doors were locked shut.

Riley struggled to slip the key into the lock. Something made a sound outside the flats — a whirring noise, like a helicopter. A crashing sound. Screams. The riots that Grandma had mentioned. That's all it was — a set of riots. Hooligans.

He pushed his door open and barged into the room.

Ted was sat in his usual spot — on a beanbag in front of the sofa. There was a permanent crater in the beanbag from where he spent his days, perfectly moulded to his fat ass. He had a greasy Xbox controller in one hand and a nacho in the other. He barely looked up at Riley as he entered the room, turning back to his videogame and cursing at the screen.

"Ted," Riley shouted. He stepped in front of the television.

"Hey, mate, watch yourself." Ted swung his head either side to get a better look at the television. "In the middle of something he... Holy shit, man. What the hell happened to you? Interview go badly?"

Riley rolled up the sleeve where Andy's teeth had pierced. There were a couple of marks from the impact, but his skin hadn't been torn. Could get by without a plaster or a bandage. The blazer could be fixed.

"Seriously, you're pale as fuck. And you're shaking. Which must mean... You've not got the job. We're going to lose the flat. We'll be selling our bodies on street corners in no time."

Riley disregarded Ted and walked to the window. He pulled open the red curtains. The streets were empty. Three helicopters hovered overhead. The doors of cars that had been trying to cross the bridge were open now, people disappearing into the distance on foot. Something had happened down by the river. Something bad.

"I've got the sickest thing to tell you. There was this dude from America on Call of Duty and we teamed up and—"

"Ted, have you seen the news today?"

Ted frowned. "Me? Seen the news? What do you think?"

Riley sighed and grabbed the remote control beside Ted, almost knocking a half empty bottle of Coke over in the process.

"Hey — what do you think you're doing?"

The sound of rifles from the videogame gave way to a rolling news bulletin. Fighting in the streets. Screaming as women held the hands of their children and sprinted away from an invisible oncoming enemy. The headline, "Violent Riots Continue to Grip Nation". There was no news commentary. Just a rolling headline and rolling footage.

"Ah man, that's boring. Everyone's rioting these days. Rioting is the new peace. Damn, man, what happened to your phone?"

Riley worked his finger across the cracked screen of his

phone. He saw his reflection. Bags underneath his eyes. Completely pale face. Fingers crossed he hadn't looked that bad in the interview.

Even if he had, he got the feeling it wouldn't matter quite so much anymore.

"Wait," Ted said. He waddled to his feet, the beanbag clinging around his wide arse. "Wait — don't tell me *you've* been rioting? Is that why you're acting all weird?"

"Ted, I..." His throat was croaky. Speaking seemed alien. Andy, tearing himself in two and dragging his upper body towards him.

"Mate," Ted said. He placed a hand on Riley's shoulder. "What's up? You... It isn't Grandma, is it?"

Grandma. Her planned celebrations. Oblivious. Unaware of what was going on.

He looked down at the tear in his blazer. Thought of the glazed, dead eyes. He'd seen this before. In films. Read it in books.

No. That was fiction. There was a logical explanation for this.

"I... Andy. He's... he's dead."

"Andy? Well, erm... that's a shame. But I, erm... I didn't realise you cared so much about the guy."

"I found him. Downstairs in the parking bay. I found his body. He's... He's torn in two."

Ted lowered the nacho from his mouth and widened his eyes. "What the fuck? In two? Why didn't you say?"

"And he's still alive."

Ted blinked rapidly. He opened his mouth to speak, then closed it again and cleared his throat. "Mate — I love you, and everything. You're my bro from another... another 'mo', right? But you really are beginning to creep me out. You're talking like a... like a crazy, or something. You aren't having problems again, are you?"

"He's dead and he's in two and he's... he's dragging his upper body along. I can't... Something's happening. The riots and the cars and the helicopters. Something terrible is happening and I don't think anybody realises how bad it is yet."

Ted picked up his Coke bottle and took a swig. He offered some to Riley, who ignored his gesture. "Listen. How about we go downstairs and we check up on this... this situation you're talking about. Okay? I'll come with you. Hold your hand and all that."

Riley shook his head. "I don't think you understand. I saw a dead man move. I..." He held his blazer sleeve up. "He tried to bite me."

Ted laughed. "Dude, he took a fair nosh out of that, didn't he? You sure you didn't, y'know, just catch it on the stair railing or something?"

"I know what I saw. We need to go back down there. We need... You need to see it for yourself."

Ted looked at the TV and gritted his teeth. Then, he tossed his Xbox controller onto the cushionless sofa and licked his fingers. "Okay. Try me. Let's do this."

Riley took a deep breath and grabbed the handle of their flat door.

The bulletin continued to roll across the television. No voiceover. Repeated images. An automated warning.

"So you're with me?"

Ted rolled his eyes. They stood beside the door into the car park. The shuffling and the groaning — it had disappeared. The only sound was that of a helicopter somewhere far in the distance. The screams down the high street had receded. No engine sounds. It felt empty. Dead.

"Don't roll your eyes," Riley said. "This is serious. It's—"

"A hungry dead Andy without any legs. Right. I mean, excuse me for being sceptical but it's hardly on my list of things I expect to see every day. Have you been stealing my weed again?"

Riley gripped tighter hold of the handle. "We go out there,

you look at him — you look at him so you can get it in your stupid head that I'm serious — and then we get back to the flat and figure out what the hell we're going to do about it."

Ted shrugged. "Lead the way, sir. No need to be so... offensive about things. I happen to have a rather clever head, I'll have you know."

"You won't be joking when you see it. Believe me, you won't."

Riley held his breath and opened the door. The dim lighting of the parking area flickered through into the stairway. The white Fiat Punto was still beside the door, painted in blood.

But something was missing. Andy was missing. Both halves.

"Holy shit." Ted staggered towards the car, wide-eyed. He reached out to touch the blood, but pulled his hand back. "We need to report this. Get the police down here right now. Maybe he's—"

"Shush," Riley said. "Keep quiet. Something's missing. The body, and the legs. They're both gone. He was here, and now he's gone."

"Okay, okay. But let's forget about your crazy talk and focus on what we can really see right now — a shit load of blood." He lifted his phone to his ear.

"Who the hell do you think you're calling?"

"The police. Who else? Hello, can I... Oh." He put the phone back in his pocket and stared at Riley. His face had lost its colour. "Voicemail."

"Emergency services on voicemail. *Now* do you believe me that something's going on here?"

Riley and Ted glared at one another. The blood reflected the light as it twinkled above. The parking area was completely silent. Completely void of life.

Ted crouched down and looked at the blood. "You say... You say this is Andy's?"

"Andy who was here ten minutes ago, yeah. Andy whose

body was in two."

"Then... then where is he now?"

Riley looked around the parking area. Just the one car. Andy could be behind a concrete pillar. Or outside — he could've gone outside. Or perhaps Riley was just going crazy. Startled by the amount of blood and projected a vision, or something like that.

"The fact of the matter is, we need to get back into that flat and decide what we're going to do here."

Ted slammed Andy's ajar car door shut. "Like, a crisis talk, or something?"

"Yes, a crisis talk. My Grandma — she... she's on her own. She has no idea about any of this. And your rents—"

"They're in Gran Canaria sunning it up. They'll be safe as houses." He started to walk towards Riley.

Somewhere in the distance, Riley thought he heard a shuffling.

"Two weeks in the land of the sun. Lucky gits—"

"Shush, one second. Do you hear that?"

Ted squinted. "Hear what?"

At first, there was no sound other than the pair of them breathing. Ted shrugged.

But then it happened again. A movement somewhere in the distance. Somewhere outside the parking area.

A nausea welled up in Riley's stomach. Ted looked over his shoulder at the doorway leading outside. He had to see it. He had to show Ted so he understood. They both needed to know what they were dealing with.

They started to creep away from the Punto. The movement was growing closer. A groan, somewhere up ahead. The hairs pricked up on Riley's arms. The groan from before — croaky, lifeless. It was Andy. It had to be.

When they reached the entrance area of the parking lot, Riley covered his mouth with his finger. Ted nodded, and the pair of them peeked out at the courtyard.

There was a trail of blood on the floor. It was roughly as

wide as a human body. Riley held his breath and dug his teeth into his lips as he began to follow it outside. It swerved to the right of the courtyard, towards the main gate. The shuffling had stopped, but the groaning was louder than ever.

Riley stalled at the corner. The groaning was so close. He looked at Ted and nodded. "One look. That's all you'll need," he whispered. Then, the pair of them poked their heads around the corner.

One look really was all they needed.

The upper half of Andy's body was at the gate. His fingers clawed against the chained fencing, propping himself up. His intestines dangled from his body and onto the floor behind him, like a tail.

And at the other side of the fence, there were a group of people crouched down on their knees. For a split second, Riley thought about calling for them.

But then he saw the blood dripping from the mouth and down the neck of a girl. The glassy, glazed over eyes. Eyes like Andy's.

But mostly, his eyes were focused on the thing they were eating.

It was a man. He was wearing a strange suit, like quarantine gear. A broken suitcase rested beside him, his fingers gripping it tightly. Through his blood-drenched white jacket, the creatures were sticking their hands in, dragging chunks of raw meat to their mouths and ravishing it.

"Oh… Oh God," Ted mumbled.

One of group turned around and faced Riley and Ted as Andy let out a large groan. Another of them let out a groan, and another followed. Soon enough, all of them were at the gate, blood-drenched bodies pressed up against it, blocking any possible form of exit.

Ted's hands started to shake. "I… I think we should go back to the flat. Crisis talk."

Chapter Four

THEY STUMBLED BACK AROUND THE CORNER and into the parking lot. Ted fell against the wall, panting. Sweat dripped down the side of his face.

And at the gate, around the corner, the groans. The rattling of the chain metal fence. Six or seven of the creatures, all lined up against it, pushing their way in.

"Come on. We've got to get back and work out what we're —"

"You saw those things. You—you saw what they were doing to that man. We've no chance, mate. We're… we're food to them. What the fuck? What the actual fuck?"

"Ted!" Riley crouched opposite him and put his hand on his shoulder. "You've got to snap out of this. I… I know it's not good what happened out there, okay? But we're fortunate. We're in a fifth floor flat. We can ride this out until…"

"Until what? What exactly are we riding out here? Because, I hate to say it, but the emergency services don't look like they're paying much attention anymore. Do you hear any sirens? See any police? And those helicopters — hear them anymore?" Ted shoved his phone into Riley's chest and barged past him. "How about you ring them and leave them a fucking voicemail?"

"Then what do you propose we do? Give up? We have to think this through, Ted. We can't go making any rash decisions. You... you've seen what these things do. We can't let that become us. And that's all I care about."

"All you care about?" Ted swung around and squared up to Riley. The groaning and the shuffling grew louder. "What about your dear grandma, hmm? Don't you care about her?"

Grandma. She wouldn't have any idea about any of this. The last time he'd spoken to her, she'd...

"Oh. Oh shit."

Riley pushed past Ted and rushed back in the direction of the exit gate.

"Woah, woah, woah," Ted said, jumping in front of Riley. "In case you haven't already noticed, there's not a fucking chance you're leaving through that route in one piece. And as annoying as you can be, I quite like you in one piece."

Riley's head throbbed. *"Somebody's at the door. Probably one of those salesmen."* Grandma's final words. "Grandma. She... she's in trouble. We need to help her."

Ted shook his head. "Of course she's in trouble. We... I think it's pretty clear we all are. But your grandma. She should be okay, man. She... she never left the house really, right?"

"Unless it was to answer the door to somebody. Shit." Riley walked back towards the stairway door. "I need to go and see she's okay."

Ted groaned and followed Riley. "The fuck, mate? She lives at the other side of town. If these... these things. If they're all over town, then you don't stand a chance."

"I have to try. She's all I have. She's done everything right for me since my parents left. You know what she pulled me back from better than anybody. I can't abandon her, not now."

He walked towards the white Fiat Punto as the roaring of dead voices continued outside.

Ted stood in the middle of the parking area shaking his head. "It's too risky. Way too risky. I hardly think the bus service will be running through all this either."

Riley grabbed the door of the Punto with his sleeve, being careful not to touch the blood. Couldn't take any chances. They didn't even know how this virus spread yet. If it even was a virus. Was that just something he was taking from TV? Inside the Punto, the car keys dangled from the engine. "This looks good enough for me."

Ted's mouth dropped. "But you... Your license. You aren't supposed to drive for... for weeks, right?"

"Ted, I hardly think chasing up license points is the priority of the police right now. Besides, I'd rather it be me driving than you." Riley closed the door of the car and walked up to Ted. "I'll go back to the flat, get a few supplies — food, drinks — and go to my grandma's."

"And the creatures outside the gate? How are you going to drive past those?"

Ted had a point. But the flat, it was positioned around the corner from the gate. "If we can drop something out of the flat window, then we can try and distract them. It's worth a shot, right?"

Ted's gaze wandered. His bottom lip shook. "Wha... What about me?"

Riley shrugged. A movement caught his eye over by the exit. It was the top half of Andy's body dragging himself slowly towards them. Stretching out his bloodstained fingers. Cracking his teeth against one another. "You can stay here or you can come with me. That's your choice. We... We're going to have to do something about him though."

Ted turned to look at Andy. The pair of them watched as he struggled ever closer. Dead eyes. Possessed muscles. Dragging his upper body along the ground with every last ounce of strength. They'd have to get rid of him somehow.

Whatever he was, he wasn't Andy anymore.

"If I can bring my nachos along, I'll take my chances on the road with you."

A tension rose in Riley's throat. "You... You don't have to do that. You know you don't."

Ted smiled and stared at Andy's half-body, edging ever closer, so slowly. "What's my other option? Who else do I have?" He walked over towards the elevator and pressed the button. "I mean, the idea of locking myself away and playing Call of Duty sounds great, but I dunno. The noises outside could get kinda distracting."

Andy was a matter of metres away now. Teeth marks across his neck. Dried blood covering his cracked head. "We'll go back to the flat. Get some supplies. Attempt a distraction. Then I'll... I guess we'll drive over Andy and put him... put him out of his misery. Elevator's still not working, by the way." Riley stepped away from the stairway door and circled Andy, drawing his retching body away so he wasn't too close.

The elevator pinged to life. "Well I'll be damned," Ted said. "Looks like it's working after all."

A sudden dread hit Riley in the stomach.

The bite marks on Andy's neck.

The gaping wound that had torn his torso in two.

Somebody had already started feasting on Andy, and they were nowhere to be seen.

"Looks like the doors are as sticky as ever though." Ted bashed his thumb against the switch and stepped back.

"Stop!" Riley rushed towards Ted, his heart racing. "The elevator — get away. Get the fuck back!"

Ted looked around, bemused. "What are you—"

Riley grabbed Ted and pulled him back as the elevator doors creaked open.

Inside, the six-strong family of Polish immigrants from the fourth floor turned around to face them.

Their eyes were glazed. Blood dribbled down their chins.

And on the floor in front of them rested a half-eaten pair

of legs.

"Get to the stairs!"

Riley scrambled to his feet, grabbing at Ted's collar. Ted was static, staring up at the six creatures in the elevator, transfixed.

The tall, bald man who looked like he was constantly ill.

The slightly chubby wife, a chunk of flesh missing from her stomach.

And their four children. Eyes glazed. Limbs bent and disfigured.

"Ted, quick! We need to get back!"

Ted's entire body shook as the creatures staggered out of the elevator, dropping Andy's missing pair of legs to the ground like leftover food. He scrambled backwards as Riley grabbed him underneath his armpits before stumbling to his feet and shimmying in reverse.

They started to run towards the stairway door, away from the crowd of oncoming creatures. Riley's heart raced. His vision blurred and every sound seemed like it was out of proportion with reality. They had to get out of here. Somehow, they had to get back to the flat and get out of here.

"Watch out!"

Ted's voice.

Something solid beneath his feet.

He looked down and he saw Andy's upper body right in front of him.

He yanked his foot backwards and jumped over Andy as his teeth tried to gnash at Riley's lower leg. *Shit. So close. Too close. Try to stay calm. Try to stay cool.*

Ted held the stairway door open and waved Riley through. His eyes were widened, focused on the creatures. The shuffling feet. The chesty cries. *Get to the stairs. Keep on running and get to the stairs.*

He reached the door and took a final look back at the room. All six of the creatures staggering towards them. Six and a half, counting Andy's half a body. All of them blocking access to the car.

The gates rattled in the background.

They were trapped.

The dialling rattled in Riley's ear.

Ring.
Ring.
Ring.

He tightened his other hand. Waited for an answer. Sweat dripped down his face and his heart crashed against his sternum, any harder and it might just explode. The empty blue screen of the television, switched to the rolling news channel, illuminated the room.

Ring.

Ted perched beside the main window staring out at the street. Occasionally, he tutted, and shook his head. Swore under his breath. The groans were still just about audible right up on the fifth floor.

"I'm sorry, but the person you called is not available at the moment. Please try again later, or leave a message after the—"

Riley hit the cancel icon and slid Ted's phone across the floor.

"No luck?" Ted asked.

Riley shook his head. "She always answers her phone when she's home. Always."

"I... I'm sure she'll be okay, mate. Maybe a neighbour went round to help her out. Maybe she's in someone's attic keeping herself safe. She's more in the countryside than us, right? She... she'll be okay."

Riley stared into space. The pride in her voice when he'd told her he'd managed to keep hold of his job. *"Oh, of course you did!"* Her faith, unwavering, but completely misguided. She should have left him to fend for himself when his parents went away. Should have left him in his one-roomed pot-filled hole to fend for himself and learn to get back on his feet the hard way, like everybody else did.

"She's a... Well, a tough lady anyway. Remember when she pushed me down the stairs when she thought I was an intruder that time? Nobody's gonna barge past your old Gran!" Ted attempted a laugh of reassurance, but his face soon straightened again, and he looked back out of the window.

"See anything out there?"

Ted exhaled and puffed out his lips. "These ghouls. Wandering aimlessly around the street. Abandoned cars. I just... I don't get it. I don't get how something like this can happen. How it can all just... just break out like this in no time?"

Riley crouched beside Ted and stared out of the window. A woman in a flowery dress, grey skinned, blood dripping from her half-eaten jaw. A man wearing a builder's cap, crouched on the ground, feasting on the remains of a body. All of their lives. All of their normal lives, gone in a violent, bloody few moments.

"I mean, do you think it's airborne? Or something in the water? Or... What about us? What if we have it?"

"I don't know," Riley snapped. "Nobody knows. The news channels clearly don't know and aren't going to tell us any time soon. The police and the emergency services — well. I don't see them anywhere. I just... The fact is, we're alive. We're not one of those things. No matter how it happened. What matters is now." He stepped up and shot across the room, grabbing what remained of the canned food from the broken-doored cupboard and stuffing it into a black rucksack on the sofa.

"What are you thinking, mate?"

"I'm getting out of here. Getting to my Grandma as soon as possible. If there's a chance she's still alive — if there's the smallest of chances — then I have to take that chance. She would've done it for me." He walked to the door and gripped the handle.

Ted's hand came down hard on his shoulder. "You saw what it's like down there. I don't... Mate, you know I love you like a bro, but this is suicide. There's six — six-and-a-half of those things down in the parking area alone, and that's before you even get beyond the gates. You aren't thinking straight. You need a plan. We need a plan."

Riley held the handle of the door. He wanted to open it. He wanted to walk on out there and charge past them. He wanted to get into the Punto and drive through them as fast as possible.

But Ted was right. It was suicide.

He moved his hand away from the handle and leaned against the wall beside the door. "We need to distract them. Somehow, we need to distract them."

"Like a pair of legs?" Ted said.

Riley frowned. "What do you mean?"

Ted shrugged and walked back into the lounge area. He picked up an empty bottle of Coke from the floor and tossed it towards the overflowing bin, where it fell atop the rest of the missed litter. "Well, I'm thinking you saw a body torn in two. And then we go down there, what — ten, fifteen minutes later? And the legs are in an elevator with a bunch of those things. Does that not say something to you?"

The realisation washed over Riley. Andy's legs. The way they were there in the parking lot, and the way they vanished. "Somebody put those legs in there with them. They... they were trying to feed them."

Ted nodded. "Maybe the elevator was on another of the floors and they were trying to draw the creatures towards it or something. An escape plan of some form. Whatever they tried, I hope it worked for them. But... Well. It didn't work so much for us."

Riley rubbed his temples. They needed a distraction. Some form of distraction that would clear a good enough path for them to get into the Punto, and then to get out of the gates. A plan was laying itself out, piece by piece in front him. Every piece he saw of it, he wanted to unsee. But it was all they had.

"Remember when you were paranoid about there being a

fire in the corridor and you… you were going on about getting a rope ladder in case we couldn't reach the fire escape?"

Ted shrugged. "Well, yeah. Still worries me to the day. Never did test the thing."

"So you *have* a rope ladder?"

Ted began to nod, but it soon turned to a shake of the head. "No. No. Whatever you're thinking, no. We can't just climb out there. You've seen the streets — it's madness. Even if there is a car out there with keys inside, we'll be torn to pieces before we even have the chance to ask 'manual or automatic?'"

Riley rose to his feet and walked over to the window. He brushed his fingers against the ledge, then tensed and lifted the window. A gust of air worked its way through the room, sending empty crisp packets to the floor.

"Oh, he's serious. He's actually serious and he's completely lost it. I will not be a part of your crazy suicide act. I will not be—"

"You don't have to be," Riley said. The unstoppable groaning sounded through the open window. Exhaust fumes were strong in the air. "One of us is going to distract those on the outside, and the other is going to deal with those in the inside. We're going to get out of here."

Ted backed away. His mouth jolted open and shut as he narrowed his eyes and squinted at Riley. "We… We're going… But who does what?"

Riley reached into his pocket and pulled out a two pence coin. He flipped it in the air and slapped it against the back of his hand. "I suppose the only diplomatic way of answering that question is the good old fashioned method. Heads or tails?"

Chapter Five

"SO YOU'RE OKAY WITH DOING THAT?"

Ted rubbed his head in his hands. His greasy fringe dangled over his fingertips as he inhaled and exhaled audibly. Something else Riley had taught him. A calming method. One of his favourites.

"I climb out of the window," Riley said. "I shout and attract the attention of the ones on the outside. Draw them away from the gate. Keep them distracted."

"And that shout is my cue. Yeah, I get it. I get it." Ted slumped back against the sofa and stared at the blue screen of the television longingly, his Xbox fan still whirring by its side. "I go down the stairs, get the Polish creatures down there to follow me, then get back here and tug the rope ladder—"

"—But call the elevator first, remember. We don't want to get caught by them waiting for the elevator. And make sure they follow you into the stairway. All of them. Okay?"

Ted sighed and shook his head. "Yeah, yeah. It's mad.

That's what it is. Mad. They might catch us when we're making our way back to the elevator. But strangely, I don't think we have much of a choice right now. And of the limited choices we do have, which as far as I can tell stops at 'die in a heap of microwave enchiladas and Gears of War', it's probably the least nihilistic choice, too."

"Right." Riley poked his head out of the window. Creatures were scattered around the street, but none of them close enough to pose an immediate threat. As he stuck his head further out, he could see the group still pressing against the gate, ten or twelve of them now, still trying to force themselves through. A bunch of them were gathered behind them, feasting on a body.

"You'll need this." Ted handed Riley the unopened rope ladder. "Never did learn how to use it, mind."

Riley glared at Ted. "You're saying you never tested this thing?"

"Hey — I'm a big-boned man, okay? I hardly wanted to risk snapping it or anything like that, unless I really had to. But you should be okay, you little runt." He jabbed Riley between his protruding ribs. "I, er… I guess I should call that elevator."

Riley nodded as Ted's eyes diverted to the floor. "Yeah. I guess."

Ted let out a sharp breath and attempted a shaky smile at Riley. "And, um. In case this doesn't work. In case anything happens. I—"

"Hey." Riley hit Ted back in his flabby stomach. "This is going to work. Okay?"

Ted turned away and walked over to the flat door as Riley hooked the rope ladder over the edge of the window. "I hope so, mate. I really hope so. I still need to get my own back for that FIFA defeat, after all."

Riley smiled. "That's the only thing I'm certain is not going to happen. Good luck, Ted."

"You too. You too." He turned the handle of the flat door

and disappeared into the corridor.

A sickness welled in Riley's stomach. For the first time since he'd become aware that something was desperately wrong, he felt alone. Completely alone.

It was the same feeling he'd felt when he'd walked away from that interview room, coffee stain spread across his crotch.

"We're coming for you, Grandma. We're coming."

He unraveled the rope ladder and watched as it fell to the ground below. Some of the creatures in the distance arched their heads to see what the movement was, but turned away again and continued to stagger around aimlessly. There was a deathly silence in the air. He'd never before thought it possible for everything to collapse within such a short space of time, but now he'd seen just how fragile the world really was. Society was just one big ant's nest, built on weak foundations, waiting for somebody to stuff their foot inside and kick it into oblivion.

Only difference was that humans had a weaker bite. Alive ones, anyway.

"Better hurry, mate."

Riley jumped and swung around. Ted peeked his head through the flat door.

"I called the elevator. If you want to avoid a date with the hungry Poles, you'd better hurry." He disappeared out of sight again.

Riley stared down at the rope ladder. The floor looked like it was miles away, growing further and further into the distance the longer he stared at it. He blinked his eyes rapidly and straightened his neck, then placed his foot onto the first of the unstable metal steps.

Deep breaths. You can do this.

Descending the rope ladder was like climbing an attraction in a children's playground. He'd always been awful at climbing frames and rope swings as a child. Even the stairs of some slides sent him a bit dizzy. A coin flip. *Fucking 'Queen's Head'.* Perhaps she'd heard his rant against the monarch in the pub a few weeks ago.

Then again, he trusted himself on a rickety rope ladder more than he trusted Ted's weight.

The further he got down, the closer the groans and the tapping of the fence grew. He glanced at the floor quickly and immediately realised his mistake. Elevated three stories into the air by an untested piece of rope. He could fall to the ground. Break his legs. They'd find him trying to struggle away. Surround him. Sink their teeth into his stomach and into his neck, piercing his jugular, and there's nothing he'd be able to do about it.

No. Keep calm. You can do this. You can fucking *do this.*

He took another few steps, and he noticed that something was different. Something in the air. The sounds.

And then he realised what it was. The rattling of the gate. It had stopped.

He bit his lip and turned his neck slowly to his right hand side. He was elevated about a storey above the pavement, high enough to stay out of reach but hardly comfortable. A breeze whistled through the street as the scattered creatures in the distance looked on at nothing in particular, glassy-eyed and dazed.

But at the gate, he saw one of them starting to turn around. Starting to edge towards him. It was a woman. The bottom half of her jaw was missing. Tears of blood dripped down her cheeks. She stepped up from beside the half-eaten man wearing a quarantine suit and pottered in Riley's direction.

Riley tightened his grip on the rope ladder and held his breath. This was it. If one came, surely the others would follow. He'd have to shout for them just to be sure. He didn't know how they worked, or if they communicated in any way. That's just something they'd have to learn over time.

If they ever got the chance to.

He started to open his mouth to shout when the creature woman let out a pained moan.

When she did, the other ten or so gathered over the body looked around. Creatures across the street started to twitch and arch their necks in the direction of the continuous moaning. The woman got closer and closer to Riley as he dangled above the street. She reached her arm out when she was directly underneath him, stretching it so hard that it looked like it might fall out of its already torn socket.

"He—Hey," Riley shouted. His jaw and hands shook as the woman's moans turned into manic screeches beneath him. The other creatures were all walking in his direction now — creatures from down the street that he hadn't seen before. Creatures from empty cars, from behind hidden corners. One by one, they started crying out, and others followed.

"Hey!" Riley shouted again. He kept tight hold of the rope ladder. A crowd of twenty or thirty were gathered underneath his feet, all of them reaching up for him, trying to wrap their fingers around the rope ladder, which didn't quite reach as far down as them. The fence was clear. If Ted hurried, they could make it out. But there was no telling how Ted was getting on. He could've just started luring them out, or he could've finished minutes ago. The Polish family could be waiting for Riley to return to his flat, biding their time…

But no. He had to think about the task at hand. He had to wait for Ted to tug on the rope ladder. He'd come good. He glanced below. The creatures were all reaching up towards him, falling over one another and gnashing at thin air with their broken teeth. Worse than the sound was the smell. A group of twenty to thirty recently deceased bodies, flesh exposed, breath pungent from their raw meat feast. Riley tried not to breathe in too deeply and gripped hold of the metal pole of the rope ladder, which swung side to side.

It could snap. It could drop at any moment, and he'd be food. Food for all of them.

No. Keep calm. Stay fucking calm.

He clenched his eyes shut and waited. Waited for a sudden shift in the weight of the ladder. Weighted for Ted's voice above him. He counted the seconds. The seconds turned to one minute. Then two minutes. The rope ladder still swung lightly from side to side. The ravenous cries continued beneath him, attempting to nip at his ankles just metres away.

Then, he felt a tugging. A slight shift in the weight above him. He looked up. Panted rapidly. A hand was holding the rope ladder. He couldn't see their face.

"Ted?" Riley called. "We ready to go, Ted?"

The hand disappeared back into the flat. Nobody responded.

The cries of the creatures intensified beneath him as he shouted out. More of them started to approach from the distance. Why wouldn't Ted show himself? If everything had gone okay, then why wouldn't he respond?

Fuck it. The creatures were probably close. Ted was probably trying not to attract the Poles' attention. He clambered up the rope ladder, and the shouting below him grew gradually further away.

He kept on staring upwards. Watched the rope ladder swing from side to side as he clambered up it. His hands shook. He had to be quick. The creatures — they had to keep focused on him. They had to stay put, or it would all be for nothing.

The window was getting closer now. He was more than half way up. The fourth storey. He could make this. He could do this.

Something snapped beneath his feet.

His body fell downwards. He gripped the sides of the rope ladder as he plunged back in the direction of the creatures. The groans got louder again. He closed his eyes and screamed out. *Fuck. Fuck. Fuck.*

Then, he stopped.

He opened his eyes. He was holding tightly onto the bottom of the rope ladder, swinging above the creatures. There was barely any ladder left to hold onto as the bloody fingernails of the dead scratched at his shoes. He pulled himself back up. Calmed and steadied his frantic breathing. *Fuck. You're okay. You're okay.*

He climbed up the rope ladder again, watching closely as he placed his jittery foot on the steps. When he got to the fourth floor, he saw one of the metal steps dangling out of the rope, torn on the left side. Good job Ted hadn't been the one to test it after all. He'd been close. Too close.

"Here, Ted." He sighed as he reached their flat window. The creatures were still gathered in a crowd beneath him, stretching and stretching as if they expected him to fall by magic, or grow wings and fly up to him. *Fuck.* That didn't bear thinking about.

He dragged himself over the window ledge and tumbled to the floor, staring up at the ceiling. But there was no time to mope. No time to calm himself down. He had to get to the elevator. Ted must be there. He had to hurry.

As he turned over, he realised he wasn't as alone as he had first thought.

A woman was holding a gun to Ted's head. Her hands were shaking, and her dark mascara ran down her pale, gaunt cheeks. "Give me the keys to the car, or I'll shoot. I swear, I'll shoot."

Chapter Six

TED WINCED AS THE GUN SMACKED against his face. He spat blood out onto the floor. A bruise was forming underneath his eye.

Riley stepped back with his hands raised. Seeing a gun in the UK wasn't the most common of events. Sure — they were all over television, videogames, films, books. But seeing one — staring into the barrel of one — the gun seemed different. It wasn't quite as taken for granted as it was in those movies. It was real. So real.

The woman snivelled. Her long, greasy dark hair dangled down onto her shoulders. Snot ran from her nostrils, mixing with tears. She had a cut above her lip. Riley thought she looked familiar. Probably seen her around the flat block at some point.

"Just give me the car keys and I'll go. That's all you need to do."

Riley's heart raced. Ted had the car keys. He must've told

her Riley had them, seeking his help or something. If he could get her to lower the gun — talk her out of it — they'd have a shot at walking out of here. All of them. "You don't have to do this. We should be fighting them, not each other."

"Do you know what I... I had to do? What I had to watch?" Tears poured from the woman's eyes. The gun shook in her hand.

Riley took a step forward. He had to try something.

"No." The woman raised her gun and pointed it at Ted's head. "Don't come another step closer. Don't."

Riley stopped and raised his hands. *Deep breaths. Keep calm.* "We aren't your enemies. And I'm sorry for what might have happened to you. But that isn't between you and us. Come on. Let's... let's all leave this room. Let's get out of here. We need to stick tog—"

"Shut up. Shut. Up. Try telling my boyfriend to stick together when they... they attacked him. Just try."

A weight welled up in Riley's stomach. His eyes met Ted's as the woman scratched her wrist. "Your... Your boyfriend. Where is he?"

The woman lowered her gun slightly. Her bottom lip was trembling. "He... He's sick. But I have to get him out. I have to get him to a hospital. I need the keys to that car. Now." She turned her gun to Ted again and smacked him across the face.

Riley winced and stepped backwards. He could still hear the creatures groaning outside. But Ted's side of the deal. Distracting the Poles. They'd be coming. If he'd carried it out, they'd be approaching them, slowly but surely climbing the stairs. They had to get to the elevator.

"Ted — did you do it?" Riley asked.

The woman frowned and looked between them. Ted nodded. "Yes. I did it. We need to be quick."

"What the fuck is he talking about?"

"Please," Riley said. He started to walk to the woman, his hands raised. "You need to listen to me. Right now, we have one chance to get out of this building. That's why I was outside and he was in here. We found a way out and past these creatures."

"Then tell me. Tell me the way out and we can get this over with and I—I can get my boyfriend seen to."

Riley shook his head and carried on walking towards the woman. Every step he took, her gun raised, but faltered soon after and lowered. "We can help you. We can help your boyfriend. We can all get out of here. But you need to lower your gun and come with us, quickly. We only have one shot at this. One shot. What do you say?"

Riley and the woman stared one another in the eye. Ted looked between them, still on his knees, waiting for their verdict.

The woman dropped her gun and covered her eyes. "Okay. Let's... Okay. But we have to help him. Please."

A weight lifted from Riley's shoulders. He smiled at Ted. Ted didn't return the smile as he rose to his feet.

"Quick. We'll get your boyfriend and we'll go to the elevator. Where's your flat?"

Ted grabbed a rucksack of supplies and the three of them rushed out of the flat. "Down there." The woman pointed to the flat opposite the staircase entrance. "I... I can get my boyfriend and then we can go. We can get out of here."

"Okay. I'll help you get your boyfriend. And then we—"

"It's okay," Ted interrupted. He stepped up to the woman and half-smiled. "We'll both help you. But we have to be quick."

"Oh... Okay." The woman sniffed and nodded. "Okay. Sorry about... about before."

"Don't mention it." Ted smiled at the woman. "On one condition — you give me the gun. I know how to use it. Videogames and stuff."

The woman shook the gun in her hand. "Well, I... Okay. If you say so."

Ted grabbed the gun. Eyed it up like it was a prized possession — treasure from the bottom of the ocean. "I had the keys all along, you know. Now come on — we don't have long."

Riley always considered his and Ted's flat a tip. Empty takeaway boxes. Half-finished bottles of flat Coke. Ted's underpants coated with a number of questionable stains.

But the woman's flat made him realise he hadn't had things quite so bad after all.

There were syringes lined along the windowsill, filled with a brick-grey fluid. Spoons covered with a brown film. A wall of sweat hit you as you walked inside.

And on the sofa, underneath a bloodstained blanket, a man lay.

A belt was tied around his neck and attached to a lamp on the wall. Another around his arms and another around his legs.

His eyes were grey. Distant.

Gone.

"Stuey, are you okay? I've got us some help, see. We can get out of here."

The man, whose cheekbones were even more protruding than his girlfriends, snapped out at her, tugging at the belt around his neck as she crouched beside him. "Oh... Okay. Quick. You have to help me lift him. He's sick and he needs help."

Riley and Ted were completely silent. They turned to look at one another, slowly. A knowing look in both of their eyes. "What's... Your name. What is it?"

The woman shrugged and shook her head. "Jordanna. It doesn't matter now. Please. We need to help him."

"Jordanna." Riley approached her as her boyfriend continued to snap, tugging to pull himself free from the ties. "We... Your boyfriend. He isn't who he once was. I'm sorry."

Jordanna's watery eyes searched Riley's face. "But you said you'd help. You said we didn't have long and we had to get out of here."

"And we do." Riley rested his hand on Jordanna's shoulder. She flinched back, looking at her boyfriend's twisted neck and shaking body. "But he can't come with us. He's gone. I'm sorry, but he's gone."

A tear rolled down Jordanna's grimy face. "I promised him I'd help him. When he got sick — he made me promise I'd get him better. I can't just leave him. I can't."

A banging against the stairway door cut through the atmosphere of the room. Ted flinched and poked his head around the flat door. "Shit. We need to hurry up in here."

Riley turned back to Jordanna as the banging continued. He lifted her chin. "Jordanna — you need to be tough here. We need to go. If we leave him here, maybe… maybe he'll be safe. We can lock the door and… and maybe when this whole thing dies down, he'll be okay."

Jordanna's chin quivered. The banging grew more frequent. They had to go. Soon. "And you say… You say we can come back for him? You promise?"

Riley tried to smile at Jordanna, but he couldn't think past the sound of the approaching creatures. "Yes. Yes we can. Now come on. Let's get to the elevator. Quick."

Jordanna laid a hand on her shaking boyfriend's body and kissed him on the side of his chest. "I'm sorry, honey. I'll be back for you. I promise." She stepped to her feet then walked to the door. Riley followed.

But Ted didn't move. He stared at the man's body, retching and struggling like a seizure sufferer. His eyes were narrow. Focused.

"Ted? You coming?"

Ted twiddled his finger around the trigger of the gun. Started to lift it out of his pocket. "These things. We're going to have to… to learn to kill them soon."

Riley grabbed Ted's hand as he raised the gun. "Not now," he whispered. "There will be plenty of time for that. But think about the noise. They seem to react to noise. So not now." He pushed Ted's hand back into his pocket. Ted pushed back against him. "We need to stic—"

A huge bang clattered outside the flat.

Then a chorus of groans erupted.

The six creatures staggered out of the doorway and into the hall.

"Those fucking Poles," Ted said. "Time to move."

Riley, Ted and Jordanna ran out of the flat doorway and to the elevator. The elevator door was sealed shut. "I thought you said you opened this thing?" Riley shouted, smacking the 'call' button. The creatures were getting closer. Five flats away. Roaring. Groaning.

"I did, but I also didn't count on having a nice little chat with a lady round the block," Ted said. He raised the gun at the creatures. "Just take a breath, and fire. Take a breath and fire. All there is to it."

"You can't do that now." Riley bashed the call button. Third floor. Fourth floor. "The sound — it'll attract the ones outside. We can't risk that."

"Then we die!" Ted said. "The rules have changed. We have to adapt, mate."

Jordanna covered her face with her hands and sobbed. The creatures were just metres away. Ted pulled the trigger.

But nothing came out. No explosion sounded.

But the elevator door pinged and slid open.

"The fucking safety," Ted said, messing with the gun and running into the elevator.

Riley smacked the ground floor and 'close door' buttons when they were inside then moved to the back of the elevator. The creatures started to turn the corner. Blood dribbled down their mouths. Chunks of flesh hung from their body.

"Holy shit, now or never…"

Riley held his breath. Tensed his muscles.

The elevator door started to close. One of the creatures — the Polish father — stuck his hand through the gap in the door and blocked it. A matter of seconds and the doors would bounce open again.

But Ted stood up and thumped the arm. Brought his elbow down on it and pushed it back as it wriggled its dirty fingers at him. "Quick! Help me out here, mate."

Riley stared on, his body frozen. Time seemed to freeze. His head spun. The blood. The bodies. All of it. *No. Not now. Keep calm. Keep fucking calm. Not now.*

In what seemed like a split second, Jordanna booted the arm through the elevator door as hard as she could.

She kicked again. The arm disappeared from the elevator door. Blood ran down the crack between the doors.

Ted and Jordanna fell back, panting and shaking their heads as the elevator began to descend.

Riley could only look on. Frozen. *Deep breaths. Keep calm. There's nothing to panic about. Nothing at all to panic about...*

The elevator rumbled and ground to a halt. All of them were silent during the descent. Blood covered the inside of the doors, a reminder of how close they had been to losing everything. If it wasn't for Ted's strength; for Jordanna's kick...

"You okay, mate?"

Riley blinked and readjusted to his surroundings. The ringing in his ears had stopped. The tingling in his fingers had subsided. *It's passed. It's gone. Over.*

Riley pulled himself away from the wall and walked to the switch by the elevator door. "I'm good. Thanks. Both of you, for, y'know."

"Don't mention it," Ted said. He stared closely at Riley. "I moved the car right in front of the elevator when I got the chance. Providing we haven't had another person decide to crash the party, I'd say we're good to go." He shot a judgmental glance at Jordanna before pressing the 'open door' button.

Riley and Jordanna caught each other's eyes. There was no hiding their apprehension.

"Oh, come on," Ted said, sensing the atmosphere. "Trust me to do this one thing right."

The elevator door slid open. Sure enough, the car was parked right in front of the elevator. The rest of the parking area was quiet. Empty.

Ted opened the front and back doors and gestured for Riley to climb through to the driver's seat. "After you."

Riley clambered through and got into position. He felt something damp against his leg: a large bloodstain was spread across the fabric of the seat. Andy's blood. He yanked his leg away and arched it so it wasn't resting against the blood as Jordanna and Ted climbed into the car.

"Woah, woah," Ted shouted. He had his hand pressed against the back door that Jordanna was about to close. "Keep it quiet. We can't attract those things."

"Okay, okay," Jordanna said. She gently clicked the door into place, and Ted followed.

"Ready to drive?"

Riley took a deep breath and gripped the steering wheel. The first time since the accident. Since the tingling had taken hold of his fingers and the freezing of his body had made its debut. He checked for the signs — racing heart, sweaty forehead — but realised that they were unavoidable given the circumstances, so didn't think too much of them. "Okay." He turned the key. "Ready."

The car crawled to life. He took a look around the parking area. The bloodstain where he'd found Andy. It seemed so long ago — like so much had happened since. And yet, deep down, he got the sense that this was only the beginning.

Over by the stairway door, he saw the top half of Andy's torso. Where his head once was, there was a mound of deep red flesh, bloody tire tracks moving away from it.

"Not... Not a lot else I could do," Ted said, stuttering. "R.I.P. Andy, I guess."

Riley nodded. Ted had dealt with Andy after all. "R.I.P. Andy indeed."

"So you just expect to drive past these things?" Jordanna said, leaning into the front of the car. "I've seen what they do.

How they react."

"We have a plan, okay? A plan that was going perfectly fine until you showed up."

"Hey — I could've shot you. If I'd wanted to, I could've just shot you and taken the car for myself. Consider yourselves lucky."

Ted tapped the gun in his pocket. "Well, you aren't so lucky anymore, are you?"

Riley held his breath as they approached the turning at the gates. Tensed his fingers. They'd been upstairs for too long. The creatures, they'd have heard the commotion. They'd be outside the gate again. Waiting.

Riley slowed the car down. "You know what to do, Ted. Hop out of the car, open the gates, then get the hell back here."

Ted shook his head. "I think she should do it. She's the one who got us in this mess. Plus she's… well, more physically built than me."

Jordanna let out a sarcastic laugh. "Should've thought about that before you ate all that junk food, you fat fuck."

Ted swung around again to lambast Jordanna.

"Okay. One of you does it. I don't care who as long as we get this done before we lose our chance. That's if we even have a chance still. So, who's it going to be?"

Ted and Jordanna lowered their heads then looked at one another, like embarrassed children who had just fallen out.

"I'll do it," Jordanna said. "I know… I know what I did in the flats was hasty. But I want to get out of here as much as you two. So I can get help for my boyfriend."

Riley waited for a few moments before speaking. "Okay. I'll go round the corner, you run to the gate, and you enter the code. 4-7-5-1. But first, you have to get out and check. Give us the all-clear. Right?"

Jordanna pulled her hair back and nodded. "Right."

"Don't you think you should worry about your appearance some other time?" Ted said, as he watched Jordanna tuck her hair into her collared white shirt.

"I'm tucking it away, so that one of those things can't grab me." She shot her hand to the side of Ted's head and tugged at a short clump of his hairs. Then, she opened the car door and crept to the wall, peeking around it.

"Do you think we've taken too long?" Ted asked, defeat in his voice.

Riley shrugged. "I guess that's what we're about to find out."

Jordanna perched at the side of the wall and arched her neck around. She kept it there for a second. Another second. What was keeping her so long? What had she seen?

"She's stunned. Fuck. She's stunned and she's... oh."

Ted was interrupted by Jordanna. She turned around and gave them the thumbs up, then walked around the corner.

Riley rolled the car forward so that it moved around the corner as silently as possible. When they did emerge, he saw Jordanna at the gate keying in numbers. There were no creatures around. None in the foreground, none in the distance. Nothing except the body the others had been feasting on when Riley had interrupted them.

Jordanna hit in a few numbers then waited. The gate didn't move. She typed the numbers in again and waited. But still, no movement.

"The fuck is taking her so long?" Ted said.

Riley watched Jordanna as she continued to input the numbers. "I don't know."

"I mean, has the code changed or something? You should know — you keep on top of these things."

Riley thought back to his conversations with the landlord. Something about a burst pipe on the second floor. Scheduled maintenance for the elevator. But nothing about a change of code. "One of us is going to have to go out there. Go check on her."

"No chance, mate," Ted said. "No chance. I've done enough errand running for today."

Riley sighed. "That's survival, Ted. That's life until they get things sorted out. One big fucking chore. One…" He stopped. Something in the distance had changed. He'd always been blessed with what he called a semi-photographic memory, and even though it didn't work for intricacies like exams, it was good for 'spot the difference' exercises. And something was different about the scene ahead. Very different.

He squinted. Looked closely at Jordanna. Stared beyond the gate and over at the shops on the other side of the road.

Then, he saw the body of the half-eaten man on the ground, and he knew what it was.

"Shit," Riley said.

The gate started to open slowly. Jordanna turned round and stuck her thumb up, a relieved smile on her face.

"Hell yes," Ted said. "Now get the hell back here."

But the half-eaten body. Its neck was arched. Its mouth was open. They couldn't hear it through the car window, but Riley could hear in in his mind, crying out so loudly.

The creature lifted itself further upright, its mouth still moving.

Groaning.

"She needs to hurry. She really, really needs to hurry."

"Ah, don't worry about it. We can take that one half-eaten fucker with the car, or just swerve around it. It's no big deal."

As Jordanna got closer to the car, there was a movement to the right of the gateway.

Then another movement. A leg. An arm. A body.

Several bodies.

Ted's face dropped as Jordanna opened the door and threw herself into the car, panting. "Sorry, I… The keypad was sticking. Looked like rust or blood or something. What…" She saw what Riley and Ted saw and went quiet immediately.

The mangled creatures were beginning to walk around the corner. Three of them. Four of them. The groans were getting louder. Nearer.

"That one creature might not be a problem," Riley said.

"But all those… they might be."

Chapter Seven

"WE'RE GONNA HAVE TO GO THROUGH them."

Riley pressed his foot against the gas. Held the clutch down. Ted was shouting words in the background — incomprehensible words. Jordanna was leaning through the gap between the front seats, pointing ahead.

Six creatures. Seven creatures. All of them shrieking. All of them stumbling in their direction.

Riley pulled his seatbelt across and started to raise the clutch. "Hold tight." The tingling in his fingers was there — completely absorbing him — but he didn't feel the same level of nerves engulfing him. *You can do this. You can keep this under control.*

He lifted the clutch. The car jolted forward.

"Oh, fuck. Fucking, fucking fuck." Ted held his head between his knees. Jordanna moved back into her seat.

Riley stayed focused. Aimed for the small gap between the oncoming creatures.

You can do this. Do it for Grandma. Do it for Grandpa. He'd have been so proud.

Nine creatures. Ten creatures.

So close. Metres away. Feet away.

He held his breath.

The right wing mirror snapped off as it cracked into the side of one of the creatures. Riley resisted the urge to lift his foot from the gas as the car jolted sideways, the left headlight smacking into another creature.

Ted shouted out, burying his head deeper between his legs, as the car plummeted further forward, crashing into more and more of the creatures. But the gate was so close. The road was so close. They could do this. They could make this.

Riley swerved to the left, avoiding two of the creatures that were directly in front of the car, and jerked back to the right. The dead fell into Riley's side window, clawing at the door with worn down nails as he shot past them and through the gate. He kept on holding his breath. *So close. So close.*

The car sped out from the gate and smacked into two more creatures, which tumbled to the ground, their heads popping underneath the tire. Riley looked to his right and saw the crowd of creatures he'd attracted to the rope ladder clambering towards the car, walking like wooden puppets.

But there were no creatures in front of them. Other than the abandoned cars ditched in the middle of the street, they were all clear.

Ted lifted his head. He still had one eye closed as he peeked through the window. "You… You did it. You fucking did it." He smacked Riley on the back and started to laugh as Riley manoeuvred past the ditched cars out of the high street and onto a main road.

Riley smiled. Tension drifted out of his body. "We did it." He glanced at Jordanna in the mirror. She wasn't smiling, but the tears had disappeared from her eyes. She nodded back at Riley, then stared out of the window at the passing houses.

Riley drove slowly for ten minutes or so. Adrenaline ran

through his body.

"What now?" Ted asked, finally breaking the euphoria induced silence. "Take the A6 down to your Grandma's?"

Cars were lined up at the side of the streets, some of them abandoned in the middle of the road. Doors were ajar as hazard lights flashed. A murder of crows cawed as they flocked on the roof of a nearby house. It was quiet. Far too quiet for a populated area.

"I'm not sure this is the best way to go," Riley said. "There's a lot of houses around here. A lot of ditched cars."

"I hardly think houses and cars are the biggest problem," Ted said.

"No, but the more populated the area, the more of those… those things there are likely to be. We need to take the back road through the countryside. It might be bad around there, but I'd rather take a chance than risk getting ambushed with nowhere to drive."

Ted shrugged. "Fair point." He rubbed his finger across the crack on the passenger window. "We got lucky once. I'm not sure how many more times that's going to happen."

"When are we getting help?"

The voice startled Riley. Jordanna had been relatively silent since they'd left the city. She sat in the back seat, arms crossed, staring out at the abandoned streets and boarded up windows. People were preparing. Fortifying.

"I… Jordanna, we're going to go to my grandma's and get her. Then we'll be able to find a little more about helping your boyfriend."

Jordanna opened her mouth then resisted. She leaned back against the headrest and closed her eyes. "Just remember you promised. I trusted you."

Riley and Ted exchanged a glance. Ted grit his teeth and shook his head. They were going to have to be honest with her eventually. There was no way they were going back into the city, not while the situation was as it was.

But they could use her help. They could use numbers. They

needed to stick together.

Riley eased the car towards the edge of the mass of abandoned vehicles which stretched right the way down the A6 main road. The left turn emerged up ahead. If they turned there, they would be able to get to Grandma's in a matter of five or ten minutes. Manoeuvring through abandoned cars would take them the best part of an hour. More if something got in their way. They couldn't risk that. Grandma might not have much time left. They needed to hurry.

"I just don't get how this can happen." Ted stared out at the abandoned cars. The ditched vehicles. The wind blew up a flurry of autumn leaves. "How does *everybody* just ditch their cars in a matter of hours?"

Riley moved around a van. Blood spread across the back doors. "I think the bigger question is 'why?'"

Ted shook his head. "I don't like it. Not at all."

Reaching the turning onto the country bypass, Riley started to turn the car when he saw something up ahead. Ted must have seen it too, because he sighed and lifted his hands behind his head.

"So, did we account for abandoned tankers blocking the road when we planned this country route?"

Riley switched off the engine of the car. Ted rubbed his temples with his fingers and stared ahead at the abandoned tanker. It was positioned across the entrance to the country road. There was no way around it in the Punto. They would have to go on foot until they found another car. Or try their luck on the main road.

"I'm sick to the teeth of this, mate. Sick to the fucking teeth."

"Well what do you suggest?"

Ted smacked his fist against the car dashboard. "We should've stayed put in the flat. Taken refuge in there. We could've sneaked out for supplies every now and then. But it had everything. A gate. Height. Fuck."

"Hey. Don't you dare drop this on me. I told you to stay in the flat with your fucking video games if you wanted to, didn't I? I gave you that option—"

"—And what would you have done without me? How would you have got out? Done a runner down the street? What would you have done without my distractions? It's fucking ridiculous."

"Well I apologise that you don't have any family in the country to look out for right now, but this is—"

Something hard smacked the side of Riley's face and stopped him speaking in his tracks.

He only realised what it was when he saw Jordanna smacking Ted in the face.

"Ow!"

"Listen — we aren't going to get anywhere sitting around in here arguing over who cares more about who. Right now, all I care about is getting somewhere we can help my boyfriend." She opened the car door and stepped outside.

"Where the hell do you think—"

"I'm going to take a look at the tanker," Jordanna said. "My boyfriend used to drive one of those things. They usually leave a spare set of keys lying around. Idiots are always losing their keys. So you boys kiss and make up and I'll see what I can find." She slammed the door shut and jogged lightly over to the tanker.

Riley and Ted looked on.

"She... She's mad. There could be one of those things out there. Does she have a death wish or something?"

Riley didn't answer Ted. He scanned the area. The abandoned cars, some of their engines still rumbling. The crows landed on the roof of a car up ahead, deeper into the jungle of steel. They needed to be fast. It wouldn't be clear forever.

Jordanna disappeared around the side of the tanker. Ted tapped his fingers against the handle of the door, like he always did when he felt guilty about something.

"Listen, I... I'm sorry for flipping. You know I care about helping your grandma out. It's just..."

"I know. I get it. It's tough. I understand that."

Ted sighed. "And you. I saw your face in the elevator. You're okay now, aren't you?"

The tingling fingers. The frozen limbs. "Yes. I'm fine. It's okay."

"Well... If you say so. I thought those turns had stopped?"

"Bloody hell."

Ted frowned and followed Riley's eye-line over at the tanker. "Holy... She did it." He wound the passenger window down. "You did it?"

Jordanna was leaning out of the tanker window. She had a set of keys in her hand and a smile on her face. "Told you I'd come good. Now if I can just start this up..."

"She did it," Ted said, smiling at Riley. "She fucking did it. Clever motherfucker."

As the engine of the tanker came to life, something else sounded. A high-pitched siren.

"She... Oh. Oh shit."

Jordanna struggled around the tanker's controls as the alarm whistled out from it. In this silence, it would echo for miles.

"Just reverse," Riley called out of the window. "Reverse the tanker and we can get out of here."

"It's too late," Ted said. He was focused up the road ahead at the mass of abandoned cars.

The crows flapped their wings and flew away squawking.

Between the cars, one by one, creatures began to rise.

In front of them. Beside them. Behind them. All of them shuffling towards the sound of the alarm.

"I guess... I guess this place isn't so abandoned after all," Ted said.

Jordanna started to reverse the noisy tanker, the siren roaring on. A small gap was forming on the right hand side.

But they were running out of time. The creatures — tens, hundreds of them — all staggering in the direction of the tanker. Soon, the gap would be filled with those things. They'd lose their only escape route out. The only route to Grandma.

"We've got to move, mate," Ted said. "We've got to get over to that gap and we've got to drive before they get us."

Riley started up the engine and put his foot on the accelerator. As he did, a group of the creatures diverted their path towards the car as it moved along the road. They were getting closer to blocking the car's way out onto the country road. The broken wing mirror of the car caught Riley's eye. The Punto couldn't take many more collisions. They needed to go.

Riley slowed down as he reached the tanker. The creatures were a matter of feet behind them. Jordanna struggled with the tanker door and stumbled out of it.

"Come on!"

A thump hit the back of the car.

"Shit," Ted shouted, spinning around to look out of the rear window. "Gotta move, Riley — now!"

Riley looked in the mirror and saw three of the creatures pressed up against the back of the car. A woman scraped her teeth against the glass, cutting her gums and cracking one of her teeth as she dug deeper and deeper into the glass.

"But Jordanna—" Riley said, accelerating forward slightly.

"We have to leave her," Ted said. "We've got no choice."

Riley's heart raced as he looked out of the side window. Jordanna was standing by the tanker door. She stared into his eyes, shaking her head.

Between her and the car, a group of creatures blocking her way.

"We have to go!" Ted shouted.

A sickness grew in Riley's stomach.

Jordanna's bottom lip was beginning to quiver. A silent word emerged from her lips. "Please." Tears were dripping down her face.

"I'm sorry," Riley mouthed, as more creatures filled the gap beside the tanker. "I'm so sorry."

He put his foot down on the accelerator and he drove down the country road.

He didn't look back in the mirror, not until they took a right onto the roundabout and towards his grandma's house. When he did look, he saw a swarm of creatures surrounding the tanker.

He didn't hear any screams. Just the continual ringing of the tanker's alarm, on and on and on.

Chapter Eight

THE ROAD TO THE COUNTRYSIDE WAS relatively quiet compared to the main roads.

They passed farms and houses on their way to Riley's grandma's. Outside, they saw men and women — living men and women — pointing at one another, shouting orders, preparing for the arrival of the creatures in their own individual ways. Every now and then, a car sped past. The creatures hadn't hit the countryside quite as hard, not yet. There were still living here.

But eventually, they would come. And he had to get to Grandma before that happened.

Ted stared out of the passenger window. He bit his nails and didn't speak. Neither of them spoke, not since leaving Jordanna behind.

The final image of her eyes, teary and bloodshot, staring back at Riley. The silent word escaping her lips. *"Please."*

They crossed the motorway bridge. On the motorway, cars

were beginning to queue up, honking their horns at one another. The queue seemed to stretch on for miles. An untouched feasting ground for the creatures. They'd be coming. That's what must have happened on the A6 main road. The majority of them had heard the pipping of horns and staggered towards the motorway.

"We did what we had to do," Ted said. He continued to stare out of the window and bite his nails. His words sounded like he was thinking aloud, reassuring himself more than anybody else. "If we hadn't done it, they'd have ended it for us all. We... We had to take that risk."

Riley gulped. Jordanna was trying to help. She'd helped them get out of the gates back at the flat. She'd found the keys and moved the tanker. And how had they repaid her? They'd left her.

"We have to be tough. We have to make tough decisions."

"But we can't make too many decisions like that," Riley said. "We need to be more careful in future. We need to hold on to our humanity."

"If we'd held on to our humanity back then, we'd have all been killed. Just saying."

Riley didn't say anything. Ted had a point. All these people — all the ones who had turned — had they been trying to hold on to their humanity? Were they the ones who had failed to make the tough decisions?

"I don't know how this started out and I'm not sure I care until it's over. But one thing I do know is that we're going to have to make tough decisions to stay alive, mate." He pulled the gun out of his pocket and rested it on his leg.

Riley's stomach turned. "The gun. You could've shot those creatures. You could have... You could have saved her."

"Right next to a tanker? Have you ever even *played* a first-person shooter? That thing would've gone up in flames and swallowed us all. I had to make the tough decision."

Riley gritted his teeth. "You don't know that would've happened. Not for definite."

"I'd rather not know than end up barbecued creature meat." He turned back to the window and stared out of it. He didn't look all that up for arguing anymore.

Riley looked in his rear-view mirror. A group of people dragging wooden boards up to their house, ready to block themselves in for days. Weeks. Months. As long as it took. They had to hold on to their humanity. They had to get through this with their sanity still intact. No matter what Ted said, they couldn't fall any further down the dark hole.

He looked at the gun as it sat on Ted's lap. They'd have to learn to use it properly. Protect themselves. But they wouldn't leave anybody else behind.

He indicated to the right by force of habit and took a deep breath as he looked down the road.

Grandma's house was on the left.

Riley stretched his arms out as he pulled up outside Grandma's house. The engine cut out, leaving the area in silence.

"You want me to go in there first and just check?" Ted asked. He had a half-smile of reassurance on his face.

"It's okay," Riley said. He stared over at the all-glass front door. "It's better if we both go. We can't take any chances doing things alone. Not anymore."

Ted nodded and grabbed the small rucksack of supplies. "It's your call." He opened the car door and climbed out, checking both sides of the car. All looked clear.

Riley got out of the car and closed the door as quietly as possible. He looked down the street. The leaves on the trees lining the pavements were crisping, falling to the floor. Cars were still in their driveways. The place was always quiet, as with every countryside suburb. But with everything they had experienced, Riley still wasn't sure whether quiet was a good sign or not.

But they had to go into the house. They had to get to Grandma. See that she was okay.

"You lead the way, mate. I'm right behind you." Ted lifted the gun out of his pocket. "Just in case. Agreed?"

Riley thought about protesting, but they couldn't risk their safety. Very few people would be carrying guns around Preston. Not even the police were allowed. They had an advantage, and they had to use it. Just sensibly. Seven bullets. Seven bullets that had to save their lives, and nothing else.

Riley walked down his grandma's driveway. Ted followed closely behind, his footsteps crunching against the gravel. The large gate in the driveway was closed. There was no sign of blood. No sign of anybody. Any thing.

As he approached the door, Riley noticed something was slightly out of place.

The realisation welled up inside him, trying to burst out. His heart started to race. He lifted his hand up and pushed against the door.

The door swung open with minimal effort. It was open.

Riley and Ted looked at one another. Ted had a concerned frown on his face. He raised his gun and tilted his head forward for Riley to continue.

The tingling sensation started to shudder through Riley's hands and arms. *No — not now. Embrace it. Embrace the fear and move on. Deep breath in, hold for four seconds... and out.* He cleared his throat and pushed the door a little further open.

The hallway was empty. The grey carpet was untouched as ever. No footprints. No blood. A good sign.

Riley took a step into the house. "Grandma?"

No reply. No sounds.

He moved further into the hallway, crouching slightly to give himself some chance of escape if something leapt out at him. He reached for the handle of the living area door and pushed it open. Ted poked the gun around the corner.

The room was empty. The grandfather clock ticked and ticked and ticked in the centre of the far wall. An empty cereal bowl sat on the mantlepiece, milk settled at the bottom.

Riley nodded at Ted and they left the room. "Grandma?

It's Riley. Are you... Where are you?"

Still no reply.

"Maybe she's gone," Ted whispered, aiming his gun around the hallway and up the stairs. "I bet she rushed out of here. She gets on with the neighbours, right? Right?"

Ted's words started to buzz out of focus as Riley stopped in front of the dining room. He stared at the handle. The tingling was engulfing his body now. His throat was swelling up. The door handle.

"Mate, what is it?"

Riley pointed at the door handle. "Blood."

Ted squinted as if to object, but when he saw it, his face dropped.

The gold metal handle was covered with bloody fingerprints. The blood dripped down the side of the door and stained the patch of carpet below. Drip. Drip. Drip.

Riley held his breath and reached for the handle, covering his palm with his sleeve. They had to go inside. They had to find her. Even if she was... One of those. He had to know.

"Are you sure you don't want me to—"

"I've got this," Riley said. He lowered the handle. It creaked as he pushed the door open.

At first, he thought she was just looking out at the garden. Standing by the window and admiring the view, like she always used to.

But it wasn't her. The body was too thin. The hair was too dark.

They turned around and gasped. Their dead eyes stared at Riley and Ted.

It was Grandma's next door neighbour, Alan. And he had a piece of flesh stuck around his four remaining teeth.

Alan started to stagger towards them. Riley's heart raced.

"Should I shoot? Mate — should I shoot?"

The blood on the floor. The drips of blood from whatever Alan had in his mouth. Small. Almost invisible.

Riley turned around and followed the trail of blood with

his eyes. It was ever so light in the grey carpet. But he saw it now. It was there.

"Mate, seriously, should I... Ah, fuck it."

One blast. Another blast.

Riley swung around. Ted's hand was shaking. His eyes were focused on the dining room.

And Alan's body was lying on the floor, blood pouring out of his head.

"I did it." Ted panted. Exhaled sharply and lowered the gun, before raising it again. "I... I shot one of them. I... I did it. I... Hey... where are you going?"

Riley reached for the kitchen door. The trail of blood was beneath his feet. The trail that led to or from the dining room. He ran through the possibilities in his head, but none of the thoughts seemed clear.

He grabbed the handle. Turned it.

"Be careful, dammit."

Riley opened the kitchen door. The first thing he saw was the wireless phone lying on the hard floor in front of him. It was covered in blood. Two numbers — '9 9' — were input on the display.

But even more eye-catching was the widening trail of dark blood leading from it.

"Riley, I should really..."

Riley stepped into the kitchen. His hands dripped with sweat. His vision was blurred and a tension engulfed his body. Grandma. She had to be okay. She had to.

When he saw her body on the floor at the end of the wide trail of blood, he thought she was just taking a nap at first. Perhaps she'd had a bad fall. Perhaps the blood wasn't hers — maybe it was Alan's. Maybe she'd hit him and the blood was his. It couldn't be Grandma's blood. It couldn't be.

Riley's body weakened. He shuffled into the kitchen. He could hear her groaning slightly. See her body starting to twist around as it lay on the floor.

"Grandma, it's—it's okay. It's me. It's—"

Arms wrapped around Riley's back. Stopped him moving forward. "Stay back," the voice was saying. Ted. But it seemed so distant. They were so close to Grandma. They'd come so far, and they were so close.

Riley struggled free of Ted's grip. Grandma's blood-drenched body started to turn even more in their direction. She was trying to say something. Wincing.

Groaning.

Riley shoved Ted back and rushed forward. His entire body shook. She was okay. She had to be okay. "Grandma, I'm here."

When her eyes met his, he felt as if he had taken a bullet to the stomach.

Her eyes were grey. They stared not at him, but through him. There was a hole in the side of her neck. A chunk of flesh missing. A chunk of flesh around the same size as the one Alan had in his mouth.

She groaned some more. Reached her shaking hand out towards him.

Riley felt the arms around his back again. Heard the words, miles away. So far away. "Come on, mate. I'm sorry. I'm sorry." Felt warm tears dripping down his face.

Ted dragged him backwards and pushed him into the hallway with all his weight. His eyes were red, bloodshot and welled up. "You know what we have to do now, man. You know, don't you?"

"She's... She might not be. We can help her. We can—we can save her."

Ted grabbed Riley's face and shook his head. Grandma continued to groan in the background. "We can't. You know we can't. I'm sorry."

The words knocked Riley back. Ted was right.

Ted pulled the gun back out of his pocket. It shook in his hand. "I'll do it. I'll finish it. And then you can... you can say your goodbyes."

"No." Riley grabbed the gun from Ted, who pulled it back.

"You know we have to do it. We can't... You can't leave her in this state. It's not—"

"I'll do it."

The words surprised Riley as they left his mouth. A weight lifted from his shoulders. Ted frowned and loosened his grip on the gun. "You... You're sure?"

Riley took a deep breath in. Pulled the gun towards him. "Yes. This is... We have to make these tough decisions. To survive."

Ted let go of the gun completely and patted Riley on his shoulder. "I'll... I'll be right here, mate. I'll be right here. I'm sorry. I really am."

"Thanks, Ted. Thanks."

Riley walked past Ted and back into the kitchen. Grandma — no, Grandma's body — dragged herself — itself — along the floor, unable to push her dead weight up. Her glassy, empty eyes gazed up into space, purple and bloodshot. The kitchen floor resembled an abattoir.

Riley's arm started to lift the gun automatically. He rattled with nerves as he aimed at her. Her dark hair, coated with dried blood. The lipstick she always wore so proudly — even if she was just spending a full day pottering around the house, watering the plants — smudged across her cheeks.

"I'm sorry, Grandma," Riley said. He sniffed back the tears as they poured from his eyes and dropped to the floor. "For everything. You were so good. You were... If it wasn't for you, I wouldn't be here. I wouldn't..."

Grandma shrieked and pulled herself further forward. She had a snarl on her face. She snapped her teeth together, shuffling towards Riley.

"I'm sorry for everything. Thank you. For being there. Thank you for being there when—when nobody else was."

Her hand smacked against the floor. She was just a few metres away now. A new trail of blood was emerging underneath her flowery dress.

"I love you, Grandma. God bless."

He closed his eyes and he pulled the trigger.

Episode Two

Chapter Nine

RILEY LOWERED THE GUN. HE COULDN'T look directly at her head, or where it once was, but he saw thick, dark blood pooling out underneath it. His bottom lip shook. His throat welled up. Grandma was gone.

"We can... I can go get something from the attic. Try and find something to put her on, or—"

"No," Riley said. He turned to face Ted and handed him back the gun. "We can't... we can't waste too much time. I'll... Pass me a sheet. Or something."

Ted looked as if he was going to protest, his wide eyes diverting to look at Grandma's body, but then he nodded. "I'll —I'll get her bed sheets. Something... something nice and warm to cover her up."

Riley nodded his head in acknowledgement. He couldn't turn around. He couldn't see her in that way. He just had to accept it — she was gone.

He looked at the kitchen worktop. Old-fashioned salt and

pepper pots. A new Kindle eReader. Grandma always loved to stay at the forefront of technology, even if she didn't know how to use it. A pile of Liquorice Allsorts. Claimed she didn't have a sweet tooth. Perhaps not, but she definitely had a liquorice tooth.

Something else caught Riley's eye at the far end of the worktop. It was an envelope. Turned on its back, the flap still not sealed. A pen rested beside it, chewed down at the end. Riley reached for it. His stomach tensed. He had a feeling he knew what might be inside.

"Got it."

Ted was by the door. He had Grandma's bedding underneath his armpit. Pink flowers patterned across it. The faint smell of Lenor. Fresh bedding.

Riley stuffed the envelope in his pocket and grabbed the bedding from Ted. He kept his head upright, trying his best not to look at what remained of Grandma's head as he crouched down and stretched the bed sheets over her.

Her hand stuck out from under the bed sheets. Grey. Wrinkled. But when he squinted hard enough, he could see it was still her hand. Warm. Tender when she held his hand as a kid, but oh so rough when she washed his hair or dried him after a bath. He reached for her hand, her golden wedding ring still wrapped around her finger, and he gripped it. It was cold. Stiff. Not like her.

"I'm sorry, Grandma. You sleep tight." Riley blew his grandma a kiss and rose to his feet. The blood from her gunshot head was beginning to creep out onto the peach coloured sheets.

Ted rested a hand on Riley's shoulder as they looked down at the mound on the floor. "Come on. We... I know it's not ideal right now, but we need to talk about the next step, mate."

Riley blinked away some stinging, warm tears and nodded. "Goodbye, Grandma."

They walked out of the kitchen and they closed the door.

The sound of the gunshots echoed for miles. Echoed against car doors. Echoed against buildings, through streets and across hills.

They staggered to their feet. Groaned.

And they walked.

When they heard something, they didn't back down.

Chapter Ten

THE HALLWAY SEEMED TOO SILENT FOR Grandma's hallway. Usually, the sound of the radio playing upstairs echoed down, adding a sense of life to the place. A sense of vibrancy. But now, nothing. No radio. No Grandma, singing and chirping away. No cars speeding past outside. Dead silence.

Until Ted cleared his throat, that was. "Like I say, mate, I don't mean to press you or anything, but what... well. Everything we had planned revolved around your grandma. We didn't think beyond that. So what now?"

"What now?" He had a point. Beyond Grandma, they hadn't really considered what action to take next. She was the end goal. The finish line.

But there was no finish line in this world. Not until the government or the police sorted it out. And right now, they didn't seem to be making much progress.

"I mean, we could camp out here for a few days, but I don't

know. We can't be sure how far away those things are."

"I'm not sure we have much of a choice," Riley said. He walked past the family photographs. Grandma and his dad. Grandma and him. Grandma and Grandpa.

"Thing is — and this is no disrespect to your Grandma's shopping — but she always kept the place a bit, well... bare of food."

"As you'd expect from an old lady living on her own and getting meals delivered, yes."

"Yes. That's what I mean." He dropped his rucksack to the ground and searched through it, pulling out bags of crisps and chocolate bars. "I have stuff here, but it won't last us too long. And we're way out at this place. Where even is the nearest supermarket?"

Riley thought about the nearest places to his Grandma's house. An ASDA, at least five miles away. Too far for them to be commuting to and from every day. "I don't know what to suggest."

"Then you'd better start thinking." Ted's voice was stern. "I'm trying my best here. Trying my best to keep us both alive. And I understand what you just had to do wasn't easy. I get that. But we have to stay on our toes. There's no time for sulking around."

A fire burned inside Riley's body and he lurched towards Ted. He grabbed him by the scruff of his collar and held him down as well as he could on the floor. "Listen. You have no idea what I just had to go through. You do not fucking 'get' anything. I just had to... I just had to shoot my own grandma. My own grandma. The only fucking person in the world who truly gave a shit about me. Don't you dare tell me you get that. Your parents are sunning it up in the Canary Islands."

Ted pushed Riley back, scratching at his neck and his face with his flabby fingers. "Oh yeah? You're wrong. Your Grandma might've given a shit. I know that. But what about me? I've put my neck on the line to be here with you. At least you *know* what's going on with the person you care about. My parents — how do I know they're okay? How do we know this thing isn't global?"

"You came here for yourself," Riley said, pinning Ted down between his legs. "You came with me because you couldn't bear being left on your own back there. You came…"

Riley stopped speaking. He felt a gust of wind brush against his back. Had Grandma left a window open? Or had he forgotten to close the front door?

"You ungrateful fuck." Ted thrashed around at Riley. "You ungrateful, fucking *fu*—"

Riley covered Ted's mouth. Ted thrashed some more. But as Riley moved away, Ted saw what Riley saw.

The front door was partly open.

And outside it, behind the frosted glass, a figure stood.

Riley and Ted looked at one another. Both of them were silent. Both of them frozen out of their argument.

With another push, the door swung open.

It was another of Grandma's neighbours. Paul Postwaite. Always visited at Easter with a chocolate egg.

He didn't have a chocolate egg today.

And he'd brought some friends along, too.

"Get up," Riley shouted. He jumped to his feet and tried to pull Ted with him. "We have to go out the back."

The creatures were spilling in through the door. First, just Gran's neighbour, Paul. Then another old lady, guts sliding out of her torso. And behind her, an old man with broken glasses. A piece of glass was wedged into his eye, eyeball fluids dripping down his face. The old person's tea party with an interesting, exciting twist.

Ted raised the gun as they backed into the dining room where Alan's body lay.

"Put that down," Riley said. "We can't attract any more of them. And we've only got five bullets left. And you wasted your first bullet. That's two good shots on a lucky day."

Ted sighed and lowered his gun. They stumbled into the

dining room and slammed the door shut.

"Where the fuck did that lot come from?" Ted asked.

Riley reached for one of Grandma's old wooden chairs and propped it against the door handle. The wood was rickety and flimsy. It wouldn't hold the creatures out for long.

"We need to get out of here," Riley said. He clambered over Alan's dead body and reached for the patio door, completely covered in glass. "We need to get to the car and drive the hell away from this place."

"And go where?"

"I don't care where," Riley snapped. "Just anywhere but here."

Ted nodded. As he did, the door began to rattle on its hinges. They both looked back at it, panic in their eyes. "Oh shit. This thing isn't gonna hold for long, mate."

Riley yanked at the patio door. The large glass windows looked out onto the garden. Specks of blood coated them. Small fragments of Alan's exploded brain. The patio door wasn't budging.

Another barge against the door. Ted backed up to it. "Gotta move, man."

"Okay, okay. I'm trying." Riley rushed to the cabinet beside the television and opened the top drawer. Nothing but jewellery. Loose change. Unattached buttons.

The door barged again. They were groaning in the hallway now. More of them could have joined since the last bunch they'd seen climb through the front door. There could be tonnes of them that had heard the gunshot. They had to be quick.

Riley searched the next drawer. Loose scraps of paper. Snapped pencils. Reading glasses. *Fuck*. Where did Grandma keep her keys?

The realisation hit him hard and sudden. "Fuck."

"What is it?" Ted asked, pressing back on the door.

Riley shook his head. Sickness started to climb to his throat. Trapped. "The keys. Grandma — she got a keyring. To carry them around with her all the time."

Ted's face dropped. "Why the fuck didn't you—"

The wood of the door above Ted's head cracked open. A hand tore its way through, clambering around for a grip on Ted, scratching at his hair. The groans grew louder when their dead eyes saw Riley standing still in the middle of the room, staring back at them.

Ted fell to his knees. The broken wood of the door was crumbling away as more and more hands shoved themselves inside, like traffic trying to squeeze its way out of a tight junction.

They were trapped. Stuck. They weren't going to get out.

Ted slid the gun across the floor as the wood continued to crumble. He was on all fours now. Dust from the white paintwork fell down and covered his wispy hair. He couldn't look at Riley. "Quick. Shoot the glass!"

Riley scooped the gun up and removed the safety. The warmth of the metal. Grandma, staring back at him, straining her vocal chords.

The tingling in his hands. The racing of his heart.

"Quick!" Ted shouted. One of the creatures shoved its head through the door, snapping its teeth just inches away from Ted's ear.

Riley took a deep breath and aimed the shaky gun at the patio glass. *Deep breaths. Keep calm.*

He pulled the trigger and the glass shattered.

"Now!" Riley swung around to face Ted.

But the creature. It was so close. Almost touching his neck. He couldn't move. He was stuck.

Riley aimed the gun again and steadied his hand before firing at the creature above Ted. The bullet pierced its neck, knocking it back into the crowd of ten or so gathering behind it.

"Now!"

Ted let out a small squeal before running towards the broken patio glass. The moment he moved, the door gave way and the creatures started to crawl into the room. He looked at the gun. Only four bullets remaining. They had to save them. Use them when necessary.

"To the car. Watch the glass."

Riley climbed over the fragments of the broken patio glass first. Several sharp shards pointed out from the bottom of the patio door, like teeth, ready to sink into the flesh of an unfortunate wrong-stepper. He ran out onto the damp grass of the garden, being sure to check the area. The garage looked clear. The garden looked clear. The driveway looked clear. They could get to the front of the house. Get to the car.

"Argghh!"

Riley swung around. Ted was on his hands and knees. Blood was spouting out of his foot. The creatures were getting closer.

"Shit." Riley sprinted back to the door and wrapped Ted's arm around his neck before tensing and pulling him to his feet.

"It's... It's stuck, man. It's stuck. Mate. Please." Ted was whimpering. A small, sharp shard of glass was sticking into the bottom of his shoe. The glass looked like a piece of red-stained window in a church.

But the creatures. They didn't have enough time to get him free. Three of them were in the room. More of them were crawling through the gap in the door.

"Fuck. Fuck it." Riley aimed at the creature nearest and fired at its head. The bullet missed, hitting its shoulder but the creature fell back into the one behind, knocking it to the floor.

Then, he crouched down while they had a bit of time and grabbed the sides of Ted's Doc Martens. "This is going to hurt."

"Quick. Just do it. Do it. Ple—aaaaarghh!"

Riley yanked Ted's foot free of the shard of glass. A piece of it snapped away, still wedged in the bottom of Ted's shoe. Blood poured out of the hole the glass had made in the bottom of the footwear.

"You take those deep breaths I told you about," Riley said, hopping along with Ted. The creatures were far enough behind them. One of them reached through the patio door and stood foot first onto the glass. It tore right through its foot and out of its thigh, and it fell down onto another piece of glass, still struggling to move forward, still trying.

Riley and Ted moved down the driveway, which was clear. The bloodstained Punto was in front of the house. They just had to hope there were no creatures around the corner, waiting to pounce.

Ted breathed in and out loudly. Tears rolled down his cheeks. He moaned with the pain, but battled on, stumbling along the driveway. A trail of blood dripped out underneath his feet, like Riley and he were Hansel and Gretel, only they were the ones leaving tasty treats for the creatures to gorge on. A candy house of blood.

"If—If you have to leave me, do it," Ted said, as they approached the front of the house. Just a few metres to go. Just a few more metres…

"Don't be stupid. We're… Oh shit."

As they turned the corner and approached the Punto, two of the creatures that were headed for the front of the house turned around. They started to groan at Riley and Ted, and staggered towards them. A woman — or what *was* a woman — with greasy long hair. A withered old man, skeletal, and completely bald presumably from chemotherapy. Given a new lease of life by death. Ironic.

"I'm gonna have to use it." Riley lifted the gun. Two bullets remaining. Two creatures remaining. "I'm… I'm just going to have to try."

"But we—we might need it. Like you said. We might—"

Riley fired at the woman first. She dropped to the floor as the bullet scraped through the top of her scalp. *Not a bad shot.* Then, he aimed at the bald man, who could barely stand with his shaky, bony bed-bound legs.

"Sorry, old fella." He fired. The bullet plummeted into the

man's chest and he too fell back, skull cracking as he hit the ground. He continued to groan on the floor. But he was down.

Riley looked at the gun. Completely empty. Used within their first hour or so of finding it. Like an armour cheat on a videogame, timed out. Fuck. He must've been hanging around with Ted for far too long to be thinking like that.

Riley opened the car door and eased Ted into the passenger seat before climbing into the driver's. He took a look at his grandma's house. The open door. Silhouettes of creatures turning back to leave the house. Shadows approaching the driveway from the garden.

And the kitchen window. She'd be in there. The only room that didn't seem to be attracting any attention. At peace.

Ted held his shoe, wincing. "What now? What—what now?"

Riley placed the gun on the dashboard. Reached into his pocket to check the envelope was still in there. Guilt welled up inside him. He opened the envelope.

Riley,

Congratulations on your new (or old!) job. So proud of you. Grandpa would be too.

All my love,

Grand-

The ink trailed off after the 'd'. Riley swallowed the lump in his throat.

He'd lied about keeping his job, but at least she'd died proud.

Ted moaned, squeezing the bottom of his shoe.

Riley started up the engine and crawled down the country road. "We get to a… a pharmacy. And we get your foot sorted out."

"Then what? We've no ammo. We've—we've—arghhh." Ted cried out as he tried to unlace his shoe.

Riley looked back in the mirror. His grandma's house behind them. Creatures staggered out into the road. More of them were beginning to appear from the old people's residency around the corner. They'd heard the gunshots. That's why they'd come for them.

But a question niggled in Riley's head. A question that had been niggling at him under the surface for some time now.

How had they all been bitten if they were out in the countryside?

"We need a plan. We—we need a—"

"All we need right now is to get to a pharmacy before you bleed out or get some infection. We take things step by step. Okay?"

Ted looked as if he was about to protest, but then he winced again and slackened his shoelace even more.

"At least you've finally got a good excuse to get rid of those fucking disgusting smelling shoes."

Chapter Eleven

THEY DROVE DOWN THE MAIN COUNTRY road for quite some time. The countryside seemed relatively clear, still yet to have been hit with the same level of force as the inner-city. Ted clutched his foot. He cried out with the pain now and then. Blood continued to ooze out of the bottom of the shoe and onto the floor. He had to get him some help. A pharmacy. A bandage and some alcohol to ease the infection.

"You holding on over there? We're almost there. It should be up here on the left."

"I can't wait anymore," Ted said. He bit his lip and started to pull his shoe away, shouting out as it slipped from his foot.

"Just keep it still, for God's sake. Keep it still."

Ted's white sports sock was completely covered in blood. At the bottom of his foot, near his toes, a piece of glass poked out. The piece that had snapped away when he'd tried to pull away from the shard of the patio.

Ted went completely pale when he saw the glass sticking

out of the bottom of his sock. "I've... I've got to get it. It's dangerous. I... I can't walk. I'm fucked, mate. Fucked."

"Just calm down, okay?" Riley looked back on the road. Despite all the twisted things he'd seen in the last couple of hours; all the mangled corpses. All the raw flesh. Despite all of that, it was the sight of a shard of glass sticking out of his best friend's foot that made him feel the most queasy. He kept his eyes on the road as his face started to heat up. *Just a wound. Just a bit of blood.*

"I'm going to have to get it out," Ted said. "I just... I just don't want to... I don't want to."

Riley saw the pharmacy approaching on the left. Two cars were parked outside. It looked quiet enough.

But the old people from the residency. The man who looked like he'd been on chemotherapy. He didn't look like he'd been savaged by these things. Maybe Ted was right. Maybe it was airborne. Maybe they were all carrying it. Or did that only happen on the TV shows?

"I'll never walk again. Never—never walk properly again. What good am I in this world? I'll just be slowing you down. I'll just be—"

"Shut up," Riley said, as he turned into the driveway of the pharmacy. It looked dark inside. The window shutters were down. A 'closed' sign dangled from the front of the glass door.

Riley opened up the dashboard. A few CDs, unlabelled, with marker pen scrawled on them. Empty tobacco packets.

And a red spanner.

Riley grabbed the spanner and turned it in his hand. Heavy head. Heavy enough to swing at one of those creatures and knock them down if he needed to.

"I can't even help now. What am I supposed to do? What am I... Hey!"

Riley opened the car door and climbed out. "I'm going to take a look inside. Grab what I can. Then I'm going to get back to this car and we're going to..." His gaze diverted to the glass wedged into Ted's food. "We're going to deal with the, um. The problem." He pressed the door shut quietly before Ted had a chance to protest.

He scanned the area quickly. No abandoned cars on the road. Crows flying overhead in the distance, cawing. Ruling from above. He peeked in through the window of the car nearest to him in the car park — a dark red Mercedes. Nobody was inside. The doors were closed. Abandoned, and never returned to.

As he started to walk towards the pharmacy, spanner in hand, he saw a movement in the upstairs window of the Chinese takeaway restaurant next door. A curtain twitched. Somebody peeked out at him, then moved out of sight. He kept on watching the window, waiting for the curtain to move again, as he walked towards the entrance of the pharmacy. Made sense. If he was shacked up in some place, running low on supplies, he'd hardly be announcing his presence to some stranger with a spanner either. He turned back to the pharmacy door and approached, slowly.

Riley pushed the door open. There was nobody at the till. The floors smelled of disinfectant. The place didn't look like it had even opened up at all today. He crept through the central aisle, squinting in the relative darkness that was caused by the shutter blinds. This place wouldn't be such a bad hideout. Secure windows. The door could easily be blocked by a shelf or two. Scraps of food — yesterday's sandwiches, cartons of juice. They could get by in here for the time being. He'd have to go get Ted. Bring him in here instead of taking the medical gear to the car.

But they still needed food. And the supermarkets would be running low on supply, if they hadn't already run out. They needed to get there first. Get enough food and water to live on for now. Then, they could think about shacking up in here. Physiological needs first, safety needs second. Maslow's Hierarchy. Some crap or another that he'd read at journalism school. Great load of good that was for music journalism. Now, however; now it seemed more appropriate.

He peeked down the aisles. It seemed clear, but he had to be sure. The cosmetics aisle was stacked with lipstick and women's hair products. They'd probably still shift, even in the middle of all this chaos. He moved on to the next aisle. He needed some bandages and some disinfectant of some sort. Did pharmacies sell pure alcohol? Was there even such a thing, or was that a thing of the movies too?

He reached the third aisle and noticed the bandages. *Gotcha.* He walked down and grabbed a pack. Underneath the bandages, a bottle of Dettol. He picked it up. *Ideal for cleaning minor wounds and areas of infection.* The glass sticking out of the bottom of Ted's foot. Was that a minor wound?

He slipped it in his pocket anyway. Couldn't afford to be selective in the apocalypse.

As he walked back to the door, Dettol in his pocket and bandages in hand, he saw a movement outside between the pharmacy and the Punto. He slowed down to a creep. Clenched the spanner tightly in his free hand. Ted would be okay as long as he'd stayed inside the car. As long as he hadn't done anything stupid.

He got closer to the door. All he could hear was the sound of his own heartbeat, thudding in his skull. That was a good sign. At least there were no groans. No screams.

Something dropped to the floor behind him. He swung around. It sounded light. Plastic. A small bottle of sun cream lay on the floor at the back of the pharmacy where he had come from. It definitely hadn't been there before.

Must've knocked it off. Unsteadied it. No big deal.

He turned back to the door of the pharmacy and pulled it open. There was nobody around the car. Nobody in the road or either side of the pharmacy. The movement must just have been his eyes playing tricks on him. Easy enough considering everything that had happened today. Even if these creatures were contained, it wouldn't surprise him if the world ended up throwing itself off a cliff through madness, not sickness.

He picked up his pace as he approached the car. He'd have

to tell Ted about the pharmacy. They could easily use the place as some sort of refuge as soon as they had some food. As soon as he'd sorted Ted's foot out. Sure — Riley was no doctor, but he could handle this. He could try.

As he crouched down to open the car door, he froze. Something was missing. Something from the passenger seat.

Ted.

Riley opened the door. Looked around the car. Checked the back seats.

"Ted?"

He checked the other side of the car but there was no trace of him. No sign that he'd tried to get away.

Except for the drops of blood leading from the passenger door.

Riley's body tensed. The drops of blood led around the back of the car. He followed them, his spanner raised above his head. A creature had tried to get Ted. He'd freaked. Hid somewhere. That's all it was. He kept low and moved round the back of the car.

The trail of blood continued. Spiralled half way down the parking area and led right to the middle of the two cars, a Previa and the red Mercedes, parked closely to one another. Riley took a deep breath and walked in the direction of the trail. He'd hid. That's all it was. He'd hid.

The crows cawed overhead as he approached the two cars. Asserting their dominance. A light breeze blew a discarded can along the pavement, aluminium scraping the concrete. He'd have to look between the cars. Take a look, and act fast if he had to.

No. Ted would be okay. He had to be okay.

He placed a hand on the boot of the red Mercedes and prepared himself. The blood pools were larger here. Collected.

Three. Two. One...

He swung around the side of the cars.

But Ted wasn't there.

The spanner dropped slowly to Riley's side as he stared at

what was in front of him.

A golden retriever was lying on its side. Its eyes were closed. The bone in its back leg was exposed, flesh torn from it.

Riley shook his head. Poor thing. But that didn't explain where Ted was.

He heard something behind him. A footstep. Or just the wind. He swung around. Nobody in sight. His fingers tingled. His body tensed. "T—Ted? Is that you?"

As he turned back round to look at the dog, he felt something smack against his chin. He flew back onto the floor.

His vision blurred. His head thumped. But he could see two silhouettes above him. Two dark silhouettes. Voices. Muttering.

He felt himself being elevated from the ground, flying away, and then silence…

Chapter Twelve

HIS HEAD POUNDED. HE WAS IN bed at his flat. Had he been out last night? He wasn't sure. But his head — splitting headache. Sickliness in his stomach. How many had he drank? Five? Six?

He could hear noises in the background. Voices, one minute sharp and the next muffled. He tried to open his eyes, but they stung. He winced. There was a dampness on the back of his head.

And then he remembered. The groans. The dead on their feet. Raw flesh. Grandma.

And Ted. Ted had gone.

He forced his eyes open. A shadeless lightbulb shone brightly in the centre of the room, stinging his eyes.

"Stan — hey, he's awake."

Voices. Movement in the distance, blurred, and just out of view. Footsteps approached him as he lay on his side, pushed back against a wall. The large figure crouched down and grabbed Riley's cheeks with his tree-trunk fingers.

"Were you bitten?"

Riley stuttered as the man looked into his eyes. He had wispy grey hair and protruding ears. A full beard sprouted around his mouth.

"Hey," the man said. He pushed Riley back against the wall. A shot of pain ran right the way through Riley's body. The place where his head had been hit, digging into the solid wall. "Were you *bitten*?"

"No," Riley said, cringing with the pain. "Nobody was... We weren't bitten. My friend. Where is he?"

The man held Riley's head against the wall a few seconds longer before letting it drop to the floor. "Weak bastard."

"Go easy on him, Stan." Another voice. The woman's voice from earlier. She was crouched over something at the other side of the room. She had long, dark hair and gorgeous auburn eyes. Riley arched himself upright, his head spinning with colours and dizziness. *He—llo gorgeous...*

"What's... Who are you people? Where am I? And my friend?"

The man called Stan tutted and pointed his finger over at the woman.

Riley followed his finger with his gaze. His vision was returning now, adjusting to the light in the room, which wasn't so bright after all.

His stomach tingled with relief when he saw what it was the pretty woman was crouching over.

Ted was leaning back against a pillow. He had a large smile on his face as the woman's hand rested near his crotch. His foot was propped up at the end of the bed, wrapped in a bandage. "Hello, mate," he called. "Sleep well?"

Riley smiled. A speck of jealousy ran through his body when he saw the woman massaging his ankle. But mostly, he felt relief. Relief that his best friend hadn't been taken. Bitten.

"Allow me to introduce you to the lovely Anna," Ted said. He grinned at woman, who rolled her eyes and smiled back at him. She had a slim face with freckles peppered across like spots on Mini Eggs. The tall, thin features of an actress.

"Hi," Riley said. He sat even further upright even though his head was searing. "I'm Riley. Pleasure to meet you."

"Okay, okay." Stan folded his arms and grimaced. "This isn't a fucking speed-dating society. You two almost caused us a load of trouble wandering into the pharmacy."

Riley looked around the room. Blinds covered the windows, although it looked dark beyond them. An orange glow emitted from a small lamp over by the mattress that Ted lay on. There was a door at the other end of the room.

"Where... When..."

"You were out cold for an hour or two," Stan said. "Whimpered like a baby when you got hit."

"I'm guessing that was you."

"Actually, that was me." Anna raised to her feet and brushed her hands together. She held one of them out to Riley. The same one that had been massaging Ted's feet. "Pleasure to meet you too, Riley."

Riley shook her hand. He had to remember to wash that later. Poor woman, messing around with Ted's feet. Lifting his slippers out of the middle of the flat was a tough enough task in itself. "And you did that because?"

"Can't take any chances." Anna smacked Stan on the shoulder. "What's grating on you, Granddad?"

"I wish you'd stop calling me that," Stan said. He kept his eyes on Riley. Held his jaw together tightly and bit at his fingernails. "I'm just not comfortable with this arrangement. We've got enough people weighing us down as it is, what with Trevor, and Claudia and her kids. We're bustling at the seams."

"The arrangement was that we helped them out. The guy's stepped right the way through a shard of glass. We owe it to him to let him rest with us, even just for the time being."

Stan tutted and mumbled. "It always starts with the 'time being'."

"Is this the pharmacy?"

Anna tilted her head to Riley. "Close, genius, but not quite. We're in the Chinese restaurant next door. The upper floor just so happens to run right the way across. Not sure I'm so comfortable about the Chinese being able to sneak into the pharmacy. Makes you wonder what they're putting in our takeaway after all."

"Or what the pharmacists are really putting in our laxatives," Ted said.

Anna smirked at Ted's joke before walking back to Stan. He mumbled something. Whatever it was, it didn't sound like a compliment. She whispered in his ear and patted him on the shoulder.

Riley stepped up and examined the room again. "This place you have here. It's good. Safe. It's not ideally close to the supermarket though, but it's one of the safer places I've seen."

"Before you ask — no," Anna said. "You can't stay. Just for tonight."

Riley thought about replying. He looked at Stan, who peered back at him. He was old, but he certainly looked like he had some steel in him. Capable of packing a punch or two. "I… We've nowhere else. The only place is in the middle of town. I don't know if you've seen it out there, but—"

"Yes. We have. I had to run on foot from those things. Got caught up in the traffic making its way over the Ribble Bridge. Wasn't so lucky as to have a car. Insurance and petrol costs never really appealed to me. Guess I can freeload now, huh?"

Riley nodded. Without the pharmacy, where did they go? They should have stayed at the flat. Ted was right all along. All the good places would have been taken. Fortified. "You say there's other people. How did you meet?"

"Unfortunately," Stan spat. "Anna and my wife, Jill, they are okay. But the others. Weighing us all down. Especially the kids. Absolute drain on our resources. No wonder we're running low."

Riley's ears pricked. *Running low.* "The ASDA. It's about five miles from here. We can help you gather some food and water. We can—"

"And how do we know we can trust you? We've got children here. A single mother who can't stop bawling her eyes out every time she sees a speck of blood. A guy who seems to want to sleep his way through this whole thing. And — and no offence here, Stan — an ageing couple. How do we know you aren't just going to try and... well. Shoot us." She pulled the gun out of her pocket and held it out like it was toxic waste.

Riley and Ted's eyes met. The gun. She must've found it in the car. "Listen. The gun — we found that by accident. We're not—"

"By accident? People count themselves fortunate when they find pound coins lying around in the road by accident. But a gun in the middle of a zombie apocalypse? What sort of accident?"

Ted slowly lowered his head back down onto the mattress, attempting to bail himself out of the debate. *Great one, Ted. Great one.* Could he tell her about Jordanna? About leaving her behind? No. He couldn't risk it. They'd almost certainly throw them both out to fend for themselves then. And with no weapon and no place to go, how would they survive?

"I'm... I stole it. I was caught in town too. And one of the police officers. They were carrying guns because of the... of the 'things'. And he... One of them was on the floor. Bitten. So I took it." He stared Anna straight in the eyes. *Hold eye contact. Make her trust you.* In the corner of his line of vision, he could see Ted peeking out of one eye. Stan muttered and cursed inaudible words beside them, and shook his head.

Anna twirled the gun around in her hands. "And what's stopping you from just 'taking' something from us?"

Riley cleared his throat. He could feel warmth working its way up his back and into his neck. "We won't. What you've got here — it's good. We... We want to prove ourselves. In any way we can."

Anna raised her eyebrows. Ted started to lift his head

again, watching Riley with curiosity. "Any way you can?" Anna asked.

Riley nodded. "Yes. Aside... Aside from being bitten. Or anything... You know. Against our morals. Morally incorrect. You know."

Anna bit her lip and looked at Stan. "Well, our food stocks *are* running low."

"We'll do it," Riley said. "We'll go to ASDA and we'll get some supplies. Food. Water. Whatever you need. We'll do it. Right, Ted?"

Ted shrugged half-heartedly. "You can do what you want, mate." He lifted his foot. "I'll just have to see how my sore foot feels in the morning. Might give it a day. Or two."

"Don't push your luck you cheeky son of a bitch," Stan said. "Lucky enough you got a doctor to see to you in the first place. Count your blessings."

Anna circled Riley, tapping the gun against her opposite palm. Through the door, Riley could hear whispering. Footsteps against the floor. Children's voices. "You're serious about proving yourself to us?"

Riley nodded. "Absolutely. What you've got here — it's not perfect, but it's as close as I think we're going to get until they sort this out."

Anna laughed.

"What's so funny?"

"You still think somebody's going to come along and sort this out, don't you? Wake up. Look around." She tapped the gun against Riley's chest before eyeing him up closely for a few long seconds. "Tomorrow. Morning. Me, you, and Trevor. We'll go to ASDA and we'll salvage everything we can."

"Trevor?" Stan interrupted. "You're not seriously taking along that mute idiot, are you?"

Anna smiled. "That 'mute idiot' is quick on his toes. Good at lifting. We need the gift of the abs, not the gift of the gab. In this case, anyway. So, tomorrow. You make sure you're awake. Then we go."

Riley's stomach rumbled audibly. "Right. Thank you. Thanks. For—"

"Thank us by proving your worth to the group tomorrow. We'll introduce you to the rest of them if you pull through." Anna walked in the direction of the door. She stopped by Ted. He grinned at her. "As for you… You'd better hope to hell your friend pulls through. I'm not dragging a big… A wounded guy out of here when the creatures come. And they will. One day." She ruffled his hair and walked to the door.

Stan squared up to Riley. "Don't get too comfortable." He followed Anna towards the door.

"Where are you going?"

Anna opened the door and smiled. "Chinese takeaway. On me. I'll save you a bag of prawn crackers. The bucket on the right — that's for pissing and shitting in. Try not to be too messy, please. Sweet dreams."

She slammed the door shut. A bolt snapped across.

Ted perched on the end of his mattress. "Mate. I think I'm in love with her. She is so, so fit."

Riley grabbed the plastic bucket. Tapped his fingers against it then dropped it back to the floor. "She's also our prison guard."

"Oh, now *that's* an image and a half. Thank you, mate. Thank you."

Chapter Thirteen

TED CRUNCHED A PRAWN CRACKER. HE peeked out of the window, squinting down the dark road. Anna had brought them a bag up not long ago. She'd also dimmed the light right down. *"Can't have those things seeing us. Sweet dreams."*

"Do you think these creatures will ever, y'know, come back to life?"

Riley reached into the bag of prawn crackers. He placed one on his tongue. Instead of sizzling and crackling, it went soggy. They tasted stale. Days old. "I dunno. It's hard to say."

"I mean, the ones who have bad bites. Obviously they... That would be difficult. But what about the ones with leg bites? Things like that? Perhaps there's a way to bring them back to normal someday. Cure them. Don't you reckon?"

Riley thought of the glassy eyed stare of his grandma. Nothing behind her eyes but hunger. "I don't know. How's the foot?"

Ted bit into another prawn cracker. He pulled away from the window and slotted the blind back in place. He lifted his foot up. A thick bandage was wrapped around it, his big toe poking out of the end. "Better than it was. Although I doubt I'll be running free for a few days."

"Well, we're fortunate. This place seems good. Elevated off the ground. And the people here — Anna, Stan… Well, Anna anyway. She seems okay."

Ted whistled in approval and grabbed the bag of prawn crackers. "Yes, she does."

"And the rest of them. Anna said there were more of them. Single mother. Children. We're lucky. They sound like they could have something good going on here. At least for now."

Ted winced as he moved his foot back down on the mattress. "Well, you'd better get proving yourself tomorrow then, hadn't you? I wish I could join you. I really, really do, mate." Ted winked and popped another prawn cracker into his mouth.

"We can do this. I can do this. I think… I think the best thing in times like these is to stick together. We have to prove ourselves." Riley snatched the bag of prawn crackers back from Ted. "Which means more than just sitting back and eating their food. You need to be productive tomorrow, too."

Ted pointed at his foot. "In case you haven't noticed, productivity isn't my strongest point right now."

"I'm not talking about supply runs or anything like that. Just make an effort with this lot. Be kind. Smile, for God's sake."

"Hey." Ted forced a wide, cheesy grin. Specks of prawn cracker were wedged between his teeth. "That good enough for you, mate? Nice big smile?"

"Don't be sarcastic." Riley walked over to the side of the room where he had woken up. He didn't have a mattress — just a thin sheet. He pulled it up to his neck and pressed his back against the wall, a shiver creeping over him.

"Hey…" Ted perched up on his pillow. "How… Are you

okay? After — well, you know. You coping?"

Riley stared up at the ceiling. He could hear voices somewhere opposite them. Floorboards creaking ever so slightly. The rest of the group.

"Because I know it can't have been easy. I know you… How much she meant to you. I know that."

Riley thought of his grandma. The kind woman who picked him up when he fell down, right from an early age. The woman who had always been there for him, no matter what trouble he got himself into. And the being on the kitchen floor. The blood. The dead eyes.

"And having to… to do what you did—"

"The creature I shot wasn't Grandma. It was her body, but it wasn't her. I… I did what I had to do. What we're going to have to keep on doing. That's how we survive."

Ted was silent for a few moments. Then, he cleared his throat and shuffled around on his mattress. "You're tough, bro. Tougher than you ever were before this shit all kicked off anyway. That pansy I used to thrash on FIFA wouldn't stand a chance in this world."

Riley closed his eyes. Felt tiredness working its way down his body. An urge to sleep. But no urge to wake up in this world. Not how it was.

But he had to try. He had to adjust. They all did.

"I'll go to the supermarket tomorrow morning and I'll earn our keep here. You just try to get that foot healed."

"Thanks, Doctor Jameson. Your words aren't quite as motivational as the hot nurse's, though." Ted groaned as he stretched for the light switch and flicked it off. The room was engulfed in darkness. "Night, mate."

Riley breathed in deeply. First night of the new world. He didn't know how long it was going to last. Nobody did.

But he had to be tough.

"Night, Ted."

A sickness thumped him in the stomach the second he

woke up.

He kept his eyes closed. The images rolled through his head like a cinematic montage. The blood — all the blood. The mangled corpses. Intestines rolling out of torsos and trailing against the floor.

The tang of stale prawn crackers in the back of his throat. He needed to puke. Soon.

He opened his eyes.

A little girl was standing over him.

He yelped, startled, as the blonde girl stared at him.

"Come on, Elizabeth. What did I tell you about interrupting the visitors?"

Riley looked up as the little girl ran to the door. His heart raced. By the door, a woman stood. Somebody they hadn't seen yet. She had greying hair down to her shoulders and was tall and slim. She grabbed Elizabeth's hand and half-smiled at Riley.

"Sorry if she startled you," the woman said.

"Mummy, is the man sick like them?" Another girl peeked around the corner. The woman reached for her and pulled her to her side.

"No, Chloë, the man is not… Sorry. I'm—Anna told me to come wake you up. So I… Yeah."

Riley sat up. At the left hand side of the room, Ted had his thick white bedding wrapped over his head. He snored and mumbled under his breath. Out cold.

Riley approached the woman. His throat was dry — he hadn't had a drink for ages now. His head thumped as nausea took a hold of him. "It's okay. Glad you woke me anyway." He held a hand out to the woman. "I'm Riley."

The woman looked at Riley's hand with reluctance. Her daughters, both at her side, stared up at Riley. After a few seconds of hesitation, the woman placed her hand in Riley's and shook. "Claudia. Claudia." She pulled away. "Come on, girls. We'd—we'd better grab a bite to eat."

"Pleasure to meet you, Claudia," Riley said, as Claudia

moved along the hallway area and down a set of stairs. Her daughters whispered at one another, turning around and pointing at Riley.

"Ssh," Claudia said. "Don't be rude. And don't go in there again without me. Okay?"

Riley sighed. He still had some trust-earning to do. But that was to be expected. Today was his big day. His big opportunity to prove to them all that he was serious. To prove to them that Ted and he were completely harmless.

The lie about the gun. That wouldn't matter. It didn't matter as long as their intentions were good. Which they were.

Riley stretched out and yawned. His shoulders cracked as he raised them. Low sunlight peered through the gap in the hallway window. Must've been early.

"If you're wondering why she's so uncertain, she's like that with everyone."

Riley swung around. He hadn't noticed the man standing at the other side of the corridor. He was shorter than him, dark-skinned and an athletic build. He had a buzz-cut. A black hoodie zipped right up to his neck.

"I... Who are—"

"Trevor." The man walked up to Riley. He avoided eye contact. "Thought I'd come say hello." He held out his hand.

Riley took it. "Riley. Pleasure to—"

"Bathroom's where I just came from. By the colour of your cheeks, I'm guessing you need it." He walked away from Riley and hopped down the stairs in a matter of seconds.

Riley whistled as he walked to the bathroom. *Frosty bunch.*

But Trevor was right about one thing. He really did need the bathroom.

Riley stumbled out of the bathroom. His throat stung after vomiting up the very little food he still had left in his system. A piercing pain shot down from the lump on the back of his head and through his body. He could feel himself shaking. Now was not the time to fall ill.

Now was not the time for the fear to set in.

Ted was waiting by the door. He yawned and cocked his leg, taking the pressure off his bandaged foot. "You okay, mate? Look a little... pale."

"I'm okay," Riley lied. "Met a few of the others."

"They okay?"

"They seem normal enough. A little bit uncertain, but to be expected I guess. We're all in the same boat."

"And it's hardly a Mediterranean party boat."

Riley frowned and shook his head. "I've got to get down there. Anna wants us to get prepared for heading to ASDA. You should rest that foot."

"And turn down a date with the lovely Anna? Who are you trying to fool?" He held his hand out. "Lead the way, cupid."

Riley sighed and walked towards the stairs, Ted following closely behind. He arched his neck as they approached the first turn in the stairs. Outside, the road looked quiet. No sign of any creatures. No sign of people. Perhaps things had gone back to normal overnight. Perhaps all was under control again.

At the bottom of the stairs, there was a double door with a large pole wedged through the handle. The door to the Chinese restaurant. He could hear voices to his left, through another door. He held his breath and reached out. "On your best behaviour, okay?"

Ted nodded. "I'm not a child, for heaven's sakes."

"Just—"

"Okay. Okay. Got it." He forced a smile.

Riley lowered the handle and pushed the door. As he did, the talking stopped.

The group was all sat around a large rectangular table. Anna at the top end. Stan and a woman — presumably his wife, Jill — to her left. To her right, Claudia sat, as the two girls chased each other at the other side of the room. At the back of the table, Trevor sat, hood up and disconnected from the rest of the group.

"Boys." Anna smiled and raised a glass of murky looking

water at Riley and Ted. "Good of you to join us. I hope you're okay with prawn crackers for breakfast — we don't have much in the way of choice right now."

Riley's stomach lurched. "I'll... I'll just have some water. Thanks."

Riley and Ted both sat at the end of the table. Trevor moved his chair away and kept his head down, slumped beneath his hooded top. Anna poured Riley and Ted a glass of water and slid them over. Riley tried to hold back, but couldn't stop himself, pouring it down his neck. It might have looked a little murky, but it was cold and it was soothing, and that's all he needed right now.

"Sleep well?" Anna asked.

Riley nodded. "Yeah. Didn't hear any... any of those things. Perhaps... Are they still out there?"

"Yes," Anna said. "I went out earlier this morning to get rid of the dog. Dunno how it found its way here, poor thing. But yes. They are still out there. Just haven't quite wandered in this direction yet."

"Foolish going out on your own," Stan grunted.

"Hey — she got back okay," Stan's wife, Jill, said. "All in one piece, eh?" She held a tissue underneath her nose and sneezed.

"I'm more worried about those things following her back here. She could've put us all at risk."

"Stan." Claudia widened her eyes and tilted her head at her daughters.

"Oh, they're going to have to find out and toughen up at some stage. You must've seen how it was in the city. When you hear them coming, you know it's already too late to do anything about them."

"We'll be okay," Anna said. She smiled reassuringly at Stan. "They didn't see me."

Stan held eye contact with Anna for a few seconds then sighed and folded his arms. Jill sneezed into her tissue again.

"Anyway," Anna said. "For those of you who haven't met

them, this is Riley and Ted."

Riley smiled at the group. Jill was the only one to smile back at him.

"Riley is going to help me gather whatever supplies we can from the supermarket this morning. Now, I know what you're thinking—" Anna held her hand up to Stan as he opened his mouth to cut in. "—It's worthless. It's where everybody else will have gone. And maybe that's true. But think about it — ASDA is kind of in the middle of nowhere. Sure, a lot of cars drive down there when things are normal, but things aren't normal. If people have tried to go to shops, they'll have picked Sainsbury's. Tesco. All in more residential areas. Or perhaps not. But we have to try. We can't survive forever on prawn crackers."

Riley nodded. That was one thing he could agree on.

"And what if you don't come back?" Claudia said. "You… You're organised. Without you, we'll—"

"Claudia, we have to start taking some risks. This isn't a world where we can sit around and starve to death. We can't risk everything being taken while we still have a chance to do something about it."

"Anna's right," Stan said. "We can't laze around on our arses waiting for things to get back to normal again, because I'm sorry to say this sunshine, but I haven't seen anything like it in my sixty years on the planet."

Jill sneezed again. She stuffed the damp, snot-ridden tissue into her pocket and pulled out another one. The space between her lip and nostrils was chapped and raw.

"Thank you, Stan," Anna said. "Claudia — I get your concern. I really do. But we have to be tough now. You have to be tough for your daughters. And they have to be tough for you."

Tears welled up in Claudia's eyes. "I… I know. I know. Pete was always our rock though, you know? I hope to God he's okay. He was…" She sniffed and wiped away her tears with her sleeves. "I know. Got to be tough for them. I know."

Anna smiled and nodded. Stan rolled his eyes and muttered something to Jill, who slapped him on the arm in return.

"It's seven a.m. now. Just gone. Stan — you grab some cold and flu tablets from next door for Jill, or something. We can't have her being ill right now."

"Right you are," Stan said. He wrapped his arm around his wife. "Can't have her feeling rough with all this going on."

"Well, mainly, we can't have her giving our position away with her constant sneezing. Or worse — passing on her cold to all of us. If it gets worse, you might have to keep her in the spare room for a while."

Stan's face flushed. "I'm not fucking—"

"No, no, Stan," Jill said, patting his arm. "She's right. Maybe I should spend the day out of the way. Don't want to make the lovely girls sick." She pointed over at Claudia's daughters. "It's that bloody flu jab again. Always brings me down."

"That can happen," Anna said. "But it's just a small dose. It won't last long. Get well soon."

Stan grumbled and peered at Riley and Ted as he left the room with Jill.

"Okay — Claudia, obviously I want you to keep an eye on your girls, but also watch the street. If anything happens, I want you to be the one to make sure everybody gets in the Previa and out of here. Okay?"

Claudia looked around the table. "Are—are you sure I can—"

"You're tough, remember? We can trust you with this."

Claudia inhaled a sharp breath. "Yes. Yes I am. You can trust me."

"Ted — darling — I want you to help Claudia on watch. If anything gets out of hand... yes. You act fast. Can you do that?"

Ted's eyes were dreamy as they stared at Anna. Way too dreamy and positive than they should be in the middle of a zombie apocalypse.

"Ted?"

"Yes. Course I can. Course."

"Okay," Anna said. "Which leaves the three of us. Riley. Trevor."

Trevor raised his head. Looked at Riley then Anna. "Me?"

"Yes, you. You're tough and you're quick. I saw how you were in the city. You can handle yourself."

Trevor shook his head and slumped back under his hood. "Don't know if I can…"

"It's this way or the road. We're all pulling our weight around here. Your call."

Trevor lifted his head and stared at Anna. Narrowed his eyes. His jaw tensed.

And then he sighed and nodded. "Okay. Whatever."

"Good." Anna raised to her feet. "Then we all know what we're doing. Trevor, Riley — meet at the Mercedes in five." She opened the door and started to walk out of it.

"And where are you going?" Riley asked.

Anna raised her eyebrows. "Getting us some equipment to kill creatures with."

Chapter Fourteen

RILEY SAT IN THE PASSENGER SEAT of the car. He gripped the wrench tightly against his legs. It was heavy enough to swing at the heads of the creatures. Not the most comfortable thing to carry, but it would serve its purpose. Finding a gun within the first few hours of the outbreak was good luck. This was reality.

Anna sped down the road in the red Mercedes. A butcher's knife was stuffed under her belt strap. Her weapon of choice against the creatures. She kept her eyes on the road. She didn't turn to look at the boarded-up windows or the gradual rise in abandoned cars as they got further out of the countryside and into the suburbs. She disregarded the slow, stumbling beings, turning their heads and clambering in the direction of the engine. She didn't drive all that badly for somebody who didn't own a car.

"We'll have to take another road back. If those creatures follow us now, they'll—"

"Let's focus on getting there first. Okay?"

Riley shrugged and looked in the rear-view mirror. A pair of furry dice dangled down from around it. He could see Trevor on the back seat, hands in pockets. Staring out as they passed the creatures, not a flicker of emotion.

"So, how did you two meet?" Riley asked in a hushed tone. The car swerved past a corpse in the road, innards spewing out. Riley tried his best not to remember the taste of the prawn crackers.

Trevor shuffled in the back seat. "In town."

"Okay... So did you guys know each other before, or...?"

"No."

Riley puffed his lips and turned to Anna, who was focused on the road. "He's a chatty one, isn't he?"

"You know as much about him as I do. All we know is that he's quick and he's tough. Helped get us out of a really bad blockage of those things. Not... I don't think a lot of people survived at my surgery. But the few that did, well. I have Trevor to thank. So he's entitled to his silence."

Riley took another glance in the mirror at Trevor. He stared back at him, eyes unmoving.

"He was covered in blood when he got to us. Didn't speak until last night."

"What if he has... like... a dark secret?" Riley whispered.

"I think we all have our secrets." Trevor cut through Riley and Anna's chat.

Riley nodded. The gun. How they'd kept hold of it. Leaving Jordanna to die. "I guess so. And the others — you know them?"

Anna slowed the car down. Two creatures were in the road, feasting on a skinny framed corpse. The gender was unidentifiable. As was the age. The creatures looked up as the car approached and gradually manoeuvred around them. "Stan and Jill were at the surgery when it... when they came. Claudia and the girls were on the street outside. So no. I don't really know them." She continued to edge the car around the feeding creatures, who rose to their feet and pressed their bloody hands against the window.

"Then why do you trust them and not me?"

Anna stopped the car. The creatures were still pushed up to the glass. They snapped their teeth and scratched at the window. Thick blood and mucus oozed out of their mouths and onto the car. Anna pulled the butcher's knife out of her belt strap and rolled the window down, then stabbed one of the creatures in its half-eaten face. "Because they didn't have a gun." The other creature attempted to pull itself in through the window, but Anna yanked her knife back and stabbed it right in its wide open mouth. When she brought her knife back again, it fell to the floor.

She closed the window and wiped the knife on a towel. Then, she slipped it back into her belt strap and smiled. "Does that answer all your questions?"

Riley looked out of the front window as the car began to pull away. "All but one."

"Which is?"

"How can a doctor be so handy with a butcher's knife?"

Anna smirked. "I guess we really do all have our secrets, don't we?"

They drove for another ten minutes or so. The numbers of creatures fluctuated as they turned off the main road and down a windy country lane. The supermarket was at the end of the road. With any luck, it wouldn't already have been stripped of its supplies. The chances of that were small, but it was the best chance they had of all the supermarkets in the area.

"What if this place is already bone dry?" Riley asked. He could see the roof of the supermarket emerging in the distance.

"One step at a time, like we agreed."

Riley nodded. Anna was right — they couldn't get too far ahead of themselves. But a sense of dread lingered in his stomach. A 'what if?' circled his head. Nine mouths to feed back at the Chinese restaurant. If they didn't manage to take much food back, he had a bad feeling Ted and he wouldn't be top of the guest list. The group could only last so long on prawn crackers. Numbers would have to be cut.

He had to prove his worth. Stake his claim in the group.

Anna turned in to the car park. There was no sign of creatures around. Several cars were in the car park. Not loads — perhaps twenty or thirty. People rushed inside, clinging to the hands of their wives, as others pushed trollies stuffed with tins and various sharp paraphernalia out of the supermarket doors.

"I guess this is it," Anna said. She opened her door and looked around the car at Riley and Trevor. "Trevor — you head for the canned aisle. Grab baked beans, tuna — anything that we can eat cold if we absolutely have to. Meet back at the car in fifteen minutes. No exceptions."

Trevor nodded and opened the car door. He slipped a knife under his sleeve and scanned the area. It was clear. For how long, nobody could tell.

"And you." Anna stopped the engine. "Get us some bottled water. With a load of contaminated bodies crawling around and bathing their feet in the water supplies, I wouldn't like to think too much about the sorts of diseases that could be spreading through the tap water."

Riley smiled and made sure the wrench was securely fastened in his pocket. "Something only a doctor would consider."

"I'm hoping that's the case." Anna opened the car door and stepped out. Riley followed.

Trevor was already several hundred feet in the distance, reaching out for a trolley and pushing his way into the supermarket.

"Told you he was quick," Anna said.

"Let's just hope he's loyal."

Anna clicked the remote car lock. "He's quiet, but he seems to have his heart and head in the right place. That's the sort of people we need on our side in these times."

The pair of them walked to the entrance of the supermarket. The people entering and leaving were completely focused on themselves, barely acknowledging those around them. Their trollies looked full. Microwave meals. Books. Video games.

"The world goes to shit and all people are interested in doing is playing video games."

"At least we haven't changed that much. Yet, anyway."

Riley grabbed a trolley and yanked it backwards. It was chained to the one in front.

Anna held a coin out. "Just because the world's gone to shit doesn't mean you can start stealing trollies." She plonked the coin into the trolley that Riley struggled with. The chain snapped free, and she repeated it with the next trolley.

"Meet you in fifteen?"

Riley examined the car park. Families stuffing the contents of their overfilled trollies into their car boots. Men barking orders. Children crying.

But no creatures. Not yet.

"Let's get this done with."

Riley shoved his way past people as he approached the bottled water aisle. He tried to remain focused and undistracted, but he couldn't quite believe what he was seeing. Men grabbing televisions and iPads, handing one each to their children. Trollies stuffed with bottles of wine and booze. Consumerism's final dying breath.

He took a right and looked at the words above each aisle. *Fruit & Vegetables.* No use. Would start to rot in no time. Would have to find other sources of Vitamin C. *Meat & Poultry.* Same as fruit and vegetables. Still, the aisle had been mostly emptied. One last fry-up to celebrate the end times. No — they'd have to find some sort of link with a farm if they wanted a meat supply in the long run. Somehow form a trust with them. Repay them in a sought after commodity. Somehow, Riley didn't expect that prawn crackers and the scraps of fried rice remaining in the Chinese restaurant would be much of a catch, but then again, business consistently surprised.

Riley started to jog. He could see the *Water & Juice Drinks* aisle emerging in the near-distance. Anna was right — they were relying on the complacency of others when it came to water. The short-sighted assumption that tap water would suffice for the immediate future.

But they didn't know how long this was going to last. Nobody did. Better to prepare for a future that might not unfold than be underprepared and dehydrated.

He turned his trolley around the *Water* aisle. All the juice drinks had vanished. All cordial and all the pure juice. But at the end of the aisle, at the bottom of the shelf, there were three packs of bottled water remaining. Eighteen large bottles a packet. Enough to get by on, for now.

Riley pushed his trolley to the end of the aisle and reached down for the bottles of water. His neck ached as he lifted the pack from the shelf and dumped it in the trolley. Must've slept funny. Or hurt it at some stage yesterday. Both were likely.

He grabbed another pack and winced as he lifted it. He could hear voices at an aisle nearby. People giving orders. Footsteps echoing against the hard floor. He dropped the second pack of water bottles into his trolley. *Two down, one to go...*

As he lifted the third pack of water bottles, he heard footsteps shuffling at the end of the aisle he'd come from.

"Just get what you can!" A voice an aisle or two away.

He looked up. A woman was at the end of the aisle. She had thin blonde hair, a gaunt and pale face. She twiddled with a locket around her neck, her fingers covered with warts. Her bottom lip shook as she stared at Riley with the third and final pack of water bottles in his hands.

The pair of them glared at one another, completely silent. But nobody had to talk. Riley knew what she wanted. The way she was staring at the water bottles, lips cracked and chapped.

She blinked rapidly. Opened and closed her mouth as if to speak.

A guilt descended inside Riley's chest. The images of the people in the supermarket stealing televisions. Trollies rampacked with excess food and excess drink and excess-whatever-the-hell-else. Pure greed. He couldn't be that man. Humanity had to stick together.

He placed the final pack of water bottles on top of the others and started to tear the plastic wrapper that held them in place. The woman watched him, closely. Silent.

"Get a fucking move on down there," a man's voice shouted.

"Ye—Yes. Almost done." The woman's voice was high-pitched. Croaky. Sounded like she'd smoked one too many cigarettes in her lifetime. She shuffled her feet on the spot. Scratched at her reddened arms even more rapidly with dirty, over-long nails.

Riley squeezed out three bottles. *Would three be enough?* It would make just a bottle and a half each for her and her husband. A bottle each if they had a kid. Less if they had two. He grabbed another bottle and held the four of them in his arms, carrying it over to her like it was a baby.

She didn't look him in the eye as he got closer. Moved back slightly.

"Here," Riley said. He nodded at the bottles. "This... It should get you by. For now."

The woman briefly looked Riley in the eye. Her eyes were watery. Dark underneath. Scanned his face inquisitively. "Tha... Thank you. Very kind. Very kind of you." She held out her weedy, shaky arms.

Riley lowered the bottles into her arms. She hunched forward slightly with the weight, then took a deep breath and pulled herself as upright as she could manage, her tendons sticking out with the tension. She smiled. "We won't forget this. You're... You're a kind man. Thank you."

She disappeared around the corner with the four water

bottles in hand.

Riley turned back around to his trolley. The fifty remaining bottles. He sighed. He could've given her more. She'd been so grateful. So appreciative. He walked back to the trolley and reached for a loose piece of card from the top shelf. He covered up the water bottles. He had to get them to the car. Anna might have been right about people's misjudgment, but he couldn't risk the woman's husband seeing him pushing fifty bottles along while he had to make do with four.

He looked at his watch as he turned the trolley around. Five past eight. He still had ten minutes remaining. He could take his time on the way back. Exit via the quietest route. He pushed the trolley forward. The first thing he'd stolen since 2000. *Kid A.* Even that, he'd stolen digitally because a major reviewing opportunity appeared and he didn't have the money to buy the album at the time. Spent it all on booze. And no matter how perfectly layered the album was; no matter how sonically brilliant and brimming with depth, he still couldn't listen to it without feeling a slight bit of guilt to this day.

This should have felt different. This was stealing to survive. But it didn't. In the back of his mind, a small part of him truly believed that everything was going to suddenly switch back to normal again. That order would return and he'd be the one caught red-handed stealing water bottles. He shook his head and carried on pushing the trolley as two men rushed past carrying a fifty inch television.

As he turned out onto the main aisle, he noticed a little green plus sign above a closed door. It flickered on and off intermittently. He moved towards it. He'd never noticed the ASDA pharmacy before. There were no lights on inside. It didn't look like anybody else had noticed it either.

He turned the handle and the door swung open. It was silent inside. No voices. All the voices and the commotion were in the supermarket area. No doubt the druggies would find it eventually. Raid it for its supplies.

But not yet, by the looks of things.

He glanced at his watch. Eight minutes past eight. He still had time to go in there. See if he could find anything to help Jill — Stan's wife — with her cold. Sure, there would be meds in the pharmacy next door to the Chinese, but supplies were limited. At least if he showed he was making an effort, Stan might warm to him. Maybe.

He moved into the dark corridor. He could see a dim light flickering on the right up ahead. The words, *Sharoe Green Surgery* were written above the lit window. He definitely hadn't been aware they'd had a doctor's surgery in here, either. Quite handy, really. Go to the doctors, get told you're not morbidly obese, and treat yourself to something from the ice cream freezers on the way out. Just make sure you carry a bag of vegetables with you to give the illusion of healthy eating.

Riley turned to the shelves on the left. Stacks of Strepsils and Halls Soothers. Sun cream and allergy repellants. Nothing too extreme.

He grabbed a few of the Strepsils and Soothers and dropped them into the trolley. They wouldn't cure any illness, but they'd help. At least he'd be acknowledged for making an effort. He swung the trolley back round and headed to the pharmacy exit door.

Something thudded behind him.

He turned around slowly. The thudding seemed further away than the pharmacy. Down the corridor.

Another thud.

It was coming from the surgery.

Riley gripped the wrench in his pocket. He didn't have to check it out. He could take the trolley and leave. Anna had made it clear — fifteen minutes and they were out of here. He couldn't take his chances.

Another thud.

He brought the wrench out of his pocket and walked slowly down the dark corridor, pulling his trolley behind him. One look wouldn't hurt anybody.

As he got closer to the flickering light of the surgery

window, he saw the door shaking slightly. The thudding noise. Something was banging against the door. Somebody was trapped inside there.

Something was trying to get out.

He held his breath and let go of his trolley as he stepped past the door. There was a note pinned up to it — *Flu Jab Season: Get Yours Here & Stay Safe for Winter!* The door shook again. Rattled on its hinges.

Riley peeked in through the window, holding the wrench tightly in his clammy hand.

The wrench almost dropped to the floor when he saw what was inside.

There were seven creatures. All of them were standing over the half-eaten body of a nurse. She had an injection in her hands. Her legs were stripped of flesh, white bones on show. Three of her ribs were also visible, the muscles in her chest and her breasts torn away from her body.

She was gasping. Gargling blood. Dead eyes. Snapping teeth.

Riley stepped to the side. Covered his mouth. *Shit.* He had to get out of here. Stay silent and get out of here.

Another thud at the door. One of them must have been pushing against it. But the others — they hadn't heard him, or smelt him, or whatever else it was they did. None of them were groaning in the way he'd heard them do so many times yesterday. He still had a chance to get out of here.

As he rushed back to his trolley, the door at the opposite end of the pharmacy crashed open. A man stormed in. He was wearing a sweaty vest, revealing the tattoos that covered both of his arms. He was muscular and well-built, with hair shaved right down. He had two bottles of water under each arm. "Hear you've got a bit more water than you're letting onto."

Riley's legs went weak. Behind him, peeking around the door, the woman he'd given the four bottles to.

The man dropped the bottles of water to the floor, eyeing up Riley's trolley. As he did, the creatures in the surgery turned their heads, like they were searching for the source of the noise. The greying eyes of the mutilated nurse on the floor stared at Riley. She raised her skeletal arm in his direction.

"Fucking selfish bastard," the man said, pumping out his chest as he got closer to Riley. He cracked his knuckles and kicked one of the bottles along the floor.

"Petey, don't—"

"You, shut up," he said, turning and pointing at his wife.

She cowered and took a step back into the expanse of the supermarket. Tears ran down her bruised face.

Riley looked to his side. The creatures were all groaning now. All walking in the direction of the glass. The one by the door had diverted its attentions to Riley — an old man in a suit, blood dribbling down his bearded chin. The others stepped on and over the nurse on the floor, who kept on falling back down every time she tried to stand on her flimsy, fleshless legs.

Pete started to approach Riley again. "I think it's fucking rude. Taking all that water for yourself and only giving my wife four bottles. Fucking rude."

"We can work something out here," Riley said. The creatures lined up against the glass. Eventually, it would crack. They'd spill out of the surgery and take the supermarket, one by one.

"Too right we can," Pete said. He grinned and nodded at the trolley full of water. "How about you let me take a look in that trolley of yours?"

Riley's heart raced. He gulped down a lump in his throat and made his wrench visible. He felt ridiculous in the process. A scrawny bastard like him standing up to this muscular, gym-crazy beast. Who was he fooling?

Pete raised his eyebrows and whistled when he saw the wrench. "Boy's brought a toy along, has he? Does the boy want to play? Huh?" He pulled a knife out of his pocket. It glistened in the flickering of the surgery light.

Riley stepped forward and grabbed his trolley. The

creatures continued to push their bodies up to the glass, desperate for a fresh meal. He could try and push his way through Pete and his wife. Charge towards him with his wrench raised and hope he jumped out of the way. Hope Pete's knife didn't stab into his leg.

Instead, he took a step back.

Pete frowned as he raised his knife. "Backing off, huh? Not want to play anymore, boy? Well, tough. Nowhere to hide down there. What you gonna do? Go running out the back door into those zombies? I'm gonna fucking cut you to pieces. Rude bastard."

Riley saw the movement in the corner of his eye as he stepped further and further backwards with the trolley. The creatures. So close. Only glass between them. Groaning. Thumping their hands against the window. Pete moved towards him. Tension welled up inside. He had to do something. He had to try something.

He knew what it was. He just wasn't sure whether he had it in him.

"Or maybe I'll take you back with us. Feed you to those hungry fuckers and keep you as a pet." He started to laugh, manically. "A fucking scrawny zombie pet!" He turned to his wife for approval. "That's funny. Hey — I said that's funny."

His wife forced a smile as her husband's tone turned angrier. Riley stopped moving backwards. Looked to his left. The creatures were still there. They weren't going anywhere soon. If Pete saw them, he'd throw Riley in there. Leave him to die. Or worse. Cut him up. Throw him in bit by bit. Force him to watch himself be dissected. A slow, excruciatingly painful death.

"Bitch needs a sense of humour." He spat on the floor and approached Riley again. "Used to be funny when we first met. Then went the way of all the whores in this place. Miserable fucking bitch. But I love her. I love her, you know?"

Riley nodded. He took a deep breath in. Cleared his throat. "Then take it."

Pete stopped. His face turned. "You what?"

"Take it," Riley said. He let go of the trolley. Adrenaline pumped through his body. He had a sense of what he was doing. A sense of a plan. But it had taken a life of its own. "Just... Just take it. I don't want any more trouble here."

Pete sniggered. "You're just gonna give that trolley up? Stand there like a little weak boy and hand it over? That's how it's gonna be?"

Riley nodded. "Yes."

Pete was silent. He observed Riley closely. Squinted and scanned his face and his body. He still hadn't seen the creatures behind the glass. The flickering light was deceptive. It made their movement look like nothing more than shadows. "Then bring it the fuck here."

Riley held his ground. Twirled the wrench around in his hand. "If you want it, you can come get it."

Pete's eyes narrowed. "Suit yourself." He walked quickly towards the trolley. He was just feet away now. The creatures at the window—he'd notice them soon.

Riley had to act fast.

Pete grabbed the front of the trolley. Pointed his knife at Riley. "You stay there. Don't move a muscle until we're out of here. Okay?"

Something thumped against the window. The light flickered to life.

Pete must have seen it because he turned his head slowly in the direction of the glass. His knife lowered, as did his jaw.

Riley yanked the trolley back. "You can have all the water you want."

Then, he lifted his wrench and threw it at the glass.

Pete barely had a chance to react before one of the creatures was on top of him. It wrestled him to the ground as he stabbed at its neck. It continued to snap its teeth above him, pushing him down as more creatures swarmed out of the broken glass and piled onto him.

Riley ran towards the door he'd come through. His heart

raced. He heard Pete scream out and the sound of flesh tearing as the creatures groaned and grunted.

Pete's wife was completely frozen. She stared at her husband as teeth sunk into his jugular, spraying blood across the walls. He was still stabbing into the thin air with his knife as the creatures chewed on his arms and legs and chest.

Riley stopped at the door. Pete's wife was still not moving. She gasped. Her face was even paler than it had been before. Snot and tears covered her mouth.

"Have you got it?"

Riley recognised the voice. When he looked up, he saw it was Trevor. He had a trolley full of tins and cans. Baked Beans. Spaghetti. Spam. Even dog food. Enough to last them a long, long time.

Riley stared back into the room. Pete's wife dropped to her knees, whimpering. The trolley was still in the room. Some of the water bottles had tumbled to the floor as the creatures had poured out of the glass.

"Ah," Trevor said, peering into the pharmacy.

Pete's knife dropped to the floor and he disappeared completely under the mob of creatures.

Chapter Fifteen

RILEY REACHED FOR THE PHARMACY DOOR. Pete's wife sobbed into her hands, crouched on the floor. He pulled the door shut as the creatures in the room continued to feast on Pete's body. There was no point going in there to try and retrieve the water bottles. That would just attract unnecessary attention. Better just to leave them to it. Leave the problem for somebody else to deal with.

Trevor stared at Riley. He had his hood up and his trolley beside him. "Better go," he said. There was an apprehension in his eyes. A wariness. Riley had screwed up and he knew it. He didn't have to go into that pharmacy. He didn't have to walk down the corridor and alert the attention of the creatures. He didn't even have to give the woman those bottles of water. He should've just walked. Taken the bottles and walked. Survival had no time for the sentimental.

Riley and Trevor started to walk away. It was thirteen minutes past eight. They didn't have much time to get to the car. They'd have to hurry, or Anna would leave. Either that, or she was bluffing. He wasn't particularly keen on finding out.

"You have to take me with you. Please."

Riley's stomach sank. He turned around as they reached the *Crisps* aisle and saw Pete's wife on her knees. Mascara trailed down her cheeks. She sniffed and sobbed.

"Please." She held her hands together. "I've... I've got nothing left. Just... Just let me come with you. You were so kind to me. Let me come with you."

Riley looked at Trevor. Trevor shook his head. "There's too many as it is. We've really gotta go."

"Please." The woman stumbled to her feet and edged towards them. "My husband — he was a bad man. But I'm not like that. I'm—I'm not—"

"We can't. I'm... I'm really sorry." Riley's head sank. "I'm sorry."

Pete's wife frowned. Stumbled around on the spot. Her face had changed. She didn't look sympathetic anymore. The pitiful expression had vanished.

Instead, she was scowling. Her bottom lip was shaking. "I was wrong about you. Thought you were a kind man. Thought you were going to help me. But no. No."

Trevor started to move away with the trolley. "Got to go. Seriously."

Riley stepped towards the woman. "We've got too many people as it—"

"Bastard. You bastard. I could've locked you in there with him. Could've locked you in there with him to die. Bastard." Her face turned again, and she started to whimper.

"I'm sorry," Riley said. "You... You have to go back home. Go somewhere safe. There are others out there. Others who can help you."

Pete's wife looked at the door. Sniffed back her tears. "There's nobody else for me."

In what seemed like slow-motion, she reached for the door handle and opened it. Then, she banged it against the wall.

"No!" Riley shouted. He tried to run towards her but he felt arms wrap around his chest. The creatures would hear the banging. They'd hear the banging and they'd come to get her. They'd get her, then they'd take the supermarket. Men, women, children—all of them.

"Time to go," Trevor said. He pulled Riley back and grabbed the trolley.

Pete's wife stared back at them with red raw eyes as they disappeared in the direction of the exit. She banged the door. Banged it again. The groans grew closer. The footsteps grew closer.

"I'm sorry," Riley mouthed. He turned away and jogged alongside Trevor.

Bang. Bang. Bang.

Don't look back. Keep on moving forward.

The banging stopped. Riley tensed his jaw. Any moment, they'd be out of the pharmacy. Hunting down their new prey with insatiable hunger.

Struggling. A thud against the hard floor.

"Best not look back now," Trevor said, as they approached the exit doors.

But he didn't have to look back. He could tell from the fear in the eyes of the shoppers and looters in front of him that it was likely happening.

And when Pete's wife started screaming, he knew it was definitely happening.

Were it just Riley and Trevor, or Riley and another member of the group, they'd have kept as quiet as possible as soon as they sighted a creature. Their experiences with the beasts over the last eighteen hours had taught them that much. Don't make a sound. Don't let them hear you.

Unfortunately, the rest of the shopping centre hadn't caught on to this idea quite as rapidly.

People screamed and barged past Riley and Trevor. They crowded around the door, clambering over fallen bodies. The creatures diverted their attention from Pete's wife and raised to their feet as soon as they heard the commotion. One groaned, and another followed. That one groaned, another followed.

"No chance we're getting out that way," Trevor said.

The main door was lined with people. They were throwing trollies at one another, punching and scratching and fighting their way out as the creatures staggered forward.

Leading the pack was Pete. Wedged between his teeth was his wife's locket, coated with blood and flesh.

"Don't see why they can't just be patient. There's only eight or nine of those things."

"Are *you* patient?" Trevor shouted.

He had a point. It was all fair and good intending to take things easy and move single file. But at the end of the day, everybody wanted the same thing — to get out of here. Fast.

"We're three minutes late. We're screwed anyway. No chance Anna's waiting around in this. But we need to find another way out of this place."

"The pharmacy," Riley said. "The way those things came from. There was a double door. A doctor's exit, or something."

"And it was unlocked?"

"We're going to have to find out."

Riley and Trevor turned around. The creatures were stumbling towards them, grabbing unsuspecting looters and biting them. Pete's wife was on her feet now, eyes glazed and arm partly dangling off.

"They're multiplying. We're going to have to get around them quickly."

Riley pointed at the *Rice & Pasta* aisle to their left. "Up there, flank them, then get back into the pharmacy."

"And if the door's locked?"

A bitten man raised to his feet and sunk his teeth into his sobbing wife's neck.

"Then it's been totally fucking bizarre knowing you these last few hours, Trevor."

Trevor pushed the trolley up the aisle and Riley followed closely.

Riley looked around as he opened the door to the pharmacy. Everybody had flocked in the other direction. The creatures followed the screaming, stopping now and then to gorge on a fallen body. Funny how life threatening the most minor of mistakes could be in this new world. Tripping over a shoelace. Twisting your ankle. Things taken for granted in the old days. Not anymore.

Trevor pushed the trolley slowly across the blood and gut stained floor and into the pharmacy. Riley cringed, trying not to look too closely at the mess below. Pete. Pete's wife. A sick, twisted way for their story to come to a close.

"Looks clear enough," Trevor whispered. "Let's make this as quick as we can."

Riley took a final look around the supermarket. The creatures continued their pursuit in the opposite direction. Blood dripped from their open wounds. It still didn't look real. They were like waxwork models. Actors. Scary, but seemingly false.

Until they had their teeth sunk into a person's neck.

Riley closed the pharmacy door as quietly as he could and turned around. The pharmacy was silent. Blood covered the floor right up to the smashed glass. A mash of innards were gathered in a pile beside the trolley of water bottles.

"Looks like some shit went down in here," Trevor said. He stopped at the trolley of water bottles, reaching down and picking one up from the floor. Blood ran down the side of the bottle like condensation.

"You could say that," Riley said. He checked the aisles. Checked to see that none of them had stayed behind. How many of them were there before? Seven? Eight?

Riley crept over the broken glass. The light in the surgery room flickered, illuminating the blood. The sign on the door — *Flu Jab Season: Get Yours Here & Stay Safe for Winter!* — had been partly torn away. He looked at the trolley that he'd left behind. Still stuffed with water bottles. Some of them had fallen to the floor, but there were enough. He grabbed the handle and pushed the trolley towards the rear door.

"Funny, isn't it?" Riley said.

Trevor frowned. "What?"

"All this panic about flu season and flu's the least of our..." Riley froze. Stopped in his tracks and stared in through the broken surgery window.

The mutilated nurse lying on the floor was gone.

"We have to leave," Riley said, pushing the trolley towards the door. "Quick. One of them can't have got out. Her legs — they were bitten down to the bone. We have to—"

Trevor lurched backwards. It seemed to happen in a blur. The creature nurse was on top of him. He pushed back her head as she snatched her teeth. He couldn't reach for his weapon. His hands were occupied holding her back. He couldn't do anything about her.

"Help!" he shouted. "Please—please help."

Riley was still, like an animal caught in the headlights. He'd lost his weapon. Thrown it through the glass. He turned around. Ran in through the broken window of the surgery and scanned the floor. It had to be here. It had to be.

Trevor shouted out as the nurse's teeth got closer to his neck. His arm shook. He was struggling to hold her back. "Please!"

A piece of sharp glass caught Riley's eye. He had to act fast.

He reached down for it and snapped it from the floor, nicking his hand in the process.

Then, he ran over to Trevor and the nurse and plunged the sharp glass through her temple.

Deep red blood spilled out of her skull, covering Trevor. He gasped, like he'd been held under water for too long, then pushed the nurse from on top of him. The glass wedged further into her head as she hit the floor.

The pair of them were still for a few moments. Riley felt a burning sensation in his palm — he'd cut it with the glass. He wiped the blood away onto his trousers and stood up. Trevor stared at the corpse of the nurse, wide-eyed.

"Come on," Riley said. He held out his good hand.

Trevor nodded and grabbed Riley's hand, pulling himself up to his feet. "Thanks."

They each grabbed their trollies and walked out of the rear exit door.

Outside, people swarmed out of the main doors like ants, retreating to their nests. Cars were stacked up in a large, spiralling queue. Horns honked. Windows cracked as people jostled their way free.

"No chance Anna's stuck around," Trevor said. He slumped against the trolley and smacked his fist into the tins.

Riley examined his watch. Twenty-three minutes past eight. Anna would be long gone. She'd probably have left before the commotion properly started. He let go of his trolley and shook his head. "What now?"

Trevor shrugged. "We take the road. Hope we stumble upon an abandoned car when we're out of this place. Priority is getting out of here."

Engines revved up. Somewhere by the exit, there was a scream. Car horns pipped and honked to their right, to their left, everywhere.

"We might find a car on the main road. But we'll be lucky. And we both saw what it was like on our way down."

A car horn continued to honk to their left. It seemed further away from the other cars. And why would it be honking?

Riley turned and saw exactly why it was.

It was the red Mercedes. Across the street, outside of the car park and away from the traffic. Anna waved madly in their direction.

"Holy shit, it's her," Riley said.

Trevor turned around, serious-faced. When he saw what Riley saw, a smile twitched at the edges of his mouth for the very first time.

Riley reached for his trolley again. Pushed it forward, over to the other side of the car park. She was a matter of metres away. All this time, and she'd waited for them.

Trevor followed closely behind. They ran over the grass, then over the pavements and across the road. When they reached the Mercedes, Anna lurched the car forward, teasingly, then reversed again. She wound down her window.

"What the fuck kept you two so long?"

Riley and Trevor raised their eyebrows. "It's a long story. But we've... we've got the stuff."

The boot clicked open. Trevor lifted it and started to throw the tins inside. Riley stuffed a few bottles of water under his arms and tossed those in.

"No trouble getting hold of bottled water by the looks of things?"

Riley shook his head. "Don't even get me started."

Chapter Sixteen

RILEY CLOSED HIS EYES AND RESTED his head against the car window. Images from the supermarket replayed in his mind's eye. The wrench, leaving his hand and crashing through the surgery window. Pete's jabbing knife dropping to the floor as his arm disappeared from sight underneath a pile of creatures. Pete's wife. Scared. Alone. Afraid.

"You shouldn't lean on the window." Anna had been relatively talkative when Riley and Trevor had got in the car. But now, she seemed more reluctant. Now she'd seen the blood on their hands, and in Trevor's case, his entire face. "Wouldn't... Wouldn't want one of those things to grab you."

Riley straightened his neck onto the headrest and opened his eyes. They were on the main road again, travelling in the direction of the Chinese restaurant. They'd be back soon. Back to normality. Except it wasn't normal. Not after the things they'd been through. Not after the things they'd had to do.

Anna slowed the car down and manoeuvred it around a

half-open door of an abandoned car. "You did good, though. Getting all that water. And all those cans." She nodded in her rear-view mirror at Trevor. Trevor stared on, silent. The nurse's dried blood coated his face. "I got us some meat and veg. A few things for the kids. Mini sausages, things like that. Hey... I had to kill one too, y'know? You aren't alone in this."

Riley gritted his teeth. She had no idea what he'd had to do.

The car sped up again. The mass of abandoned vehicles grew smaller as they left them behind. Anna tutted and exhaled, agitated. "You're going to have to toughen up if you want to survive this. Can't start moping every time we go on a supply—"

"I let two people die," Riley said.

Anna turned slowly and looked at Riley. She cleared her throat. Tried to disguise her shock. "You... Are you okay?"

He stared out at the road. The fields passed by. Wooden blockades covered the windows of the various country houses. He'd partly told the truth. He'd killed Pete — as good as. He'd allowed Pete's wife to be devoured by her own husband.

But it was Jordanna who still haunted Riley. Her wide, bloodshot eyes as Ted and he accelerated away from her, trapped at the side of that tanker.

Then looking back and seeing the mob of creatures crowded around her. Lost in a sea of agony and death.

"Well, hey. If you need to... y'know. Talk it out or whatever." She rested her hand on his forearm.

He flinched slightly, then allowed it to stay there. He looked at her nervously, his eyes twitching, and half-smiled.

"I let my friends die."

The voice startled Riley at first. He turned around. Trevor was still staring into space. He rubbed his temples with the ends of his fingers.

"You—"

"In the city. There were four of us. Fooling around. Free running and parkour and all that shit. And then this man comes up to D-Job... Dave. This man comes up to him and wraps his arms around him. Me and the rest of the boys are all laughing. Shouting at him and cussing. But then he looks up — this old fella, tramp sort of guy — he looks up and he's got a chunk of D-Job's neck in his mouth." Tears rolled down Trevor's cheeks. His bottom lip quivered.

"And then the other boys. Pal and Little Si. They go up to this tramp and start kicking the shit out of him. But I froze. The blood — it froze me. And then... D-Job bit into Pal's ankle. And then it was just Little Si and he was cornered and I..." He gulped. "I ran."

Riley turned to Anna and back to Trevor. He had his head in his hands. He pulled his hood up and sat back. The tears crawling down his cheeks were still visible even though his eyes were covered.

Riley nodded. "You did what you had to do. We... We've all had to make some tough decisions. But they don't define us. What we were, when this whole thing broke out. That's not us now. It can't be. We have to be strong. But we have to be open. Right?" He looked at Anna for approval.

Anna's eyes were welled up. She remained focused on the road. They were deep in the countryside again now. An element of peace returned. Fewer abandoned cars. Fewer bodies staggering around the streets. "Do you really believe that?"

Jordanna's face. The fear. *"Please."*

"I have to. We all have to."

The Mercedes pulled in beside the Previa in the Chinese restaurant and pharmacy car park. Trevor got out first and headed straight for the boot, bundling as many tins and cans into the bottom of his hoodie as possible. Stan was peering out of the upstairs window as Riley and Anna stepped out and picked up some shopping of their own.

The front door of the Chinese restaurant opened.

It was Ted.

Riley rushed towards him and dumped the water bottles into his hands.

"And there I was thinking you were going to give me a hug!" Ted said. He smiled at Riley and nodded. "You... okay?"

Riley looked back at Anna, who threw various items of food into a large, white carrier bag. They exchanged a brief glance.

"Haven't gone and pulled the fit nurse while you've been away, have you? Please say no. I mean, fair game if you have, but... Oh, hello little one. What do you think you're doing here?" Ted patted Claudia's daughter, Elizabeth, on the head. "A right handful this one. But she's my mate, eh?"

Elizabeth giggled and shook her head. "Me and Chloë think you smell!" She ran back into the kitchen.

"Making friends I see?" Riley said.

Ted laughed. "Something like that. They're okay really. Stan's a tough nut, but he's a big softie deep down. I think. And Claudia and her kids — they're just regular people."

"Okay, okay, time for catch up is later," Anna said. She shoved past Riley with her carrier bag full of goods and walked into the restaurant.

"Pleasure to see you too, darling," Ted said.

The pair of them walked to the boot of the car and grabbed the remaining water bottles and tins.

"The black dude. What's his name?"

"Trevor," Riley said.

"Trevor. He... What's with him? He looked a mess. Drenched in blood."

Riley slammed the car boot. Looked down the street. Still all clear. Birds chirped in the trees. Decidedly normal considering the circumstances. "We had a rough run at the supermarket. But we're here. And that's the main thing, right?"

"Right," Ted said. They walked through the door. Riley breathed in deeply. Smelled like home. Almost.

Claudia poked her head around the top of the stairs. Her other daughter, Chloë, was beside her. "You're back." She smiled.

"Indeed I am," Riley said. "Everybody keeping okay?"

"As well as we can be. Ted's great with the girls though. Isn't that right, kids?"

Chloë stuck her tongue out at Ted. He put his hands behind his ears and waved them like he was a monster.

"I… I guess you'll be staying?"

Riley and Ted turned to one another. Shrugged. "I think so. If that's okay with—"

"If I had it my way, you wouldn't have even had a chance to prove yourself in the first bloody place."

Riley's stomach sank. *Stan.*

He pushed past Claudia and climbed down the stairs before squaring up to Riley. His cheeks were red and his eyelids twitched. "These idiots had a lot of hope in you."

Riley held his stare. Swallowed the lump in is throat. "And I came through. I—"

"But," Stan said, holding his hand in Riley's face. "You came through. You came back with food and water. So fair play for that." He held his hand out.

Riley examined Stan's extended hand with surprise for a few moments. He turned to Ted and to Claudia, almost expecting some kind of trick. He grabbed it, and shook.

Stan tightened his grip and stepped closer to Riley. "But I'm watching you. Closely. Any fuck ups and you're out of here. I don't care how sore your friend's foot is or how much of a clown he's being with the kids. No screwing up. I'll see to it myself if I have to."

Riley grimaced as Stan's grip tightened. His hand stung and he yanked it back.

Stan looked down at his hand, frowning. There was a line of blood across it from the cut on Riley's palm. Stan noticed the cut, then exhaled loudly out of his nose and shook his head.

"I'm sorry, I—"

"We'll let this go," Stan said. "Just this once. But only

because I have a bed-ridden wife to check up on." He turned away and climbed the first few steps.

"Let me," Riley said. "I… I'll check on your wife. See she's okay. It's… It's the least I can do. I got her some cough sweets."

Stan peered at Riley, as if he was looking inside him for some sort of ulterior motive. He grunted. "I guess. Just don't get too close or she'll coat you in germs. As much as I'd like to see that, it wouldn't be ideal right now." He walked back down the stairs and headed for the kitchen. "I'll get started on lunch and dinner. Ted, Claudia — a hand, please?"

Ted rolled his eyes. "Like I said. He's all soft inside really."

"Yeah. He really seems it."

Ted smacked Riley on the arm. "Good to have you back, mate. Get something on that hand, though. Can't have these things sniffing us out."

"They aren't *sharks*, Ted."

Ted stuck his bottom lip out as he walked into the kitchen area. "How do you know?"

Claudia followed Ted into the kitchen. "Thanks again," she said as she passed Riley. "We… we really appreciate what you've done. For us. It's good to be able to… to trust someone."

Riley nodded. "Any time. Just not too often."

Claudia grinned. "Come on, girls — let's help The Grinch cook some food."

"'The Grinch?'"

Claudia put her finger over her lips. "Between the four of us, okay?"

"Did somebody say 'Grinch'?" Stan shouted.

Riley, Claudia and her two daughters all silently sniggered before the latter three joined Ted and Stan in the kitchen, leaving Riley on his own.

Riley climbed the stairs. He felt a smile on his face. A true, warm smile. Ted was right — these people were okay really. Stan was a tough nut, but a group needed that sort of character in times like these. Claudia and her daughters, they were sweet. Maintained a sense of hope within. And the others — Trevor, Anna — they had their secrets but their motives were in the right place. Anna was right — everybody had their secrets.

Riley whistled as he reached the top of the stairs and walked down the corridor. The room Ted and he had slept in was on his right. The bathroom was at the end. He could hear a shower — either Anna or Trevor had beaten him to it. He allowed himself to consider Anna showering her smooth skin for a few brief seconds before stopping at the door opposite his room where Stan's wife, Jill, was resting.

He knocked on the door. "Jill? It's Riley. The... The new guy. Just checking you're okay?"

No reply.

Riley waited a few seconds. She was probably sleeping. He knocked on the door again and turned the handle. "You okay in there?"

The smell hit him first. He tumbled back and covered his mouth and nose. A rotting stench. He raised his head, still covering his mouth. Heat radiated from the room. A tiny speck of light peeked through the dark curtains.

"Jill?" Riley stepped into the room. He could see her on the bed. She was lying on her back underneath the flowery quilt. Her feet, which poked out of the end of the quilt, moved, and she rolled onto her side.

Riley stopped. His hand lowered from his face, almost automatically. Dread welled up inside him. His heart raced. His fingers tingled. His head grew heavy, as if the ceiling was falling down on him and the walls were closing in.

Jill let out a pained groan.

Riley turned on the light switch as Jill tumbled out of the bed and stepped up.

Her eyes were grey and glassy. The flower prints he'd thought he'd seen on the bed were not flower prints, but blood. There was a hole in her flabby upper arm.

She growled at Riley and lurched forward, bearing her dentures. Pieces of flesh were wedged between them. Her own flesh.

"Everything okay up there?" Stan called.

Jill *was* sick. Very sick.

"Ye... Yes," Riley shouted, as Jill let out another throaty groan and staggered towards him.

How the hell had this happened?

Episode Three

Chapter Seventeen

THE DARKNESS WAS CLOSING IN EARLIER every night as autumn progressed. Crispy brown leaves brushed along the ground in the cool breeze. Eight to nine hours of daylight was all people had. After those eight to nine hours were over, it was time to hide inside. Close the curtains. Tape them together to make sure the tiniest cracks of light were kept inside. Lower tones to a hush. It was hardly the most aggressive form of warfare, but it was the most logical.

The A6 running through Barton used to be lively at six p.m. on a Friday night. School kids would gather on the park to celebrate the end of a long and arduous week of double mathematics and after-school detentions. Young professionals would rush into the Chinese takeaway for a fried, soy-sauce-drenched end of week treat. The place was alive. Not buzzing, but alive.

Now, it wasn't quite dead yet. Not like the rest of the surrounding areas. But it was close. Everything died at some stage.

The bicycle moved slowly down the street. The pedals squeaked slightly as they turned, but only loud enough to keep the creatures curious. Quiet enough to give the cyclist enough time to do what they had to do.

They reached into the basket and cringed. The animal was still damp with blood. There was no guarantee this was even going to work. It hadn't worked the last time they'd tried.

But perseverance was key. That's what they'd been told. They'd catch them off guard, eventually.

They pulled the dead squirrel out of the basket and dropped it onto the road. It plopped onto the concrete, its tiny worm-like intestines spewing out of the cut down its chest. Poor thing. It was a shame that animals always had to be the subject of human experiments, even in this new, developing world.

But this was a much more important study than cosmetics testing.

They wiped their bloody hands on their coat and closed the basket. No time for hanging around. The results of this experiment would be visible tomorrow morning. If it worked, it would be clear to see.

They stepped on the pedal, winced as they cycled over the animal, and moved further down the road. When they were ten metres or so ahead, they stopped again, reached into the basket, and pulled out another dead animal.

They looked back down the road. The animals were running low, but this should be close enough. Especially with the raised voices. The clearly visible lights and silhouettes moving in the window. Foolish. Although naivety was easy to sympathise with, there was no room for it in a world as dangerous as this.

They shook their head, closed the basket, and cycled away.

Several hundred metres behind, a creature feasted on a

dead rabbit. It groaned, and another creature joined it. Fresh meat. Not live, but close enough. Still warm. The creatures jostled over the dead animal before one of them followed the tire tracks of blood with their tongue.

At the end of this trail of tire tracks, the creature found a treat of its own. Groaned as it sunk its teeth into the brittle skull of a blackbird. The other creatures heard the noise, and they followed.

The process went on like this for another hundred metres. Find, eat, follow, groan. If the creatures thought, they'd likely think it was endless.

But it did come to an end.

The creature at the front of the group finished feasting on its final snack — a squirrel, intestines exposed — and looked around. There was no more blood.

But the muffled voices in the building on the left. The shouts. The movement in the window.

The creature stepped to its feet, fluff from a squirrel's tail spread across its lips. It let out a cry, and it walked.

Behind it, a trail of a hundred or so followed, towards the red Mercedes, towards the white Fiat Punto, towards the Chinese takeaway restaurant...

Chapter Eighteen

NINE HOURS EARLIER...

RILEY CLOSED THE door slowly. His heart raced. What he'd seen flickered in his mind, images engrained on his eyelids.

She smacked against the door. He stepped back, frozen. Behind the door, Jill let out a low, deep groan, right from the pit of her stomach. She'd turned. Something had turned her.

"Riley, get your ass down here. Tell my wife to shut up if she's nattering on."

Riley edged away from the door as it continued to bang. He could hear the water still flowing in the shower. He gripped the packet of cough sweets in his hand. It was just a flu. A bad cold. That's all it was.

Riley turned away from the room Jill was in and headed towards the stairs. He'd worked up an appetite on his trip to the supermarket, but that had diminished in a flash. The sight of Jill. A chunk of her own flesh in her mouth. He needed to speak to Ted. Work out what to do about this.

The banging of the door had stopped, but she was still in there. Waiting.

Riley descended the stairs and walked into the kitchen area. Chicken sizzled in a frying pan, coughing up white smoke in Stan's face. Claudia grinned, and her daughter, Elizabeth, giggled beside her. Ted had a smile on his face too. He was content.

"Oh, here he is," Ted said. "Jill keep you talking?"

Riley's face was cold. His eyes were wide and burning. The whole room seemed to be spinning around. Less than a day and the very thing they'd battled to keep out was in the bedroom.

"Grab this," Stan said to Riley. He placed a wooden spoon in his hands and stepped away, wiping his greasy hair back. "I'm not the chef of our house for a reason. Jill would go crazy if she knew I was cooking her chicken. Ask her about the last time that happened. Actually, don't."

Claudia laughed as she stirred a red, tomatoey sauce. "You got that, Riley?"

"Looking a bit peaky. Caught my wife's cold already?"

Riley examined the wooden spoon in his hand. The chicken was beginning to brown. The smoke was growing thicker and darker.

"Jesus, mate." Ted rushed over to the pan and pushed it out of the way to stop the chicken burning. "You should go get a lie down or something. You don't look your best."

"I... We need to talk about something."

Ted frowned. "What is it?"

Claudia and Stan were looking at Riley now. All the eyes of the room seemed to be on him. He couldn't tell Stan, not yet. How would he explain it? He needed it to be somebody else's decision too. He needed a second opinion.

"Upstairs. Please."

Ted turned to the food and the others and sighed. "Right.

But I'm starving, so let's make this quick, okay?"

Stan watched Riley and Ted with narrow eyes as they left the room. Chloë, Claudia's oldest daughter, skipped down the stairs and into the kitchen. Claudia brushed her hair out of her face and cleared her throat, still looking at Riley. "That cut. On your hand. You should get Anna to see to it."

The words clouded in Riley's head. "Right," he called. "Thanks. I will. You... I'm looking forward to the food." He forced a smile back into the kitchen and walked up the stairs with Ted.

"The fuck's wrong, mate?" Ted said. He stumbled beside Riley up the steps.

Riley didn't respond. He held his breath. There was nothing he could say to Ted. Ted only understood things — believed things — when he saw them. Like Andy's body, split in two. Like the creatures feeding on live bodies.

"Did something happen on the road? Is there, like, something I should know about the others?"

They reached the top of the stairs.

"Holy... What happened there?"

Riley froze.

There was a pool of blood outside the room that Jill was in. A pool of blood that wasn't there before.

"Mate," Ted said. He punched Riley's arm. "What's happened?"

"I don't... She was..." Riley walked slowly towards the door. Maybe she'd pressed up against the door. The wound in her shoulder — that was severe enough to cause a high level of bleeding.

The sound of running water started from the shower again. Riley and Ted approached the room. Ted squelched the shoe of his good foot into the patch of blood. It was still damp. Like a spilled drink of juice on a living room carpet. The banging had stopped.

"Mind telling me what—"

Riley held his hand up to Ted's chest and reached for the

handle of the door. "Ssh."

He turned the handle, on his side, and moved back as it swung open, just in case Jill was waiting for them, propped up against the door, ready to pounce.

But she didn't fall out of the room when the door opened. Nor did she groan.

She was on the floor. There was a large crack right in the middle of her head. Fragments of skull stabbed into her exposed brain. She was still. Completely dead.

Ted heaved and moved back with his hands over his face.

Riley squinted. The shower stopped and started again. He couldn't quite process what was happening. Somebody had killed her. Somebody had finished her off.

The door opposite Jill's room opened. "Everything okay out..." Anna stopped talking the second she saw Jill's dead body. Covered her mouth with her hands.

The door at the other end of the corridor swung open. The bathroom door. Trevor stepped out, wiping his hands with a towel. He stared at Riley, Ted, and Anna—wide-eyed. He didn't say a word.

"Somebody... We need to—to tell Stan." Anna started to push the door back, hiding Jill's dead corpse. Ted leaned with one hand against the wall and heaved up saliva and phlegm.

"Tell Stan what?"

All of them turned around. Stan was at the end of the corridor. He had a bowl of chicken and tomato sauce in his hands.

He could likely tell from the way they were all looking at him that something was wrong. Desperately wrong.

"Don't look at me like that. What... What's going on? Is it Jill? Is she... Is she okay?" He walked up the corridor. Riley stepped to one side as Anna approached Stan.

"I think you should probably head downstairs, Stan," Anna said. "We should talk."

Stan frowned. He stopped in his tracks and looked past Anna. "Is nobody going to tell me what's happened here?"

Riley was silent. Ted was silent. Trevor was silent.

Stan shrugged and started to turn away. "Then I guess I'll just have to find out for myself." He barged past Anna and jogged down the corridor.

Riley tried to reach for the door but he didn't have time to close it properly. Stan had already seen the blood outside the room. And seconds later, he'd seen where the blood was coming from.

The bowl of chicken and sauce dropped from his hand and spilled out over the floor. He dropped to his knees.

"What... Jill? This can't... Jill?"

He started sobbing. Stood back up and reached for her head, but pulled away as he likely realised there was hardly anything to hold. He grabbed her hand. Rubbed his shaking fingers up and down her bare arm. "Jill," he sobbed. "I don't... I can't."

Riley turned to the others and took a few steps away from Stan.

Ted stared at him. Trevor stared at him. Anna stared at him.

A speck of blood dripped from the cut in Riley's hand.

All of them watched it fall to the floor.

The five of them were silent.

Silent, except for Stan. He rested his head on his dead wife's chest and sobbed loudly. Anna bit her lip. Reached out to place a hand on Stan's shoulder, then thought better of it. Riley could feel the glances. The eyes looking at him as he squeezed the cut on his hand.

Somebody had finished her off.

"How—" Ted started. He pulled away from the wall, doing his best to avoid eye contact with the body. "How did this happen? Riley?"

Riley frowned as Anna and Trevor both looked at him. "Why look at me?"

"I'm just saying, mate," Ted said. "You were the one who

came downstairs all pale. You brought me up here to see her."

"But not like this." Riley shook his head. "This... this isn't what I was showing you."

"Then what were you showing him?" Anna interrupted.

Riley paused. Took a deep breath in. "She... Jill. I came to give her the cough sweets and she... she was one of them."

Anna frowned. "One of 'what'?"

Stan continued to sob onto Jill's chest.

Riley cleared his throat. "One of those—those things. The creatures. She'd turned."

Anna, Trevor, and Ted looked at one another. Stan started to lift his head.

"I don't know how it happened but she was one of those things and I... I came downstairs to ask for help. I needed a... a second opinion."

"You say you knew and you didn't tell me?" Stan turned around to face Riley. His bottom lip quivered. His eyes were bloodshot.

Riley glanced away. "I would have done. I intended to. But —"

"You say she... my Jill. You say she was one of those things and that's why you... you killed her?"

"No," Riley said. "I didn't kill her." He turned to Anna and to Trevor for support. They were the only ones out of the kitchen at the time. Both of them lowered their heads and didn't speak. "I found her, but I didn't... I wanted you to decide... what to do with her."

Stan squared up to Riley. His breathing was fast and shallow. "You... You know what I say?"

Riley gulped. "I... I'm sorry. I'm sorry she—"

"I say... bullshit."

Riley felt something hard smack against his cheek. He tumbled back against the wall, banging his already sore head in the process.

"You murdered her!" Stan lodged his boot into Riley's side. Trevor threw himself at Stan and tried to pull him back, but he was like an escaped zoo animal, unstoppable. "She—my Jill—she was never bitten. You murdered her. You fucking murdered her."

"Get back," Anna shouted. She too tried to pull Stan away. Ted joined her. Claudia rushed up the stairs to see what the commotion was. The look of curiosity soon turned to a look of shock and horror when she saw Jill's body, her skull cracked like a broken egg.

Riley winced as Stan was pulled away. His ribs and right arm stung. He rolled onto his back and stared up at Stan, who frothed at the mouth.

"Come on, Stan," Claudia said. She placed a hand on his shoulder and he lashed back at her.

"He did it... He killed her. He killed her. Twisted fuck."

Claudia held her cheek where Stan's flailing arm had knocked and stared at Riley. He was in too much pain to protest.

"Come on," Claudia repeated. She took her chances and reached out for Stan again. At first, he looked like he was going to push her away, but he fell into her arms. "My Jill. My Jill. She's gone."

Claudia and Stan walked down the stairs, Trevor escorting them. Every few steps, Stan turned around with a furious expression, but Claudia whispered in his ear and he carried on walking, caught between grief and fury.

Anna, Ted, and Riley were the only ones left upstairs with Jill's body.

"I guess we should... we should get Jill... her body. I guess we should get rid of it." Ted stared into space.

"Not until we've cleaned your friend up," Anna said. She held out a hand for Riley. "Better check you aren't too broken."

Riley gasped as he grabbed Anna's hand and rose to his feet. His legs wobbled with a combination of the beating and the shock. Ted's eyes wandered, avoiding contact.

"We'll go into your... your bedroom," Anna said. She tilted her head at the door behind Riley where Ted and he had slept last night.

Riley nodded. "I'm okay. But… but Stan. He needs to understand. He needs to understand. She'd turned."

"That can wait," Anna said. She looked Riley directly in his eyes. It had to be her or Trevor. But if it was, then why was she so understanding? "But he needs time."

Riley sighed and turned to the room.

"Mate?"

Ted rubbed his arms. Shuffled away from Jill's bedroom door. He looked uncertain. Twitchy.

"Yes?"

"It wasn't you. Was it?"

A weight fell to the pit of Riley's stomach. His own best friend, staring at him with more uncertainty than he'd ever before seen. He shook his head. "I wouldn't lie to you." He turned away and Anna and he stepped into the bedroom.

Chapter Nineteen

Anna dabbed the sponge against Riley's eye socket. He held his breath and bit his lip, every little nudge of the material against his exposed flesh sending a stinging bolt of pain down his face. Anna didn't ease off. She didn't speak. Both of them were silent.

Outside the room, Riley could hear noises. Male voices — Ted and Trevor. Something heavy being dragged along the floor. Jill's body.

"Just hold still, please," Anna said. She squeezed some cream out of a small tube and prodded it against his eye socket. She'd already stuck a plaster on his palm and taken his watch from his bruised wrist, so didn't have much cleaning up left to do.

"I didn't do it. In case you were wondering."

Anna didn't react. She dabbed another speck of soothing cream onto her index finger and tilted Riley's head back. "Shouldn't need any stitches. Gonna hurt for a couple of days, but it's manageable."

Riley tried to make eye contact with Anna. "Did you hear me? I didn't kill Jill. What I told you and Stan — I found her like that. That's the truth."

Anna took a moment to consider, then shrugged.

"Is that all you think of this? A shrug?"

"Quite frankly, I don't think it matters what I think," Anna said. Her tone was sharper and more abrupt. "I think right now, it's Stan you should be proclaiming your innocence to."

Riley tutted. "He's had it in for me since the moment I stepped in this place. This is perfect for him. Something to pin on me."

Anna's eyes finally met Riley's. They narrowed. "Stan's just found his wife with her head caved in. This is not perfect for him. Not in the slightest. And excuse him if he's a bit tetchy, but I think he's entitled to that."

Riley tensed his jaw. Anna was right. Stan had every reason to feel the way he did. He'd just lost his wife. The circumstances were unexplainable. "She'd turned. She... The chunk of flesh missing from her arm. She was... I saw her eating herself. I don't get how it—"

"There's a lot we don't understand. And that's how it has to be. We have to focus on surviving. Living together. Understanding comes second."

Riley shook his head. "She'd turned. And that's the real focus here. Not who... who finished her off. But something turned her. And if she wasn't bitten, then it makes me wonder how else this thing spreads."

"Maybe that's your priority," Anna said. She squeezed the bloody tissue firmly against Riley's bruised cheek. "But, try telling Stan that. We need to find out who did this. Why they did this. And nobody's talking. Which makes me think—"

"—That somebody has something to hide."

Anna and Riley's gaze met for another brief moment.

"Where were you when all this happened, anyway?"

Anna stepped away. "I was in here having a lie-down. I

didn't hear anything. First thing I heard was Ted cursing when you guys… when you found her."

"Are you sure?" Riley asked.

Anna frowned. "What are you? An investigative journalist or something?"

"Close enough. Music journalist."

"Not really close then, is it?"

Riley shrugged. "They share some traits."

Anna raised her eyebrows. "Don't flatter yourself. Look — you've only been here a day and already you've caused an upset. You did good at the supermarket, I'll give you that. And, strangely enough, I believe you. I don't think you're the kind of guy who'd go around hitting old women over the head for no reason."

"Thank you," Riley said. "Means a lot."

"And I know you say she'd turned, but we aren't in… in much of a position to understand that right now. We need to take things step by step. Who else wasn't accounted for other than you?"

Riley puffed his lips out. "Well, erm, you. And there was Trevor. He… he must've been the one in the shower." The sound of the water starting and stopping. "We'll need to talk to him."

"Nobody else? Ted? Claudia?"

"They were in the kitchen. No way could they've done it."

Anna paused. "And Claudia's girls?"

Riley felt himself knocked back by the question. "No. They couldn't. They…"

He thought back. Remembered the people in the kitchen. Elizabeth and Ted teasing one another. Chloë running down the stairs and joining them.

"Chloë. But she can't have. She—"

"Everybody needs to be accounted for. Just in case they… they saw anything. Right?"

Riley's stomach sank. "Right."

Anna picked up her medicinal gear and threw the green

rucksack over her shoulder. "We stick together through this. We need to find out why this happened. I... I believe you that Jill had turned. But we need to find out who finished her off. For closure. You understand?"

Riley started to nod. "Right. I—"

"Anna! Riley! Someone!"

The scream came from downstairs. A female voice — Claudia. Anna and Riley's eyes widened. Riley jumped to his feet as Anna ran through the door and he followed her down the corridor and down the stairs.

When they reached the bottom of the stairs, there were pots and pans spread across the floor. The front door, previously blocked by a tumble dryer, was wide open. There was a bloody fist mark on the white-tiled wall to the side of the door.

Claudia was on the floor. Trevor rested his hand on her shoulder.

"What happened here?" Anna asked.

Claudia pointed at the door. "It's Stan. He went crazy. And he's gone."

Riley picked up a pan that Stan had sent tumbling to the floor and hooked it up in the kitchen area. Claudia whispered to her daughters in a reassuring tone. Trevor and Ted stood in the doorway, arms folded.

"He must have said something," Anna said. She slammed her hands down on the top of the kitchen worktop. "Something about where he was going or what he had planned. He can't just have taken off on foot. That's madness."

Claudia shrugged. "I already told you. He—One minute he was there and the next he was gone. I don't know what else you want me to say."

Anna sighed and shook her head. "None of you heard him mention a thing? You know what he's like with his big mouth. Surely if he knew somewhere close to here he'd have mentioned it by now, right?"

Trevor and Ted looked at one another and lifted their shoulders. "Sorry," Ted said. "He... he didn't say anything. But maybe it's not such a... a bad thing."

Anna frowned. "You what?"

Ted scanned the floor with his eyes. "Well, I just think, he was a little... a little off the rails. And with..." His eyes met Riley's briefly. "With, um. With what happened. To Jill. I don't know whether we'd be able to all just get on again. You know?"

Anna squared up to Ted. She eyed him up from head to toe. "What sort of a coward are you?"

"Maybe Ted's right," Trevor interrupted. "And it's not like we've any real choice. He's gone. Nobody knows where."

Anna moved away from Ted and stared at Trevor. "So, we just leave him out there? Leave the... the grieving old man out there to get torn to pieces? Is that what you think is right?" She stepped closer to Trevor and lowered her voice. "Tell me — where were you when Jill was killed, anyway?"

Trevor's eyelids twitched. "It doesn't matter who did that. If she turned, she turned. No room for sentimentality."

Anna shook her head. "Is that a confession?"

Trevor remained completely still. "No. But I don't think that's the issue right now."

Anna opened her mouth to respond but closed it and stepped away from Trevor. She approached Claudia and the girls. "You got any thoughts on this? You think we should just leave him out there too?"

Claudia shrugged. "I don't... I don't know what to suggest. But I just think that looking for him is going to be difficult when we've no idea where he might be."

Anna nodded. Forced a smile across her face. "Right. So it's just me then. Just me that after two days, hasn't lost her sense of—"

"Stan said he had a dairy farm."

The voice was unfamiliar. Everybody's attention turned beside Claudia and to her daughter, Elizabeth.

"What did you say, darling?" Claudia asked.

Elizabeth squeezed her hands together. Her cheeks went slightly pink. "He... He said he had a farm nearby. And I asked if I could go see the cows one day but he said I had no chance."

Claudia turned to the rest of the group. "Nice of him to let us know he had a farm, wasn't it?"

"Stevens' Dairies," Anna said.

"What?" Riley asked.

"Stevens' Dairies." Anna shook her head. "Of course. Stan and Jill's surname was Stevens. Stevens' Dairies — you've seen the vans, right? They... they're based in Barton. Short trip around the fields should take us there, I think." She walked over to the front exit door.

"Wait," Riley said. He stepped in front of her. "We can't act on a hunch. There's no guarantee he's even gone there."

"Riley's right," Ted said. "And we don't know how many of those creatures are out there now. They could be growing in number. You could be cut off before you even have the chance to get back."

Anna pushed past Riley. "Well, that's just a risk I'm going to have to—"

"Who is Stan to you, Anna? Really?"

Anna stopped in her tracks. She turned around, slowly. "What... What do you mean?"

Riley cleared his throat. "I can't blame you for looking out for us. I'd like to think you'd do the same for me. But you're being rash. Which makes me wonder whether you're closer than you let on? The Anna I met yesterday, I don't think she'd do this. You have to think about this. You can't just go running out there. We need a group. We need to figure out who's doing what." He reached out and rested a hand on Anna's shoulder. "We need to *think*."

Anna looked distant. Her eyes were wide and she seemed deep in thought.

Then, she pushed Riley's hand from her shoulder. "Then what do you suggest?"

Riley turned around. Claudia and her girls stared back at him. Ted and Trevor looked on from the doorway. All eyes on him. All ears waiting for an answer, from him. "I'll go."

Anna frowned as Riley edged past her. "You what? Just you? But that's... that's mad."

"It's not," Riley said. "I'm solely responsible if I'm on my own. And he blames me, so I need to prove myself to him. But logistically, too. Ted would be my first choice, but he's still hurt."

Ted held his foot out as if nobody was already aware. "Man, I'd... I'd love to but... Alone? You can't. You just—"

"Claudia has her daughters to look after. And you're tough. A good organiser. I want you here."

Anna shook her head. "I'm better out there. I'm—"

"This group needs you," Riley said. "They need you. And you should be here. Okay?"

Anna looked like she was about to protest but she backed down and nodded once.

"Good. Now... now I'll take the Punto and I'll check out this farm or dairy place. Anna — you'll need to draw me up a map or something."

"What about Google Maps?" Ted asked. He pulled his phone out of his pocket. His face dropped. "Oh. Yeah. Scrap that. Network is... it's completely down."

"What about me?"

Trevor shuffled. Looked around the room at the others.

"I'm not sure I can trust him around my daughters," Claudia said.

Riley walked up to Trevor. "I don't care whether you did or didn't kill Jill... Jill's creature. I saw it too. I know she'd turned. And I know you're a... you're a good guy. You helped me out in the supermarket. But just don't do anything stupid. Okay?"

Trevor peered into Riley's eyes. "I'm not the one going out into the middle of nowhere to search for a missing man."

Riley tilted his head. "Suppose you're right."

"Riley," Anna called.

Riley turned around. "Yes?"

Anna's eyes were welling up. She opened her mouth, and then closed it again, shaking her head. "It's nothing. Just... say you do find him. What makes you think he'll just come back with you?"

"Yeah," Ted said. "He seemed pretty pissed at you. The guy's flipped his lid. Just... be careful. Okay?"

Riley nodded. "You keep an eye on this place."

Ted attempted a smile. "I'll make a decent carer when the world goes normal again, right? Finally a job I'm good at."

"Consider this work experience. Least it's got you off your arse. Sort of."

Ted jabbed Riley in the arm. He coughed and smiled. "Good luck. If... Right behind you."

Riley turned around. Saw Claudia and her daughters. Trevor. Anna. All of them looking at him, waiting for him to make the next call. He'd never really fancied being a leader before. But he'd always been the one that people seemed to turn to in group meetings and the like. Never figured out why, and always hoped that wouldn't be the case were the apocalypse to arrive, but beggars couldn't be choosers.

"Okay," Riley said. His voice squeaked slightly, which didn't add much authority to his position. "I guess I'll grab some water, take the Punto and check this place out. If it gets dark, keep... keep the outside light on for me."

"You know we can't do that," Anna said. "Can't risk the things seeing us."

Riley winked. "Correct answer. Just testing."

Riley splashed his face with hot water. Condensation coated the bathroom mirror. He wiped away a patch with his wrist and stared back at himself. Bags under his eyes, bigger than ever before. His skin, pale and washed out. There was something different about him. The way he looked at himself — he truly saw his face. Every crevice on his forehead. Every prickly hair on his beard. He lifted his hand — it wasn't shaking. His heartbeat was there, but it wasn't too strong. He'd faced his fear. Stepped up. Spoken up and taken charge of the room.

And now he was going to go for a little drive. That's all it was — a little drive on his own.

He inhaled the steam from the hot water right into the bottom of his lungs and felt a wave of calmness splash over him.

"I've got you those directions."

Riley jumped around. Anna was stood at the door of the bathroom. She had a small piece of note paper in hand. She stared beyond Riley. Right through him.

Riley pulled his shirt back on and grabbed the directions from Anna. "Thanks. I—"

"What you said before. About knowing Stan better than I was letting on."

"Ssh," Riley said. "Like we said, we all have our secrets. We can't just expect one another to suddenly open up. We've only known each other a day. Trust builds."

"I don't know him. But I…" She froze. "I… He reminds me of someone. Yeah. And I guess I don't want to let that go just yet."

Riley held his breath. His hand started to rise, almost automatically. He rested it on Anna's shoulder. She flinched a little, then let it rest there. "I'll do my best to bring him back. I'll try the farm. It's a long shot, but it will be worth it."

"Do you really think that?"

"Think what?"

"That it will be worth it?"

Riley lowered his hand. "I suppose I've done a lot these last two days. More than I ever did stuck at an office desk. There's a strong chance I've absolutely lost my mind. But maybe that's a good trait to have in this new world."

Anna half-smiled. "Maybe it is."

Riley and Anna were silent for a moment. They looked at each other. Riley could see something behind her eyes.

Something deep and dark beneath that stare. Something behind her quivering lips. A secret. Some kind of secret.

"You'd better—"

"Yeah," Riley said. "Get to the car, get on his trail."

Riley brushed past Anna. As he did, she grabbed his hand. "Thanks. For… Thanks."

Riley looked back at her and nodded. "We're all entitled to our secrets." He walked down the corridor and hopped down the staircase.

Anna watched him as he disappeared down the steps. A sickness welled up inside her. *"We're all entitled to our secrets."*

She slammed the bathroom door shut and rushed over to the taps. She let the hot tap run for a few seconds, water splashing out of the sink and covering her clothes. She stuck her hands under the water, biting her lip as it scolded her palms, and threw it over her face. She gasped. Looked at herself in the mirror.

"We're all entitled to our secrets."

Would he feel the same way if he knew the truth?

"Looks clear."

Riley and Ted examined the road outside the house. Empty plastic packaging scraped against the tarmac, blowing gently in the breeze. The playground just up the road was empty. A family of ducks pottered up from the pond, curious as to when their next helping of bread was going to arrive.

"Good luck, mate," Ted said. He patted Riley on the back. "And sorry. I can't… I can't be more useful. I feel like such a letdown."

Riley nodded at Ted. "You just gradually get yourself used to walking again. It's better if just I do this, anyway. Less fuss."

Ted stared closely at Riley. "Is that what this is really about?"

Riley's cheeks warmed. His stomach tensed. "Yes. Yes. Why wouldn't it be?"

Ted shook his head. "Just be careful. I... The Punto. I wouldn't want to lose it." He winked at Riley then disappeared back inside the Chinese restaurant.

Riley breathed in deeply. The way Ted had looked at him with those pitiful eyes. He knew what he was implying. The accident. The sound of metal crunching against concrete. The guilt he'd felt in that hospital bed, everybody visiting him. And although they didn't say anything at the time, he knew what they were thinking. *Why did you do it? Are we not good enough for you?*

He let go of his breath and walked towards the car door of the Punto. That was the past. The rules were different now, in this new world. Who he was, that was irrelevant. Same went for everybody. In these days, it had to be about who you *were*, and what you were willing to do to hold onto that sense of identity.

He opened the car door and threw his rucksack onto the passenger seat before sitting down. Andy's blood had dried up, but the rest of the car was a mess. There was a patch on the passenger footwell mat where Ted's foot had dribbled blood out of the bottom of his shoe. But it would do the job. Get to the dairy farm, look for Stan, and get him back. He was on foot, so he couldn't be much further ahead. And maybe it was a shot in the dark. But he had to try. He couldn't allow Stan to die believing that Riley was responsible for his wife's death.

He raised the clutch and started to reverse out of the parking area when he heard something scraping underneath the car.

Then, the vehicle jerked backwards and forwards. Something wasn't right.

Riley stopped the car and climbed outside. He could see what the problem was right away. Ted reappeared at the door. "Everything okay, mate?"

Riley's heart began to thump. Nausea built in his chest. He turned around and looked at the other cars. The Previa. The red Mercedes. All of them the same.

"I... I think I know why Stan went by foot," Riley said as he jabbed his finger into the slashed tire of the Punto.

Chapter Twenty

"THE BASTARD. THE ABSOLUTE BASTARD."

ANNA leaned her head against the round table in the dining room. The others were also gathered in the room, agitated, uncertain.

"What do we do now?" Ted asked.

Claudia sighed. "There's not a lot we can do. Stan's… He's made his choice. And he's made our choices for us. We can't let a man like that back here."

Anna smacked her hand against the table. "We can't be certain it was him. He—"

"Come on," Ted said. "You saw how he was when he took off. Who else would do that?"

Anna shrugged. Her eyes were bloodshot. "I dunno. The same person who left the dead dog?"

"Nobody left the dog," Claudia said. Chloë rested on her knee. "Don't start that crazy nonsense again."

Anna rubbed her fingers against her temples. "We need to

work out what we're going to do. We... we need to come up with some sort of plan."

"The way I see it, we don't have many options." Trevor broke his self-imposed silence. "Our tires are slashed. We're stuck here. That's that."

Anna shook her head and turned to Riley. "You. What do you... you've been acting like you're some sort of leader these last few hours. So go on, Mr. Leader. What do you suggest?"

Riley looked around at the group. Anna's concerned eyes stared at him, desperate for some sort of answer. He swallowed the lump in his throat. He knew what he had to do, but he had to be careful how he approached it. "I... I think we should draw up some plans. Plans of action for if we have to leave this place."

"No," Anna said. She shook her head. "This place is as good as we're going to get. We need to hold onto it."

"Riley's right," Trevor said. "We need to prepare. Just in case."

"I'm not living my life as a 'just in case,'" Ted interrupted. "I'm not doing this. We've got something... something good here." He looked at Riley and attempted a reassuring half-smile. "I'm sorry, mate. But that's what I think."

Riley nodded half-heartedly. He turned to the dining room door and started to walk out of it.

"Where are you going?" Anna asked.

Riley seemed to awaken to his surroundings. The wooden doors, the dull smell of cooking, the autumn sunlight peering in through a crack in the window at the top of the stairway. He knew what he had to do. And it had to be him. They couldn't let every bond they'd worked for fall apart already.

"I'll be back soon," Riley said. He stared Anna in the eyes and nodded his head. "Just going to collect something."

He closed the dining room door.

Then, he took a deep breath, and he ran.

Deep breath in, deep breath out...

Riley hopped across the fence and onto the field behind the Chinese restaurant. He jogged, maintaining a steady pace. He couldn't run too fast and risk tiring himself out. The last thing he wanted was to find himself in the middle of a large group of creatures and with no energy to run from them. But at the same time, he wanted to get there and check the dairy farm out as quickly as he could. He tried not to think about Ted and Anna's reactions when they saw he was gone. Claudia, her daughters, Trevor. The cursing, the arguing, the disagreements. He needed to try and find Stan. Maybe he was mad. But at least he was doing something proactive.

He looked at the directions that Anna had given him. The dairy farm was directly behind the Chinese restaurant, across a bunch of fields in the distance. If Stan had gone by foot, then this had to be the route he'd taken. The fields would be relatively safe. Low on people, so low on creatures. Hopefully.

He squinted ahead. He had another couple of fields to run through, but it all looked clear. To his right, he could hear a cry somewhere in the distance. A woman, shouting and struggling, her words inaudible and muffled. But she was far enough away. Better her than him. Was that selfish? Maybe he had to be selfish to survive in this world.

Then again, if he was selfish, he wouldn't be trying to save a missing old man who wanted to kill him.

He reached the stile between the field he was in and the next field. He rested his hands on his knees and leaned forward to catch his breath. They'd definitely have noticed he was gone now, back at the restaurant. But they were strong enough without him. Strange. He'd never been considered particularly strong before. Did a few push-ups every now and then, and used to run distance. But the way the group was starting to look at him, waiting for him to make calls, relying on him. It was unfamiliar. Something he wasn't used to. If only they knew everything about him. Wouldn't be trusting him to make their calls then, that's for sure.

When he raised his head, he could see the grey metal roof

of the dairy farm up ahead. If he maintained the pace he had been running, he could be there in ten minutes or so. Enough time to get inside, then get back out again.

He readied his legs and prepared himself to run the final stretch. His breathing was still shallow. He was getting worse at these runs with age. Age, what a bastard.

Then, something moved up ahead.

He froze. Lowered his leg slowly. Something had definitely twitched in the long grass of the next field. He could hear something, too. A moaning. An animal? A person? Maybe it was Stan?

Not a creature. Anything but a creature.

Riley started to move slowly into the field. He flanked to the right slightly, out of the direct path of the movement. He jogged, slower than he had before, and reached into his pocket. A screwdriver he'd found in one of the kitchen drawers. He'd use it if he had to.

As he got closer to the source of the movement, he saw another twitch. He stopped. There was definitely something there. He crouched down. He could feel his heart beating against his shirt. He stepped towards the movement, keeping low in the long grass. The song of insects was almost deafening, as was every step in the dry, lifeless grass.

He took another few steps closer to the movement. It was a matter of metres away now. Whatever it was let out another noise. He raised his screwdriver. Tensed all the muscles in his body. Reached for the grass blocking his view.

Three, two, one...

He pulled the grass aside and yanked the screwdriver ahead of him.

His muscles eased off. It wasn't a creature. It wasn't a human.

He lowered the screwdriver and stepped towards it.

It was a cow. It lay on its side, shaking its front leg and letting out low, raspy moans. One of its back legs was snapped out of place, at a right-angle in the opposite to natural direction. Riley sighed and stepped closer.

The cow's intestines were spilling out of its front. The white fur on its body was matted and damp with blood. It huffed and puffed when its bulging black eye saw Riley, and let out another low moan.

A lump grew in Riley's throat. He could feel his eyes beginning to sting. It was a cruel world. It always had been before these 'Dead Days,' or whatever they were. But now, it was particularly cruel. The gruelling conclusion of the life of a farmyard animal was there for all to see, instead of hidden away in an abattoir like a dirty secret and served up on a plate with chips and peas.

The cow let out another low moan and kicked out its front leg.

Riley looked around. The area was clear enough. Whatever had got this cow had long moved on. Maybe it was a creature. A stray farmer who'd somehow got bitten and made his way back to his field, attacking his livestock before moving on to something more… alive. Or perhaps it was a human. Somebody trying to catch and stock up on fresh meat while the government — wherever they were — figured out how they were going to tackle this outbreak. Perhaps they'd found the cow to be too heavy to drag any further. None of them had the guts to kill it.

Riley lifted the screwdriver. The singing of the insects grew louder. He'd have to move on. He couldn't get distracted.

He pressed the screwdriver against the side of the cow's head where it seemed softest. His hand shook as the cow shuffled its body, begging for some sort of release from the pain.

"I… I'm sorry," Riley said. He stroked the cow on its bloody head and turned away.

Then, he lifted the screwdriver, and he brought it back down into the cow's head.

The cow twitched and struggled for a few seconds as Riley twisted and turned the screwdriver, clenching his eyes together as warm tears built up behind them.

And then the cow stopped twitching.

He looked back at the cow's head. Felt the sticky blood coating his hand. He tugged the screwdriver away and closed the cow's eyelid. "I'm sorry."

He rose to his feet and wiped his eyes with his clean sleeve, and dabbed the bloody screwdriver on his trousers. He kept his focus away from the cow. It had gone now. It was at peace, finally. No more pain, no more struggling. Bailed out from a harsh world. The easy road.

He stretched his legs and started to jog again, through the long grass and in the direction of the dairy farm.

"Is that him?"

They stared through the gap in the fence and watched as he jogged through the field. Blood coated his right-hand sleeve. He was heading right in the direction of Stevens' Dairies.

"Yes. That's him. That's the fucker."

The pair of them were silent for a few seconds as they watched through the scope of their guns.

"And… and what do you think we should do about him, hmm?"

The other person gritted his teeth. Teased the trigger with his fingertips, lowering the aim to the running man's knees and feet. "We follow him and cause him a world of pain for what he's done." The person rose to his feet.

"Are you sure that's a good idea?"

"We follow closely. Make him think he's got a chance. Then see how he handles the nasty surprise we've got lined up."

The reluctant person shook his head and grabbed the others' hand, standing up and watching as the bearded, skinny man got closer and closer to Stevens' Dairies.

"He's no idea. Absolutely no idea. But he'll pay for this."

They lowered their guns and they walked in the direction

of the dairy farm.

Riley slowed down as he approached the dairy farm. Everything seemed quiet. There was a long, winding road leading up to the main road, but providing there wasn't much life around here, no creatures would have wandered down. Regardless, he crept up to the back of the dairy farm and leaned against the metal walls of the building, screwdriver in hand.

He took a few steps closer to the farm entrance. There were no cars in the parking area. A sign with Stevens' Dairies swung above the doorway in the gentle breeze. At least he'd got the right place. That was a start.

He took another couple of steps closer to the side entrance of the farm. The building was quite big. Thinking about it, Stan must have been quite well off. Stevens' Dairies provided milk to lots of the supermarkets around Preston. Perhaps they were even national. He'd have to ask him, if ever he got the chance.

Riley poked his head around the large, open doorway. There were seven cows all lined up in individual pens. One of them mooed when it saw Riley. Another shoved its head inside its empty food tray, trying its best to lick any remaining scraps up.

One of the pens was empty. The gate was open. Must've been the cow he'd killed in the field. Somebody had let it out. Or something.

He crept through the main area and towards the room at the back. He could see a door, partially open. It looked like an office area. But the place was big. Perhaps it was where they put the milk in to bottles. Regardless of what or where it was, only one thing really mattered: finding Stan.

The cows' eyes stared at Riley as he passed. Usually, they had nonchalance about them. But these cows were focused. Curious. He dreaded to think what they might have seen, if they'd seen anything. The creatures didn't seem to have reached the countryside yet.

But Jill. The way she was dead in the room. No possible way she had been bitten. There were things they didn't know about the virus — or whatever it was — yet. Things they didn't understand.

As he pushed the door at the end of the room open, he heard something clatter behind him.

He swung around. The main doors were still wide open. He couldn't see anything down the street. The cows stared back at him. It must've been the cows. Must've just been one of the cows searching for food.

He breathed in deeply and returned to opening the door.

The room was dimly lit and narrow. A long corridor led right down to a turning. Either side of him, blankets hung down, covering the contents of shelves. He started to lift one of the blankets. Perhaps there'd be something in there that would come in handy. Some bottles of fresh milk, or eggs.

As he lifted the blanket, he jumped back as something screeched out at him.

His heart thumped. His hands tingled. "Fuck. Fuck." He wiped the sweat from his head and took a few moments to compose himself, lifting the blanket again. Just a hen. It was a dairy farm. Dairy farms supplied eggs. Something to remember in future. *Idiot.*

He continued moving along the corridor and towards the turning at the end. He saw twitching underneath the rest of the blankets. The hen whose blanket he'd lifted continued to cluck. Best not wake all of them up.

Another clanging noise sounded from the cow area. He turned around again. He couldn't see for the door. Had he closed it that much? Yes. He must have. No other explanation.

"Stan?" he whispered. He gripped the screwdriver tightly in his hand. Where would a runaway man go to hide, anyway? Maybe Riley had been hasty coming to this place. But at least he'd tried. At least he could take some milk and eggs back. Another contribution to the group.

As he reached the end of the corridor, he looked either

side. On the right was a door, but it was padlocked. He sighed. This place might have been big, but he was limited in where he could search.

He turned to his left, and his body froze.

Behind a wide-open wooden door, there was a figure. Riley couldn't make it out properly for the poor lighting, but he could tell he had a bulky build and thin, grey hair. The figure had his back to Riley and to the door, and was sitting completely still.

"Stan?" Riley got closer to the door. A chorus of mooing cows cut through the silence. He reached the door. His hand was gripped so tightly around the screwdriver that it felt like a natural extension of his body. "Stan? It's… it's me. I've come to… to help you. To say sorry and to bring you back. If you want that."

Stan didn't respond. He remained completely motionless. A streak of light just about cut through the murky darkness as it shone in through the dusty window.

A hen started to cluck. And then another, and another.

Riley reached for Stan's shoulder. He was sitting in the middle of the room on a wooden chair. Every few seconds, he twitched. Mumbled. It sounded like he was whimpering.

Riley looked around the room. A sense of dread began to work its way through his body. An overwhelming foreboding emotion that he really, really shouldn't be here.

"Stan, let's… let's get you out of here. Okay? Let's…"

When he saw Stan from the front, he realised why he wasn't talking.

Stan's mouth was covered with duct tape. Blood-laden tears seeped out from his bulging eyes. His feet and hands were tied around the wooden seat with thick layers of tape. He shook his head at Riley and tilted his head at the door, shouting and mumbling beneath his gag.

Another hen clucked.

"Shit, Stan, what… what happened here? What's…? Come on. Let's get you out of here. Let's…" Riley tried to break the duct tape from Stan's mouth with his shaking hands. He could see equipment hanging from sharp nails on the wall. Scissors. A hammer. An axe.

Riley yanked the duct tape away from Stan's face. Stan gasped. Congealed saliva and blood seeped from his swollen, chapped lips.

"Let's get you out of here. It's… It's not safe. Let's—"

"You shouldn't have come here," Stan said. His bottom lip quivered. "You should go. Go while you can."

Riley rushed to the wall and grabbed the scissors. "I'm not leaving without you. I'm not—"

"Well, hello there."

Riley froze. The hens had stopped clucking. He turned around slowly in the direction of the unrecognisable voice.

It was a man. Skinny. Wore a cap and a bloody vest. Greasy hair dangled onto his shoulders from an unkempt ponytail.

And he had a gun pointed directly at Riley.

"Aaron, kid — it looks like we've found our animal killer."

Chapter Twenty-One

"PLEASE, THERE DOESN'T HAVE TO BE any—"

"Shut up." The ponytailed man aimed his gun directly at Riley. It was long and thin, like a rifle. "Just shut up and drop the scissors."

"You shouldn't have come here," Stan mumbled. "Shouldn't have fucking come here."

The ponytailed man slammed his boot into the leg of Stan's chair. "Since when did I say you could talk old man?"

Riley's body trembled. The scissors slipped out of his hand. He couldn't move. He couldn't think.

Another man poked his head around the door, presumably 'Aaron.' He had mid-length ginger hair and a freckly face.

"What took you so long?"

Aaron looked at the floor in disappointment. "I... I was just checking if this thing was loaded."

"Well, it is loaded, okay? I told you it was loaded before. Got a problem with this?"

"No, Sam, no. Let's just... let's just get this done with." He started to approach Riley. He was holding a smaller gun. There was some tape dangling from his belt. "Keep still. Not a flinch."

Riley couldn't flinch if he wanted to. Aaron checked his pockets and pulled out the screwdriver, tossing it over to Sam. Fear pumped through Riley's body. Aaron grabbed his wrists and pushed him back towards the floor. Riley crumbled backwards, like a statue without support.

"Tie him up," Sam said. "Tie him up and we'll decide what to do with them."

"Please," Riley whimpered as Aaron lifted him back onto a chair and tied up his wrists while Sam kept his gun on him. It didn't seem real. Everything that was happening was like a blur, or a dream. This couldn't be happening to him. "Just— please. Let us go. We haven't—"

"Haven't what?" Sam said. He squared up to Riley. "Killed our animals? Fucked with our produce?"

Riley tried to speak but an invisible grip tightened around his throat. "No, we... No. No."

"No?" Sam said. A little smile emerged on his face. "You haven't? Really? So that cow we saw you lurking around just before. You didn't shove a screwdriver into its head, did you? Hmm?"

Riley stared back at Sam. The cow. Dying, suffering. He had to put it out of its misery. He had no choice.

"The cow, it... something had already—"

"Bullshit." Sam smacked the butt of the gun against Riley's face. "Y'know, once upon a time, maybe I'd have believed you. Given you the benefit of the doubt, or whatever. But what about the rest of our animals, hmm? What about the others? Were they all suffering too?" He stepped up to Riley and squeezed his cheeks tightly. "What about my Trudy, hmm? Lovely golden retriever. What about her?"

Riley's stomach sank. The Labrador he'd seen outside the Chinese restaurant. Dead, the bone in its back leg exposed.

"No. That wasn't... We didn't..."

"We? I'm hearing a lot about 'we.' Just you and the old man, is it?"

Stan stared over at Riley. He had been silent up to now. His jaw shook. It looked like he was holding back an explosion of words and emotions.

Aaron finished strapping Riley to the chair and stepped back. Sam looked from Riley to Stan. "Well?"

"We have a group," Stan's voice bellowed through the room. Riley frowned. What the hell was he doing? They couldn't give anything away.

"Oh really?" Sam approached Stan and crouched in front of him. He pointed the gun in between his legs. "And where would we happen to find this 'group'?"

"Stan, don't—"

"Shut the fuck up," Aaron said. He aimed the gun nervously in Riley's face.

"Old man? Care to continue?"

Stan glanced at Riley and cleared his throat. "They're tough. Six or seven strong. And when they find out what you've done to us, they'll come for you. And by the way — these are *my* fucking animals, not yours." He spat in Sam's face.

Sam barely flinched. He wiped away the stringy phlegm with the back of his hand and examined it, nodding his head from side to side. "They might have been your animals once upon a time. But the rules have changed, in case you haven't noticed. The flesh eaters, they are the government now. And they don't give a fuck whose dairy farm this *was*." He stood up and nodded at Aaron.

"What do you want from us?" Riley asked.

Sam narrowed his eyes. He waited a few moments before responding. "I'm not totally sure yet. I haven't quite decided whether you'd miss an arm or a leg more. But you're going to pay for slaughtering our animals. Come on, Aaron. Let's decide what we're going to do with these fuckers."

Aaron nodded a little too enthusiastically and led the way out of the room. Sam rolled down the blackout blind at the grimy window, then followed closely behind. He stopped at the door.

"By the way," he said. "Don't bother trying to scream or anything like that. Wouldn't want to attract any flesh eaters now, would we?" He winked at Riley and slammed the door shut.

The room was plunged into darkness.

"You okay, Stan?"

Stan was silent. Every now and then, he let out a wince, and shuffled around in his chair. They'd been locked away in this room for what felt like hours. Now that Riley's eyes had adjusted to the darkness, he could just about make Stan out in the dim light peeking around the sides of the blackout blind. Somewhere in the distance, he could hear voices. Debating and arguing. Sam and Aaron deciding what to do with them.

"Stan, I... I don't know how to say this but—"

"You shouldn't have come here," Stan snapped. "Putting everybody at risk."

Riley wasn't particularly fond of what Stan was implying, but he was relieved to finally hear him break his silence. "I didn't know anything like this had gone down. And... and I couldn't just leave you. Not on those terms."

"'Those terms,'" Stan scoffed. "Which terms? The, 'my wife was murdered' terms?"

Riley sighed. "I'm not here to argue with you. And I... I am really, genuinely sorry about what happened to your wife. But you have to believe me when I tell you that I didn't kill her. I found her... I found her turned. Into one of those things. I walked downstairs and I was... I wasn't thinking straight. I couldn't tell you, not yet. I couldn't understand it myself. So I got Ted and when we went back, she was... yeah."

Stan took a few moments to mull over Riley's words. "And you thought by coming out here on a little suicide mission, you could win me over, hmm?"

"I guess." Riley tugged at the tape around his hands. He was completely stuck to the chair. "Would've been nice of you to tell us about having a dairy farm, though. Milk. Eggs. Meat. Just saying."

Stan snorted. "I've only known you people a day. I needed a backup for me and… for me and Jill. In case things went awry. Besides, you can't tell me you don't have any secrets of your own. The gun that you suspiciously picked up from a zombiefied police officer? How about that for luck?"

Riley felt as if Stan had grabbed a baseball bat and swung his own perusal of the truth right back into his face. Very hard.

"You know, me and Jill were actually going to go abroad in December. We… we've got family. Daughter and her son-in-law. They live in Canada. Lived there for three years now. Haven't seen them once since they left. Jill, she… she never liked flying. But she'd got over that this year. Went for some hypnotherapy shit and strangely enough, it seemed to do her good."

Riley didn't say anything in return. Best to leave him speaking now he'd finally opened his mouth.

"I just—" Stan sniffed back. His voice was croaky. "I just wish we'd had the chance to go see them. Both of us. A chance to go see them just once in Canada. But…" He stopped and sniffed again.

"I understand, Stan. I understand."

"What the fuck do you understand? How can you possibly understand?"

Riley took a deep breath. "My parents walked out on me seven years ago. I was in a bad place. Drank a lot. Did a few drugs. And they just decided one day that enough was enough. They couldn't look after me anymore." He gulped down the lump in his throat. The tingling sensation had returned to his arms. "So one day, I got up in the afternoon again, and there was just a note… a note on the side. A note saying that they'd gone away. Left the country. Been planning it for ages. And that the house was on the market so I'd have to get out of there. They left me with nothing. I was officially homeless."

"Sounds to me like a perfect kick up the arse."

"It was. I got a job. Dream job—music journalist. At the local paper, but still. Everything I'd ever dreamed of. But was I happy? Truly? No. I was living at my... my grandma and grandpa's. And they were great for me, but I was a loner. I had nobody, not really."

"Did you... did you ever see your parents again? Or have you, should I say?"

Riley smiled. The memories flooded back to him at full force. "Yes. And no. I... I had a car accident a year ago. Was in a coma for... for a couple of days. And they visited me there, but I never saw them. So, yes and no."

Stan sighed. "It... it sounds like your grandparents are good people."

"Were good people." Riley didn't have to elaborate. Stan would understand.

"I... I suppose that's why I get on with Anna so well. She reminds me of my daughter a little. Attitude. And my daughter's a nurse too. Jill always liked it when Anna gave her the jabs. Must've been the same for her."

Riley started to reply but something stopped him. An image in his head. Or, at least, a series of images.

The elderly creatures swarming out of the residence around the corner from his grandma's.

The signs in the supermarket pharmacy: *Flu Jab Season: Get Yours Here & Stay Safe for Winter!*

Jill sneezing into a tissue. *"It's that bloody flu jab again. Always brings me down."*

And Anna. *"I guess we really do all have our secrets."*

"Riley?"

Riley jolted from his daze. Adrenaline rushed through his body. The flu jab. The creatures—they had to have something to do with the flu jab. "Stan, what... When did Jill have her... her flu jab. When did she—"

"Slow down," Stan said. "What are you talking about?"

Riley's mind spun with theories and memories. The lack of clear bites on the creatures in the pharmacy. Jill's body, clean except for the self-imposed bite on her arm. Anna's description of the outbreak at the surgery. It had to be related. It couldn't be a coincidence.

"Riley? What is it?"

"I think I—"

The door swung open. Sam charged in, gun in hand.

"It's your lucky day," he said. Aaron sneaked in beside him and started to untie their feet, keeping his gun on them. "We've just about decided what we're going to do with you."

"And?" Riley said.

Sam snickered. "You're no use to us alive. But we have a couple of friends who you could be good use to."

Aaron yanked Riley to his feet and held the gun against his back as Sam did the same to Stan.

"Let's go," Sam said. "There's a group that would really love to meet you."

Stan nodded at Riley. His face was awash with fear. The nod was a sort of, "If I don't see you again, goodbye" kind of nod. Riley wasn't sure whether he liked it, but he returned it out of kindness.

Sam pushed Stan first. He walked with his shoulders broadened out, his rifle in one hand. They moved past the corridor with the covered up chickens and towards the locked up door at the opposite end.

"Give it here," Sam said. He held his hand out and Aaron tossed a set of keys over to him.

"You sure this is… this is the right way to—"

"Yes, Aaron," Sam said. He stuffed the keys into the padlock and turned them. "They took something from us, so we'll take something from them." He pulled the padlock away from the door and gripped the rusty metal handle. "On your best manners, boys."

He pulled the door open.

Stan stumbled back. Riley tried to move free of Aaron's grip. His eyes locked on what was ahead. "Please," Riley said. "This... We haven't done anything. I swear to you." He pushed himself back against Aaron, whose gun dug further and further into his lower ribs.

"Amanda, Beatrice, and Jenny — meet your new friends. But no fighting over them. Not too much, anyway. Bring the young one through, Aaron."

Riley dug his feet into the ground. He tried to stop himself moving but Aaron was pushing too hard.

"What's the matter? Not like your new friends?" Sam laughed as Aaron pushed Riley closer and closer towards the room.

Inside, there were three women. All of them were dangling from meat hooks, which were wedged through their necks.

And all of them were lurching forward, growling, and snapping their jaws.

Chapter Twenty-Two

RILEY DUG HIS HEELS INTO THE floor. "Please," he begged. "You don't have to do this. We can help you. Please."

Aaron continued to push Riley into the room where the creatures hung from meat hooks. Sam smiled as he held his gun at Stan's head, dragging him closer to the room too.

The creatures edged forward. The skin around their neck, where the sharp meat hooks were piercing through, split as they stretched themselves further and further towards the humans, their eyes glazed yet focused. As they groaned, blood dribbled out of the hole in their necks and down their already blood-soaked dresses.

Sam applauded and laughed. "This is gonna be fun. Screw TV—this is gonna be real live entertainment, right here. Come on, Aaron, get him in here."

Riley could still feel pressure against his lower back, but it wasn't intensifying. It had stopped. He turned his head to look at Aaron.

"What's keeping you, little bro?" Sam asked.

Aaron's bottom lip was shaking. The gun lowered from Riley's back. Aaron couldn't make eye contact with anybody. "I... I can't. I can't."

Sam frowned and glared at Aaron. "The fuck do you mean you can't? You can. You fucking weak piece of shit. You can. Okay?"

Riley and Stan exchanged a wary glance. Sam's attention had waned. He pushed Riley to one side. "You, stay put, or I'll make the fuck sure you go through a world of pain, okay?" He squared up to Aaron and lifted his chin. "Hey, little bro. Come on. You're tough, deep down." He punched his chest. "I know you are. Wuss on the surface but inside, you're like me. Brutal. Y'know?"

Riley and Stan looked at one another again. Sam's gun was still pointed in their direction. Riley's heart raced as the creatures continued to groan, continued to stretch themselves towards the humans, more and more of their neck muscle tearing as they did. They couldn't run. The passage to the exit was narrow. Sam would shoot the second they flinched, and he wouldn't miss.

Aaron's gun was by his side. He shook his head. "I can't. I won't. When the government and the police come back. They'll... They'll find out about this. They'll find out."

"Bullshit." Sam pressed his forehead against Aaron's. "You just don't have it in you to make the tough calls. These fuckers have been killing *our* animals. Trying to fuck over our livelihood. So now we've gotta fuck with theirs."

"But Dad. Mum. How would they—"

Sam smacked Aaron across the face with his rifle. He dragged his head back to face him, then turned around and pointed the gun at Riley and Stan just to make them aware that he was still keeping an eye on them. "Don't fucking talk about Dad and Mum. Dad and Mum were too weak for this. And those sisters of ours?" He jabbed the gun in the direction of the meat hooks. "Look what happened to them. Bitches.

Always were Dad and Mum's favourites. But they're gone and we're still here. So what does that say to you? Hmm?"

"Please, we can—"

"Shut the fuck up," Sam said. He swung around and planted the end of the gun against Riley's forehead. "If you don't want to play with my sisters, you can fucking get screwed. Little bro, you need to toughen up. Get this gun. Hold it. Now."

Aaron's eyes widened. They met Riley's. Held for a few seconds. "But... but I..."

"Do it. *Now.*"

"I'm not going to stand for this," Stan said. He lurched himself at Sam.

But Sam acted fast. He swung the butt of the gun at Stan's head. Stan dropped to the floor. His eyes were closed. He was still. His feet were by the room with the creatures in, who pulled themselves further forward, almost tasting their prey.

"Stan!"

"Shut up or I'll make *you* eat him instead." Sam loaded the gun. "Little bro, you're going to have to toughen up in this world. Things, they ain't like they were before. There's no room for anybody who can't make the tough calls."

Aaron snivelled and whimpered as Sam held the gun to Riley's head. "Please, Sam. Please."

"Just let us leave. Please." Everything was like a blur to Riley. Something he was watching on television. He was just a music journalist. Things like this, they didn't happen to people like him. To normal people. "Please."

Sam shook his head and winked at Riley. "Treat this as a lesson. Take this lesson to the grave with you. Do *not* fuck with somebody else's property. Do not fuck with—"

A gunshot rattled through the air.

Riley clenched his teeth. Closed his eyes. Waited for the pain to claw its way through his skull and into his brain.

But his ears were still ringing. The gun that was prodded against his head had gone. Something heavy thudded to the floor.

Riley opened his eyes.

Aaron's mouth was wide open. He was holding his gun with both of his trembling hands. He gasped. Stepped forward a little, then backwards.

At his feet, his brother's body lay.

Riley closed the door to the room where the creatures on meat hooks swung towards them. The second the door slammed, their groans were drowned out. He lifted the padlock from the floor and stuck it back across the handle, throwing the keys to Stan, who was on his feet again. "We'll take what we need and we'll get out of here. Take more care of these keys in future, too."

Stan stared, wide-eyed, at Sam's body on the floor. Blood pooled out of his smashed skull, seeping in between the cracks of the dusty tiles. Aaron was completely static, breathing heavily and loudly. He lowered his gun.

Riley approached him. He remained wary of the gun in Aaron's hand. He'd just shot his brother, so anything was possible. He lifted a hand, trying to zone Aaron back into the room again. "Hey. You okay?"

Aaron lifted his head. Blinked, as if waking from a long nap. "I... He's dead. I killed him."

"We're... we're going to get out of here." Riley nodded at Stan. "We're going to take some supplies of our own and we're going to leave this place and you aren't going to bother us again."

Tears streamed down Aaron's cheeks. He fell to his knees and rested his head on his brother's stomach, solid and lifeless as a stone. The bullet had pierced right the way through his skull. He wasn't coming back.

"I'll check the hens for eggs. Few of 'em will have been at bursting point yesterday. And I have some crates of milk lying about." Stan moved to one of the hen covers and lifted it. The hen immediately started clucking. "Hey, girl. Keep yourself calm. What've you got for Daddy?"

Riley crouched beside Aaron, who sobbed onto his brother's chest. Sam's eyes were bulging. A genuine look of surprise washed across his greying face. Blood-splattered, brain-coated surprise. "If it's any consolation, I sort of know how you feel."

Aaron lifted his head. His cheeks were reddened and damp. "What do you know about this? What can you possibly know?"

"I killed my grandma," Riley said. "She'd already turned, but… but it wasn't something I was comfortable with doing. And if it's any consolation, I think you have a better shot on your own."

Aaron shook his head. "He was the tough one. Always went on about how he could make the tough calls, even before all this. I don't stand a chance on my own."

Riley sighed. Images of Jordanna, surrounded by creatures as he accelerated the car away from her. Pete's wife in the supermarket, screaming as the biters pushed her to the floor, her husband tearing a chunk of flesh out of her neck. "But maybe you don't have to be on your own."

Stan turned around with a handful of eggs. "What? I hope you aren't suggesting what I think—"

"It's about time we started letting people in, Stan. The kid's got a good shot."

"He tried to *kill* us," Stan roared. "I knew you coming here was too good to be bloody true. I knew in the back of my mind that somehow, you'd find a way to royally screw things over."

"I—I didn't want to kill you," Aaron said. "I swear. That was all my brother. And… and look." He gestured to his brother's dead body on the floor, which twitched and shook every few seconds. "Look what I did. Because… because I knew what he was going to do wasn't right."

"Sometimes you have to do stuff that isn't right."

"Preach. I just shot my brother."

Stan was speechless. He looked at Riley then at Aaron, before shaking his head and waving an egg-filled hand in their direction. "Whatever. Whatever." He stormed off to the main room with the cows.

"Where are you—?"

"Getting some milk." He disappeared into the next room.

Riley nodded at Aaron. "I think that's a yes."

Aaron took a few forced deep breaths in and out and wiped his tearful eyes. "I swear I mean what I said. I wouldn't do anything to hurt no-one. I swear."

Riley cringed. "On two conditions. Okay?"

"Whatever. Whatever you need."

Riley grabbed the gun from Aaron's loose hand. "First, you let me keep hold of this. For now. I have to fight your case to the rest of the group. Being in possession of a gun isn't the best welcome gift."

Aaron nodded reluctantly. "And the second thing?"

Riley stuffed the gun into his pocket and reached for the rifle, which was still wedged between Sam's stiff fingers. "Brush up on your double negatives. There's a big difference between 'not hurting no-one' and 'not hurting anyone.'"

Aaron frowned in puzzlement.

"Oh, and um... what would you like to do? With your brother's body?"

Aaron placed a hand on his brother's shoulder and rose to his feet.

Then, he swung his foot right into the side of his chest.

His face was red. His eyes were bloodshot. Saliva sprayed out of the corners of his mouth.

He gasped as he stopped, catching his breath.

"Everything... okay there?" Riley asked.

Aaron shook his head. "I've always wanted to do that. Always. Goodbye, bro." He stepped over his brother's body and walked towards the covered up hens.

"Okay," Riley said, staring down at the dead body. "Looks like you'll be sleeping alone, Sam, old pal. Look after the place.

And thanks for the weapons."

He followed Aaron through past the caged hens and into the room with the cows.

Stan lifted a large bottle of milk. Dried blood was still trailing down his face where Sam had hit him. He patted a cow on its head. "Good girl. Good girl."

"Ready to move?" Riley threw the rifle to Stan.

Stan grunted, catching the rifle in his free hand.

"These your guns?"

"No, they're ours," Aaron said. "Mine."

"Was going to say. Dairy. Guns. Anything else you're keeping from the group, Stan?"

Stan turned and shook his head at Riley, refraining from reacting. "We take the milk and eggs back to our place." He poured some food into the metal trough where one of the cows was. "I'll leave the cows with enough food and drink and they should be okay. Might have to head down here to clean them every couple of days, but that's manageable."

"Manageable? What if more people decide to take this place for themselves?"

Stan shook the gun from side to side. "We're armed. The stakes are different. Say, kid — where do you get your ammo?"

Aaron looked from Riley to Stan with apprehension. He lowered his head.

Riley sighed. "You're going to have to tell us if you want to save your own neck. You're one of us now. Start acting like one."

"Okay, okay. There's… there's an old bunker. Couple of miles from here in Goosnargh. Sam bought it a few years ago to stash his old equipment in. That's where we… where we were trying to stay. But we got stuck on the road, ran into the field and found this place. Spent the night here. But you… you came. For our animals."

Riley shook his head. "I killed that cow because it was suffering. It was in pain."

"Suffering?" Stan interrupted. "One of my cows?"

"I'm not just talking about the cow. That was just the proof. But Trudy. The way she…" His voice quivered. "The state she was in when she showed up in the field this morning. Why did you have to do that?"

Trudy. The golden Labrador retriever Sam had mentioned earlier. The one that was outside the Chinese restaurant, its leg chewed down to the bone.

"That wasn't us," Riley said. "We found her, but one of our group — they took her away. So her body didn't start, y'know. Smelling, or anything."

Aaron inhaled sharply and nodded. "I thought… After seeing Trudy's body and then the squirrels and then you with the cow… Sam was mad and I thought the same as he did."

"Well you're…" Riley froze. "Wait a second. Squirrels?"

Aaron nodded. "Yeah. The dead squirrels around the farm first thing this morning. But I figure you were just trying to take the dairy farm back. Right?"

Riley and Stan looked at one another. "No. That wasn't us."

"Okay," Stan said. He lifted another bottle of milk up and started to walk towards the main entrance. "All this squirrel murder talk is starting to creep me out. It's time we left. Riley — you grab the box of eggs. Kid — you—"

The bottles of milk tumbled to the floor.

Stan fell backwards onto the ground.

At first, Riley couldn't quite process what was happening. Everything seemed to be unfolding in slow motion.

But then, when he saw the teeth gnashing, getting closer and closer to Stan, he understood.

"Stan!" He ran towards him and raised his gun. Stan pushed the creature back, his flabby muscles tensing as much as they could.

Riley took a deep breath. Raised the gun.

One, two, three…

He pulled the trigger. The gun knocked him off balance. The bullet went flying past the creature's head and out through the wide doorway into the open.

Riley rushed towards Stan as he wrestled with the creature. "Stan, just—"

"No, Riley!" It was Aaron. His voice sounded desperate. Pleading.

When Riley looked up at the main door, he realised why.

A crowd of creatures were staggering towards the main door. All of them were focused. All of them were walking in their direction. And all of them were groaning.

"Arggggh!"

Riley looked back down at Stan. The creature was still on top of him, wrestling away.

But blood was squirting out of Stan's shoulder. His face had turned pale in a matter of seconds.

Stan was bitten.

Chapter Twenty-Three

"GET TO THE DOORS!" RILEY SHOUTED.

Aaron stumbled towards the double doors. The creatures outside were getting close. Tonnes of them — ten, twenty, maybe more. They'd found the countryside. At last, they'd found the countryside.

Riley aimed his gun at the creature's head, which gnawed at Stan's shoulder and neck. His gun hand was shaking. He had to keep cool. Keep cool, stay grounded, and do this.

He pulled the trigger. The creature slammed forward into the floor, bits of brain and muscle splattering over Stan's already-bloody white shirt. Stan winced. Cried and blabbered like a baby, gripping his shoulder as blood continued to fountain out of it.

Riley looked up at the doorway. Aaron was struggling to pull the shutters across. The few creatures that weren't already staggering in the direction of the farmhouse all were now, groaning and reaching out as Riley pulled Stan from underneath the rigid body of the creature.

"They won't fucking close!" Aaron shouted. He stepped back from the doorway and turned to Riley. A look of desperation was washed over his face. "What the fuck are we going to do?"

Riley's heart pounded. He grabbed the rifle that had dropped from Stan's hand and slid it across the floor to Aaron. "Hold them off. Just keep them away."

Aaron's eyes widened. "But I can't. I—"

"Just do it."

Aaron lifted the rifle and messed around with it before aiming at the crowd of oncoming creatures. A shot rattled through the air. One of the creatures tumbled to the floor.

"Please... Please..." Blood dribbled from Stan's mouth. Riley wiped his sleeve against it, but he spluttered and coughed up some more bubbles of thick blood. The bites were deep — right into Stan's neck and shoulder blade. Even if infection didn't spread, he'd die through blood loss.

He was a lost cause.

Another shot sounded through the air. Riley looked up and saw that two of the creatures had fallen to the floor. Aaron was gradually stepping backwards as the creatures got closer to the entrance of the farmhouse, picking them off one by one. But ammo would run out. Soon, it'd be all gone. They had to get out of here. Somehow, they had to leave.

"Kill me. Please... Please. Kill me."

Riley swallowed the lump in his throat and placed his hand on Stan's head. He was burning up. "You... I'm sorry this happened to you, Stan. I'm so sorry."

Another shot blasted. "Running low on ammo!" The creatures stepped across the entrance. They were inside.

Dread took a hold of Riley as he looked down at Stan's dying body, then at the cows, cowering in their pens. He knew what he had to do. Just like in the supermarket, moments before he'd thrown the wrench through the glass, he knew exactly what he had to do.

But his morals. Their humanity. They had to hold on to that.

"Please…" Stan spluttered. More colour diminished from his cheeks. "I… I don't want to turn… Please…"

Riley wiped a tear from his eye and raised his gun. "You won't know a thing. I promise you won't know a thing."

"Need the fucking pistol!" Aaron stepped further back as five creatures walked into the farm entrance, all focused on him, all groaning.

Riley patted Stan on the shoulder and smiled. "You'll be with Jill soon. I promise."

He jumped to his feet and pulled open the gate where one of the cows was.

The cow let out a loud moan and sprinted out of its pen. This had to work. It had to.

As Riley reached for the gate of the next pen, he heard a scream.

When he turned around, he saw that Aaron was on the floor.

The cow sauntered past the creatures, who scratched their fingers into its sides half-heartedly. It ran into the distance, knocking a bunch of creatures to the floor. Some of them paid attention to it, but their focus was elsewhere. Their focus was on Aaron and his screaming. Riley's Plan A had failed.

"Please!" Aaron shouted. Another creature pressed against the back of the one already on top of him, sinking him further into the ground. "Shoot them! Please!"

Riley looked at the creatures, all walking towards Aaron, who shouted and screamed. He looked at Stan on the floor, pulling himself onto his side, dragging his body weight over to the opposite side of the room.

And then he saw the gap in the main entrance. A gap that wouldn't be there for long. A gap that the runaway cow had formed.

"Please!" Aaron screamed as another creature appeared beside him. "Pleaaaaase!"

Riley held his breath. Let the fear and the tingling sensation and the nausea in the pit of his stomach take over him.

And, with his gun raised, he ran.

He reached the door. A couple of the creatures turned and looked at him. He couldn't shoot. He had to save the bullets for when he absolutely needed them. He pushed past one and rammed into the stomach of another, knocking them both to the floor.

Most of them were still staggering in the direction of Aaron's screams, and their fellow creatures' groans.

Riley sprinted and sprinted until he reached the fence. He didn't look back until he was over the fence, until he was out of the main crowd and half way up the field. He didn't look back, but he could still hear Aaron, screaming away.

He fell into the long grass. Sweat dripped from his head. His body crumbled to the ground, and he started spluttering. He looked at his hands—drenched with blood. Stan's blood. Aaron's blood. Pete and his wife's blood. Jordanna's blood. He could have saved them. He could have tried to save them. But he'd run. He was a coward. A failure. Not fit to lead anybody.

Something tickled his back. He jumped and jolted forward. The cow that had escaped the dairy farm was sniffing him, a curious look on its face. Riley sank his head into his knees and let out a sigh of relief before standing to his feet, the cow watching his every move very closely.

"Least… Least you're okay, eh? Least you're okay. And I'm speaking to a cow."

Riley stared in the direction of the dairy farm. The screams had stopped. The creatures were all pretty much inside now bar one or two lone stragglers. They'd feed on Aaron's body, then they'd move on to Stan, and then when they realised there was no more human meat, they'd feed on the cows, and the chickens, and then Sam's dead corpse, head cracked as he lay on the floor. A pointless death.

He looked down at his hands. The blood was beginning to

dry. So much of it that it looked like it would never wash off.

"When you hear them coming, you know it's already too late to do anything about them."

Stan was right. Except this time, they hadn't even heard them coming.

It was always too late to do anything about them.

Riley patted the cow on its side. "You go find some... some grass to feed on. Or something." He waved his hand at the cow. "Go on."

The cow crept away, still focused on Riley. A witness to his crimes. A witness to his guilt and his grief.

Riley took one last look at the overrun dairy farm, the sun making its final descent behind it. He took a deep breath, and walked back in the direction of the Chinese restaurant as the cow wandered off in the other direction.

"We can't just give up on them."

Anna smacked her hand against the wall. "Then what do you suggest, Ted? Going out there yourself with your foot in the fucking state it's in?"

"Anna," Claudia said. She pointed at her daughters.

"Oh shut up, Claudia," Anna said. "Just shut up. Your daughters are going to see horrible things. Horrible things worse than any fucking swear word. Grow up."

Claudia's mouth dangled open as her daughters, Elizabeth and Chloë, sniggered behind her.

Ted loosened the bandage and pressed his foot against the ground, wincing and hobbling slightly, but managing to walk at a steady pace.

"Trevor — please, tell him," Anna pleaded. "We have to stick together. Stan and Riley — they made their choice. But we need to stick together. What we've got here — it's good. We can't just let all that go to waste."

Trevor shrugged as Ted approached the door. "I can't stand in anyone's way. People make their own choices."

Anna dropped her head into her hands. When she moved

them away, tears were covering her cheeks. "It's been a—a long day. We're all tired. The sun's setting, so let's just... let's just eat, sleep, and think about it."

Ted stopped by the door. "Eat, sleep and think about it?" He stepped closer to Anna. "Eat. Sleep. And think about it?"

Anna looked him in the eye. Nodded her head. "Yes."

Ted swung a hand across her face. "Eat? Sleep? Think about it? My fucking friend is out there." He felt arms grab him from behind as Trevor pulled him back. Claudia covered her mouth with her hands and grabbed her daughters.

"My only fucking friend is out there looking for Stan all because you went and fucking killed his wife."

Anna was turned to one side, soaking up the impact of the slap. She lifted a hand to her face and moved her sweaty hair out of her teary eyes. When she lowered her hand, a cut was visible on her left cheek. "You think I killed Jill? You really think I—"

"Yes," Ted spat. Trevor continued to pull him back. "Who else? Who the fuck else? Because it wasn't Riley. I swear it wasn't Riley."

"Ted, come on, man," Trevor said.

Ted swung around and pushed Trevor up to the wall. He pressed his forehead up to Trevor's. Stared into his eyes. "What about you then? You were unaccounted for, weren't you? Did you do it? Slip a knife in the old lady's neck when she wasn't looking?"

Trevor took calm, collected breaths. "No. I didn't."

"Well it was either you or her," he said, pointing at Anna. "One of you did it. Riley insisted to me he hadn't, and I believe that dude 'cause he's my mate and he'd never lie to me. I believe that dude because he's—"

"Ted, please," Claudia called. She gripped her girls close to her chest. "You're scaring the girls. Please."

"He doesn't care," Anna said. Her face twitched and her jaw clenched. "He just wanted to use us. Get his foot sorted out, and use us."

"Fuck off," Ted said. He tossed Trevor back against the wall and turned around to face Anna, head on.

"What single productive thing have you done for this group since yesterday, hmm? Played the clown with the girls? Sat on your arse and let your best friend make all the tough decisions?"

"Stop it," Ted said. He squared up to Anna.

"Ted, please!" Claudia shouted. Elizabeth started to cry.

"Or what?" Anna said, moving closer and closer to Ted. "You gonna hit me again? Let everybody witness what a pathetic, weak man you really are? Does your best friend know you hit women? I bet he has no idea. I bet if he knew, he'd throw your fat little ass to the biters too."

"But he won't. Because he isn't here. Because he's cleaning up your mess. Cleaning up after *your* killing."

"Go on," Anna said. She pressed right up to Ted, her sickly sweet breath blowing into his face. "Do what you have to do. Hit me again. You weak, pathetic piece of shit."

"I'm going to go out there and I'm going to find my mate. And if he's dead — if he's dead or if he's turned — I'm going to kill you. I'm going to kill you because if you hadn't started this fucking chain of events, this wouldn't have happened. I'm going to—"

"Stop!"

The voice was initially unrecognisable. Ted thought it was Claudia at first, but it was too high-pitched even though it came from her direction. He looked over, as did Anna and Trevor.

Chloë was standing in the middle of the room. Tears streamed down her cheeks, tumbling down onto her furry slippers. Her bottom lip wobbled as she held her hands behind her back and sobbed. "It was me."

Ted frowned. Claudia's eyes widened.

Claudia reached a hand out for her daughter. "You... What was you? Darling?"

"It-it was me," Chloë said, stuttering her way through the

tears. "Jill... she came at me, and I... She was one of those things. But it was me. I killed her."

A bang rattled through the silence of the room. It came from the door. Ted swung around.

"Holy shit," Anna said, as Trevor rushed over to the door and opened it.

Riley staggered in. His hands and arms were drenched in blood. His hair was coated in sweat. He gasped and sniffed and shook his head.

"Riley... you're... you're alive," Ted said.

Riley dropped to his knees and collapsed on the floor.

Chapter Twenty-Four

A SHARP PAIN CLAWED THROUGH RILEY'S head. Visions danced in his mind. The dairy farm. Aaron's screams. The creature sinking its teeth into Stan's neck and tearing away his flesh. Running, running, running away. Not stopping for anyone. Not stopping for anything.

He knew where he was. There was no confusion about the situation he was waking up to anymore. No confusion about the state of affairs outside. The creatures were out there. They were coming. And eventually, they'd find them, and they'd kill them. Trevor. Ted. Anna. Claudia. The children. All of them.

He opened his eyes. The dim light pierced through his blurred vision. He was on Ted's bed, elevated off the ground. Ted was sat on the edge of the bed, head in hands.

Riley lifted himself upright. His head felt weak and dizzy.

"Oh, hey," Ted said. He nodded at Riley and reached for a half-empty bottle of water, pouring some out into a plastic cup. "You should drink. You… you don't look great, man."

Riley grabbed the plastic cup with his weak, jittery hand. The dried blood covering his arms caught his eyes. But no. He couldn't dwell on that now. What was done was done. He held the cup to his mouth and poured the cold water down his dry throat.

"You… you were out for a good few hours. Trevor thought you'd turned but… There's no bites. But you haven't been… bitten. Right?"

Riley shook his head.

"Good," Ted said. "One thing to be positive about I guess. Hardly… hardly wanted you to wake up as one of those things. Not that it'd make much of a difference. I'm dead anyway. Oh, and erm… Anna. She's got the gun you brought back with you."

Although Riley understood the words that Ted was saying, they didn't really resonate inside him. Didn't create any sort of emotional response. He felt numb. Cut off. Dead to the world. The things he'd seen, they'd made him more of a zombie than any of those creatures.

Voices echoed up the stairs from the lower section of the Chinese restaurant. Raised voices. Shouting. Anna. Claudia. Trevor. Children crying.

"They… We had a fall out. I did something stupid, mate. And—" He paused. Gulped. "Chloë. Claudia's… Claudia's daughter. She killed Jill. Said she'd turned and came at her and… yeah. Self-defence. Kid was too scared to say anything."

Riley stared up at the ceiling. In the corner of his eyes, he saw a streetlight flicker to life outside. A breeze swept the autumn leaves down the road, further into the darkness.

"Anna's pissed. I… I don't know what to do. I… Riley. I hit her." He stared at Riley with a pained grimace, as if he was waiting to be torn to pieces for his actions.

Riley could only shrug.

Ted frowned and shook his head. "I didn't mean to do it. I was just… Mate, I was worried about you. I thought she'd killed Jill. I thought she did it and I just flipped. I… I know it's stupid. But I just want you to know I'm sorry. Because... well. I don't know how much longer they're going to let me stay here."

Riley kept his mouth shut. Ted's words swam around his mind, distant and unconnected. Diluted and watered down. The events at the farm. The blood and the screams and the struggles.

But more than anything, it was his realisation that spun around his mind. The flu jab that Jill had taken. The advertisement for the flu jab outside the room where the creatures gorged on a nurse, who held a syringe.

And Anna's words. *"I guess we really do all have our secrets."*

"I hate to go into this, but Stan. Is he... gone?"

Riley nodded.

Ted sighed. "And you... Are you—?"

Riley nodded again.

"Just if you want to talk about things. Because we're going to have to talk about things at some point soon. Okay?"

Anna's words. The look of guilt in her face when they'd stood in that bathroom before he left.

Ted tutted and hopped off the bed. He winced as he landed on his sore foot. "Look — I know what you've been through was no doubt bad, but now's not the time to start cutting yourself off and hiding away from things. We're in the shit. Okay? Deep, deep shit. You hear them downstairs? You want to know what they're arguing about? They're arguing about what to do with us. And no, not whether we're staying or not, but whether to send us packing without any supplies or to tie us up to a railing and leave us to die. We're in the shit. So you can't just sit there and—"

"I just watched a man get torn to shreds by those creatures instead of shooting them. Instead of helping him." A burning sensation rushed all the way through Riley's body. He climbed off the bed. "I could have helped him. I could have. And maybe we'd both have got out of there. He was only a kid. Shot his own psycho brother because he didn't agree with him.

Saved Stan. Saved me. And I let him die. I listened to him scream and I didn't do anything about it. And Stan, too. I could have shot him. Put him out of his misery. But what did I do? I saved the bullets. So sorry for my silence, Ted. Sorry for not being all bubbly or all, 'Oh, I'm sorry Ted, don't worry, Ted,' but I'm dealing with some shit of my own here. I…" He looked at the dried blood on his hands. "This world. It's two days in and I've already let so many people die. I've allowed that to happen. I haven't wanted to, but I've had to. What does that make me?"

Ted stared at Riley. He was silent for a few moments. Then, he cleared his throat and placed a hand on Riley's shoulder. "Alive. That's what it makes you. Alive." He turned away from Riley and walked towards the bedroom door.

"Where are you going?"

Ted stopped at the door. "I'm going to the bathroom and then I'm leaving this place. You… you should stay. You're good with these people. You'll be better here with them."

Riley walked after Ted, swaying a little. His head spun and his stomach churned. "You aren't going anywhere. You don't have to leave."

Ted turned to Riley. His eyes were bloodshot and his face was grey. "I *hit* Anna across the face. Bruised her. Right in front of… of the girls. That's the image this group has of me now. That's who Ted is. Not the clown who keeps the kids entertained. Not the fat slob who lazes around while his best mate does all the hard work. I'm Ted the woman-beater. And even in this world, I can't come back from that image."

Riley stared down the corridor. The voices grew louder and angrier. "There's a few things in this world we can't come back from." He walked down the corridor towards the staircase.

"Where are *you* going?" Ted shouted. "There's… Now's probably not the best time to go down there. You need to rest. You need… The blood on your hands. You need cleaning up."

Riley let Ted's words disappear into thin air and climbed down the stairs. The arguing voices and the crying got closer.

Through the window at the top of the stairs, he could see nothing but complete darkness. He had to mention what was on his mind now. He couldn't let it brew inside him any longer.

"Riley, come on, man. This is ridiculous." Ted's new training shoes that Trevor had grabbed from the supermarket for him squeaked against the stairs. "We need to do this together. We need a plan."

Riley pushed the door to the reception area open. The room went silent.

Behind the counter, Anna was crouched opposite Claudia. Tears streamed down Claudia's cheeks as she held Chloë in her arms. Trevor paced around the room with his hands behind his head. Elizabeth sat on her own by the front door, sulking.

"Nice of you to join us," Anna said, rising to her feet. "I suppose your friend's told you everything there is to know about what's going on here?" She pointed a finger at her face. A red bruise was protruding from her cheekbone.

Riley walked further into the room. His heart raced. Adrenaline rushed through his body. Claudia looked at him as she held her daughter. There was no reassuring smile or nod, not anymore.

"And you've got a nerve showing your face in here again," Anna said. She looked past Riley.

"I've told him what's going on," Ted said. "I tried to stop him. I—"

"The truth is, Riley, your friend here showed his true colours. In front of all of us. I don't want a person like that staying with us. Claudia, the girls — they've been through a lot. And I don't trust him. I'm sorry."

"Okay," Riley said.

Anna looked taken aback. "Is… I'm not sure you understand what I'm saying here. You have a choice. You can take the road with your friend, or you can stay here with us."

Riley stuck his bottom lip out. Nodded his head from side

to side, weighing up Anna's proposal. "What if I choose another option?"

Anna frowned. Trevor and Claudia looked on, silently. "Which is?"

Riley stepped up to Anna. Stared her in the eyes. "Remember in the bathroom before I left to find Stan? Remember what we spoke about?"

Anna narrowed her eyes. Squinted as if searching her head for the memory. "I'm not sure what you—"

"Secrets. We talked about secrets. About how we're… how we're entitled to our secrets. Remember?"

Anna's cheeks flushed. She turned to Claudia and then to the floor. "I don't get the relevance to be honest."

Riley smiled. "Well, I was wrong about secrets. I said we're all entitled to them. But I don't think that's true anymore. Look at what secrets have done to us. They got Stan killed."

Anna lifted her head. "Stan… he's…?"

"Yes. He is. And I'll tell you another secret of mine." Riley raised his blood-coated arms. "I let somebody die today. I could have saved him, but I didn't. I chose my own life instead. And when we met you people. The bullshit I told you about finding the gun on a police officer—that was a lie. The truth is Ted and I bumped into a girl. She had a gun. She got out of our car to save us and we let her die to save ourselves."

The rest of the room looked on.

"So there. That's my big secret. I'm a coward. I've let people die. Now, you know who I am. You can judge me. Does anyone else have any secrets they want to share? Trevor? Aside from the letting your friends die thing, anything else?"

Trevor flinched and shook his head.

"What about you, Claudia? Have you anything you want to tell us? Nothing you're hiding, is there?"

Claudia glanced at Anna then back at Riley. "No. No, I don't."

Riley nodded. "Good." He stepped back up to Anna. "And what about you, Anna? Doctor Anna. Do you have anything you want to tell the rest of the group?"

Anna raised her head. Her bottom lip quivered. Riley knew she was hiding something just by the way she peered at him.

"Nothing at all? Nothing… flu jab related?"

Anna's shoulders dropped. She shook her head. "Don't. Don't."

"What are you talking about?" Claudia asked.

Riley turned to Claudia and Chloë. He took a deep breath. The words were spouting from his mouth like somebody else was speaking through him. A man possessed. "Chloë, I know you think it was you who killed Jill, but it wasn't. Not really."

"Please," Anna said. She grabbed Riley's arm. "Please."

Riley stared at Anna. He had to tell the truth. There could be no more secrets. It's all they had left. "Jill was already dead when you found her. I know that and you know that. And that's because—"

"Arrrgh!"

Glass smashed at the front of the Chinese restaurant.

Elizabeth fell to the floor.

"Holy shit," Trevor said. He rushed over to Elizabeth and scooped her up. "Upstairs! Now!"

The sound of footsteps running up the staircase echoed behind Riley. Blurred faces rushed past him. Voices called out. The children screamed.

"Riley, quick!"

He stared at the smashed glass of the restaurant door.

A creature pulled itself in.

Another followed.

And another.

"Riley, we have to close this door. Get in here, now!"

Riley stumbled back as more and more creatures swarmed into the entrance area. Ten. Fifteen. Twenty. Groaning. Walking in his direction.

He ran through the door to the stairway and slammed it shut.

"We've lost this place," Trevor said. "We've lost it."

… **EPISODE FOUR**

Chapter Twenty-Five

"RILEY, WE NEED TO GET THE hell upstairs. Now!"

The groans grew in number behind him. It sounded like a deathly choir. A sing-off. The sheer number that had crashed their way through the entrance. More than ten. More than twenty. And there were more of them behind him, all making their way in the group's direction. They'd seen which way the group had gone. They'd heard it, too.

There was only one place the group could go, and that was upstairs.

Riley rushed up the staircase. Trevor was at the top, following the rest of the group. The children cried out and shouted at one another in panic. Anna swore and bossed people around at the top of her voice.

"Then where the fuck do you suggest we go?" Anna struggled with the window at the end of the corridor. "You've seen them — they're coming for us. And unless we move, we'll be one of them too."

Ted shook his head. "I just think we should talk about this. Properly."

"We don't have *time* to talk about this, 'properly.' We have to move. Riley?"

Riley stared down the corridor at the group. All of their eyes were on him. Even after what he'd told them about abandoning people. Even after how close he'd come to exposing Anna's secret in front of all of them. Still, they looked at him. Looked to him.

"I... I think—"

The door crashed at the bottom of the staircase. The groans were getting clearer, which meant the door must have cracked. So many of them, like flies buzzing 'round shit. All their supplies. Everything they'd worked for. All of it, gone to waste.

"We need to try and salvage something," Ted said. He limped down the corridor in the direction of the staircase. "Everything. The food and the water. We can't just let that go. We have to collect what we can while we can."

Trevor held his hand up as Ted started to walk past him. He shook his head. "You can hear those things. We can't go down there."

Ted opened his mouth to protest. His eyes reddened. He looked past Trevor and at Riley. "Mate? What d'you say? The stuff you came back with. The run to the supermarket. We can't just—"

The door downstairs crashed again. Wood cracked and even more groans and cries echoed up the stairway. Claudia held her hands over Elizabeth's ears. She tried to get Chloë to join her too, but she looked on, wide-eyed and distant.

"I'm sorry, Ted," Riley said. "We can't risk it. We can't lose anything else."

Ted cringed and shook his head. "Damn. Damn it. Then what—"

"Get back!" Anna shouted.

Riley spun around. A creature was waddling up the stairs. It looked like it had been a bald man once upon a time. Fresh blood and bits of skin were smudged across its mouth. Cracked glasses sat on its nose.

Anna struggled with the window some more. "We've no choice. No fucking choice." She pulled the gun that she had taken from Riley out of her pocket and aimed at the glass.

"We need to get in the bedroom," Claudia said, backing up towards Anna with Elizabeth's hand in hers. "We need—we need to hide. Somewhere. Anywhere!"

Behind the bald creature, another emerged. A woman with thin peroxide blonde hair. Huge chunk missing from her neck. A wonder her head was still balancing on her shoulders.

A loud bang exploded. Glass shattered and rained out of the window that Anna shot. Shards sprinkled to the ground outside like icicles on a cold day. Anna leaned out of the window and squinted into the darkness.

"Can we make it?" Ted asked. He lifted his foot. "It's just… my foot. It's…"

Anna narrowed her eyes at Ted. She didn't say anything, but she didn't have to. The look said it all. *Tough.*

Another creature staggered up the staircase, tumbling forward and knocking the other two down, like dominoes.

"Mummy, I don't like them."

"Don't be so soft," Chloë said to her sister as the three of them moved right up to the smashed window. "We have to learn to be tough!"

Riley's heart raced as he watched the creatures get further and further up the stairs. And yet, he felt strangely calm. Strangely in control. The moans of the creatures seemed to blur into the background. He looked down at his arms. Stared at the sleeves of dried blood. The things he'd done, he wasn't proud of. Nobody could be. But Ted was right. He was alive. That's what his decisions made him.

"Riley? Mate? We don't have long."

Riley turned away from the growing queue of creatures and walked up to the smashed window. He placed his hands on the edge and stuck his head out. A wall of cold hit him as he stared down into the darkness below. No groans. No light. Nothing.

"We need to find a pipe. Some way of getting out there."

Riley took a deep breath in through his nostrils and swung a foot over the side of the window ledge.

"Wait — Riley! What are you—"

He closed his eyes and he fell.

Chapter Twenty-Six

"MATE, WHAT THE *FUCK* ARE YOU doing?"

Riley gripped his shoulder. A shooting sensation rushed down it as he winced and stood to his feet. Ted's head was sticking out of the window above. Anna was beside him, frowning into the darkness as shouts and screams sounded behind her.

"Is he—what did he—"

"I'm okay," Riley called. He kept his tone hushed and gripped hold of his ribs. The impact had hurt, but he'd been sure not to tense any muscles as he tumbled to the ground. A school friend of his used to sleepwalk as a child. Jumped out of a third story window several times and didn't break a single bone. Decided to show off to his mates at a party and ended up breaking his legs and shattering his pelvis. Doctor told him it's because he was tensing his muscles when he was awake. The key was to be as floppy as a rag doll.

But that wasn't easy.

A gunshot sounded in the window above. And another. The creatures were getting closer to the group. They had to get out of there. They couldn't all jump — it was too risky. Not everybody would be able to quit tensing like he could. It was a relaxation trick he'd learned. *Focus on the breathing. Steady the mind. And... release.*

"Riley!" Anna shouted. "I... We can hold them off for now but..." Another gunshot fired. "Shit. We're gonna have to jump too."

Riley's heart raced. He looked around the area in front of him, lit up by the bright light of the full moon. An abandoned white minivan. On top of it, a ladder.

Another gunshot. Trevor shouted out. "Back up! I can kick them down but... you have to back up."

Adrenaline raced through Riley's body as he stared at the ladder atop the van. If he could get to it, he could bring it over to the window and they could all climb down.

But the groans. The throaty, raspy cries of the creatures. He could hear them to his right, around the corner of the wall. He had to be careful.

He slowly crept towards the corner of the wall as the struggling and firing continued above. He held his breath and poked his head around the corner.

A crowd of creatures all made their way through the smashed glass of the front door. They were all coming from down the road, all stumbling in the direction of the Chinese restaurant entrance. Why the fuck were they coming this way? What had attracted them? Could it be the horde from the dairy farm? Had they followed him back?

"Get the kids in the bathroom," Trevor shouted. "Quick!"

Riley looked down at his hands and gulped. The dried blood of too many people. People he'd abandoned. Let down.

He could come back from this. He couldn't just run away.

He moved from the cover of the side wall. He remained crouched, keeping his focus on the white van up ahead. He didn't turn to his right to look at them. If there was one on his left and it ambushed him then so be it. But he had to get there quickly. He had to stay focused.

An intense fear gripped hold of him as he reached the middle of the road. His right ear was deafened by the sounds of their groans. Were they getting nearer to him? Approaching him? *No. Keep calm. Keep focused.*

The van was just metres away now. The commotion of the Chinese restaurant seemed further and further away every step he took. He just had to get the ladder then get back to the restaurant. He could do this. He could save them.

When he reached the van, he stopped and took in a couple of deep breaths before rising slowly to his feet. Almost automatically, he looked to his right, and regretted it immediately. The crowd of dark silhouettes and figures pouring in through the door, their blood-drenched clothes illuminating in the moonlight. He turned back to the van and rushed around to the other side of it where he would be protected from view. The upstairs light of the takeaway shadowed as shots continued to fire and voices muffled.

Riley reached and grabbed the top corner of the ladder, wrestling with the holder to set it free. The creatures weren't approaching him. The gap between the Chinese restaurant and the van was still clear. He could do this. He had to.

As he unclipped the fourth corner of the ladder from the holder, he felt something grip hold of his leg.

He looked down and almost tumbled over.

A creature's hand pushed through the glass of the van window. It pressed itself up against the cracking glass, sticking its tongue out at full stretch, the glass severing and slicing it.

Riley kicked out and shook his leg free. His foot clanked against the side of the van. He looked up at the crowd of creatures — still focused on the restaurant. *Fuck.* He kicked at the gripping hand again and struggled free of it, climbing on top of the minivan, exposed in the bright moonlight.

The van shuffled from side to side as the creature tried to pull itself out.

Please don't notice. Please don't...

In the distance, near the back of the long, winding queue of creatures, one of them strayed from its Lemming-esque path and started to stagger in the direction of the minivan.

Another followed.

And another.

"Shit." Riley gripped hold of the ladder and jumped off the side of the van as the creatures heading towards him started to groan. More of them changed their course of direction as he sprinted across the road and towards the window. They were screwed. What use were ladders if they had no escape?

"Get yourselves ready!" Riley shouted. He knew the creatures had already noticed him, so he could shout as much as he liked. They'd be surrounded. The creatures inside the Chinese restaurant. The creatures outside, all gathering around the ladder. They were trapped.

But perhaps they didn't have to climb out after all.

Riley crouched down in the alley at the side of the restaurant and extended the ladder with his shaky hands. "Coming up. Keep them back."

"They're not stopping, man!" Ted shouted. "They—they're not stopping."

Riley rested the ladder against the wall, where it fell just short of the window ledge, and put his foot on the first step.

As he did, a small crowd of creatures stepped around the corner and walked in his direction.

He rushed up the ladder, which shook from side to side the further he ascended. His heart raced. His palms dripped with sweat. He could do this. They could do this.

The creatures were so close. Hungry. Noisy. Unforgiving. They were coming for the ladder. They'd crash into it and they'd knock it down — knock him down.

He took another step and felt the ladder start to fall to the right.

He jumped up and gripped the window ledge. The ladder disappeared beneath his feet as he dug his nails into the window ledge, crying out as his clammy fingers slid away.

The ladder clattered to the ground. Something gripped his hand.

He looked up. It was Claudia. She nodded at Riley and pulled him through the window with all of her strength, back in to the corridor and back to where they'd started.

Trevor and Ted were at the other end of the corridor, knocking the creatures down the stairs. Anna was assisting them, gun raised.

"What the hell was that about?"

Riley watched Ted as he smacked the shrinking crowd of creatures to the ground, the groans building outside the window.

"Saving this place," Riley said.

Riley rushed down the corridor towards Ted, Anna, and Trevor.

"Be careful," Claudia called. "It's... it's no use. They're coming. They're—"

"Those creatures are all outside the window I just climbed through. I want you to keep them there."

Claudia's eyes watered. "And... and how am I supposed to do that?"

Riley shrugged. "Improvise." He carried on walking to the others as they battled with the creatures, pushing them further and further back down the stairs.

"Mate, you—you're okay." Ted hit a creature over the head with a spanner and sent its limp body tumbling down the steps, joining a pile outside the door. There were only three more creatures. The numbers were diminishing.

"You need to back up," Riley said.

"Back up?" Anna frowned. She smacked the butt of her gun against the chin of a creature and knocked it back. "But they're coming. They're—"

"They're by the window," Riley said. He pointed at where he'd come from. Claudia leaned out of it, waving and shouting at the creatures below. "I... I drew them to the window. Claudia's keeping them there. We have to back up while we still have a chance to fortify the front."

"Fortify it?" Trevor said. He shook his head. "The front door — it's gone. Smashed in. They might have moved for now, but they're coming back. You've seen how they are."

Riley looked down at the pile of bodies built at the bottom of the steps. "Maybe so. But if we act fast, we can do this. Trevor—you come with me to the front door. We'll cover it up as well as we can. Stay upstairs if we have to."

"And the bodies?" Anna said. "We can't live here with—with all these dead things lying around."

"We'll burn them. Throw them out of the window and burn them."

Ted nodded. Sweat dripped down his face. "We can save this place. We can do it."

Anna shook her head. "We need to move on while we still can."

"And go where?" Ted asked.

"Anywhere we can. The creatures — they're coming from the city. We can head further into the country. Towards... towards the canal. We can get a barge and—and sail up to Lancaster. Riley?"

Riley stared at the bodies on the floor. The door to the reception area, half open, battered by the force of the creatures that had piled through it. Claudia's voice, shouting at the creatures to distract them, rang around his skull.

He took a step down the stairway.

"Where do you think you're—?"

"Trevor and I will close up the doorway as well as we can. The shelves in the kitchen—we can move them. If Claudia keeps those things outside distracted, we can do this. There might be one or two loose, but we can handle those. Right?"

Trevor paused, then offered a single nod back at Riley. "If you say so. Lead the way."

As Riley began to descend the stairway, he felt a hand on

his shoulder. It was Ted.

"Let me... let me help. Please."

Anna rolled her eyes and sighed. "You? Help? Don't think I'd trust you to."

Ted's eyes were bloodshot. He had that desperate look on his face, like when he'd begged Riley to let him stay in his flat with him. Like when his benefits had been cut and Riley was forced to contribute more towards the flat rent. Except he wasn't the one asking for help this time. Ted was the one asking *to* help.

"You give Anna a hand clearing up the bodies," Riley said. "But keep it quiet. And make sure Claudia keeps their attention. Okay?"

Anna shot a disgusted glance at Ted. The bruise on her face was growing purpler. "And why should we work together?"

"Because we have to," Riley said. "We're a group. We help each other out."

A creature groaned in the reception area. It was wandering through on its own. A woman with a deathly pale face, dressed in her pajamas. Teeth-marks all over her forehead, hair torn from her head and her scalp gnawed at.

Riley and Trevor exchanged a glance. Trevor lifted his spanner, ready to approach the creature.

"Take this." Anna held the gun out to Riley. She bit her lip and avoided looking him directly in the eye.

Riley took the gun. "How many bullets left?"

Anna shrugged. "A few. But you'll need it more than I do. Good... Good luck."

Riley nodded at Anna, then at Ted.

"Ready?" Trevor asked him.

Riley took a deep breath. "Ready."

The pair of them clambered over the mound of rancid dead bodies and into the reception area as Claudia's cries of distraction continued to sound.

Trevor swung his spanner at the head of the oncoming

creature.

The spanner smacked against it and sent fragments of skull inward towards its brain. Trevor yanked the spanner back, blood pouring out of the creature's head, and the creature dropped to the floor in a lifeless heap. Trevor stepped away from the creature, turned to Riley, and nodded.

Riley followed Trevor's lead and entered the reception area. He held his gun up and scanned the room. Bloody footprints were spread across the floor from the smashed glass of the main door, like mud on a rainy day. His shoes squelched through the slippery dampness of water and blood as he stepped closer to Trevor. There were no groans inside anymore. No sign of creatures by the door.

"We need to grab what we can from the kitchen," Riley said. "As many counters as we can push up against that door."

Trevor moved over to the kitchen door. "And how do you propose we get out of this place? For food? Supplies?"

Riley shrugged. "We'll find a way. We... This place. We're not going to find anywhere better than this. We need to hold on to what we've got. Ted's right."

Trevor tilted his head. "And this has nothing to do with you throwing yourself out of a window, hmm?"

The question caught Riley off-guard. He had acted quickly. He'd put his own life on the line. But it turned out he'd done the right thing. He'd given them a chance. A chance to do something. "The plan was to get out of here. But we might not have to."

Trevor shook his head and grabbed the handle of the kitchen door. He reached into his pocket with his free hand and shook a pack of cigarettes. "If we make it out, we're smoking one of these. Think we've earned it after today."

Riley nodded and aimed the gun at the door. Still no sign of any creatures at the main entrance. "I... I would. But, I quit smoking a while ago."

"Well you're going to un-quit smoking, just for me." He smiled at Riley then pulled the door open.

At first, Riley couldn't quite process what it was he was seeing.

Trevor tumbled back, covering his mouth with his sleeve, coughing.

A thick black cloud of smoke drifted out of the kitchen door. The smell of burning strengthened in Riley's nostrils.

The kitchen door slammed shut and Trevor struggled to his feet, still coughing up the smoke he'd inhaled. He pointed at Riley, his eyes watering. "Need to... need to get upstairs. Need to leave."

Riley frowned. "What... What—"

"Fire. Fire." Trevor staggered past Riley and towards the stairs. "Need to leave. Now."

Riley shook his head and rushed back over to the kitchen door. Dread built up inside of him. "We can put it out," he said, grabbing the handle. "We can deal with it. We can..."

As he opened the kitchen door, his stomach sank.

The fire was spreading around the kitchen worktop. Climbing up the walls and across the ceiling. A flaming frying pan sizzled in the middle of the black smoke.

A groan emerged at the side of Riley. He turned around and saw a creature at the main door, stumbling in the direction of the smoke and the burning.

"They're coming back!" Claudia shouted. "Riley, Trevor — they're coming back to the front!"

Riley closed the kitchen door.

"We've got to leave," Trevor said, shaking his head. "Sorry, but we've got to leave."

Chapter Twenty-Seven

RILEY AND TREVOR RAN BACK UP the stairs. The smoke was beginning to work its way out from underneath the kitchen door now. The groans of the creatures were returning to the front of the Chinese takeaway restaurant. They had no choice. They had to go — or at least try to go.

"Claudia — get the girls and keep them close. Anna — find a weapon."

"What's going on?" Claudia asked. Chloë and Elizabeth appeared from the bathroom.

"We're going to have to leave. There's a fire in the kitchen."

Claudia's face dropped. "The... the pan. I left the pan on... Oh god. I—"

"No time for tears," Trevor interrupted. "We've gotta leave."

Riley heard a groaning by the door again. One of the creatures waded through the smoke, which filled the entire downstairs area now. They needed to get out while they still could.

"Claudia — the creatures. How many of them have moved?"

Claudia shook her head and looked back out of the window. "I—Ten. Twenty. We can deal with them. Most are staying put. But... but not if we don't hurry."

"Right," Riley said. "We leave. Now."

Anna stepped up to Riley. She had a pipe in her hand, presumably yanked from the bathroom somewhere. "I thought we were defending this place?"

"The rules have changed. Soon, there'll be nothing left to defend. We have to go."

Anna nodded. Gripped hold of the metal pipe. "Got it."

"Good. Ted? Foot okay?"

Ted spun the fire safety axe around in his hands. His jaw was visibly shaking. "Yeah. I... It better be."

Riley nodded. The smoke and the lone creature were making their way up the steps. "Right. Then we go. I'll take this first creature and lead the way. Claudia and the girls go in the middle. We need those kids to be the hardest ones to get to."

"No," Trevor said. He placed a hand on Riley's chest. "I'll deal with this one. Save the ammo for when you need it. Okay?"

Riley half-smiled at Trevor and nodded. "Okay. Cover your mouths. Let's... let's get out of here."

Trevor zipped his hoodie over his mouth and rushed past Riley. He knocked the creature down with his spanner, splitting its fragile skull. Then, he turned around to the rest of the group and waved them down, clouded by the murky smoke.

Riley covered his mouth and raised his gun as he jogged down the stairs. The smoke was rising to the upper floors. In a matter of minutes, the place would be too toxic to survive in. They could attempt to extinguish the fire if they had the luxury of time, but unfortunately they didn't have that luxury in this world.

"Keep your—" Riley coughed as he stepped into the reception area. "Keep your wits about you. Run for the door and cross the road and—" He coughed again. "And do not turn back."

Ted appeared beside him. He patted Riley on the shoulder, coughing and spluttering. His eyes were dripping with tears from the smoke.

They ran into the reception area and moved around the counter. Four creatures were visible ahead of them, but it was hard to say given how thick the smoke was. They snapped their cracked teeth as they moved through the darkness of the smoke. Riley raised his gun at a chubby one that waddled in his direction.

But before he had the chance to fire, a thick pole smacked into its head and sent it falling to the floor. Anna nodded at Riley, covering her mouth with the top of her jumper.

Riley nodded back in approval. Conserving their bullets was a wise move.

The group jogged through the smoke and towards the door. A small creature — possibly teenage — threw itself at Ted, but he reacted fast, swinging the axe at its head and sending its jaw out of the opposite side of its face. Riley turned around. Chloë was trying to drag herself free of her mother, who wrapped her arm around a crying Elizabeth. Trevor was beside them, acting as their personal bodyguard. After they'd cleared the area, he rushed ahead to the door, knocking down another two creatures with his spanner in the process.

"Everybody make their way to the other side of the cars," Trevor said. "Just stay low. Keep going and going. Come on — Anna, Ted, you go first. Then Claudia and the girls. Riley and me, we've got this."

Anna and Ted looked at one another cautiously, then back at the group. "If we don't see you on the—"

"You will. Go," Riley said.

Anna nodded, pushed past Trevor and disappeared out of

the door. Ted followed closely behind. He took one final glance into Riley's eyes before he left the blanket of smoke, vanishing into whatever lay ahead.

"Mummy — fire! Fire!"

Riley swung around.

An orange glow covered the door.

"Shit. It's spreading. You've got to go. Get out of here."

Tears ran down Claudia's cheeks as she held Elizabeth in her arms. "But we... we might not make it. We might— Chloë!"

Chloë broke free of her mother's grip and rushed out of the smoke. The sound of struggling outside. Heavy things falling to the ground.

"Claudia, you've got to go," Riley said. Trevor was still perched by the door. He was growing less and less visible as the smoke spread.

Claudia coughed, kissed her daughter's head and grabbed her hand. "We've got to be strong now. Okay? Strong, like your sister. You can do that, right?"

Elizabeth sniffed and shook her head. "I... I can't, Mummy. I can't."

Trevor smacked another creature back as it stumbled in through the front door. They didn't even know if the rest of the group had made it out there.

But they had to go. Soon.

"Claudia, Elizabeth — we don't..." Riley spluttered. "We don't have much time. That fire is spreading. You have to take a chance. You have to go."

Claudia wiped a tear from her daughter's face and smiled at her. She whispered something in her ear then lifted her onto her shoulder and stepped up to the door.

"Take this." Trevor held the spanner out to Claudia. "You'll need it."

Claudia took it from Trevor. "Thank you. Thanks. We... Come on, darling. Come on." She took a few deep breaths then ran outside into the darkness.

Flames flickered and worked their way up the side of the doorway. The foundations of the building creaked, preparing to crumble.

Trevor pulled out his pack of cigarettes and threw one at Riley. "Just in case. I'm a man of promises. We moving?"

Riley slipped the cigarette into his pocket and lifted the gun with his unsteady hand. He aimed it out of the door. "Let's go. Run for the opposite side of the street. Work it out from there. Okay?"

Trevor stuck a cigarette between his lips and nodded. "Go."

Riley held his breath and rushed out of the door. The first thing he noticed when he stepped outside was just how much heat the fire had provided when he had been inside. The cold gripped hold of him, sharp in his lungs.

He saw the others up ahead. Claudia and the girls, crouched in the grass. Ted and Anna, a large gap between them. There were no creatures in the way. He turned to his left. The bulk of the creatures were congregated around the side alleyway still. The group could run up the road and the creatures wouldn't notice. They could get out of here.

Riley smiled at Ted as he got closer. Ted probably wouldn't see for Riley had his back to the glowing flames at the restaurant, and the moonlight wasn't strong enough. But he smiled because they'd got out of there. They'd made it. Finally, they had something worth smiling about.

And then Riley noticed something else.

A screeching alarm sounded to his left.

It was the white minivan that he'd grabbed the ladder from. The vehicle was shaking from side to side as its captive creature tried to struggle out through the window. The group started to whisper. Shook their heads and bickered with one another.

Riley turned around slowly. Trevor was just starting to make his way from the front of the restaurant, but he had frozen on the spot. He stared at the minivan. Riley's heart raced. They could still get out of here. The creatures — they

didn't necessarily notice alarms.
>Not necessarily.
>But in this case, one staggered around the corner.
>*Please don't groan. Please don't notice.*
>A small crowd followed the leader.
>All of them had noticed.
>And they were heading in the group's direction.

Chapter Twenty-Eight

THE CREATURES STAGGERED TOWARDS THE GROUP as they crouched at the side of the road.

Commotion began to rise behind Riley. Voices of discontent. Anna bossing the rest of the group around as Claudia attempted to calm her children down. One child, at least. Presumably Elizabeth.

Trevor stood frozen just outside the front of the Chinese restaurant. The flames were starting to spread up the sides of the building, the smoke blocking the view of upper floor. With nobody to see to it, the place was going to fall. Its structural foundations didn't have long left.

"Riley, mate — we need to go," Ted shouted. "We need to go or… or they'll catch us. They'll get us."

Riley stared at Trevor as the creatures disregarded him and walked in the direction of the van alarm; in the direction of the group. Bloated flesh. Mucus and blood-laced cries emerging from their throats. There were too many of them.

Too many to deal with. It didn't matter how far they ran—they'd follow.

Riley turned around to the group. Tears ran down young Elizabeth's face as she kept tight hold of her mother. Chloë sat away from them, plucking grass from the ground and nonchalantly glancing up at the oncoming creatures. Ted and Anna bickered with one another. Naturally.

"Riley—you know we can't run from these things," Anna said. The groans were getting closer behind Riley's back as the fearful eyes of the group stared past him. "You—you know they'll just keep on coming. We need a distraction. Some sort of distraction."

"And what do you suggest?" Riley asked.

Anna's eyes diverted over Riley's shoulder again. "Trevor. He... he's over there. He could help us. He's stuck." She took a large gulp. "He can... He can help us."

Riley's stomach tightened. "No. I will *not* leave Trevor behind. No way."

"That's what I said," Ted interrupted. "But... but it's survival now, man. It's not about sentimentality. It's about survival."

"Can we just stop talking and start deciding, please?" Claudia shouted.

Riley turned around. A dozen or so creatures were closing in, blood running down their faces. Through the gap between them, Riley could see Trevor. He was crouching down in the glow of the flames and the moonlight, weaponless after giving his spanner to Claudia. He couldn't allow him to become another Jordanna. Another Pete's wife. Another Aaron. He looked down at his arms. He couldn't quite make out the dried blood that he'd gathered on his trip, but he knew it was still there. He felt it, deep inside, ingrained on his soul. He couldn't let Trevor become another distraction.

"You know it's what's right," Anna said. "Deep down, Riley. You know there's no other way about this."

Riley looked at his gun, then glanced down the road to the

left. It looked clear. There was no telling in the dark, but he couldn't hear anything from that direction, so he had to try.

"Mate, come on—"

"All of you, I want you to run down the road," Riley said, pointing to his right. "Run down the road and—and shout as loud as you can." He stepped up and started to flank to the left.

"Riley, what are you—"

"Run," Riley shouted. "Try and circle back here so it—it draws them away from this place then head back here. Go round the backs of the houses. And if it seems impossible… well, run. Head for—for the railway line. Down the road on the left. If in doubt, we meet there."

Claudia tried to grab Chloë's hand but she skipped away and stood with Ted and Anna. Both of them looked on at Riley with open-mouthed concern.

"Mate," Ted said. "If… Yeah. You know. You know."

Riley nodded. "I do. Now go."

Ted and Anna exchanged an understanding glance. Then, they started running, shouting at the top of their voices, disappearing into the darkness.

Riley crouched down and moved to the left of the creatures. They seemed to be following the footsteps and cries of the group, aside from the occasional straggler that got distracted and disoriented by the van's alarm.

He kept his gun raised and crept down the road. He could see Trevor clearly now, crouched down by the door of the flaming Chinese restaurant. He could get to Trevor. He could help him. Bring him back. He didn't have to leave him behind.

When he got around the creatures, the majority of which wandered off in the direction of the moving voices, he waved at Trevor. Trevor pulled his hood up to his face as he tried not to cough and distract the creatures.

But his eyes were red. His head was shaking. He didn't look good, not at all.

Riley stopped beside Trevor. The heat of the flames kissed

against his face. He placed his hand on Trevor's back. "Come on," he said. As he did, he felt the heat and smoke flooding into his lungs. Trevor had been exposed for way too long.

Trevor waved a hand and pushed Riley back. Tears streamed down his face. He shook his head, tried to stagger forward, but dropped to his knees.

"Trevor, you have to come with me. The shouts — that's the rest of the group bringing the creatures around in a circle. They... they're risking everything. We can't just leave you here."

Trevor moved the material of his hoodie away from his mouth. Blood and snot ran from his nose. His lips quivered. "You... You have to—" He coughed loudly.

Riley turned to the road. Some of the creatures diverted their attentions. One of them — an old man who looked relatively clean and bloodless — started to move slowly in their direction in his dressing gown and slippers. But the bulk of them that hadn't followed the group's cries were being distracted by the van alarm, caught in a confused stasis.

"Come on," Riley said. He pushed Trevor forward, but Trevor tumbled back down to his knees. He coughed and spluttered onto the road. A thick string of saliva trailed out of his mouth. He raised his shaking arm and pointed to the other side of the road. "Go. Get the others. Go."

As he prepared to protest, Riley realised that something had changed. Something in the air. The creatures were beginning to groan. The group's cries were louder and clearer. The flickering of the flames and crumbling of the Chinese restaurant's foundations more violent. The van alarm...

His stomach sank. The van alarm had stopped.

He held his breath, raised his head.

The twenty or so creatures that had been gathered around the sound of the van's alarm were all walking back in the direction of the Chinese restaurant. All of them were groaning.

"Go," Trevor said. He sat upright on his knees and nodded

his head. His bottom lip quivered.

Riley saw the other group members appear behind the crowd of creatures. Anna and Ted looked on with fear. They'd finished their cycle. They had to go.

"Go!" Trevor shouted. He picked a cigarette out of his pocket and dangled it between his lips, lighting it on a flame that had spread to the door. "Just go."

Riley shook his head and swallowed the lump in his throat as the groans got closer to him. He had to run. He had to go. "It's... it's been... it's been totally fucking bizarre knowing you, Trevor."

Trevor pulled himself to his feet and took a puff of his cigarette. He smiled. Tears streamed down his face. "You're a good man. Be tough for them, yeah?"

Riley nodded, and started to jog around the side of the creatures, who turned to follow him. He held his breath. Tears dripped to the ground.

And Trevor shouted out at the top of his voice.

The creatures diverted their attentions from Riley as he sprinted past them and back in the direction of the group. He wasn't leaving Trevor behind. This wasn't his decision. This was Trevor's decision. This time, it wasn't on his conscience.

Riley dropped to his knees as he reached the group again, who crouched down behind a low garden wall at the other side of the road.

"You... you okay?" Ted asked.

Riley stared back at the flaming building. Trevor was still at the door, but moving further and further into the flames. Every few seconds, he took a puff on his cigarette. The creatures followed him, every one of them.

"We've distracted them but they'll be back," Anna said. "There's too many of them. We... we have to go, Riley. I'm sorry, but we have to go."

The last of the smaller group of creatures stepped inside the flaming Chinese restaurant.

Trevor was out of sight, but he continued to scream.

"We've got to go, mate." Ted said. "We've got to go."

Riley lit the cigarette that Trevor had given him with his shaking hand and stared at the wreckage of the building in front of him. That's all he could do. Stare. Everything they'd built—all the trust, all the doubt. All the supplies they'd worked so hard for, gone. Jill, Stan, and now Trevor—gone.

"Riley, we have to go, mate. You have to snap out of this. I'm sorry."

He recognised the voice, but it floated in through one ear and out of the other as he inhaled the smoke of the cigarette. A buzz enveloped him. A calmness that he hadn't felt in days. Weeks, even.

"Have you got that fucker out of his trance yet?" In his head, it sounded like Stan. The sort of thing Stan would say. But Stan was gone. They were all going, one by one.

Another voice, further away. More screaming. More sobbing.

A hand rested on his shoulder. "Mate, I'm being honest with you here. There's nothing left of it. It's no use. I'm so sorry, but we're going to have to go."

A windowpane crumbled to the ground. A child cried behind him. The smoke disappeared into the night sky, from his cigarette, from the building. How had it ended up this way? After everything they'd worked for — everything they'd struggled so hard for — why did it have to come to this?

"Oh, fuck. Fuck, fuck, fuck." Another voice. Anna. "Bottom of the street. We've gotta go. We've really gotta go."

To Riley's right, at the bottom of the street, he could just about make out their shuffling in the glow of the flames. Their groans growing closer. Like ants, all of them headed in one direction — their direction.

'When you hear them coming, you know it's already too late to do anything about them.'

He dropped his cigarette to the ground and turned to the rest of the group. The ones left of them, anyway. The way they stared at him. The way their eyes scanned him, wide and desperate. A longing for him to join them. A longing for his company. How things had changed.

"Are you coming?"

Riley took a deep breath. The warmth of the burning building stung his skin as if standing too close to a bonfire. And the groans. The feet. Ten. Maybe twenty.

He had no choice, not really. It was run or stand still. And when you stood still, you were torn to pieces.

He nodded and he walked.

'When you hear them coming, you know it's already too late to do anything about them.'

Perhaps Stan was right about that. But one thing that he was wrong about was his declaration that he'd outlive the rest of the group.

They ran into the night, away from the approaching creatures and the burning glow of the building, into the darkness, into whatever else the Dead Days had in store for them.

Chapter Twenty-Nine

THE FOLLOWING MORNING...

DAY THREE

THE sound of the birds tweeting brought Riley back to his senses.

He breathed in deeply through his nostrils. A gentle breeze crept up on him. It smelled of cut grass. Cutting grass. An action once so intrinsic to society; so taken for granted, now nothing more than a ghost. Something that people would no longer attend to, not anymore. That was the old normal.

He squeezed his eyes together and realised how cold he was. His arms were wrapped around his body, his head resting against the cold, hard concrete floor. If he closed his eyes hard enough, he could be anywhere. Out camping in the woods in the middle of winter. A warm shower waiting for him when he got back home.

But that was gone now, too. The closest thing they'd had to home in the last couple of days was the Chinese restaurant, and that was gone. Burned to the ground. Dead.

Riley opened his eyes. The low sun stung through his eyelids as it peeked in through the glass door of the railway shelter. They'd spent the night there after running from the creatures. Lost them when they'd reached the train tracks, walked until their feet were sore with their weapons raised, flinching at every single sound that surrounded them. Every rustle in the leaves, every movement up ahead. As fatigue intensified, so too did the fear.

And then they found the shelter.

Riley pulled himself upwards. Claudia and her two girls were cuddled up together at the opposite side of the room. Claudia's eyelids were twitching, like Riley's did when he was pretending to sleep. It couldn't be easy for her. She didn't just have herself to worry about — she had her daughters, too. Elizabeth wasn't adapting too well to this new world. Chloë was doing better, but it still couldn't be easy. Good job he'd never met anybody worth settling down and having kids with.

He stretched and looked to his right-hand side. Anna had her back to him. She was completely still and silent. She must have sneaked back inside in the middle of the night. They'd agreed on a rota. Anna first, Ted second. Riley tried to contribute, but they told him he'd contributed enough over the last couple of days, so had earned the rest. Claudia and her girls went without saying.

Riley tried not to make too much of a sound as he stretched to his feet. Unfortunately, he'd always suffered from the rare, bizarre phenomenon that was clicky knees. Didn't matter how fit or healthy he was feeling, his knees always made a sharp clicking sound when he crouched and stood. Not so noticeable in everyday life, but always seemed a lot louder when he really didn't want them to. Lucky they hadn't caught him out so far.

He checked to see he hadn't woken anyone in the room and grabbed the metal handle of the door, lowering it and shielding the bell from making a clinking noise, and he walked outside.

The cold breeze that had found its way underneath the gap of the door was strong outside. The brown leaves on the trees danced in the wind, a bitter chill stinging the back of Riley's throat upon deeply inhaling. It wasn't quite the thick of winter yet, but living in the wild would be difficult to handle when winter did come.

No. He couldn't think like that. It could all be solved by then.

He walked around the front of the shelter cabin, which looked out over the railway. Ted was perched up to the wall. The gun dangled from his trigger finger as his head buried itself in his knees. His cheeks looked pale. It had been cold last night. Very cold. And they'd had a tiring day yesterday. A little fatigue could be forgiven.

Riley crouched beside Ted and patted his arm. At least he'd been the one to find him sleeping on watch and not Anna. "Ted?"

Ted jumped and gripped hold tightly of the gun, looking around with confusion. "Yes? Yes? Oh... Oh." He winced as he propped himself further up against the wall. "Mate. I... I didn't sleep long. I swear."

Riley raised his eyebrow as Ted stood to his feet and let out a yawn. Ted's breath frosted in the air as he exhaled. He rubbed his hands together and breathed on them. They were red and verging on chapped.

"Cold... cold out here. Can't do this every night."

Riley stared down the railway. It was endless, disappearing between trees gradually losing their orange leaves. Motionless. "We'll find something. There's still time until winter really kicks in. And they might sort things out by then."

Ted's eyes narrowed. "You really think so?"

Riley sighed. "No. But I don't know what else to suggest."

Ted brushed his fingers through his hair and stretched out. "At least… at least we're still here. I guess." He gulped. His eyes were glassy. Dark underneath — darker than Riley had seen them. Distant.

Riley held his hand out. "I'll take the gun. If you want."

Ted shook the gun in his hand then plonked it into Riley's. "Starting to get bored of holding it. I just want to go back to fake guns. Fake zombies. Call of Duty style. Right?"

Riley slipped the gun into his pocket and crouched down at the side of the railway shelter. "Right."

The pair were silent. The breeze was the only thing that cut through the nothingness. There could be creatures surrounding them, making their way down to the railway line. But the group wouldn't know. No groaning, and they wouldn't know a thing. They could've come in the night. Sunk their teeth into their flesh while they were sleeping. But they didn't. They were still here.

"I'm just… I'm just getting sick of having no end goal," Ted said. He paced from side to side.

"Is that what this is really about?" Riley asked. He tried to make the question sound as unsuspicious as he could. But the way Ted turned around and peered at him made him realise he'd probably failed.

"What are you trying to say?"

"Well, what we spoke about last night. What happened… with Anna."

Ted waved his hand at Riley. "That was a mistake. We were all tense. It won't happen again."

"No. It won't. But I just… I never thought you could do something like that. I never thought you had it in you to hit anyone. Let alone—"

"And I never thought you had it in you to try and kill yourself," Ted snapped.

Riley tried to speak but the words weren't coming out of

his mouth. His cheeks heated up, resisting the cool wind that blew against them. Ted stared at Riley. His eyes were bloodshot and watery.

"I never thought you'd drive a car into a brick wall. There — I said it. I always thought you were tougher than that. So don't talk to me about what I do or don't have in me, okay? Just... just don't."

Riley was silent for a few moments. He could hear movement inside the shelter — voices. Life. The images began to flicker through Riley's mind again. The collision. The pain he'd felt when the car had crashed against the wall. The rehabilitation, the recovery. But worse than anything, the looks he got from those closest to him. The reluctance of people who knew what he'd really done to joke around with him, or throw banter in his direction in fear that it would crack him like an ornament falling to the ground. The sense that, as much as he said he was okay, they really didn't believe he was. The old Riley was gone. The new Riley was tainted.

Ted stared down the railway and shook his head. "I'm sorry. I didn't mean... You know you're my best mate and I don't mean anything by it."

"Don't apologise," Riley said. He rose to his feet and stood beside Ted. He stared down the railway line. A section of the line was missing beside them. But the rest of the line — completely clear. No sign of creatures either side of them. A moment of respite.

"Just... just sometimes I think it's mad, that's all. Like, when I see you making these decisions. Running out on your own after Stan. Dangling out of the window on the rope ladder. A part of me wants to believe you're just trying to help. But another part of me... Yeah."

Riley's throat began to well up. Ted faced the ground, unable to look Riley in the eye. Riley planted a hand on his back. "Whatever happened then, it happened. Nothing can change that. But now?" He could still see the bloody marks on his arms, but they didn't trigger the same images of betrayal and abandonment that he'd grown so accustomed to. "Now, I'm different. You're different. We all are. We have to be."

Ted raised his head. His eyes were filled with tears and his lips were shaking. "I just don't want to be the bad person. I just... I want to be the good guy."

Riley nodded. The decisions he'd made. The decisions he'd made to survive, sometimes at the expense of others. They were clearer now. Made more sense. "We all want to be the good guy, Ted. We all want that. You... you should apologise to Anna. If we're going to make this work, you should apologise."

The door of the railway shelter cabin squeaked open. Ted looked over Riley's shoulder and rolled his eyes. "Speak of the devil..."

Riley turned around. Anna was at the door. She stretched her left arm out, followed with her right arm, before doing a little jog on the spot. "Morning, boys."

Riley nodded at Anna. He looked at Ted and gestured at Anna, widening his eyes.

Ted took a few deep breaths and straightened his back, then walked in Anna's direction. "Hey, Anna... I just wanted to—"

"Don't," Anna said. She half-smiled at Ted. "We were stressed. I can give you the benefit of the doubt for now." She stretched her right leg out in front of her. "Just don't do it again. Don't even dare."

Ted nodded. His eyes were focused on her long legs underneath her tight jeans. "I... I won't. I wouldn't. I'm not... That's not me."

"Whatever," Anna said. She finished her stretches and scratched underneath her eye. It was bruised where Ted had hit her. "Hey... Riley. Can we talk?"

Riley and Ted exchanged a glance. A look of rejection in Ted's eyes. He couldn't be cast off anymore. He couldn't let his friend be somebody who was tossed onto the sidelines.

"Ted can be a part of this too," Riley said. "He's a good guy. Smart. Might not show it sometimes, but he is."

Ted scoffed. "Might not show it?"

Anna's eyes twitched between the two of them. "Okay. Well... It's about last night. About what you said to me. About... about the flu jabs." She lowered her gaze.

Riley gulped. Anna knew something about the flu jabs and their relation to the creatures. They way Jill had died just a day after being injected with the vaccination. The creatures in the supermarket pharmacy. Anna was a doctor. She knew something about it.

"When we... when we received the latest batch of vaccinations, we were put under specific order to give them to the most vulnerable. The old. The weak. Standard procedure for flu jabs. But... but something was strange. We were told only to use this experimental batch — that's what they call all new batches — over one specific week. This week. And then we were to stop."

Riley frowned. "So you're saying the jabs definitely had something to do with this?"

Anna shrugged. "I... I can only guess. I started giving my patients the jabs three days ago and it was two days ago that the reports started flooding in. And then I gave Jill her jab two days ago, and it took her a day, so... yeah."

Ted's eyelids twitched. The three of them stood completely still at the side of the railway line. "You... You knew about this?" Ted started. "You knew and you—"

"No," Anna interrupted. "I put two and two together. But I didn't *know*. And I thought maybe it wouldn't affect everyone. I dunno."

"You should have told us. If you'd told us about Jill, we'd have been able to do something about it quicker. She could have killed somebody. Destroyed the group."

Anna lowered her head like a disciplined student in the head teacher's office.

"She didn't tell anybody because she wanted to see if Jill turned. Isn't that right, Anna?"

Anna shook her head. She brought her fingers through her

dark hair, which was shiny with grease. "I didn't want her to kill anybody. I hoped it wouldn't get to that point. But I suspected and I... I needed to see. See how it worked. Try and figure out if—if there was a way of reversing it. That's why I had her go in the room on her own. That's why I was upstairs having a 'lie-down' after the supermarket trip. Just so happens I did fall to sleep, dammit, and you went and found her first and complicated the situation."

Ted turned away and shook his head. He kicked a stone into the railway track. "When you were at the supermarket, she could have turned. She could have turned and got us all. What then?"

Anna stared at Ted. Her big, brown eyes were glassy and distant. "I... I hoped that wouldn't happen. I really did. But... but sometimes we do things we're not proud of. We're all guilty of that."

Ted shook his head and sighed. The door of the railway shelter creaked open again. Claudia and her daughters stepped out. "Everything... everything okay?" Claudia asked.

Riley and Anna's eyes met. They'd all made rash decisions. Decisions they were uncomfortable with. But Anna was being honest now. She was opening up. There was no more room for secrets. Just had to get Ted to see things that way too.

"We... We're just discussing our next move."

Riley and Anna swung around. It was Ted who spoke. He was facing Claudia, chin up and smile on his face. He stuck his tongue out at the girls. Elizabeth grinned while Chloë frowned and rolled her eyes.

"Probably a good idea," Claudia said. "That place — it's good. Good shelter. But it was cold last night. And it's only going to get colder as winter progresses."

"Plus, we're down between two ditches," Anna interrupted. She pointed up at the mounds of dry, dying grass either side of the railway line. "If any of those zombies find their way to the top and surround us from either side, they'll have the advantage of the upper ground. We'll have nowhere to run, not really."

"The question is, where *do* we go from here?" Ted asked. He looked down both sides of the railway line.

Anna sighed. She pointed in the direction they'd come from last night, once they'd found their way off the road and away from the crowd of creatures. "No use going back the way we came. It's a death trap. Gradually gets busier and more populated the further we head that way, so that's a write off. Agreed?"

Claudia nodded her head fast. "Yes. Yes. Agreed."

Anna turned to the other direction and lifted her arm. "That way takes us towards Garstang. It's less busy there, but it's still a risk. Right now, we're in pretty much the best place we could possibly be, but it's not ideal. Nowhere near."

Ted shrugged. "Then where do we go? What next?"

"A kid I met mentioned a place," Riley said. "When Stan and I were… when we were at the dairy farm. A kid we met. He didn't make it, but he mentioned somewhere they were headed to. Some disused old bunker that the family owned."

"The old MOD bunker?" Anna interrupted. "Yeah. It's down by Goosnargh. Probably a good five mile walk across the fields though."

"This kid," Claudia said. "How… how do you know we can trust him?"

Riley thought back. Aaron holding the gun in his hand, pulling the trigger. His brother falling to the floor. "He… he tried very hard to save me and Stan. Kept me alive. Stan wasn't quite as lucky. But I'm here because of him. And what other option do we have?"

Anna paced around with her hands on her hips. She nodded her head. "If the family owned it, there's a good chance it hasn't been taken yet. And it's way in the country, so that gives me a bit of hope."

"But what about keys?" Ted asked. "Surely these places have, like, keys? I'd like to think if I'm going into a bunker that I'm locked in, anyway."

"Yeah," Anna said. "Did this guy say what they used it for?"

Riley shrugged. "Stashing ammo, old equipment, something like that. Why?"

"I remember hearing about this bunker," Anna said. "MOD put it up for sale a few years back. Restaurant owner put a bid in for it but couldn't get the proper planning permission. As far as I know, nobody won the bid for the place."

Ted shook his head. "But Riley just told you — this guy's family…"

"Right," Anna said. She smiled at Ted and Riley. "Did this bloke strike you as the sort of bloke who might use somewhere that isn't technically his?"

Riley remembered Sam. The way he'd hung his 'sisters' up by the flesh of their necks on the meat hooks. "He'd pretty much claimed Stevens' Dairies as his own. So yeah."

"Then I don't think we'll be needing a key after all," Anna said.

Claudia sighed a huge breath of relief. A grin spread across her face. "We have a chance? We have a chance. You hear that, girls? We'll be able to be warm tonight."

"I don't care about being cold," Chloë said. She folded her arms and frowned. "I'm tough. Not like this softy here."

"Hey!" Elizabeth said. She smacked Chloë on the arm. Chloë squared up to her and tugged her hair.

"Girls!" Claudia stepped between them. "Chloë — apologise to your sister now."

Chloë turned away and walked up to Anna. She tried to grab Anna's hand, but Anna flinched her hand out of the way as if her reflexes had been triggered. "I'm tough like Anna. All *she* ever does is moan and cry."

Claudia narrowed her eyes and clenched her jaw. She gripped Elizabeth's hand. "Just because you… because you've dealt with one of those things doesn't automatically mean you can be horrible towards your sister. You're still my little girl. Remember that."

Chloë mumbled something under her breath. She looked up at Anna and smiled.

Anna smiled back at Chloë with uncertainty before nodding her head at Claudia. "So…" She cleared her throat. "We head to this bunker. It's a long walk and we need to be on our guard. We all know damn well after last night how those things can just appear out of nowhere. Trevor… he—he found that out too well."

Ted sighed and nodded. "Seemed a good dude. Wish I'd had a better chance to get to know him."

"And there's no guarantee we'll even be able to get into this bunker once we get there. It might be locked up. It might be taken. But I'll wager a bet that it isn't. It's in the perfect location. Better than the restaurant. But we just need to be aware that this might not go to plan." Anna looked directly at Claudia. "Okay?"

Claudia nodded her head in understanding. "Yes. Yes. I understand. We have to try."

"Good. We'll cross the road and make our way through the fields. I have a rough idea of where it is. We're going to have to cross a motorway to get there, though. That's not going to be easy, but…"

Anna's words drifted away. Her mouth continued to move, and the others carried on nodding in approval, but something else had Riley's attention. Something in the distance, at the bottom of the railway line, moving towards them. The railway line was beginning to vibrate. A high-pitched screeching sound was heading in their direction.

"Riley? You got that?"

He lifted his arm and pointed down the railway line. "Train."

Anna and Ted turned and squinted down the line. "What—"

"Train. It's… It's a train."

The curiosity on their faces disappeared the second they saw it. Heard it. Felt it.

The train was heading in their direction. Which meant that somebody could be alive inside, driving.

But the speed. The vibrations. The high-pitched screeching getting closer and closer.

A sense of dread started to build up inside Riley's body as he looked down at the missing piece of line in the train track right beside them. The train was heading right for it. It didn't look like it was slowing down.

"We need to get away from here. Quickly."

Chapter Thirty

"QUICK, UP THE DITCH!" RILEY SHOUTED.

"What about the weapons?" Anna asked.

"No time. We've got the gun. That will have to do. Go!"

Claudia made a run with Elizabeth for the grass verge that ran along the side of the railway line behind the shelter they'd stayed in last night. The train was speeding towards them. The front of the vehicle looked like it was wobbling from side to side. Wherever it had come from, it didn't look like it was stopping. And it was heading right towards a sudden break in the line. It would explode. Send debris flying at them. They had to get away.

Ted and Anna jogged up to the side of the railway line, Chloë beside them. "We make a run for the field up on the left," Anna shouted as she started to climb the verge. "We can get to the bunker if we all head in that direction."

But something else caught Riley's eye. They looked small in the distance, standing atop the sides of the railway. But gradually, more and more of them appeared as the train whistled past them. Creatures. All of them walking in the direction of the noisy train, tumbling down onto the railway, and falling in front of the train.

"Got to go!" Riley called, as he clambered up the muddy verge. He pulled the gun out of his pocket with his shaky hand. If there were creatures following the train further down the line, then there could be some nearby. The group that they thought they'd shook off last night. It must've been them. It had to be.

Claudia rushed over to the fence that led into an abandoned field when she reached the top of the verge. She helped lift Elizabeth over. Ted and Anna panted as they, too, reached the top of the grassy hill. Ted turned around and looked down at Riley as he made his way up it, his feet slipping on the sloshy mud.

"There's creatures," Riley said as he reached the top. He pointed down the line. "The sound's attracting them. If they hear the train crash, they'll—"

Riley felt himself knocked to one side. Something was holding his arm. The gun slipped out of his hand and tumbled down the verge, clinking as it bounced across the concrete below, then down onto the metal of the railway line. His stomach sank. Their only real weapon, lost again.

But he couldn't dwell on it for too long because one of the creatures was on top of him.

"Riley!"

The creature pressed him down into the unstable mud. It dug its thick, sharp nails into his shoulders. He pushed his arms up against it, but they felt as weak as jelly. The creature was female. Hair matted with mud and blood. She snapped her ground-down teeth at Riley, her tongue hanging on by a few stray pieces of flesh and tendon.

Riley pushed back as hard as he could. His heart raced. The train was getting closer. More creatures would be getting closer. The group had to do what he'd done to Stan. To Aaron.

They had to leave him. They had to save themselves. They had to make the decision to survive.

He closed his eyes and kept on pushing the creature back as the blood from its tongue dribbled onto his face. *Keep calm. Deep breaths. All over soon...*

Suddenly, the weight above him seemed to recede. He felt a damp and cool sensation dripping against his head. Heard a loud squelching beside him.

He opened his eyes. Ted was kicking his shoe into the side of the creature. His eyes were bloodshot. He looked like he had been taken over by an external force as he rammed his foot further and further into the side of the creature. It dug its fingers right into the muddy verge, slipping down towards the railway line. The train was so close now. The line was rattling. Shaking from side to side.

"We need to get away from here!" Anna shouted.

Ted pulled Riley to his feet. He nodded at him, sincerity in his eyes. "Gotcha," he said.

Riley nodded in return, and the pair of them ran over the fence, away from the small crowd of oncoming creatures, away from the train. They hopped over the fence. Riley crouched down in the tall grass. The train was too close. Even if they ran, they wouldn't make it far enough away to escape the explosion. "There's no time. Just... just get down!"

Claudia held Elizabeth in her arms and curled up in a ball. Chloë, wide-eyed, covered her eyes. Anna placed her fingers in her ears and tensed her jaw. Ted sat with his eyes closed, waiting for the collision.

Riley peeked through the grass at the small group of four creatures staggering in their direction from the cul-de-sac road beside them. When the train whooshed towards them, they turned around and staggered down the side of the ditch, slipping onto the track like rag dolls.

The train came into view. He could see the gun on the line. A part of him wanted to run on there and grab it, but he knew it was too late. That would be suicide. Maybe suicide was the only option.

No. Not anymore. Not in this world.

"Here we go…"

In what seemed like slow-motion, the train slipped off the line. Hovered in the air. The sound receded. The vibrations stopped. Riley held his breath.

Then, the train crashed against the opposite side of the track.

The first carriage crumbled to its side, speeding down the line like a fireball. The screeching noise was louder than ever, piercing and sickening. Pieces of hot debris flew up into the sky as the second carriage followed the first in tumbling to its side. Metal rained down around them, into the distance, small man-made meteorites. Riley covered his head with his hands. A pointless but surprisingly faith-inducing activity. He heard thuds beside him. Debris falling to the ground. He peeked to his left hand side as the deafening sound of the crunching train intensified. There were no creatures beside them. They'd presumably fallen to their death. The train had proven an adequate distraction after all.

Riley looked around at the rest of the group. Ted squatted down with his hands pressed up to his eyes. Anna cringed as the screeching metal continued.

But something wasn't right.

Riley stared at Claudia. She didn't have her hands over her head. Tears were running down her face. Blood covered her shirt. She was shouting something inaudible as the sound of the train drowned out every single word. Chloë stood by her side, pale-faced. Her cheeks were quivering.

Riley stood up and walked over towards Claudia. A large chunk of hot metal debris was on the floor between them. It had made a dint in the ground. A film of red lined it.

Riley's stomach sank when he pieced the clues together. Saw the reason for the tears. The reason for the drowned-out shouting and the shock on Chloë's face.

Claudia was holding Elizabeth in her arms. Elizabeth's

eyes were closed and her body was completely still.

Blood trickled down her forehead.

It wasn't long before the screeching of the train stopped and Riley could hear again.

His ears were ringing. His head was light and faint. But he could hear the moaning now. The crying. Claudia gripped hold of her daughter's limp body and sobbed into her chest.

"Please, Elizabeth. Please. Please be okay. Please be okay."

The rest of the group stared at Claudia now, they too distracted by her cries. Anna covered her mouth with her hands in shock. Ted's eyes watered. Chloë stood staring at her mother cradling her sister, her face pale. The blueness of her eyes seemed to have faded away. Knocked out of her by the shock.

Riley took a step towards Claudia as she gripped hold of her daughter. "She… Her heart. Her breathing. Anna?"

Anna still had her hands covering her face. She turned to Riley then to Claudia, moving her hands away and wiping her eyes. "I… Yeah," she said, stepping forward then backwards again with hesitation. She took a deep breath and crouched beside Claudia, who continued to hold her daughter to her chest, blood from her head seeping across her shirt and onto the ground.

"Claudia, I… Let me take a—a look at her." Anna reached for Elizabeth's chest.

Claudia yanked her daughter out of Anna's grip. She looked up, fear in her twitchy eyes. "I… My girl. My little girl. Please. Please."

Anna tried to smile and nodded at Claudia. She squeezed Claudia's shoulder. "Just let me take a look at her. Okay? And… and we can decide what to do then. But I need to look at her."

Claudia mumbled a few words under her breath and loosened her grip on her daughter. Ted walked over to Chloë, who was completely stationary. He reached to place a hand on her shoulder then lifted it back and scratched his head. Riley just waited. Stood and waited as the train grumbled on behind them. Waited for the inevitable.

Anna diverted her gaze from Elizabeth as she placed her on the grass. Her hands hovered around above Elizabeth, unsure of where to touch. She inhaled a shaky breath and lifted her wrist. Stared at Riley as she checked for a pulse.

Riley could tell from the way Anna stared at him, her eyes growing gradually more bloodshot, that the news wasn't good.

Anna lowered Elizabeth's wrist as Claudia sobbed beside her.

"She... Please. My angel. She's—she's okay. She's okay, isn't she? We can make her better. Can't we?"

Anna gulped. She checked Elizabeth's neck for a pulse, but it was clearly in vain. Riley didn't want to look too closely at Elizabeth's head. He didn't have to. He could see the blood pooling out onto the grass. Spread across Claudia's arms and shirt. Another loss. They couldn't take another loss.

Anna held her hand against Elizabeth's neck. Kept it there for a few moments. Then, she sighed and pulled it away. She lifted her head and looked into Chloë's eyes. "I'm... I'm sorry. I'm so—"

"No!" Claudia cried. It was a sickening, deafening moan from the pit of her stomach, filled with hurt and grief. Anna was crying now too. She grabbed hold of Claudia and held her. Claudia tried to struggle initially, desperate to be reunited with her little girl. But Anna held her. Whispered in her ear. And eventually, Claudia gripped back and cried onto Anna's shoulder.

Riley stepped up to Ted. The pair of them stared down at Claudia and Anna as they held one another. Chloë stood over her dead sister's body. She was frozen, like a victim of Medusa, focused on the body. She wasn't crying. She wasn't flinching. She just stood and stared.

"Chloë... are you... I'm sorry." Riley placed a hand on Chloë's shoulder.

Chloë knocked it away. Spun around to face Riley and Ted. Her eyes were still wide and focused, as if she was in a trance.

Ted cleared his throat. "I... We're sorry. I just... We just want you to know we're here, like. Here for you."

Chloë switched her gaze from Riley to Ted and back again. She stared right at them, the muscles underneath her eyes twitching as if she were trying to read a foreign language.

"Ted... Ted's right," Riley said. Claudia sobbed and blubbered some inaudible words in the background. "Anything you need. Anything you need and we—"

"She was weak," Chloë interrupted.

Riley's skin crawled. The hairs on his arms and his chest stood up. A lump took hold of his throat. "What... What do you...?"

"She was weak," Chloë repeated. Life was returning to her eyes now. She bobbed her head, justifying what she was saying to herself. "She—she was never going to make it. This was quick for her. It... She's gone and it's quick for her and... and it's better for everybody."

Riley and Ted exchanged a wary glance. He wasn't sure what to say in these situations. Elizabeth had struggled to adjust to the harsh nature of the new world, but that didn't justify Chloë's stance. It wasn't a normal reaction to a death of a sibling.

"You shouldn't... you shouldn't say those things," Riley said. "You don't have to pretend to be tough. It's... it's hard for all of us. Hard for your mother. You can cry if you want to."

"I don't want to cry." Chloë stared Riley directly in the eyes. "Crying... crying got Elizabeth killed. It..."

"You what?" Claudia said. She had a frown etched across her forehead. Old mascara dribbled down her cheeks. "You... What did you say?"

"Claudia," Anna said. "Don't—"

"No." Claudia pushed Anna to one side. "You let me talk to my daughter. Okay?"

Anna bit her lip and shrugged. She stepped to one side.

Claudia walked around Elizabeth's body and stared down at Chloë. "Well... Do you... Do you want to repeat what you just said?"

Chloë stared at her mother's feet. She looked like she had slipped back into a trance again.

"Claudia," Ted said. He approached Claudia with his arm raised. "She's upset. We... we all react in different ways when we're upset."

Claudia shoved Ted away and grabbed her daughter's wrist. Chloë struggled and pulled herself free as her sister's blood pressed from Claudia's hand onto her skin.

"Your... your sister has... She's gone. She's gone. And what did you have to say about it? Go on. If you can tell them, you can tell me."

Chloë held her wrist and looked up at her mother. Their stare connected. Searched one another's face for a reaction of some sort. "I... Elizabeth was weak. She—she didn't understand them. The zombies. She didn't understand them and... and she wasn't ready for this world."

Claudia paused. Blinked rapidly as she processed her daughter's words. Then, she huffed. Turned around and looked at Riley and Ted with a faux smile on her face. "Well that's okay then, huh? She was slowing us down. She was weak. So she... What happened to her was a good thing?"

"I didn't say that," Chloë said. "I'm just trying to say—"

Claudia cracked a hand across Chloë's face and pushed her to the ground. She tugged at her hair and shouted into her ear. Her eyes were manic. Saliva dribbled from her mouth. "You little bitch! You little, fucking bitch! Don't ever speak about your sister like that. Don't ever speak about her in that way again."

Anna rushed over to Claudia and tried to pull her back, but Claudia had tight hold of Chloë's hair. Chloë wasn't fighting back. She wasn't making a sound and she wasn't kicking up a fuss. She was just taking it, tearless, wordless. It sent a cold shiver down Riley's spine.

"I have a right mind to leave you here," Claudia shouted. "Leave you here to fend for yourself. See how you cope then because you're oh-so-strong."

"Stop this, Claudia." Riley joined Anna in trying to pull Claudia away from Chloë. Elizabeth's body lay completely still behind them. "This is about Elizabeth. Think about your two little girls and what you really want for them. Think about Elizabeth and what's best for her."

Claudia's hand began to shake where it held Chloë's hair. She wasn't speaking anymore.

"Think about Elizabeth. Come on. Let's decide what we're going to do with her."

Claudia loosened her grip on her daughter's hair. A tear dropped from her face onto Chloë's chest. "I..." She started to speak, then pushed Chloë away and jumped up to her feet. She looked like the grieving mother again, not the manic psychopath, as she approached Elizabeth's body.

"We need to decide what to do," Ted said. "With... with her bo—"

"Okay," Anna snapped, glaring at Ted. "Just... just give Claudia a moment. Please."

Riley ran his fingers through his hair and reached a hand out for Chloë, who lay in the mud. She examined it, then grabbed it, pulling herself to her feet and brushing her dress down.

"It'll be okay," Riley said.

Chloë let go of Riley's hand and picked up where she'd left off before the confrontation with her mother, staring at her sister's body as Claudia crouched over it.

Riley took a deep breath in. The air was thick with smoke, which tickled the back of his throat. Pieces of debris were scattered around the grassy area. Small chunks. Large chunks. They were lucky that only one of them had been hit, in truth.

But no. There was nothing lucky about this scenario.

He walked to the edge of the verge. The train carriages were piled up diagonally. A fire spread from the front of the train through the first carriage and down to the rest. Only one of the six carriages was still standing. Nobody to clean it up. Nobody to care.

Just as he was about to turn back to the group, he saw something move underneath the third carriage. The third carriage was nearest to them. It was on its side. The windows were smashed and the front end of the carriage looked like it had twisted with the impact into the back of the second carriage.

But something was moving by the window.

Reaching a hand out and tugging itself free of the debris.

"Guys," Riley said. "We've got compa…"

He stopped. He noticed another movement. More movement further down the carriage. Another hand, laced with glass and sharp metal, pulling itself out from the wreckage. And then a head. Relatively undamaged. Climbing out onto the wreckage and tumbling down onto the railway. It had one arm.

It looked up the side of the verge. Clambered up the railway line ridge.

And it let out a throaty groan.

Ted appeared at Riley's side. "What did you… Oh. Holy shit. Will we *ever* get a fucking break?"

"We have to move," Riley said, as more and more creatures pulled themselves from the wreckage and staggered towards them, groaning.

"Riley!"

Riley turned around. Anna was pointing into the distance across the field.

Riley's stomach sank. His chest tightened.

A horde of creatures were heading in their direction.

"We're… We're surrounded," Ted said, as the creatures closed in on them from both directions. "We're stuck."

Chapter Thirty-One

RILEY BACKED OFF FROM THE EDGE of the verge. Ted backed into him, facing the oncoming horde of creatures in the other direction. At least ten of them. Raw flesh dangling from the bones on their arms. Blood dribbling from their yellowing teeth. Men. Women. Children. Or what were men, women, and children. All directions. No escape.

"We… Oh God." Claudia whimpered. "We're stuck. This is it. This… this is it."

"Just calm down," Anna said. She backed up against Ted and Riley too. Her eyes were wide. Her heartbeat was visible through her white shirt. It was clear that she was anything but calm, as the groans got closer and closer. "The gun — Riley? Can't you—?"

Riley pointed down the side of the verge towards the railway line. "Dropped it, remember? Fucking dropped it."

Ted shook his head. His body was shaking and twitching. His eyes were focused on Elizabeth's body, alone on the floor in the grass. There was something in his eyes. An idea of some sort. Something he didn't seem completely comfortable with as the ghastly singing of the creatures approached. "We… We've got to try something. We have to—"

"And what do you suggest?" Anna said. She looked either side and scanned the area. No way of escaping via the way they'd come, as more and more creatures spilled out of the windows of the wrecked train. Chloë stood alone, rubbing her hands up her arms. She still wasn't crying. Wasn't shaking. No emotion in her glassy, distant eyes.

Ted tilted his head at Elizabeth's body. He looked at Claudia then the rest of the group. "Her… Elizabeth's body. It —"

"No," Claudia snapped. She turned and faced Ted directly, drowning out the oncoming creatures. "No."

"Ted might have a point," Riley interrupted. He thought of the times he'd made the tough decisions. The things he'd had to do. The humanity he'd had to sacrifice. *'Alive. That's what it makes you. Alive.'* "If we want to live… we have to make the tough calls."

Claudia shook her head. Her head shakes were becoming slower and less convincing with every turn. Her chin started to wobble. The creatures in front of them were only ten metres or so from them now. "We… It might not work. It might not…"

"But we have to try," Anna said. "I'm sorry, Claudia. I'm—"

An explosion rattled through their conversation. At first, Riley thought it was from the train, but it couldn't be because the noise was up ahead, in the group of creatures that were crossing the field.

And then he saw a flicker of light. The loud cracking continued to split through the groans. The creatures fell to their knees, blood and flesh splattering from their bodies.

"Is that…" Anna started.

"Yes," Riley said. He focused up ahead. Took a few steps forward. "I… I think it is."

Beneath the loud mini-explosions and the chorus of

creature voices, which were diminishing, the rumbling noise of an engine approached. The creatures in front of them started to scatter. Some of them turned around but were soon after sent flying to the ground as bullets cracked into their heads.

The group looked on with wide-eyes and open mouths as the vehicle came into view. It was a green armoured vehicle with a large grill on its front. Camouflage green was painted across its sides. On top of it, there was a machine gun attached, a silhouetted figure with a helmet firing rounds at the rapidly decreasing creatures. In the passenger seat of the vehicle there was another figure holding a handheld automatic rifle and firing out of his side window. The driver was similarly unidentifiable, enveloped by the low winter sun over their shoulders.

The vehicle came to a stop in the middle of the remaining few creatures.

"Shall I do the thing?" the man on the top shouted.

"Do it," one of the men in the seats said.

The person manning the machine gun edged forward and pointed the gun at two creatures that were totally focused on the camouflaged vehicle now. The creatures stumbled over detached limbs and sloshed through the blood of their compatriots, surrounding the vehicle.

"Might want to get down," the guy manning the gun shouted, tilting his head in the direction of the group. "I'm a good aim but you wouldn't want to get in the way of this." One of the creatures grabbed the end of his gun and scraped their teeth against the tough metal.

Riley looked over his shoulder. A number of creatures had reached the top of the verge. They couldn't crouch down. The creatures would get to them.

"Quick!" the man behind the gun shouted as creatures overwhelmed his gun.

Riley and Anna exchanged a nervous glance. Then, Riley sighed and nodded. "Everyone — down!"

Riley and the others crouched down and lay on their

stomachs. The groans behind them were getting closer. Soon, they'd be snapping at their heels. Ripping their Achilles from the back of their legs.

But then, he heard the firing of the gun again. The sound was spraying in all directions. Chunks of grass and dismembered limbs flew up in the air and rained down on them.

"Is he doing what I think he's doing?" Ted shouted. His hands were over his eyes.

Riley peeked through the grass. The man atop the vehicle was spinning the machine gun in a circle. Bullets were spraying in all directions. The creatures that had surrounded the men were on their knees now, heads severed from their necks. The stench of dead, dead bodies engulfed the area.

The man on top of the gun raised it even higher as he continued to spin around. "Might wanna keep down now."

Riley lowered his neck. He heard shots fly over the back of his head and plummet into the creatures behind them.

"Too many that way — you got them, Ivan?"

The side door of the vehicle opened and the man with the machine gun hopped out. He was dressed in full army gear, a helmet and glasses covering his eyes and head. He crouched as he approached the group.

"Thank you," Claudia said. "Thank yo—"

"Get to the vehicle if you want to live," Ivan barked. "And I mean live, not *re*live."

Ivan disappeared behind them and fired the machine gun at the line of creatures. He held his ground and sent a wave of bullets flying into their heads, knocking them all down the verge as they clambered up it.

Riley rose to his feet. "Come on. This is our way out. Come on."

Anna stepped to her feet slowly and chewed her lip. "I... We can run, Riley. The abandoned MOD bunker. We can go there now. Our path is clear."

"We're safer with them," Ted said. His eyes were wide and

his face awash with awe. "I mean... did you see what they just did? They're here for us. The army. To help us."

Claudia pushed past Chloë and reached down for Elizabeth. She held her daughter in her arms and started staggering over the mounds of mangled corpses, towards the army vehicle.

"We'll do better on our own," Anna said. She shook her head. "We—we don't know these people."

Riley took a deep breath. Examined his surroundings. The cloudy sky. The deathly grey grass speckled with splashes of blood. "It's time we started trusting," he said. "These people helped us. It's time we gave a little back."

He exhaled and ran towards the armoured vehicle.

The engine started up. The large circular headlights flickered to life. "Get on board," the man atop the vehicle shouted. His face was also covered by large tinted glasses.

Riley turned around. Ted was close behind him, wincing as he stepped on his injured foot. He climbed up the side of the open-top vehicle and joined Claudia, who stroked Elizabeth's hair as her limp body rested on her knee.

Anna and Chloë soon followed. Anna had a look of uncertainty on her face. A look of reluctance. Chloë kicked the innards as she clambered through them. She focused on them. Squinted and watched the body parts split and spew blood with fascination in her wide eyes. They reached the side of the vehicle and climbed up onto it.

"This is right," Riley said as Anna pulled herself onto the vehicle. "It's right for—"

"Okay," Anna said. She didn't make eye contact with Riley as she pulled Chloë up. "Okay."

Ivan stopped firing the machine gun and kicked a creature down the side of the verge. He spat at it as it descended, wiping stray saliva from his chin. Then, he turned around and gave a thumbs up as he ran back to the armoured vehicle.

"Hold on tight," the man on the gun said. He removed his helmet. A shiny, sweaty bald head hid underneath. "Pedro's the name. Make yourself comfortable."

Ivan climbed onto the vehicle and pulled off his helmet. He rubbed his fingers through his slick, dark hair, huffing and puffing.

"All this running still knackering you?" Pedro said. He had a grin on his face.

Ivan raised a finger and removed his glasses. He took a close look at the group. Narrowed his eyes and nodded at Riley. Scanned Anna's body from head to toe. "Ready to go," Ivan shouted. "As for you guys — consider this your lucky day."

The engine rumbled into full force and the tyres of the vehicle crunched against the detached bones of the creatures. The group drove off the field and onto the road, away into the distance.

Ivan pulled a blanket from the front of the vehicle and handed it to Claudia. He offered a gentle smile of reassurance and nodded his head at Elizabeth's body. "For... for your little girl."

Claudia snapped out of her trance as she continued to stroke Elizabeth's hair. She took the blanket from Ivan and wrapped it around her daughter as the vehicle drove on. They had been driving for the best part of ten minutes and they'd still yet to be met with a distraction. They'd also barely spoken.

"So," Ivan said. He removed his glasses and slipped them onto the collar of his army uniform. "You people been out here long?"

Anna and Riley shot a glance at one another. Riley could tell from the way Anna arched her body away from the others that she hadn't warmed to the idea of joining the new group. Maybe she was right. But they'd helped them out. There was no denying that if they hadn't shown up when they did, they'd have been torn to pieces. All of them.

"A day. Or so." Ted peered up at the gun on top of the vehicle. "Say, how often do you use this thing? I never knew they had like, proper armed vehicles in Preston."

Pedro, who remained in the elevated seat, patted the side of the gun and grinned. "Didn't get much chance to try this thing out before things went to shit. Think the end days are a good enough reason though, huh?"

A glimmer of a smile crept across Ted's face. It was everything he'd ever dreamed of seeing. Real-life Call of Duty. Shame about the timing and the circumstances.

"So you've been out here for a day or so." Ivan polished the end of his machine gun with a small, dirty cloth. He had thick black bags underneath his eyes. A badly styled moustache on his top lip. "How were you surviving out here?"

"We had somewhere," Riley cut in. "Somewhere safe. And…"

"It turned out not so safe, huh?" Ivan lowered the gun and wiped his hands on the cloth. "Seen that way too many times these last couple of days."

"So what are you? Army?"

Ivan and Pedro looked at one another and then Ivan nodded. "Yeah. Squadron down at Fulwood Barracks. Funny, really. I chose not to go on tour to Afghan. Conscientious objector, or whatever the hell they call us. Wanted to stick around for my family. Turns out the bigger war is on the home front."

Riley nodded. "Sounds familiar."

"Where have you guys been?" Ted turned from Pedro to Ivan and back again. "Like, we've been out and about for days and—and there's barely been any military presence. Maybe a helicopter, or something. But nothing else. Shouldn't you be the ones fighting these creatures?"

Ivan snickered. "Hear that, Pedro? 'Where's the army fighting these things?'"

Pedro fiddled with the rear of the mounted gun and shook his head. "You'd think we were warmongers or something."

Ivan leaned in to Ted and Riley. "Truth is, the armed forces — we're just ordinary people too. Now the public, the civvies, they don't want to believe that. But it's true. Y'know, I was at the barracks when the news came out. News that these—these walking corpses were taking over. There were another sixty of us. Maybe seventy. And y'know what the first thing the bulk of those people did when they were sent on immediate call to get into the city and deal with this threat?"

Riley nodded. "I can probably guess."

"Yeah. They went home. Went home to their families. Same with the police. Truth is, nobody's got any power when there's no power system in place. When something so... so unfamiliar attacks, nobody wants to fight it because nobody wants to risk making it worse. Making it angrier. So they go home and they go to their families and they die anyway."

Ted shook his head. "And you're the ones who didn't go home?"

Ivan smiled again. He tumbled to his side slightly as the vehicle swerved around an abandoned car on the main road. "Would've loved to have a family to go back to. But we were too late. Creatures were already at the barracks before we had a real chance to leave. Me, Pedro, Stocky—" He pointed at the driver, who had yet to introduce himself, with his thumb. "— We were trapped in that barracks with a few others and we had no idea what to do. Used to taking orders, y'know? But all of a sudden, we're the highest rank."

Riley's throat tensed. Everything he'd feared — everything he'd ever believed in — was all crumbling to pieces. "The... the army. It's gone? Completely?"

Ivan nodded. "The only organised army right now are these beasts. And they're winning."

Riley stared out over the side of the vehicle. As they got further into the suburbs, they drove past houses, front windows smashed and laced with blood. Dead bodies feasting on dead bodies. Television static crackling in the uninhabited houses. Life put on hold for now and forever.

"How did you find us?" Anna hadn't spoken up to now, but her tone was stern. She leered at Ivan. In the few days of knowing Anna, Riley knew one thing about her — she'd get an answer if she wanted it.

"Well," Ivan said. He stretched out his arms and looked up at Pedro again. Pedro cleared his throat and perched on the gun seat, swinging around and aiming ahead. "We were out and about and we heard the train accident. Figured we'd see if there were any survivors."

"And were there any?"

Ivan opened his mouth then closed it again. He pushed his greasy jet black hair back and shrugged. "We found you. We made you our priority."

Anna glared at Ivan with a cold, hard face. Then, she nodded her head and broke the stare. "Okay." Her inquisition looked like it was over. For now.

"Is… My daughter." Claudia's voice caught Ivan's attention. Elizabeth was covered up now. "These barracks. Is there anywhere I can… I can bury her?"

Ivan sighed. "Of course there is. We can even… We can cremate her, if you'd like that? And then at least you can have her ashes. Right?"

Claudia shook her head. "No. We should bury her. We should—"

"Elizabeth always said she wanted to be burned." Chloë broke her own self-imposed silence as she sat alone at the very back of the vehicle. "Just saying."

Claudia stroked Elizabeth underneath the blanket. She inhaled a shaky breath. "Then we'll cremate her." Her voice sounded stronger. More affirmative. A sign of strength in the hardest and cruelest of times. She glanced at Chloë and smiled. Chloë smiled back at her. The first positive contact they'd had in quite some time.

"Aw, shucks," Pedro said. He stumbled to his feet and twisted the gun back to the front. "Got some company. Hold on tight."

Ivan gripped the back of the vehicle and examined the rest of the group. "We're going to get you somewhere safe, dear.

Somewhere with food. Water. A nice cosy shower and bed. I promise you that." He smiled at Chloë. "But for now, you might want to cover your ears."

"Why?" Ted asked.

The gun on top of the vehicle rumbled to life. It fired deafening shots up ahead, where a group of creatures rose from a corpse they were fighting over in the middle of a mini-roundabout.

Ted stuck his fingers into his ears and stuffed his head between his knees.

Ivan chuckled. "That's why."

Chapter Thirty-Two

THEY DIDN'T HAVE TO DEAL WITH many more distractions before reaching the barracks.

The vehicle slowed down as it crept up the pathway. The outside of the barracks were grey-bricked and tall. A Great Britain flag flew at full-mast above the gates, which were closed. Two patches of grass lined the pathway into the barracks. On the right-hand side, a stack of charred bodies were piled up on top of one another. At the opposite side of the road, a banner was spread across the roof of a row of terraced houses. *'Save Us Please'* was scribed across it in a conspicuous shade of thick red paint.

"Got to deal with the walking corpses somehow," Pedro said, pointing at the stack of burned bodies. "All of 'um are those things. The ones we dealt with outside the gates. Figure we'll start doing daily runs eventually and get 'um out of our face soon enough."

Riley stared at the gates as the vehicle got closer. It looked like there were two sets of gates — a larger, more traditional set surrounding the exterior of the main building, then a smaller set just inside. Two men were standing by the second set of gates, starting to open them as the vehicle approached.

"Now we've got some good people here," Ivan said. He smiled at Chloë. "Some good people who will look out for you. Keep you safe."

"We'll earn our place," Riley said. "We—we owe you that much. For helping us out back there."

"That's good of you. But we take things step by step." He pointed at Elizabeth's body. Blood was starting to seep out of her head and onto the blanket that Claudia had covered her with. "We put the girl to rest first. And then you get some rest. You look like you could do with some."

Ted yawned as the vehicle stopped at the first set of gates. "You've no idea."

Pedro hopped down from the vehicle and walked towards the gates. He laughed and shook hands with the armed guard who opened the first set, then pointed at the group in the back of the vehicle. The armed guard looked over Pedro's shoulder and smiled at the group, and the vehicle came back to life.

"Of course, I have to ask you before we proceed. I have to ask you whether you're willing to be a guest here. And by that, we mean you stay here. At least, until things get a little less hectic outside these walls."

"That sounds more like we're opting to be kept prisoner," Anna said.

Ivan puffed out his lips. "Tough nut to crack, dear, aren't you? But that's a good thing. It's good to be suspicious in this world. But no — the reason you have to comply to this little house rule is simply because we don't want anybody else putting themselves in jeopardy. And that includes us. If one of you decides to go on a little run outside, who knows what you might bring to our doorstep? Make sense?"

Ted shrugged. "Sounds reasonable enough."

Anna and Riley watched one another. Waited to make the

call.

"You don't *have* to come with us. But we're just trying to help. If you think you'd be better on your own, you can—"

"No," Riley said. A weight lifted from his shoulders. "No. We're happy with this. You... We're grateful for what you did. Getting us out of that situation. And I don't think we'll find anywhere else as safe as this outside."

Ivan nodded in agreement as the vehicle moved through the first set of gates. "You're probably right. Well, say goodbye to the outside for now."

Riley turned around. Watched as the outside grew more distant and less visible through the small tunnel leading into the barracks. The dead creatures on the grass. The plea for help on the houses. The outside world — the dangerous outside world — behind them.

The gates slammed shut. Anna flinched.

"And welcome to your new home," Ivan said.

After the vehicle pulled in to the parking area, the group climbed out. They shook hands with the two guards that had let them in, faceless and void of identity as they wore the same glasses that Ivan and Pedro had worn upon their arrival. Another couple sprinted over — a shorter, chubbier man called Chef, and an older gentleman with a twirly moustache. They exchanged pleasantries and were escorted through the courtyard and into the building on the left.

Ivan took Elizabeth's body from Claudia before they entered. Claudia was reluctant to give her up, but eventually, she saw sense. She did what she had to do. Made the tough call, like they'd all had to do.

Riley rested a hand on her shoulder as Ivan handed Elizabeth's body to 'Stocky', who pushed her away on a trolley.

"You've been tough. Real tough."

Tears trickled down Claudia's face. She sniffed and watched her daughter disappear further and further away from her. "I... I've been awful."

"You're grieving. We all are. She... Elizabeth. She was a lovely little girl." He looked at the door. Chloë stared at her sister being wheeled away. Her bottom lip quivered. Her eyes were welling up. The first flicker of emotion she'd shown in hours. "But you have to stay tough. You have another beautiful girl to look after who's hurting and who's very confused about... about this new world. And she needs her mother there for her. She's seen things no kid should have to see. You need to keep her grounded. She's a tough kid. But she's still a kid."

Claudia huffed out a nervous breath. "A passer-by would think you're a father or something."

A nervous tingling sensation ran through Riley's chest. Heat began to cover his face. "No. No, I'm not."

"You'd make a good one."

She hadn't noticed. Thank God she hadn't noticed. "Yeah. Well, it wasn't for me. And I guess I don't have much choice now."

Claudia smiled at Riley. "I don't know. You and Anna seem to have a good bit of chemistry going on."

The heat that had cooled down from his cheeks fast returned. And this time, Claudia did notice.

"Never underestimate the power of a blush to reveal a thousand emotions." Claudia moved away from Riley and stepped over to Chloë. "You okay, darling?"

Chloë had her head down, focused on the ground. She nodded, but her chin was shaking and her bottom lip kept on revealing itself.

"Come here, angel. Come here." Claudia wrapped her arms around her daughter.

Tears streamed down Chloë's face. "I shouldn't... I shouldn't cry. We should be tough. We should be strong."

"I know, my sweet. I know."

Chloë continued to cry into her mother's arms as the pair of them watched Elizabeth disappear inside the opposite building of the barracks.

Ivan led the group up the stairs and towards the room at the end of a long corridor. The wooden walls were lined with medals and images of war heroes past and present.

"Always fancied myself on these walls one day," Ivan said. "Might get a shot if those walking corpses find a way inside here. As in, I'll actually be spread across the walls." He stopped and hesitated, noticing Chloë. "Sorry, I didn't—"

"It's okay," Chloë said. She walked hand in hand with her mother. "I killed one. I know how it is."

Ivan raised his forehead and carried on walking. He looked taken aback by Chloë's words. "Anyway, your bed's are up here on the left. Bunk beds, I'm afraid, but plenty of them. And we'll give you a living quarter to yourselves. We respect your privacy."

Riley stopped and looked in the room. Stacks of bunk beds with perfectly made bed sheets. None of them recently occupied. "Where is everyone?"

"Like I said. Not everybody chose to stay. But I guess that means more for you. Right?" He held his arm out towards the room.

Claudia and her daughter entered first. "Thank you. I'd just about stopped believing in miracles after… Yeah. But at least we have some hope."

Ivan shook his head. "It's the least we can do. Really."

Ted, Anna and Riley followed. Anna was still quiet, but she managed to offer a half-smile at Ivan as she walked into the bedroom. Ted winced as he pulled his training shoe from his foot. A small patch of blood poked from his bandage.

"Need any help with that foot?"

Ted grimaced as he untied the bandage. "It's… it's just…"

"We can have our medic take a look at it later. For now, you people should get some rest. There's a shower room two doors down the corridor. And we'll be serving up a nice hot lunch in an hour or so. Sandwiches. Chicken. Anyone hungry?"

Ted's tender foot dropped and he didn't even flinch. "Yes.

Yes, we are."

Ivan smiled and turned away. "Well, make yourselves comfortable. I'll be downstairs if you need me. Oh, and um. Your daughter's ashes. They... We should be able to get them to you in about an hour. That okay?"

Claudia gripped Chloë's hand, took a deep breath and smiled. "Yes. That would be lovely of you."

"Right," Ivan said. He raised his hand and waved as he walked away. "I'll leave you guys to whatever it is you do. See you soon."

Ivan's footsteps echoed down the corridor and down the stairs. Riley faced the group. Ted rubbed his rumbling stomach in anticipation of their meal. Claudia and Chloë snuggled up to one another on a bed, pulling each another through their loss. Anna was at the back of the room. She peered out of the bolted windows at the courtyard.

"You okay with this?" Riley sat on the bed opposite hers.

"I'd rather take top bunk but I fell out of one once, so this will do."

Riley edged back. "I don't mean the bunks. I mean—"

"—Being here. Yeah. I... I wasn't sure. But for what it's worth, I think you've made the right call."

Riley rested against the pillows. They felt plump and soft, especially compared to the cold frostiness of last night's stay at the railway shelter. "I'm sorry. About... about the fallout at the Chinese restaurant."

"It's okay. We were all at each other's necks. Just a shame we don't all get the chance to have a go at one another again."

Riley closed his eyes. Remembered Trevor as he stepped back into the flaming Chinese restaurant, luring the creatures inside. A selfless act. A truly selfless act that hopefully none of them would have to do again.

"You're a good guy, Riley. Thank you."

Riley thought about replying but when he opened his eyes, Anna already had the quilt pulled up to her neck and her eyes closed. The sunlight peeked over the tops of the barracks, bathing her in a thin film of light.

Riley took a deep breath and closed his eyes. Despite everything they'd lost, everything they'd had to go through, at least they still had each other. At least they'd made it through. They were safe for now. They were safe for now, at last.

Ivan whistled as he walked into the canteen. He rubbed the grime from his hands onto his uniform. Hated clammy palms. Never could stand them. No matter how many greasy-as-fuck rifles he'd had to carry, he always washed his hands at every opportunity. Germs, they spread. Spread like flies around shit. Nobody needed germs, not in a time like this.

"Chef — you got the girl?"

Chef closed his copy of FHM and raised himself from the canteen table. He shook the small black urn. *'Remembering You...'* was etched across it in chipped, tacky gold lettering. Sentimental. Perfect.

"Good." Ivan grabbed the urn and slipped it in his top pocket. "Good indeed. Where did you find it?"

"Oh, lying around. Like a needle in a haystack full of needles." Chef sniggered through his buckteeth.

Ivan cringed. "Don't fuck around. In fact, don't make jokes. They don't suit you. Have you got the girl?"

Chef scooted off to the other side of the canteen and pulled out the trolley. He pushed it towards Ivan, being sure to adjust it so the girl's body wasn't visible.

Ivan grabbed the trolley and started to push it towards the canteen exit. "Make sure you cook our guests an absolute feast this afternoon, right? We need to make them feel at home. They deserve it after everything they've been through."

Chef bobbed his head and crouched back down. Stupid fat little rodent. Fortunate to make the cut. But he was a good cook, and that worked in his favour. Needed something to keep their spirits up in here.

Ivan pushed the trolley out of the canteen and down the corridor. He started whistling again. Always had been a good whistler. If he hadn't gone into the army, he'd have become a pro whistler. If there even was such a thing. If there wasn't, there should be.

He stopped at the door at the end of the corridor. Checked to see all was clear. When he saw it was, he slipped the key in the door and pushed it open.

"Alright, Ivan?"

Ivan's heart sank. He pulled the door back and turned around.

"Don't worry. Just me." Pedro stepped towards him.

"Thank fuck," Ivan said. His heartbeat slowed down, back to normal pace, whatever normal pace was. "Shouldn't do that lurking around thing, though. It'll get you killed some day."

Pedro shrugged. "Served me well so far. That the… the girl?"

Ivan gulped. "Yeah. Might as well get her dealt with."

"You're doing the right thing," Pedro said. "I know you might not think so at times, but you are. I've got your back."

Ivan half-smiled at Pedro. "Thanks, Pedro. Thanks."

"Just quit that bloody whistling. Now *that* will get you killed someday." He scooted off down the corridor in the direction of the canteen.

Ivan took a few deep breaths. The corridor was completely silent. Completely dead. *'You're doing the right thing.'* Easier said than believed.

But he had to believe it. It was his decision, after all.

He opened the door and the cold air engulfed him.

He pushed the trolley inside. The freezing cold air of the freezer room was a bitch. Stung right at the back of his throat and tickled his lungs. He reached for the switch on the wall and flicked it on.

He saw them stacked up at the back of the room. Remembered them in their camouflaged uniform. Familiar faces. Weak faces. Plump faces. He'd made the right call. He had to.

He turned away and lifted the girl's body from the trolley.

He avoided looking at her. "Just... just pop you over here. Over here with... Yep." He placed her on the floor and rushed back to the door. His heart raced. His palms were clammy despite the sub-zero temperatures of the room. *Keep calm. Deep breaths. Get out.*

He slammed shut the door of the freezer room. Tried not to picture their faces. Tried not to picture them as humans. Because they weren't humans anymore. They were dead. They couldn't view them as humans, not if they were going to survive. Like a piece of beef on a plate. Disassociation with the cow.

He reached into his pocket and pulled out the urn. *'Remembering You...'* He shook it and heard the pieces of ash rustle from side to side. The mother wouldn't know. She'd have no idea. He'd tell her they'd only been able to put a part of her daughter in there, and that's why the urn was so small. Some accident happened. She was enamoured by them, after all. Thankful for their 'heroic actions.' And grieving, too. That helped.

He placed the urn back into his pocket. She'd have no idea it contained nothing more than dust.

Then, he grabbed the trolley, and he started whistling.

Episode Five

Chapter Thirty-Three

SUNLIGHT BATHED THE GROUNDS OF THE barracks. Frost coated each individual blade of grass. Birds swooped down from the blue late autumn sky, winter growing ever closer. They sang songs jovially, like they always had before the Dead Days. Before the fall. And they'd keep on singing those songs, no matter what happened to humanity.

The road was as quiet as ever. The hand-made banner, the words *'Please Save Us'* written across it in thick red lettering, was starting to slide off the roofing of the terraced houses. They hadn't seen any sign of life across there. They'd watched and they'd waited from a distance, but they hadn't seen anything worth investigating. No movements. No twitching of the curtains. Nothing worth venturing outside the walls for.

Riley held the gun tightly as he lay on his stomach. Kept his breathing deep and rhythmic. At first, it had been hard to get the hang of. There was much more to pulling a trigger than wrapping your finger around the metal and firing into the distance. There was the aim. The careful, steady aim. The deep breaths. The check and the double checks and the double-double checks to see that the target is definitely in sight.

"On the right."

Riley adjusted his aim. Titled to the gun slightly to the right and squinted out of the lens. "Where am I looking?"

Pedro was still. Focused. A bead of sweat dribbled down the side of his bald head. "By the old milk van. Your call, soldier."

Riley turned the gun to the milk van and he saw it. A lone creature staggering from side to side. No groans. No real sense of direction to its movement. Lost in a world without end goals. Without purpose.

Riley took a deep breath. "There's just the one. We can leave it to walk, or we can… Ah."

As Riley adjusted his vision, he saw the other creatures behind the loner in front. They, too, looked lost but there seemed to be a method to their movement. A strange sense of group logic, like a pack of birds migrating overseas for the winter. They stumbled into one another, disregarding each other like ghosts.

"How many do you reckon?" Pedro asked.

Riley focused on the mass of creatures. "Forty. Fifty. Too many to deal with."

Pedro sighed. "And I was looking forward to a shootout. This seems to be happenin' every week now."

"But at least we know what to do," Riley said. He lowered his gun. Pedro kept focused on the oncoming group of death. A sight they'd grown so accustomed to over the last two weeks. "We can't risk firing at them. We don't want a repeat of last Thursday."

Pedro tutted and dropped his gun. "Lance and Stu were good soldiers. They died out there doing what they had to do."

Riley stood up. He looked over the wall. The creatures were like specks in the distance. He wasn't sure what their field of vision was like, but it seemed like they reacted more to sound than anything else. *'When you hear them coming, you know it's already too late to do anything about them.'* Stellar advice that would forever stay with him.

"Shall we alert the others?" Pedro asked.

Riley nodded and climbed onto the ladder leading down to the entrance area of the barracks. "I'll mention it. Just keep an eye on them. We'll get a couple of people on rota. Just stay cautious for now. If they get too close, we'll have to talk about going into lockdown."

Pedro shrugged. "Worked well enough last time."

"Right. And if they get *too*, too, close, well…"

"We won't let that happen."

"Indeed," Riley said. "Let's hope not. Laters." He stepped down the ladder.

"Oh, Riley?" Pedro called.

Riley climbed back up the ladder and poked his head over the side. "Yeah?"

Pedro smiled. "Glad you guys made it here, y'know? Safety in numbers, all that. Been nice mixing with the civvies."

"We didn't 'make it here.' You and your people saved us. We owe a lot to you. Thanks for giving us that opportunity. See you at lunch?"

Pedro's smile faltered slightly. "Yeah. Yeah, I will. Catch you later."

Riley descended the ladder and hopped onto the ground. He looked ahead at the sun-soaked barracks courtyard. Claudia and Chloë were hitting a tennis ball to one another with wooden beach bats. Ted was still figuring out the controls of the lawnmower. Anna was chatting with a few of the soldiers. Riley breathed in deeply. The last two weeks had been better than anybody could imagine. Things hadn't been easy, but they'd improved. They'd had warm beds to sleep in. Warm showers. Warm food on the table. And sure — there had been a couple of security breaches — but they'd managed it. They were all pulling their weight. There was a niggling sense of normalcy about it. New normal, anyway. Every day when Riley woke, the dread in his stomach grew smaller and smaller. The guilt over the people he'd left behind and the hard choices he'd made also shrank.

He stepped across the grass and towards Ted, who wobbled from side to side on the ride-on lawnmower.

They were holding on to their humanity. They were pulling through the darkness. There was hope for them yet.

Ivan rubbed his fingertips against his temples. His heartbeat pulsated in his neck. He stared down at the empty freezer and his throat welled up. The inevitability of what they'd have to do. The decisions he'd have to make to keep them alive.

"And you're sure this is all the food we had?"

Chef nodded and slammed the portable freezer lid shut. He dabbed a speck of ice from his index finger with his tongue. It melted on contact. "All out. Which means… we might have to think about backup. Another food source."

Ivan turned to look down the corridor outside of the canteen. The secrets he'd been hiding in that freezer. The truth that only a couple of his most trusted were aware. The soldiers who had agreed with him. The tough call he'd made. Everybody had to make tough calls. "I just don't want to rumble the ship. After how far we've come with the new people. I don't want to risk losing that."

Chef sighed. His head was shiny bald and his face deathly pale. "Need I remind you your original plans for the group in the first place?"

Ivan gulped. "Plans change. Circumstances change. We've come a long way since then."

Chef placed a hand on Ivan's shoulder. He moved close to his face. His breath had a sickly sweet peppermint tang to it. "Sometimes we have to take a step back to move forward. You know that better than anybody."

Ivan bit his lip. The screams as he'd rammed the knife into their heads. Gutting them. Lifting them off the trolley and into the freezer. He'd hidden it away. He'd hidden it away for all these days in the back of his mind, pushed away in a padlocked room. He'd hidden it away but it was resurfacing, like demons always did.

"So would you like me to get the first… the first meat? Or would you like to explain to the others why we've suddenly run out of food despite all those 'heroic supply runs' you told them about?"

Ivan stared Chef in the face. Chef stared back at him, emotionless. "You really are a cold bastard, you know that?"

Chef sniggered. "I will be once I've been in the freezer." He reached for the trolley beside the counter and started to push it in the direction of the corridor. "Are you going to give me a hand with this?"

Ivan looked out of the window. Ted mowing the lawn. Claudia and her little girl playing together. Giggling. Smiling. Family stuff. He had to keep them happy. He had to keep them fed.

He nodded. "We have to do what we have to do."

"We do indeed," Chef said.

The pair of them walked out of the canteen, into the corridor, towards the freezer room…

Chapter Thirty-Four

TED WAS STILL STRUGGLING WITH THE ride-on lawnmower as Riley approached. The mower was edging from side to side. Ted bit his lip and cursed as he tried to get it on course as a circle of grass formed beneath him.

"Did your parents never have you do any jobs around the house?" Riley asked.

Ted stopped the lawnmower and puffed a large sigh out as he hopped off it. "They made me do stuff around the *house*. Emphasis on house. Always more of an indoor type. I'm through with this thing. What ever happened to the good old fashioned handheld lawnmowers, anyway?"

"Just as well you're through with it, actually. Got a group of creatures dangerously close to heading our way in the distance."

Ted tutted. "How many?"

"Fifty. Maybe more. Pedro's keeping an eye on them. If they get too close we'll have to lock up inside and keep noise at a minimum. Don't want a repeat of—"

"—last week. Right." He wiped his grass-stained hand against his shirt. "We coped well with everyone inside last time though. As long as there's food and water, which there is, we'll be cool inside for a few days."

"Always the indoor type, like you said."

Ted twiddled his thumbs. "Not my fault the army boys love a good game of FIFA. Who am I to refuse?"

Riley smiled. He looked around at the others. All of them were wrapped up in army camo coats. The winter chill had really taken a hold these last two weeks. If they'd still been stuck at the railway shelter, life would have been difficult. If the creatures hadn't already attacked them, they'd have frozen to death. Drowned on melted icicles in their sleep.

Riley tilted his head at Claudia. She and Chloë were giggling as they smacked the tennis ball to one another. "How are they doing today?"

Ted leaned against the lawn mower. "Getting better by the day. Chloë's really come out of her shell. Claudia, she's hurting obviously. But it's good that they've got each other. Don't know how they'd have survived otherwise."

"Chloë's tough. But she deserves a childhood. Glad to see her getting a chance at that again."

Ted gripped the back of the lawnmower and yanked it away from the badly-cut spot underneath. "Claudia's tough too. Come a long way. I think being in here has done her good. A hand?"

Riley crouched in front of the lawnmower and started to push it. "When we need to leave this place, it's good to know she's—"

"*If* we need to leave this place," Ted interrupted. He stopped pulling the lawnmower and stared directly at Riley. "'If.' Not 'when.'"

Riley shrugged and held back his thoughts as he continued to push the lawnmower towards the yard. They were going to have to leave this place at some stage. The food supply — it had served them well so far, but that would run out. Ammunition would run out. Water would run out. Nothing was infinite in this world other than the world itself. Infinite, endless nothingness. The Dead Days had powered on for over two weeks now. The TV stations were still down, the radios were down, the mobile networks were down. Nobody knew anything about anything.

"You boys need a hand there?"

Riley and Ted exchanged a disgruntled glance then tried even harder to move the lawnmower. "We've got it, Anna. Cheers."

Anna held her hands on her waist. She examined the spot that Ted had attempted to mow with her eyebrows raised. "Yeah, good... good job, Ted. Definitely proving as useful an asset as ever." She had a small smile on her face.

Ted rolled his eyes. "Yeah. Ha ha. The 'Ted's a useless fat slob' jokes. They didn't get old a week ago."

"Well, I'm just saying," Anna said. She widened her arms and laughed at the mess Ted had made of the lawn. "Seeing is believing, I think the saying goes."

"I was doing just fine, actually," Ted said. His voice sounded irritated, like it did when he was losing on a video game. His cheeks reddened. "But there's a ton of creatures outside. So by all means go deal with them if you have to, and I'll finish my job. What do you say?"

Anna's smile dropped. She sighed, looked at Riley, and shook her head. "And there was me thinking we were going to be treated to another day of peace. How many of them?"

"Fifty. Sixty. Probably more."

Anna stuck her bottom lip out in consideration. "Not great. Could be worse though. Should be fine as long as we get inside and keep ourselves quiet."

Ted held his arms out. "Which is why we're wheeling the lawnmower back. Happy now?"

Riley and Anna peeked at each other. Riley held back his laughter. It always was amusing seeing Ted so wound up, especially when it was by a woman he clearly had the hots for.

"Does Ivan know?"

"On my way to tell him after we've put this away. Hey, any progress with the vaccine?"

"I wish. Me and Barney are at a dead end, really. Not a lot we can do without the flu jab. And, even then, it would be nigh on impossible to do any sort of medical research in this place."

"Before you suggest anything, no. We can't leave."

Anna tutted. "It's just—"

"You know how they are about leaving this place. And with reason. It's not worth risking any unnecessary attention. It was dangerous enough Lance and Stu leaving the gates. Lucky we got away with that. So no. Not until we absolutely have to."

"You've changed your tune," Ted said. They reached the concrete ground and stashed the lawnmower into the garage. "Only a few minutes ago you were talking about scooting on out of this place."

Riley lowered his head to avoid eye contact with Anna.

"Oh really?" Anna said. She walked up to Riley. "That's interesting."

"I'm talking about food," Riley said. "Food. We need it to survive."

Anna pointed at the greenhouse in the corner of the courtyard. "That's what that place is for. Besides, Ivan said there's plenty to last us the winter."

Riley tensed his jaw as Ted, Anna, and he stepped out of the garage and stared out at the courtyard. "I hope that's the case. I really do. Anyway, I'd better go speak to Ivan."

"In his yoga hour? You'd have to be mad to interrupt that."

Riley looked at his watch. Ten minutes to ten. "I'm sure a horde is worthy of a bit of yoga postponement. Catch you guys inside."

Riley walked away from Ted and Anna and towards the entrance of the main building. The building wrapped itself around the courtyard in the middle. Riley and the group he'd come with had a room to sleep in in the west side, which was where most of the living quarters were. Ivan, on the other hand, slept alone in the corridor leading down to the canteen. He treated the room as an office, a gym, and a recreational area as well as a display room for some ancient weapons like C4 and AK-47s. He claimed the C4 was still active. Every man needed a way to keep his sanity at the end of the world.

Riley stepped into the main building and into the canteen. There were two soldiers at the back of the room, hiding from the sunlight, playing chess. They glanced up at Riley as he passed and tilted their heads slightly. Riley offered a smile in return. Truth was, there were only a dozen or so left in these barracks, and not all of them were ultra-friendly. But that was understandable. Everybody had lost something. Bonds took time to grow.

As Riley walked out of the canteen and towards the corridor leading to Ivan's room, he could hear the sound of metal slicing through something. He looked over his shoulder and saw Chef behind the counter of the canteen in the kitchen area with his back to the rest of the room. Diluted blood dribbled down his hands as he sliced through the meat. He moved around the table, noticed Riley and smiled.

Then, he stepped up to the kitchen door and pushed it so it was closed, and returned to chopping.

Riley frowned as he headed down the corridor. Chef always had seemed a bit of an oddball. Completely pale bald head. Hunched shoulders, like a little squirrel or other kind of fat rodent. But he was a decent cook. Made some good stews and the occasional deep fried dish, as well as all the necessary things like fruit and vegetable smoothies. The kind of guy who was handy to know in a zombie apocalypse.

As he continued to head towards Ivan's door in the dimly lit corridor, which was on the left, he noticed something up ahead. The usually padlocked door was ajar. A cloud of cool air was seeping out of it into the corridor. Riley slowed down as he approached it. He never knew it was a cold store room. He always assumed there must be a freezer somewhere, but this door was usually padlocked shut. Why the extra security measures for food? Control? Keeping things in order? Made sense.

He slowed down as he approached the door. He noticed something on the floor beside his feet. It was just a small speck at first, and he thought it was a mark on the tiles. But as he crouched down and dabbed his finger in it, he knew exactly what it was. Red. Thin. It trickled down his fingertip. Blood.

"Everything okay there?"

Riley jumped up and spun around. Ivan was standing by his door. His eyes diverted to the usually padlocked room then to the blood on Riley's fingertip. He started to approach Riley, slowly.

"What's... This blood. Where is... What is it?"

Ivan pushed past Riley and grabbed the handle of the door. He slammed it shut. Then, he leaned against the door and folded his arms, staring right into Riley's eyes. "Look, I didn't really want to let anybody in on this, but I suppose I'm going to have to be completely honest."

"Has... has something happened? Has somebody been bitten?"

Ivan smiled. "No. No. Nothing like that." He moved away from the door. "Look — this room here is our freezer room. This is where we've been storing our meat. All that nice food that Chef's been cooking." Ivan crouched down and wiped the specks of blood from the floor with his sleeve. "I didn't want to say anything but I... A small group left the barracks first thing today. We had to. Food, it was getting low. And they knew of somewhere with... with some fresh meat."

Riley's muscles loosened. "Why didn't you say anything? We could have helped. We could have—"

"It was too dangerous," Ivan said. He stood up again. "This group that went out, they weren't even sure if they were going to find anything... anything live. But they found some meat. Dragged some frozen cow and pig from meat hooks in this store room they knew of. Brought it over here. And yeah. I guess they just didn't clean up so good after themselves." He raised his sleeve. The deep red blood stained right through it.

Riley shook his head. Heat burned through his cheeks and his chest. "We just want to pull our weight around here. You… You've got to let us try to do that sometimes."

Ivan planted a heavy hand on Riley's shoulder. "You are pulling your weight. But you aren't soldiers. So stop pretending that you are. You're good on wall watch. The rest — they're good at their own individual things. Seriously, let us do the stressing out about the technicalities. Um… did you want something, anyway?"

"Yeah, the… Wait. You said a small group went out. Who were they?"

Ivan grinned and shook his head. He eased Riley around and walked back in the direction of the canteen, his hand on Riley's back. "Like I said, don't worry about these things. Let us do our job, and you keep on doing yours. Now what's the problem?"

Riley remained silent for a few moments. Ivan might not have been completely open about the supply run, but he had every right to stay silent, really. He was trying to run this place. Trying to keep it calm. He couldn't have people panicking over food. He couldn't have a crisis from within. The humanity of this place — that was its strong point. "And we have enough food? To last us?"

Ivan winked. "Yes. But I'd say that even if we didn't. So you'll just have to trust—"

The canteen door barged open. It was Pedro. He was panting, out of breath as sweat dripped down his face. "Thank God I found you. Thank God. Have you told 'im?"

Ivan frowned. He looked from Pedro to Riley and back again. "Told me what?"

Riley's stomach churned. He hadn't even told Ivan about the horde yet. But they weren't so close. It wasn't a major emergency. "Oh — I… There's a horde in the distance. Over by the shops. Just thought we should keep an eye out and stay on guard just in case—"

"Yeah. That was five minutes ago." Pedro rested his hands against his knees and winced. "But—but something caught their attention. They noticed something, and… and…"

"Slow down, Pedro." Ivan stared down at Pedro. "What is it?"

Pedro took a few long, deep breaths and pulled himself back upright. "We need to lock down. The horde. It's coming our way."

Chapter Thirty-Five

"EVERYBODY INSIDE!"

RILEY FOLLOWED PEDRO AS he sprinted across the grass. The gentle November sun and the way the clouds calmly floated across the sky placed a blanket of false security over the barracks, and over the whole of the city. It was easy to forget there was even a world gone-to-shit out there when everything seemed so peaceful inside here.

"What is it?" Claudia asked. She gripped the two bats as Chloë tossed the tennis ball in the air.

"Get inside." Riley pointed to the door. "Take everybody inside. We've got a horde."

Claudia's mouth opened wide. She looked at her daughter in disbelief, then back at Riley, snapping her mouth shut and nodding her head. "Right. Sure." She ran off in the direction of the greenhouse where a few of the troops were gathered.

"Stocky, Gaz — get a move on."

Stocky and Gaz were pulling large plastic covers over the

front gates. When the horde had arrived last Thursday, they'd all lined up against the gates, there for everybody to see. A teasing reminder of the dangers on the outside and how close the danger actually was. They couldn't make the same mistakes again.

"What the hell caused them to change route?"

Pedro hopped up the steps beside the wall and shrugged. "You tell me. You know how they are. Maybe they caught sight of a little movement in here. Or smelled us out. I dunno."

Riley struggled to accept the logic in his own mind as he followed Pedro up the steps and towards the ladder leading to the watch point on the walls. "And how close are they?"

Pedro handed Riley a scoped rifle when he reached the top of the walls and pointed out through one of the small crevices that they rested the guns on. "See for yourself. Although I doubt you'll need the scope."

Riley pulled himself around to the crevice and started to raise his gun. But he soon realised that Pedro was right — he didn't need a scope after all.

The horde of creatures were heading in their direction. They were visible — their bloodstained clothes, their exposed guts — from this distance. Fifty. Sixty. Seventy. It was going to be a repeat of last Thursday. The illusion of safety they'd managed to form inside the barracks was about to crumble apart.

"I just don't get it," Riley said. He peeked out of his scope. "I don't get why they're heading in this direction."

"Well they are. And they ain't quitting. What d'you reckon? Is this a job we can handle from here or are we going to have to open the gates?"

Riley bit his lip. "You know how Ivan feels about opening the gates."

Pedro grumbled. "If only Lance and Stu hadn't taken that gun-mounted vehicle out there we could've blasted them from the entrance."

"Didn't work so well last time," Riley said. Lance and Stu,

two of the remaining soldiers, had opened the gates to fire at the creatures as they piled up against the barracks. They'd fired and fired at them, sending them to the ground.

But the bodies were stacking up. The creatures were blocking any form of exit. If they'd shot any more, the gates weren't going to close. So they drove off. Off out of the barracks, distracting the creatures as they fired at them. Got as far as Sainsbury's, which was just around the corner, before they presumably ran out of ammunition and were overwhelmed by creatures. But it bought enough time for the group to clear the dead creatures and close the gates again. Enough to go inside for a couple of days and lie low. Enough to rebuild their confidence. Again.

The sound of footsteps below Riley and Pedro interrupted Riley's thoughts as he peered out of the scope at the approaching creatures.

"All covered up!" Stocky shouted.

"Good," Pedro called. "Then get back to the main wing and make sure everyone's okay."

No response for a few seconds. "You… you sure you don't need a hand up there?"

"We've got it. Now go."

Footsteps echoed around the courtyard, which would be empty of life by now. The front of the barracks was about to become a lot emptier of life, but full of death.

"We need to make a decision here," Pedro said. "Fuck. We should have been ready for this. We should have been fucking ready for this."

Riley scanned the approaching creatures. Men, women, and children. Lifeless and lacking any sort of complex communication skills, and yet resembling one automatous being and mass brain as they marched in the direction of the barracks. Their mouths were opening. Their groans were becoming audible. They were coming, there was no doubt about that.

"I mean, we can go inside and pray. But the noises they

make. They'll—they'll send us mad. And then there's the others they'll attract. They'll pile up against the gate. We'll just be waiting for somebody else to pass and distract them. And there's no telling when that will be."

Riley remained focused. Observed the front of the barracks. The black mound where they'd burned the creature bodies. The grass, laced with dandelions as usual gardening duties were neglected. Something had to have drawn the creatures. Something had to.

"Or we can go out there. Distract them. But you know what that means. You know how it is. If we leave here, we don't come back. And even then it might not work."

Riley lowered his gun. There was nothing visible out there. Nothing he could see. He shook his head. They'd seen them somehow. They'd heard them. The group had hoped they could just monitor them and let them wander past, but that wasn't happening.

"I think we should get the hell inside." Pedro dropped his gun. "Get the hell inside and if it gets too bad, we drive on out of here and distract them. Can't think of any other way. Fuck those cowards in the government who barely left us any gunned vehicles. Fuck them."

Something caught Riley's attention.

Amidst the groans, there was a high pitched squeal. Somebody was out there. Somebody was shouting.

"I mean, if we need to, we open the gates and we mow them down. Mow them down with our guns and—and if ammo runs low then so be it. We—"

"Wait." Riley raised his hand at Pedro and peeked out of his scope again. The sound was definitely close by. And it was saying something. *"Help! Somebody, please!"*

"There's somebody out there," Riley said.

Pedro struggled for his gun and he too raised it and peeked out. "Where? I don't see anyone. I don't see a thing. We need to go, bruv. Get the hell back to—"

"Just be quiet a minute." Riley's heart raced. He squinted at the grounds and at the road. Looked up at the terraced houses opposite. Still nothing. But there was somebody out there. Somebody alive. Somebody drawing the creatures towards them.

"I'm going. I'm sorry, but I'm going."

"Wait." Riley stopped moving his gun. His stomach turned. He saw where the noise was coming from.

"What is it?"

"By the tree," Riley said. He was completely still as he focused on the oak trees that lined the road down to the barracks. "The second tree. About a third of the way up. See them?"

"I don't... What... Oh."

Riley nodded. He kept his focus on the tree as the screams grew louder and louder, and the groans got closer and closer. "That's our problem. That's what's drawing them, right there."

Pedro lowered his scope. "So what do we do about them?"

Riley stared at them. A woman clinging on to the flimsy branch of the brown-leaved deciduous tree. A young boy pushing his face into her stomach, shaking his head from side to side. The creatures were getting closer to them. They were the ones they were groaning at, not the group. Not the barracks

"What do we do, bruv? What do we do?"

Riley tensed his jaw. The creatures were getting closer to the woman and her child stuck up the tree. Their cries were drawing the attention of the horde, not any sound from the barracks. The creatures hadn't noticed the barracks. They didn't have to notice the barracks.

Pedro crouched down so that he was out of sight of the creatures, just in case. He leaned back against the wall. "We need to go inside. Stick around with the rest of the group until this... until all this is over."

Riley shook his head. Guilt welled up inside him. Memories of the people he'd left behind, time and time again, all because he wanted to save his own neck. And the way that Ted had battled that creature from on top of him back on the railway verge. He'd looked out for him. Covered him. Riley wasn't sure if he could say the same for anybody. "We have to try something. They're... It's a woman and kid. We can't just leave her."

Pedro scoffed. "Are you mad? We can't just go out there. Right now, the creatures sure don't look like they know about us. Dumb shits. But the second we open these gates and run on out there, they'll know. God knows how long it'll take them to give up and back off."

"I just... We can't leave them behind." Riley's heart pounded. He wanted to fire the gun at the oncoming horde. Take down every single one of them. But he knew it was unfeasible. Ammunition had to be protected and conserved, even in a place like this. It might have been an abundant commodity, but they didn't know how long they were going to be stuck in a world like this. No army. No police. No rule. Nothing but the dead.

"We can't leave them behind? Or *you* can't leave them behind?"

The words hit Riley right in the chest with an intense force. "I..." He stuttered. He couldn't quite process the words. Pedro was right — it was his own guilt that he was feeling. His own guilt over his inadequacies.

But that didn't mean he couldn't still try something.

"We have to consult with Ivan. The least we can do is work out if there's anything we can do to help."

Pedro tutted. "Such as?"

Riley shook his head. "I dunno. Drive something out there. Lure the creatures away and help them out of that tree."

Pedro stared at Riley. A look of sympathy built up in his eyes. "I respect your morals, bruv. I really do. But they'll follow. The zombies always follow."

Riley sighed. The woman and the young boy gripped hold of the flimsy looking tree branch, tears rolling down their cheeks. He couldn't tell what the woman was saying, but she was whispering things in her son's ears. Reassuring him. The horde of creatures would reach them in a matter of minutes. This is what it looked like to stare death right in the face.

Riley turned away from the wall and stepped down the ladders.

"Where you going?"

"Ivan," Riley said. He started to jog. "We can work something out here. We can try and help them. Somehow."

Pedro opened his mouth and looked like he was about to shout but closed it, likely realising that doing so would only attract the creatures. Instead, he sealed his lips and shrugged as Riley sprinted towards the main wing of the barracks and towards the others.

Ivan was right by the door when Riley got there.

He stared at Riley with a frown. His damp fringe flopped down onto his forehead. "Something wrong? What's it looking like?"

Riley caught his breath and shook his head. Others from behind Ivan looked at him with curiosity on their faces. Claudia. Chloë. Ted. Anna. The rest of the soldiers.

"Is something—"

"We need to go out there. You need to go out there," Riley said. He pointed his arm in the direction of the wall.

Ivan followed the path of Riley's arm and shook his head, slowly. "You aren't implying what I think you're implying, are you?"

Riley gripped hold of Ivan's arms. The soldiers behind him flinched and moved towards Riley. A bolt of courage and anger and frustration crashed through Riley as he stared Ivan in the face. "There's two of them out there. A mother and a child. Stuck up a tree. And unless we get there fast, they're going to die. The creatures, they aren't coming for us. They're... they're going for these two. But we can't let them die. I can't let them die."

Ivan widened his eyes and examined Riley's hands as they

rested on his upper arms. He brushed them away as if he were stuck in a trance then nodded his head once at Riley. "Show me them."

A gentle sense of surprise knocked Riley back, kicking away his frustration. "You... You want—"

"Show them to me. Quick." He grabbed his silenced pistol out of his pocket and pointed at the door.

The two soldiers that had approached Riley shuffled their feet. "Want any help?"

"No," Ivan said. He jogged over to the door. "Keep it calm in here. We'll be back soon. Riley, lead the way."

Riley nodded his head hesitantly then jogged out of the door, the tension from his legs seeping out as he ran back across the courtyard, Ivan's footsteps behind him.

Pedro's eyes widened as Riley and Ivan approached the wall. Pedro looked from Riley to Ivan and moved his mouth, struggling for words. "Boss... Ivan, you—"

"This group," Ivan interrupted. He stopped as he peeked over the wall. The groans were loud now. So close. A soundtrack to the greying winter sky. "Up the tree?"

"That tree," Riley said. He pointed at the middle tree. The woman and her young boy were still there, holding on to one another. The creatures were almost at the grass at the front of the barracks. They'd reach the tree soon. Send it tumbling towards the floor with their sheer might and strength in quantity.

Ivan sighed. He rubbed his hand through his greasy hair and pushed his fringe back onto his head.

"We can help them," Riley said. "We can go out there and we can help them. Distract the creatures somehow. They don't have to die. Think about us. What you risked to save us. We can help them too."

Ivan turned to Pedro. Pedro had a pained look in his bloodshot eyes. His bottom lip was quivering.

"We can help them," Riley repeated. "Ivan, we can—"

"We can help them," Ivan said. He looked at Riley and

half-smiled. It was full of pity. "We can help them."

Then, he raised his silenced pistol and he fired in the direction of the tree.

A sense of dread engulfed Riley. Butterflies swarmed around his stomach. He threw himself at Ivan, who fired another shot, but Pedro pulled him back and held him to the ground. He covered Riley's mouth.

"Shut up," Pedro said. "Come on, bruv. Keep quiet. That's right."

Riley's shouting continued inside his head as Ivan fired another shot in the direction of the tree.

He lowered his gun. Stared out into the grey-skied distance for a few seconds.

He turned to Riley. "I'm sorry, Riley. I'm really sorry. But that's the only way we could help them."

He patted Pedro on his back and hopped down the ladder as a sprinkle of rain fell down on Riley's cheeks.

Chapter Thirty-Six

"YOU UNDERSTAND I HAD TO DO it. Right?"

Riley and Ivan sat on their own in the corner of the canteen. The sky outside had turned a complete shade of grey as rain spat down on the barracks courtyard. The lighting inside was dim, as the survivors gathered around the tables. Some of them looked with cautious expressions over at Riley and Ivan. Claudia whispered to Ted. Ted kept his focus on them. Riley knew Ted had his back if he needed it. He was good like that.

Ivan sighed and scratched his forehead. "Talk to me, Riley. Don't go silent on me now."

"The family. The boy and his mother. You killed them. What else is there to say?"

Ivan narrowed his eyes. The words seemed to knock some colour out of his cheeks. "You know I did what I had to do. I helped them out."

Riley shuffled his chair to one side. "Oh, please. Spare me

the bullshit."

"No," Ivan said. His voice was raised. "I shot them. Clean shots to the head. Saved them a world of pain. If those things had got to them, you know what they'd have done. Torn them to pieces. You wanted that?"

"I wanted to help them. Bring them in here. Give them a chance. What you did. It was murder."

Ivan smiled. A little laugh came out from the back of his throat. "Murder? Riley, don't tell me you haven't had to make a difficult decision in this world. I know for a fact you have. You told me. So don't take the moral high ground. It was them or us. I chose us."

"And how do you know we couldn't have saved them? How do you know that there was no chance?"

"Because there's no way we were sending more of our men out there. Not after last time. We lost last time. Lucky enough we managed to distract the walking corpses enough to keep them away. We don't get lucky twice. Nobody does." Ivan stepped up from his chair and faced the rest of the canteen. The strong winter wind rattled against the windows. "You people have all had to make tough decisions. The soldiers — my soldiers — we've had to do things we're uncomfortable with. Right?"

Two of the soldiers sat in the nearest seats to Ivan, Ken, and Bill, who kept themselves to themselves, shrugged and returned to their game of chess. Ken, who had a beard that looked unshaven in months rather than weeks, lifted a white king and jumped over the top of his opponent's piece.

Ivan nodded. "And you people. Claudia. Anna. Ted. Little Chloë. All of you. You've done things you'd rather not have done. Right?"

The four of them looked at one another then tilted their heads to the ground.

"Right," Ivan said. The silence gave him the answer he needed. "So when I say I was acting in the best interests of the group, I mean it."

"But was there no way you could, like, have helped?"

The room looked around at Ted. He didn't return the stare.

"Ted, I promise you," Ivan said, crouching down opposite Ted. "If I could have saved them, I absolutely would have. But I weighed things up. Riley saw that. And so did Pedro. I saw the horde of creatures headed towards the tree. I saw how flimsy looking that tree was. And I saw nothing but death for them. So I figured I'd give them the more humane option. Would you not have done the same?"

Ted's vision wandered up and met Ivan's face. He looked over Ivan's shoulder then wiped his cheeks and let out his answer. "Yes. I guess."

Ivan patted Ted on the shoulder and returned to his feet. "Yes. You would have. Claudia? Would you have done the same?"

Claudia turned to her daughter, who sat silently staring at the table. She gulped and cleared her throat. "I... If there was no other way, then I think you probably did the right thing."

Ivan lifted his shoulders and turned back to Riley. "You see? I did what was... No. Not what was right. But what I had to do. It's not about what's right or wrong anymore. It's about what keeps us alive."

Riley swallowed the lump in his throat. Ivan was right. Or he was right about doing what he had to do, anyway. Sending a group out there was stupid. It would only go and get them into more trouble. But the way he'd done things, he'd given the group a chance of survival. It wasn't right, no. But Riley saw shades of himself in Ivan's decision. His unwavering commitment to lifting that pistol and pulling the trigger.

And that's what scared him most about Ivan. Up to now, he'd been calm. Controlled. Almost too idealistic. But he saw a mirror image of himself. A reflection of what he was when he'd left Jordanna behind. When he'd left Stan and Aaron to die. He saw himself, and it absolutely terrified him.

"I don't think you made the right call."

The voice startled Riley. He lifted his head. The rest of the room turned around.

"What did you say, Anna?" Ivan asked.

Anna lifted herself from her seat and walked around the canteen table. She squared up to Ivan. Scanned his face. Anna was the last person Riley expected to stand up for him when it came to morals. She'd always been the one that seemed almost too eager to make the difficult decisions. "I think you could have tried to do more. You did more for us. Came all the way out to an old stretch of railway. Makes me wonder what you wanted from us."

Ivan's eyelids twitched. It took a few moments for him to reply. "Things have changed in the last two weeks, Anna. You know that as well as I do. Maybe two weeks ago, we would have tried to save them. Maybe even last Thursday we would have done it. But things have changed. We've lost more people and lost more supplies. We couldn't take that risk."

"Then why did you send a group out to gather food earlier today?"

The question seemed to come from nowhere out of Riley's mouth. It was as if somebody else was asking it through him. The information Ivan had told him earlier about sending a group out to gather food still intrigued and baffled Riley.

Ivan turned around. Frowns were etched on the faces of his soldiers. Stocky, Gaz, and Pedro exchanged a confused glance.

"What's this about?" Anna asked.

"Yeah," Ted said. "What is this about?"

Ivan faced Riley. Peered at him with an unwavering intensity. It looked as if he was trying to transmit his disapproval of Riley's words via telepathy. From the twitching and reddening of his face, Riley didn't think he was doing such a bad job.

"The barracks were running low on food this morning," Riley said. He stepped from his chair and faced Ivan. "We weren't kept informed about this. And Ivan didn't seem to have much difficulty making the 'difficult' decision then. The decision that 'puts us all at risk.' Which makes me wonder what else you're keeping from us."

Ivan looked completely baffled. His face was as still as a stone, or a victim of Medusa's gaze. Riley had him right where he wanted him. Adrenaline pumped through his body from head to toe. He was winning this argument. He had to, for all of their morals' sakes.

A smile twitched across Ivan's face. "Riley. You don't have to question anything like that. You know how open I am with you people."

"No," Riley said. He squared up closer to Ivan. He could smell Ivan's sickly sweet breath in his face. Pedro moved away from the window ledge, like a bouncer keeping an eye on troublesome youths. "I don't think you are being completely open. Something doesn't strike me as right around here. Not after today. We've been living in this bubble. This idyllic bubble. And after this, it's burst. And I think I can see something isn't right. I wanted to believe it was, but now I'm not so sure."

Ivan waited before responding. The rest of the room stared on, waiting for the stand-off to continue. "Such as?"

"I don't know," Riley said. He looked around the canteen. Looked down the corridor near Ivan's room and to the freezer room that he hadn't even known about before a matter of hours ago. "But this group you sent out this morning. I'd like to know who they were. That would be a start."

A door clattered open at the canteen area. Riley turned around.

"Sorry. Have I missed something?" It was Chef. Sweat dribbled down his shiny bald head. His typically pale face was greyer than ever. And his fingernails were coated with blood.

Ivan cleared his throat. "Chef, I was just telling Riley and everybody here about the… about the run this morning. For food."

Chef wiped his hands. "Yes? About it? I managed to make a lovely stew out of it, if that's what you're wondering?"

"How low on supplies were you?" Riley asked as he walked

in Chef's direction. "Low enough that it was worth 'putting us all at risk' to send some people out there? Low enough that we can so suddenly become completely comfortable allowing a child and mother to die in cold blood? Low enough to—"

"We were empty."

Pedro walked up to Riley. He bit his lip.

"We were all out. Completely empty. And I... I went out there this morning. I went alone. I knew a place that I figured would have some meat lying around. And I got it all and I brought it back here."

Pedro's words knocked Riley back. He hadn't been expecting Pedro to be the one keeping things from him. "But... Weren't you on the wall?"

"I covered for him," Ivan said. "Skipped my early jog."

The room descended into silence again. Guilt welled in Riley's stomach. He'd caused a fuss over nothing. They were completely empty. They absolutely needed to leave for food.

"But... but if we were completely empty," Ted said. His jaw shook. "What's to stop us getting empty again?"

"I assure you Ted, that's not going to—"

"We can't go starving here," Gaz, one of the soldiers, said. "Didn't sign up to starve."

"We've—we've got enough now," Ivan said. He was trying to smile but the voices began to rise in volume as the room became awash with panic.

"What about if we do run out? What then? What do we —"

"We've got enough!"

Ivan's voice brought the room to an abrupt silence. It took Riley by surprise, too. It was the first time he'd seen Ivan flip. He didn't think he had it in him.

Ivan huffed and puffed. His cheeks were red and his body was fidgety. He didn't look like the same man who had been trying and failing to restore a sense of order just moments earlier. "We've got enough. You have to trust me with that. And when we do run out, we go out again. That is just the way things work now. And you have to deal with that." He paced around the room like an angry teacher. "We don't have an unlimited supply of food. We had a good supply of food, but nothing's unlimited. Nothing. Never was, never is. So we cope. We've got the greenhouse set up now. We've got fruit and veg growing in there. It won't be a fast process, but we cope. We survive. But I am *not* risking the safety of this group on a heroic power trip." He turned and faced Riley. His eyes peered right through him. "I hope you're proud," he whispered, before storming out of the canteen and slamming shut the door of his private room.

The canteen was silent. The wind had dropped. Nobody was looking at one another. The strange, taken aback sense of calm after the storm.

"Well," Chef said. He rubbed his hands together and stepped back into the kitchen. "Suppose I should get that stew warmed up."

He disappeared into the kitchen and the room descended into silence once more.

Chapter Thirty-Seven

RILEY LAY WITH HIS HEAD ON his hands and stared up at the bunk bed above him. At first, he'd heard the groans outside, in the distance but so present. But they'd faded away now. The sun had moved over to the window side of the barracks, which meant it was afternoon. Nobody had bothered him, not since the dispute with Ivan.

The door creaked open. Riley closed his eyelids and tightened them together so that whoever it was would just leave him alone. He just needed some time on his own to work things out in his head. The mother and child, screaming for help. Ivan's coldness as he lifted the gun and pulled the trigger, not a glimmer of doubt in his eyes. And the way he'd defended his actions. The way he'd covered up Pedro's little run for food earlier that day. They'd been living under a curtain of security for two weeks now. When things were good, they were good. But when the apple cart rattled from side to side, sending a few ripe pieces of fruit to the ground, tensions always rose.

But nothing like today.

"I know what you look like when you're pretending to sleep."

Riley sighed and opened his eyes. Anna was standing with her arms folded at the foot of Riley's bed. She had a look of mischief on her face. A little smile in the corners of her mouth, but it was fading. Faltering after the stresses of today. A forced illusion of safety and peace shown for what it was: a sham.

She fell back on her bed and yawned. "Don't mind me. Just don't think I could take another game of fucking chess."

Riley turned onto his side. "When the world goes to shit, play a game of chess. That the new motto of this place?"

Anna puffed out her lips. "Something like that."

The pair was silent for a few moments. Anna tapped her fingernails on the metal headrest at the top of the bed.

"Thanks. By the way. For before."

"For what?" Anna asked.

"For having my back. With regards to… to the woman and her boy. Thanks."

"You sound almost surprised that I'd stick up for you."

"Well," Riley said. He perched up on the bottom of his bed. "Not to pull a bunch of examples out of the bag, but you were the woman who told me that if I didn't finish my duties in that supermarket quick enough, you'd leave without me. Warm girl."

Anna raised her eyebrows. "And did I abandon you?"

Riley smiled. "Fair point."

Another awkward silence. Except Riley couldn't tell whether it was really awkward or not, or just one of those silences that apparently were comfortable. Riley never found any silence comfortable, unless it was self-imposed and on his own. How could silence with another person possibly be comfortable?

"Listen," Anna said, thankfully breaking the silence. "I know things were tough today, and I know I was the first person to doubt the legitimacy of this place, but it's okay, you know?"

Riley turned to the door. He could hear laughter downstairs. One of the soldiers, no doubt. A sense of normalcy returning to the place. Or, at least, as normal as it could get anyway.

"And…" Anna gulped. "I guess that attitude I have. I've been thinking about it."

"Holy shit," Riley said. "You're admitting you have an attitude problem? Well that's a start. Hats off to you."

Anna sent daggers in Riley's direction. "I said I have a bit of an attitude. Not a problem. There's a difference. Don't make me prove it."

Riley raised his hands as if to calm Anna down. "Okay, okay. Carry on."

Anna exhaled and returned to her laid down position. "I dunno. I guess I've been thinking a lot. About how I can… how I can be a bit short. A bit defensive. And—and I think it's gone away a little since we came here. Since I started… started trusting people."

Riley thought about making a jokey comment about how it was rare for Anna to be opening up, but he could sense in her voice that there was sincerity about it. He got the impression that she didn't open up all that regularly. He was a fortunate one. A chosen one.

"I've spent my life fighting. Fighting to prove I've made the right decision. When I was growing up, it was just me, my mother, and my sister. And my sister was always the more academic one. Naturally academic one. Anyway, I'm blabbering on. But I guess what I'm trying to say is… that fight in me. That scepticism. I had to do it when I was growing up. I had to do it when I was getting into nursing. I worked hard. And then I became a nurse and all of a sudden I was the achiever in my family and my sister's working in a clothes shop. And then… and then this. And all of a sudden I'm forced to fight again."

Riley wasn't sure whether now was a good opportunity to

make a comical remark or whether he'd have to maintain the serious tone. He never was sure.

Anna sat up again and stared out of the window. The sun was peeking through the clouds again. The rain had stopped sprinkling to the ground. "I won't go on, anyway. Just… I don't think people get that sometimes."

"I get that," Riley said. He didn't, but it seemed like the right thing to say in his head. "You… you struggle getting the correct image across to people. People interpret you as aggressive when really, you're just trying to prove yourself to them. Prove yourself to… to yourself." Riley cringed. The words sounded better in his head. She'd know he was just rambling now.

But to his surprise, Anna's eyes met his. They were watery. Her face twitched and she nodded, then turned away, her cheeks blushing. "Yes. That's… that's about right."

Riley cleared his throat and tugged at his shirt collar. Maybe he was getting good at this motivational talking stuff in the apocalypse.

"Anyway," Anna said. She stood up from the bed and brushed down her clothes.

"Yeah," Riley said. He pretended to look at something on the wooden table beside his bed, as if he were preoccupied with something else.

Anna walked over to the bedroom door. Towards the voices down the corridor, and down the stairs. She stopped by the door. "Thanks, Riley. Thanks for understanding. It's not easy. Knowing I might have been involved in this virus or whatever it is in some way."

Riley nodded. Offered a reassuring smile. "You weren't to know what was in those jabs, if that's what it is that caused this thing. You were just doing your job."

Anna bobbed her head. Smiled back at Riley. "Yeah. I was. Game of chess?"

Riley looked around his bed for some sort of excuse to get out of the banal, mind-numbing activity that was chess. "I, er... I—"

"Scared of being beaten?" Anna winked.

Riley took a deep breath and stood to his feet. "Go on. Why the hell not?"

"Checkmate."

Ted pumped his fist. Anna had a grin on her face, as did Barney, who watched them closely. Barney was a little older than the others. A self-proclaimed chess expert, or 'chesspert,' as he called it. Sounded like something out of a Steve Coogan sitcom, and yet he still continued to tag himself with that label, time after time.

Riley stretched out. Darkness had descended on the barracks. The groans had all disappeared. Pedro had been out earlier and confirmed that the horde of creatures had 'finished their jobs here.' Riley thought of the woman and the child and shuddered. He knew exactly what Pedro meant.

"You might as well have stayed in bed," Anna said. "An empty chair might have done a better job than you."

Riley mimicked Anna's jibes. The rest of the table had smiles on their faces. In fact, the whole of the canteen area looked in better spirits after the heightened tensions of earlier. They'd had some food in their stomach. A nice beef stew. The meat was richer than anything they'd had in the previous couple of weeks. More tender. Maybe Pedro's venture out of the barracks hadn't been such a bad idea after all.

"Up for a thrashing?" Barney asked. He peered at the others through his bristly grey eyebrows. "Or you lot afraid of the chesspert?"

Riley cringed.

"I'll give you a game," Ted said. He re-laid the pieces and shuffled over so he was opposite Barney.

Riley looked around the canteen. Although the majority of the room had returned to good spirits, with Claudia and Chloë laughing as they were entertained by Stocky and Gaz, Ivan was missing. He usually had a couple of hours to himself in the evening, but not when everybody else was around. It was uncharacteristic. Riley thought back to the way he'd stood up to him earlier. The embarrassed look on Ivan's face as he stormed into his room. He hadn't seen him since, not even for dinner.

Riley raised from his chair.

"Off somewhere?" Anna asked.

"Yeah. I should... After earlier. I should go see Ivan."

The words went over Ted and Barney's heads, who were already deeply engrossed in their game of chess.

Anna whistled. "Courageous git. Good luck."

"Oh," Barney said, as Riley started to walk towards the corridor. He searched his pocket and pulled out a key. "Replacement key for him. Old one went and snapped in some padlock. Tell him I got it sorted for him."

Riley grabbed the key and shoved it in his pocket. "Thanks. I'll make sure I get it to him."

He smiled once again at Anna, who tilted her head in a 'good luck' sort of manner.

"I'll need it," Riley said, as he walked out of the artificially lit canteen area and into the corridor leading to Ivan's room.

As he walked down the corridor, he steadied himself with a few breaths in through his nostrils and out of his mouth. Deep breathing techniques were something he'd been taught by the doctor after the accident. *Accident.* Who was he kidding? Himself? There was nothing accidental about slamming one's foot on the accelerator and plummeting a car into a wall. *Accident.* Everybody referred to it in that way, even him.

He stopped outside Ivan's door. The lights in the corridor hadn't been switched on yet. It was completely silent in there, the only sounds the gentle hum from the end of the corridor from the generator room, and the echoes of the cheerful voices in the main canteen. He raised a hand and started to move it towards Ivan's door.

But then, an idea came into his mind. He turned to his right. The door that he'd found open this morning. The room where they were storing things. The room with the blood outside. A freezer room, judging from the way clouds of cold air puffed out of the door earlier.

Riley reached into his pocket. The key that Barney had given him. *"Replacement key for him. Old one went and snapped in some padlock."* He looked at the key. Long, silver, and perfectly shiny and smooth. And he looked up at the padlock. There was nothing wrong with him taking a look, right? A brief peek around the door, just to check how much they had in the way of supplies.

Right?

He moved away from Ivan's door. There were no sounds inside. No hints of movement or life. He could be sleeping. Doing his meditation thing that he always seemed to rave on about. There was nothing wrong with a quick look. He could take a look, and then he could leave. Simple.

He stepped down the corridor. The gentle humming noise grew closer and closer as he approached the padlocked door. He squinted in the darkness. The voices seemed further away. He could hear and feel nothing but his heart racing in his chest, and yet he still couldn't work out why.

He grabbed the padlock. It was rusty. Rough around the edges.

And he heard footsteps close by.

He stopped. Turned his head towards the canteen door. Held his breath.

A soldier whose face he couldn't recognise scooted past and pushed through the double doors into the canteen. The sound from the canteen picked up again, then dropped as the double doors swung shut.

Riley exhaled. His pulse rattled around his head. He gripped the padlock again and moved the key towards it. It might not even fit. It might be the wrong door.

But the key slotted into place. Fit snugly, like a glove on a hand.

Riley stepped back. He shouldn't be doing this. He'd come

to apologise to Ivan. To put things right and try to talk out a diplomatic solution of some sort. He shouldn't be snooping around. It wasn't the right way to go about things.

But still, he grabbed the padlock again and turned the key.

Nothing wrong with a look.

Just one look.

He pushed the door open. His body tensed. A cloud of cold air engulfed him, making him shiver right away.

But as the door swung open, something else made him shiver. Made his muscles loosen. Made an intense sense of dread claw its way up through his legs and into his stomach, turning every area it touched into jelly.

He dropped the key to the ground. It echoed against the floor. Bounced on the hard tiles. He couldn't understand it. Couldn't comprehend it.

Bodies. Legs and arms intertwined. Faces coated with specks of frost. Eyes as hard as glass and skin so pale that it looked like it might crack like an eggshell if something brushed against it. Army uniforms. Pained faces. Missing limbs.

Somewhere behind him, as he stared at what was in front of him, unable to turn away, he heard a whistling.

And then a door to his right opening. Movement.

Then, the whistling stopped. The movement stopped.

"I wondered when you'd find out," a voice said.

Chapter Thirty-Eight

RILEY TURNED AWAY FROM THE ROOM and looked back inside. He blinked rapidly. Held his eyelids shut for a few moments in hope that the images in front of him would just wash away.

But they were real. Very real.

The freezer room was filled with bodies. Dead bodies. Preserved bodies. Bodies of soldiers, some of them still clothed. Other bodies, unidentifiable.

"I didn't want you to find out, but I knew you would eventually."

Riley turned around. Ivan stood by the door of his room. His face was pale and his arms were covered in goose pimples. The fear was prominent in his dark, deep-set eyes.

"I wanted to tell somebody. At first, I thought maybe I should be open about it. Because that's what we are, right? Open?"

Dread spread through Riley's body. Took a hold of his

throat and prevented him from speaking. The cold air seeped out of the door beside him. A faint smell of wretched, frozen death was ripe in his nostrils.

Ivan approached him slowly. He was wearing his usual green camouflaged uniform. He always wore it. A sense of authority. A sense of order. But there was nothing ordered about this.

"How did… Why did…"

"I've not been completely honest with you, Riley. And I'm sorry to have to tell you that, but it's the truth."

"Too right. Too fucking right." An intensity spread across the muscles of Riley's chest. "You've got… you've got people in there. Dead people. What—"

"Ssh," Ivan said. He raised his hand. The voices from the canteen were muffled behind the double door. Happy voices. Cheerful, optimistic voices. A whole world away from what Riley had seen. What he knew.

"When we heard the news at the barracks," Ivan continued, "some of us left right away. And that's the truth. I've always been honest about that. Some soldiers went back to their families. Some probably got caught on the road. But there were about forty of us left. Thirty or forty. And we were penned in here. We were penned in and—and we were struggling."

Riley started to move his head from side to side. He knew where Ivan was going with this. He could sense it. Nausea crept up his chest. His stomach began to churn.

"And sure — we had some food. Yes, we had food. But we were worried. Worried about what would happen when we ran out. Worried about… about what we'd do if we could never make it out again." He paused. Took a deep breath. "So we killed them."

Riley was speechless.

"I killed them. Me and a couple of others, anyway. Went in their dorms in the night and slipped a knife in the side of their heads. Wouldn't have suffered, not for long. And… and then we threw them in there. Gutted them when it was appropriate. Threw them in there just in case. We didn't want to have to… to delve into the… the human meat. We thought we had enough food to last us some time. But then you people joined us. And food started going quicker. Faster."

The words buzzed around Riley's head. He understood what Ivan was saying, but he couldn't comprehend it. It didn't seem real. This sort of thing didn't happen in a real world. Things were meant to be okay now. A sense of order was supposedly restored. But so much started to make sense.

Ivan reached down for the shiny key that had tumbled from Riley's hand when he opened the padlock. "I'm not proud of what I did. It haunts me every moment of my life." He slipped the key into the padlock. "But I did it because I was looking out for my people. And I know you are one of my people now. But before, back before we met. How far would you have gone for your people?"

Riley was still struggling to speak, but images were coming back to him. Little memories and things he'd noticed over the last two weeks. Incidents that were barely weighty enough to warrant the name, but in light of what he now knew, so significant. "Pedro didn't go on a run for meat this morning, did he?"

Ivan sighed. Shook his head. "No. He didn't."

"Which is why you didn't save the mother and child. I just thought you were insensitive. Leaving this place to feed us and not look out for others. I couldn't understand it. But… but actually, you're terrified. Of leaving here. That's what it comes down to. Right?"

Ivan diverted his gaze away from Riley. He didn't have to answer. His subdued body language said it all.

"And… and that look in your eye. That disappointment at having to shoot the mother and child. You weren't bothered about them. You were… You were just more concerned that we'd missed out on fresh meat. Right?"

Ivan's head sunk further into his chest. He looked like an

embarrassed school pupil shown up in front of his friends by the teacher. "I had to do something. We couldn't just risk starving through the winter."

"And how did you decide?" Riley's skin burned with adrenaline. His voice sounded like it was full of rage, but he was shaking. Fearful. Completely and utterly stunned. "How did you decide who died? Who you killed?"

"We voted. The least fit. The least useful."

Riley shook his head. The echoes of the voice in the canteen. The meat they'd eaten tonight. So different to the other food. So much richer. Riley's stomach churned. He needed to puke. Badly.

"But only… only tonight. Only tonight did we have to start delving into… into there. I promise. We… we cooked and prepared when you people were sleeping. There was no fuss. And everything else you ate was—"

"Nothing else matters," Riley said. He squared up to Ivan. As commanding a presence as Ivan usually was, he seemed completely broken down. His justifications to Riley sounded more like justifications to himself. "All that matters is that you've deceived us. Who else knows? Who else?"

Ivan sighed. Took in a large breath. Exhaled. "Pedro. And Chef." He paused for a moment. "And that's it."

Riley shook his head. Pedro knew. All this time, sitting atop the wall and guarding the barracks with him, and he knew. "You think you're strong. You think you have the last word here. But when those soldiers in there find out what you've done to their friends… when they find out, they're going to kill you. You know that. Right?"

Ivan trembled. "I was just trying to do the right thing. The right thing for all of us."

Riley barged past Ivan and headed in the direction of the double doors. "Spare me the bullshit."

"Where are you going?"

"To tell everybody, that's where. To tell them what's going on in here. And then we're going to pack our bags and we're going to leave."

Ivan jogged after Riley. "Wait!"

Riley shook his head and went to push the double door. The voices got louder and clearer as he did. They were disorienting. Made him feel even more nauseous as he still got to grips with what he'd discovered.

"Claudia. Her little girl. Elizabeth. She's in there."

Riley froze. A laughing emerged from the canteen. The sound of chess pieces clinking against one another. Cursing.

He turned around. Ivan was standing upright. His eyes were narrowed. The colour had returned to his cheeks. "What did you…" Riley started.

Ivan pointed at the freezer room. "Claudia's girl. Elizabeth. She's in there. Couldn't have her going to waste."

Riley's knees went weak. "But… the urn. The ashes—"

"Oh come on, Riley. Don't insult your own intelligence. It's a wonder what a little dust and a fancy container can do, huh?"

Riley shook his head. The tingling sensations moved down his hands and up his arms. His breathing was speeding up. His heart raced. *Keep control. Stay in control…*

"You hear that? In the canteen?"

Laughter. Raised voices. Good spirits.

"I hear it too. So by all means go in there and tell everybody about this. But just think of the damage you'll cause. Just think of how hard we've worked to keep the spirits up. The stress we've been through today. Just think about that before you go storming on out there. Okay?"

Riley stared at his hands. He couldn't see any blood anymore. He didn't get the guilt running through his mind over the difficult choices he'd made. But if he walked on out of here and kept this a secret, that blood would splatter all over him again.

"Just rest on it. And if you decide you want to leave, then… then we can talk about that tomorrow."

But if he went out there and told them, it would shatter the happiness. They'd had a taster of that before. Earlier, when the arguing over the mother and child's fate started. They'd stared back into the darkness again, and it didn't look good.

"I'm just trying to do the right thing, Riley. Just trying to do the right thing."

Riley pushed the double doors open.

The sounds of the room erupted around him.

Laughter over at the chess table in the far right corner.

Chattering between Claudia and her daughter and a few of the other soldiers.

And the clattering of pots at the far side of the room. Chef cleaning the dishes. Pedro behind the counter with him.

Riley stepped into the room. Warmth ran through his body. The sickness returned to his stomach. He needed the toilet. He needed to get out of here. Fast.

"You okay, Riley?"

He looked to his side. Claudia was staring at him.

Elizabeth's body was in the freezer. He had to tell her. He had to tell her.

The laughter at the chess table.

Riley wiped his forehead and nodded. "Yeah. Yeah. Just feeling a bit sickly. Need a lie down."

"Well I hope you get well soon," Claudia said, as Riley rushed past her and headed straight for the canteen exit.

Riley lay back in his bed. He covered his eyes with the quilt. Tried to drown out the sounds from downstairs. Laughter. Messing around. The happiest and most upbeat they'd sounded in days. The incident with the family had proven nothing more than a welcome eye-opener. A necessary explosion of tensions triggering a reset button. Now, the honeymoon had set in.

But not for Riley.

He tried his best not to think of the images. The things he'd seen. The bodies, stacked atop one another. The sickly rich taste of vomit in the back of his throat. He'd had to spew it up. He couldn't keep it in his system, not now he knew.

The door creaked open. He made sure the quilt cover was pulled right up to his neck. He didn't want to talk to them tonight. Ivan had told him to sleep on it. Consider his response the following day. But, of course, he'd told him to sleep on it. That was the easy suggestion to make, considering he wasn't getting a wink of sleep tonight.

"Ssh," somebody whispered. "Don't want to wake Riley up."

Riley's stomach turned. Claudia. The way she sat the urn on her bedside cabinet. A reminder of what she'd lost, but also a reminder of hope. *"It makes me realise that there's some truly good people out there."* She was so grateful to the soldiers — to Ivan — for giving her little girl a civilized send-off. A send-off that barely anybody was fortunate enough to get these days. She'd been so strong.

She had no idea that the urn contained nothing but dust. That her little girl was in that freezer, waiting and waiting to be cooked. Consumed. Defecated.

Riley gulped. Squeezed his eyes shut. She couldn't know. She'd come so far. She couldn't find out, not yet.

More footsteps shuffled through the bedroom doorway. The voices had disappeared from the canteen below. Riley wasn't sure how long he'd been in bed, but he figured everybody was coming to sleep.

Sleeping on a full stomach. A full, rich stomach.

"I'll beat you next time," Ted said. He winced as something sounded like it punched him. Presumably Anna.

"Night."

Riley peeked out of one eye over at Ted. He fell flat on his bed and rubbed his stomach, which still seemed to be rather plump despite a significant fall in fried and fatty foods these past two weeks or so. But it was the smile on his face that caught Riley's attention. The smile of content. The smile of not knowing the truth or the secrets behind these walls.

"Just think of how hard we've worked to keep the spirits up..."

Ivan's words. Begging. Pleading Riley not to tell anybody

about what he'd found. Because in some twisted way or another, telling everybody the truth made Riley the guilty one.

But what was the least guilty route? Hiding what he knew from the others and keeping them happy for the time being, or telling the truth and destroying their happiness?

His heart pounded as he tightened his eyelids together and everybody settled down in their beds. He needed to decide. He needed to do the right thing.

He opened his eyes and looked around the room. Everybody was in place. How best did he tell them? One by one? Or announce it to the room like he was some sort of film character, all high and mighty? No. He'd speak with Anna. He'd speak with Anna and they'd go from there. He wouldn't mention Elizabeth first. Fuck. How was he supposed to bring up Elizabeth? After how far Claudia had come, how was he supposed to tell her the truth about the fate of her little girl? And Chloë — she'd just about settled back into some sort of normality. Playing tennis with her mother, reading whatever stories they had stashed in the barracks. She was becoming a little girl again. Growing down. What would learning about her sister's death do to her?

As Riley raised from his bed, his head throbbing, he noticed something was amiss. Something was different in the room. Ted was in his bed. Anna was in hers. Chloë was there, too.

But Claudia. Claudia wasn't in the room.

Riley's hands started to shiver. She'd definitely entered the room. She'd told Chloë to quiet down — that was definitely her. But now she was gone. Nowhere to be seen.

Dread built up inside Riley as he stepped to his feet. Nobody else in the room flinched, as they held their eyes shut. A bad feeling spread through his body. He couldn't quite make sense of the feeling, but he knew something wasn't quite right.

The bodies. The soldiers. *Fuck.* Having a semi-photographic memory was more a curse than a blessing.

He crept towards the bedroom door and pulled it open.

The corridor light flickered on. Somewhere behind him in the bedroom, somebody yawned and shuffled around.

"Mate, what are you doing?" It was Ted.

Riley ignored him. Stared down the corridor. The stillness of the buzzing bright lights. The closed doors. And the silence right the way down the stairs and into the canteen area.

"Mate, what's—"

"Where's Claudia?" Riley asked, as he turned around to face Ted.

Ted shrugged and looked over at Chloë.

"She went to say thank you to Ivan for everything," Chloë said, as she lay beneath the covers.

Utter dread kicked Riley in his stomach. *"We cooked and prepared when you people were sleeping."*

But before he had a chance to consider his options, a blood-curdling scream cut through the silence of the barracks. A woman's scream. A mother's scream.

Claudia's scream.

Chapter Thirty-Nine

RILEY STORMED DOWN THE CORRIDOR TOWARDS the screams. His heart raced. His head went dizzy. Claudia knew. She'd been downstairs when they were moving the bodies — gathering more food — and she'd found them.

"What the fuck was that? Riley?"

Ted rushed out of the bedroom and caught up to him.

"Where are you two going? Did you hear that too?" Anna appeared at the door and followed down the corridor.

"Was that my mum?" Chloë peeked out of the door. She too followed. She couldn't follow. None of them could see this. He was supposed to tell them first. It wasn't meant to happen like this.

Riley tried to descend the staircase but Ted blocked his path. Another door opened up behind them. Soldiers awakening from their slumber. Spectators to the show.

"You have that look on your face," Ted said.

Riley stepped around Ted but Ted moved so he couldn't pass him. The screaming and crying was dampening downstairs. Somebody was making sure that was the case.

"You tell me what's wrong. Right now."

Riley squared up to Ted. Stared him in the eyes. The others gathered behind them as they stood at the top of the staircase in stasis.

"Tell us, Riley," Anna said. "Just tell us."

Riley turned around to the others. Barney was frowning as he stood behind the group. He, too, looked completely puzzled by the situation. What did he say? How did he say it?

He looked at Ted again. "You need to see it. You need to —"

"No," Ted said. He didn't flinch. His voice was stern. "You tell me if you know something. Tell us all. Right now."

Riley sighed. He gulped down the sickly taste in his throat. He had to tell them. There was no other way about it. "I wanted to… I tried to tell you. I tried, but—"

"Just tell us. What is it?"

Riley looked down at his feet. He should have told them earlier. He should have walked on in to the canteen and told them when he'd had the chance to. They'd see this as him telling them because he had to. He'd lose them for this.

"I… The food. The food we ate tonight. The food that Ivan told us was—was meat he got on a run. That Pedro got on a run."

"Riley, what are you trying to say?" Ted asked. His eyes were watering. Riley got the sense from the look on Ted's face that he understood that something was desperately wrong now. "You're freaking me out, mate. What is it?"

Riley gulped down the lump in his throat and just let the words exit his mouth. "We ate dead bodies for dinner. Dead human bodies. The freezer room — it's stacked with troops. The troops Ivan told us had left. It's stacked with them. And…" Riley could hear a whimpering downstairs. Claudia. He had no idea what they'd do now she knew. They needed to get down there to her. Ted needed to move. "And Elizabeth," Riley said. He tried not to look at Chloë.

Everybody was completely silent. Anna's face grew pale. Ted's eyes widened and he lurched to the floor and spewed up the brown, greenish contents of his meal.

"But what..." Barney said. He looked stunned. "My friends. The—the others. What... Ivan said they'd left. Said they'd all... all left. Right?"

Riley shook his head as Ted continued to throw up beside him. "I'm sorry. But we need to get to Claudia. She... she's in trouble. We need to get to her and then we need to leave."

Riley pushed past a sickly Ted and hopped down the stairs. The group behind him was in a complete state of shock.

When he reached the bottom of the stairs, he stared into the canteen. Claudia was in the kitchen in hysterics. Pedro and Chef were trying to calm her down as she threw herself onto the floor. Pedro covered her mouth. Held his finger to his mouth. He was silencing her. Doing all he could to silence her.

"Typical, isn't it?"

The voice caught Riley by surprise. He turned around and he saw Ivan standing by the door of the freezer room. Ivan's face was pale. He looked just as sickened as everyone else. The door to the freezer room was wide-open. The cold air seeped out and clouded Ivan in a conspicuous mist.

"You work so hard for something. So hard to keep something secret. And then one little accident like this happens." He shook his head and approached Riley. "One little accident. We didn't have to keep the girl in there. We could have done as we'd said. Burned her. Cremated her. But we were thinking about the future. I was thinking about the future. I didn't want anything to go to waste. And I guess I just... I made the wrong call. But I tried."

Riley tensed his grip and shook his head. Anna appeared beside him from the staircase and stared ahead at Ivan as he stumbled in their direction.

"I tried. You know that, don't you?"

"You sick fuck," Riley said. "You... You are sick. Truly sick."

"And yet you didn't tell 'your' people when you had the opportunity. You had the chance to walk out of this corridor and into that canteen there and tell everybody a couple of hours ago. And yet you didn't. Why is that? No, wait. I'll answer that. It's because you know all of this made sense. Horrible sense."

Riley shook his head. Barney and Chloë joined Riley outside the canteen door. Ted was still lurching somewhere on the floor above them.

Ivan got closer and closer to them. More cold air clouded out of the freezer room door.

"You're holding on to something that's dying, Ivan," Riley said. He held his hands up and pointed at the medal-laden walls. "You're holding on to a dream. We all have been. We're all guilty of that. But we have to leave these walls at some stage. You know that."

"No," Ivan said. He shook his head. "You see, that's where you're wrong. There's—there's enough in there to last us the winter."

"And what about when the winter ends?" Riley shouted.

Ivan's gaze moved around the rest of the group. Looked at Barney. Looked at Anna. Then fixed on Chloë for a few seconds. "We... Then we decide. Who's strongest. And who's... who's willing to help us sustain our society."

Anna's jaw had dropped so much that it looked like it was scraping the floor. "You... You're fucking insane. You're a fucking lunatic."

Ivan shrugged. "Maybe. Maybe not. But aren't we all in this new world? Don't we all *have* to embrace a bit of lunacy to survive? Especially when you're leading. Like me. You have to make the tough decisions. Everybody knows that."

Riley backed up into the others behind him. Claudia was still in the canteen with Pedro and Chef, struggling to break free and shout out. "We're going to walk. We're going to leave this place and you aren't going to try and stop us."

Ivan laughed. He frowned and shook his head. His laughter was so sincere that it was chilling. "Why do you think we brought you here in the first place, hmm? I mean, it wasn't ideal having to… to do what we did to the troops. To the weaker ones. But we never intended that, not at first. Did you really think we'd just move on out of those walls to—to save people? To save you?"

Anna's jaw shook. Her cheeks had turned so red that they were bordering on purple. "You… You didn't want anything with us."

Ivan rolled his eyes. "Anna. Dear, dear Anna. Of course we wanted something with you. We wanted something with you from the moment we had a scout cycle outside that lovely restaurant you were shacked up in. We wanted something very important from you. Your… your contributions." His wide eyes scanned her bare skin on her neck. Her perfectly slender legs.

Thoughts spiraled around Riley's head. He remembered Aaron's words at Stan's dairy farm. *"The dead squirrels around the farm first thing this morning."*

"You… The dairy farm. And the horde that—that attacked the Chinese. You were responsible for that?"

Ivan tilted his head from side to side. "'Responsible' would be flattering. But we had somebody run a very successful job. Just a pity that tensions flared later that evening, huh? Maybe some of our soldiers didn't have to die. But there weren't enough of you to last us the winter. Not after all your little heroic missions."

Riley was speechless. The Labrador outside the Chinese restaurant when they'd first arrived. The way the horde of creatures had stumbled out of nowhere and attacked their countryside Chinese restaurant home. The lives that had been lost. All of it, linked. Linked by a psychopath who just wanted an endless supply of food for his troops. And then killed the bulk of his troops anyway.

"But you proved me wrong, to your credit," Ivan said. He stopped at the wall and leaned against it. "Proved to me that you were good people. We had a nice couple of weeks, didn't we?"

Riley shook his head. He wanted to beat Ivan to a pulp. Torture him for the things he'd done. For the loss of life he'd caused. "We're supposed to be human. We're supposed to be different to them."

"And we still can be. Well, at least, the soldiers of mine who aren't awake can be. How many is that? I make it eight. Nine. Enough."

"They won't trust a word that comes out of your mouth," Barney said. His lips quivered. Tears streamed down his cheeks from his bloodshot eyes. "You killed 'em. Killed our own. Won't trust a word."

Ivan's cheek twitched. "Oh really?" He reached into his pocket. "We'll see about that."

He lifted a pistol and he fired at Barney's stomach.

Barney tumbled onto his knees. He stared at the bloody mark on his shirt with confusion, then looked back over at Ivan. Ivan rushed over to him and cradled his head.

"Ssh, now," Ivan said. He lowered Barney to the floor. "Hush. It'll be over soon. It'll be over."

Barney winced and smacked his head against the floor as he gripped the slowly bleeding hole in his stomach. Ivan looked up at the group. Chloë hid behind Anna. Ted continued to heave at the stairs. Everybody was in shock.

"I suggest you walk into that canteen right now and start making your excuses fast," Ivan said.

Footsteps sounded above. The remaining soldiers inevitably awakened by the gunshot.

Ivan held the gun against Barney's head. Barney's eyeballs rolled upwards as he coughed up thick blood and tensed his body with the extreme pain. "The rest of my men aren't going to be happy when they see what you've done to poor old Barney."

He pulled the trigger. Riley flinched. Ivan closed Barney's eyes and sighed. Then, he checked the gun and pulled the trigger another couple of times. Empty. He stuffed the gun into Riley's top pocket and squared up to him. "Better run."

Riley, Anna, and Chloë rushed into the canteen area. Pedro and Chef swung around, surprise on their faces.

"We know," Riley said as he approached them. "No bullshit. We know."

Pedro let go of Claudia and threw her back to the floor. "Fuck. Fuck."

Chloë rushed over to her mother and into her arms.

"Oh, my darling. I'm glad you're okay. I'm glad you're okay." She looked over her daughter's shoulder. Her eyes were black underneath. "They... My Elizabeth. They've... I saw her. I—"

"I know," Riley said. He glared at Pedro and Chef. Chef's white apron was splattered with blood. "We all know."

Footsteps clanged down the stairway. Voices shouted out.

"Pedro," Riley said. He stepped up to Pedro and stared him directly in his eyes. "I know there's... somewhere deep down, there's a good man in there. The man I sat atop the wall with. The man I confided in. I know he's in you, somewhere."

Pedro's eyes teared up as the voices and commotion grew louder in the corridor. He wiped his cheek then opened his mouth. "I—"

The door clattered open. Ivan and four soldiers walked in. They had anger spread across their faces. Gripped onto guns that Riley hadn't even known about.

And at the foot of the door, Riley could just about make out Barney's body, as thick blood trickled out of his skull and stained between the cracks of the tiles.

"What's... what's happened?" Chef asked.

Ivan raised a finger. Pointed it directly at Riley. "This man. And her. That bitch. They killed him. They killed Barney."

Pedro took a step back. He shook his head. "Barney? But... Oh shit. Oh, shit, shit, shit."

"It didn't happen like that," Riley pleaded. "Seriously."

"Then how the fuck did it happen?" Pedro asked. He

pushed his forehead up to Riley's.

"You know how it happened," Riley said. "You know damn well what's going on here—"

A gunshot rattled through the room. Gaz had his pistol raised up towards the spotlights on the ceiling. "I think we should deal with them right now. Make 'um pay for what they did."

Riley backed up. Anna followed. "Please," Riley said. "You have to see what's going on—"

"Shut up." Riley felt something smack across his face. Tasted metal in his mouth, as Pedro knocked him to the ground. His head stung with the sharp pain of the butt of the gun. He looked up at Ivan, who was approaching, slowly.

"I don't think you're wrong," Ivan said. He had another gun in his hand. A handgun almost identical to the one he'd killed Barney with. He aimed it at Riley. The other soldiers looked on, guns raised. They were screwed. There was no escape. This was it.

He lowered the gun and pressed it again Riley's forehead as Pedro covered Riley's mouth. He tried to struggle from side to side, but it was in vain. "I think we should make this one suffer. I think we should make him pay for what he's done. Gaz — give me the knife."

Gaz lowered his gun nervously. "But... But Ivan—"

"Give me the fucking knife."

Gaz hesitated then reached into his pocket. He pulled out a large knife with serrated edges. Tossed it over to Ivan, who weighed it up in his hands.

"Please, don't—" Anna begged, before going silent as another of the soldiers wrapped a hand around her mouth and held her down, gun to her head. Claudia mumbled. Chloë mumbled. All of them were silenced, and they'd soon be silenced in a completely different way. A final way.

Ivan approached Riley, knife in hand. "Now lift his shirt."

Riley screamed out against the material that Pedro had stuffed into his mouth and tried to shake from side to side.

Pedro pulled Riley's shirt up and exposed his skinny chest. There was no getting away. Struggling would only make things worse. There was no getting away from Ivan's approach. From the anger in his eyes.

Ivan crouched down in front of Riley and tapped the sharp metal blade against Riley's bony chest. Riley could feel his heart plummeting against his ribcage. He could see it, too. See it as the knife approached. And he'd see it as the knife stuck into him, blood spilling from the hole between his ribs.

"Treat this as a lesson," Ivan said. His bottom lip shook as he twirled the knife between his fingers. "A lesson to mind your own business. A lesson to… to trust those who trust you. Yeah. To believe in people. To know when it's your turn to just let things progress behind the scenes. Huh? You listening to me?" He slapped the side of the knife against Riley's right cheekbone. "You need to learn where your leadership ends and where mine starts." He pressed the blunt edge of the blade against Riley's pale, exposed skin. It tickled him with the coldness. "But I guess none of that will matter anymore. Right."

He flipped the blade over and sliced Riley's chest.

Riley wasn't sure what to make of the sensation at first. The first thing he noticed was just how much blood must have been in that one small area of his chest, as Ivan worked the knife further and further across his skin, scratching against the muscle and bone. It didn't look like it was happening to him. It looked like he was just a spectator to somebody else's misfortune.

But then the pain started to kick in as his brain overcame the initial shock.

He screamed at the top of his lungs into the material that Pedro was holding across his mouth. He clenched his eyelids. The whole room seemed to blur into the background, like it was just him and the pain. The hot, sharp, searing pain, spreading right through his body.

"Ivan, don't you think that's—"

"Shut up," Ivan said. He pulled the bloody blade away and wiped it against his uniform. Then, he brought it back towards Riley's chest. "We're just getting started."

Riley's heart raced as tears of blood slipped down his chest. His body shook like a malfunctioning machine as he struggled and struggled to break free. He couldn't take another bout of that pain. He just couldn't do it.

He focused on the shuffling feet in the room. The sounds of muffled cries and soldiers muttering to one another. The distant humming of the generator down the corridor. Ivan's breaths, short and throaty, as he prepared to stick the knife back into Riley's chest.

He'd be home soon. The job he'd started when he'd driven that car into that wall at the speed he had. The closing of his eyes as the impending death got closer and closer. He knew that feeling. It was familiar to him. He'd experienced death already, or the closest thing to it.

Only this time, there was no coming back.

As he held his breath, he noticed one of the sounds give way.

The hum of the generator.

He opened his eyes. The room had been bathed in darkness. Complete, total darkness. Voices became audible. Anna's voice. Claudia's voice. The soldiers, whispering and chattering to one another in confusion.

"What the fuck's going on?"

"Where'd the lights go?"

In the distance, Riley heard another noise. It was a noise he hadn't heard all that often since they'd got inside the barracks, but he remembered it from that first day they'd got here. The screeching against the ground.

"Oh fuck. Fuck." It was Ivan. He moved away. His silhouette stepped up against the window and peered out. "That fat fucker. That fat fucking bastard."

"What is it, Ivan?" Pedro asked. "What's going on?"

But Ivan didn't need to respond, because Riley understood

what was happening already. He knew what the sound was. He remembered it so vividly. The generator hum had disappeared. The lights had gone out. And the gates were opening.

Riley laughed. He shouldn't have laughed, but it felt completely right. Tears of joy streamed down his face. Relief at surviving death twice. He disregarded the searing pain in his chest as the tears dripped against his exposed flesh.

"What the fuck is—"

"Ted's switched off the generator," Riley said. He laughed again as the whispers started to pick up around the room. "He's switched off the generator and tripped the gates and—and now you're fucked."

A loud thump echoed through the courtyard as the gates finished opening.

And the groans started to approach.

Chapter Forty

"FUCK," IVAN SHOUTED. THE COMMOTION WAS at full force in the canteen area. The conflicts and preoccupations of moments ago slipped away into the background. It had gone from humans against humans to humans against the threat outside the walls. The threat staggering in through the front gates. No matter what issues the group had with one another — no matter what pain Ivan had caused that seared through Riley's chest — they had to deal with the most immediate threat. Fast.

A lamp came to life to Riley's left. It made him realise just how affected his vision was. The pain was getting to his head. It still hurt in his chest, sure. But it was the nausea that hit him most. The dizziness. The feeling of just wanting to lie down and sleep for days. Weeks. Forever.

Chef shined the blue-tinted fluorescent lamp around the room. The soldiers had backed off from Riley's group, but Anna was still on her knees, wide-eyed. Claudia and Chloë held one another's hand.

"The fat shit has done this. He's fucking done this." Ivan stepped from side to side scratching his head.

"That's not what we worry about right now," Pedro said. He pointed out of the window. In the moonlight, the creatures were walking in through the gates and heading in the direction of the wing they were in. They must have heard the gunshots. The commotion. They heard a lot, that much was certain.

Ivan stepped up to Pedro and grabbed the scuff of his neck. His hands were soaked with Riley's blood. "You don't tell me what to worry about. Don't you fucking dare tell me what to worry about. I'll worry about what I want."

"I'm just saying," Pedro said. The other four soldiers looked at one another, uncertain. "We have a threat heading right through our gates. It's hard to tell how many there are. But we need to deal with them. Or at least decide what we're going to do before we—"

Ivan pushed Pedro back. He turned to the rest of the group, his face lit up by Chef's lamplight. "Then deal with them."

The remaining soldiers shuffled their feet. Gaz took a fearful glance out of the window. "But they… It's dark. And those things, they—"

"If you want to save this place, you'll deal with them." He stormed over to the door of the canteen.

"And where are you going?" Anna shouted.

Ivan turned to face her and his nostrils twitched with disgust. He looked as if he had forgotten she and the rest of the group were in the room, even though Riley's blood still dripped from his knife. "I've got business to attend to. Now get the fuck out of here and see to those invaders if you want to survive." He stormed through the double door and disappeared down the corridor.

Riley's heart thumped. He knew where Ivan was going. He knew what the business was he was attending to. Ted. He had to find him before Ivan did. Find him then get the hell out of here while they still had some sort of chance. Maybe even their best chance.

But he was losing blood. His chest was burning up. He wasn't going to make it, not without medical assistance.

"Well, what are you waiting for?" Chef said. The words slipped off his tongue like grease. Even with everything that was going on, he still seemed as manipulative and scheming as ever.

Gaz exchanged a glance with Pedro, who in return took a deep breath and nodded at the other soldiers as they gripped their guns.

"What are you doing while we're out there?" one of the soldiers asked.

Chef placed the lamp on one of the canteen tables and shone it up against the ceiling. He looked at Riley. At Anna. At Claudia and Chloë. "I'll deal with our guests."

The soldiers grumbled and headed towards the door.

"I don't know how you can do this," Anna shouted at Pedro. "After everything we've been through. Everything we've worked together for."

Pedro looked back at her. He smiled sympathetically. "Sorry, love. Sorry."

He closed the door and, with the rest of the soldiers, ran outside to deal with the growing crowd of creatures, like blots in the horizon. They had no idea how many of them there were, but Riley figured from the loudness of the groans at that distance that they were dealing with more than just a couple of lone stragglers.

Anna raised to her feet. She looked around at the blood dripping from Riley's chest, then turned to Chef. A bewildered expression covered her face, as well as the blue florescent lamp. "You can't just keep us here. You can't—"

Chef pulled a bandage out from the front of the canteen with his shaky hands. He dropped it to the floor and cursed before picking it up again and crouching opposite Riley.

Riley frowned. "What are... what are you—"

"When Ivan finds your friend, he's going to gut him. He's going to take his guts out and spread them all over the walls as a reminder of what happens when somebody defies him. I don't want that to happen." He pressed the bandage against Riley's chest which sent a sharp stabbing pain right through his body.

"Why are you doing this?" Anna asked. Claudia and Chloë were silent. They held one another. They looked like mother and child again, confiding instead of bickering. After what Claudia had seen in the freezer room, she needed her daughter right now.

Chef finished applying the bandage to Riley's chest. "Now I can't promise that won't get infected. Fortunately for you, he didn't cut too deep. But all we can do for now is stop the bleeding. Especially now we've lost Barney."

Riley frowned. Chef looked more humane than he'd ever looked. Sweat coated his bald head like condensation on a window.

"You didn't answer my question," Anna said.

Chef stood back up. He wiped the blood from his hands onto his already bloody apron. The footsteps sounded outside the barracks. Gunshots started to fire and specks of light glistened in the distance, over by the main gate. "It doesn't matter why I'm doing it. Just that I am doing it. We've lost enough humanity as it is. With... with the things I've done. Just save your friend and get the hell out of this place. I'll deal with the repercussions. I always do." He held a hand out to Riley.

Riley examined it. The hand that had cut up the bodies. Thrown them into a stew. The hand of a man that was responsible for so many bad things. A man that seemed shady right from the start. But the offer of a hand regardless in the toughest and most loyalty questioning of times.

Riley grabbed Chef's hand and winced as he rose to his feet.

"It will hurt for some time. But you know what you need to do right now. You know."

Riley nodded. He held Chef's hand for a few seconds after he'd made it to his feet. His knees were wobbly like jelly, but he was on his feet. He was alive. He still had a chance here, they all did.

"What about the rest of us?" Claudia asked. "What do we do?"

Chef clattered around the canteen counter as the explosions of gunshots rattled through the serene nighttime air. He pulled a set of keys out of a drawer and shook them. "This is a key to the basement passage. It'll take you right out to the main gate. It's not safe right now, but it's the best chance you're going to get."

"Basement passage?" Anna asked. "Since when was there a basement passage in this place?"

Chef threw the keys at Anna, who caught them. "Only problem is you... you have to go through the freezer room to get there. Emergency exit of sorts. Underground safe spot in case of crisis."

"And what about you?" Claudia asked.

Chef sighed and shrugged. "I figure I'll have to explain your absence. If anyone can calm Ivan down, it's me."

Anna stuffed the keys in her pocket and nodded. She didn't thank Chef, but a nod of the head was enough coming from her.

Riley stumbled towards the door. He could feel the strength returning to his legs with every step he took, but he wasn't sure for how long that was going to be the case.

Anna placed a hand on his back as he reached the double doors leading out to the corridor. "You be careful," she said. "And if we don't see you again—"

"Get into that basement passage," Riley said.

Tears built up in Anna's eyes. "But... But if we do, we might have to leave. We might get split up."

Riley looked around the room and rubbed at the bandage

on his chest. "Then so be it. Just get to safety. I need to find my friend. I need to help him. Don't wait for me."

He pushed through the double doors and turned towards the staircase.

When he looked back at the double doors, swinging as they shut, he saw Anna staring back at him, fear in her eyes.

"Be tough," Riley muttered under his breath. "Be tough."

Riley staggered over Barney's body and out into the corridor. The gunshots and cries from outside were totally audible inside these walls. He'd check the generator room then he'd go up the stairs. Go upstairs and look for Ted in the darkness. Hope he got to him before Ivan did.

And if he didn't, at least try and make Ivan see sense. He was human, after all. He'd done some terrible things. The pain in his chest said enough about that. But things had reached a climax. They didn't need to go any further. Riley and his group could walk out of here through that basement and never turn back.

But somehow, Riley couldn't imagine Ivan agreeing to let potential meals on a plate walk out the front door all that easily.

He reached the end of the corridor, being sure not to look inside the freezer room as he passed. The generator room was empty. The humming noise had receded. Riley held his breath. Closed his eyes and squinted as he tried to hear through the buzzing noise in his ears and the commotion outside.

Nothing.

He turned away and walked to the stairs. Turns out Ted's interest in electrics and computers had come in handy after all. If Ted had interrupted the generator, chances are he'd hidden somewhere. Climbed out of a window or locked himself in a room. But Riley needed to know. For certain.

He pulled himself up the staircase, gripping the railing. The slice on his chest ached and throbbed as he ascended. He took a few breaths. He could handle the pain. It could have been worse. And it could still get worse. But while it was the way it was, he had to find Ted.

When he reached the top of the staircase, he stared down the corridor. The window at the end of the corridor let in a small amount of light from the starlit sky. The doors on the left and the right — bathrooms, living quarters — were mostly shut. He crept across the creaky wooden floorboards. Ivan had to be here somewhere, and so did Ted. He couldn't have got too far away.

He held his breath as he pushed open the door to their bedroom. He thought he saw a movement in the corner of his eye, and swung back round to look down the corridor. Nothing. Just a trick of the light. Just the darkness playing tricks.

But then he heard the floorboards creaking in one of the rooms on the right.

The tingling sensation that he'd grown so accustomed to engulfed his body, wrapping him in a blanket of pins and needles. But that didn't matter anymore. He could pull through that. Deal with it. It was only a mental thing, anyway. He crept down the corridor. The floorboards were definitely creaking in there. Somebody was inside.

Riley jumped as he heard the double doors swing open downstairs. It would be Anna, Claudia and Chloë leaving through the basement door. He'd join them later. That was the only way for it. He had something else to see to right now.

He placed his hand on the cold, hard wood of the door to the room with the creaky floorboards. Something was still moving in there. It could be Ivan, searching for Ted. If he saw Riley, he'd finish him off, just like that.

Or it could be Ted. Hiding. He was a heavy guy, so it made sense that the floorboards might creak if he were moving around.

Riley bit his lip. Nerves held his chest and stomach tightly. He needed to go inside. He needed to see.

He pushed the door open.

At first, the dim glow of the light took him by surprise. There was a candle burning on a table beside a window. Wax dribbled down the side of the holder. It was a smaller living quarters, with just two bunk beds and wooden floorboards.

And at the opposite end of the room, by the window, Ivan was holding a knife to Ted's neck.

Ted's eyes were filled with fear. He tried to shuffle free of Ivan's grip, but whenever he moved, the sharp edge of the knife nicked his skin.

Riley was completely still. He couldn't move. His heart raced. He had to play this right.

Ivan looked up from Ted to Riley. His jaw was shaking and he was exhaling loudly as he held the knife against Ted's neck. Tears streamed down Ted's cheeks and snot spewed out of his nostrils. He blubbered, trying to speak, but he couldn't.

"Please," Riley said. He felt completely weak, seeing his friend in this situation. Fear surrounded him. He couldn't think rationally. He hadn't prepared for this.

Ivan tried to smile at Riley. A reassuring half-smile. He was crying too, as the gunshots and screaming outside drifted into the background.

"We need to defend this place," Riley said. He raised his hand and took a step towards Ivan. "We… We can start again. It doesn't have to be like this."

Ivan sniffed and kept the knife against Ted's neck. "I worked so hard. We all did. Worked so hard for—for things just to be normal. Just for a little longer."

"And they still can be," Riley said. He took another step closer to Ivan. Ted's breathing was calming. Becoming more rhythmic. He'd sealed his mouth shut and he wasn't talking or muttering anymore.

Ivan edged the knife away slightly. Nodded his head. "Yes. Yes."

"That's right," Riley said. He reached out for Ivan. He'd grab the knife. Take it away from him. Do what he had to do. "Just… Just put that down. Please."

Ivan moved the knife further away then stopped. He looked Riley in the eye. The room seemed to freeze. "I'm sorry. But there's no going back."

He brought the knife back to Ted's neck and he slit his throat.

Riley rushed towards Ted. Everything felt like it was moving in slow-motion. Riley screamed out at the top of his lungs. The pain vanished from his chest. Everything else in the room — the candle, the bunk beds, even Ivan — blended into the murky background.

Ted fell to his knees and then to his back. Blood splurged out of his neck. He looked up in fear, trying to speak, but couldn't for the mass of blood in his throat.

Riley gripped hold of him. Grabbed his big, damp, sweaty shoulders. "Please, Ted. Please. Please."

But Ted's spluttering slowed down. His struggling grew more and more half-hearted. Quarter-hearted. Eighth-hearted.

"Please, Ted," Riley said, holding his head against Ted's chest. "Please."

Ted's arm stopped flailing and moving.

The spluttering stopped.

Ted was still. Completely still.

Episode Six

Chapter Forty-One

THE GUNSHOTS OUTSIDE THE BARRACKS GOT louder and louder. So, too, did the screams. The shouts. The orders as the groans got closer. There could be tens of them. Hundreds of them. It could be the group from earlier that had wandered in the direction of the mother and child, torn the dead flesh from their bodies. It could be another group.

But none of it seemed to matter.

Riley held his head against Ted's chest. He wasn't sure how long he'd been there. He waited for a breath. Kept his eyes tightly shut and waited for Ted's heartbeat to return, like it always seemed to in Hollywood movie characters. Ted was his friend. His best friend. His only friend. He couldn't be gone. There was no world without Ted.

He heard footsteps creak past him. He knew whose footsteps they were. He knew exactly what he had done. What he'd done to Ted. He knew exactly what he wanted to do to him for it. To ram a knife into his skull. To beat him repeatedly into the ground.

But he couldn't do it. He pushed his head into Ted's chest. He had to wait for a heartbeat. Waited for him to wake up. Like in the movies.

The door to the bedroom creaked open. As it did, the gunshots and commotion outside seemed to amplify. It must have been bad. The creatures must have heard the gunshots from the barracks earlier, or Claudia's screams, or both. Ted had sent the generator into meltdown somehow. His final act a selfless means of distraction. He'd paid the ultimate price. He hadn't survived. That was all there was to this world now — survival. There was no room for selfless acts.

But Ted had saved them all.

"I am sorry. Sorry I had to do that."

The voice was muffled and the words jumbled as they entered Riley's ears. He lifted his head from Ted's body. His face had turned pale, and thick, dark blood reflected from the deep gash across his neck in the glimmer of the candlelight. His eyes were wide and lifeless, like stones. Eyes that had played so many video games; eyes that had seen Riley at his lowest points and helped him pull through. All of those experiences and images, gone.

Riley turned around. Ivan was standing by the door. He was pale, too, as he fidgeted with the bloody knife in his hand. He stared down at Ted's body, totally fixated, almost as if he himself couldn't believe what he'd done.

"I was just really angry," Ivan said. His lips shook. "Really, really angry at him. For what he did. For letting them inside. Careless. Careless." Saliva dribbled down his chin. He looked like a rabid dog as he attempted to justify his actions to himself.

Riley's shock began to boil into anger. Every muscle in his body felt as if wire had tightened around them. "You—you murdered him. You murdered him." Talking wasn't easy. Saying the words out loud added a reality to the situation. Ted was gone. Dead. Never coming back.

Ivan moved his head from side to side. He took a sharp, deep breath in through his nostrils and nodded. "I did what I had to do. For the safety of the group. For the safety of—"

Riley shot to his feet. He was possessed with rage. The vein in his head pulsated. "You killed him. Fucking killed him. My friend. My—my best friend. You fucker. You fucker." He threw himself towards Ivan.

Ivan took a step back and raised the knife but Riley threw himself at him anyway. His mind only wanted one thing, and that was Ivan to pay for what he'd done. He plummeted against Ivan, barely missing his knife, and pushed him to the ground. The gash on his chest stung, but it didn't matter.

"You fucking killed him," Riley shouted. He held Ivan by the scruff of his collar and thumped him in the eye. It cracked his fingers. Riley's chest seared with pain as Ivan dug his fingernails into him and pushed Riley back as he made another swing at Ivan's face. "You—you killed Ted. You killed Ted."

Ivan threw Riley off him and pressed him down against the floor with his forearm across his neck. His eyes were bloodshot and the skin surrounding his eye was beginning to bruise from Riley's punch. But he had the strength. He held Riley down. "And I'm going to do it to the rest of you. I'm going to—"

Something clattered downstairs. The previously unclear gunshots and shouting became much more vibrant. Much closer.

"*Get back inside!*" one of the guards shouted.

Ivan frowned. He turned to look down the corridor, keeping Riley pinned onto the floor. Riley attempted to scramble free of Ivan's strong grip, but it was no use.

The gunshots built in number and in clarity. More voices entered the barracks.

"*There's too many of them!*" another voice shouted. "*Back inside.*"

Ivan stared down at Riley. He looked preoccupied,

mumbling barely audible words. "Got to protect... can't come inside..."

Riley continued to scramble free of Ivan. "You'll pay for this. You'll fucking—"

Out of nowhere, Ivan yanked Riley to his feet and propped him up against the doorway. It was as if he had found a sudden bout of strength and energy; a determination to protect the sick fantasy world of the barracks that he had built.

"You won't—" Riley's words faded out as Ivan pushed him further back into the room. "You won't—"

Ivan threw him onto the ground. He grabbed the door handle and lifted his gun out of his pocket. "You'll stay right here. I'll be back for you."

Then, he slammed the door shut.

Riley stared up at the door as the lock made a clicking sound. Ivan's footsteps resonated further down the corridor and down the staircase, towards the shouting, towards the nearing groans.

Riley was alone again. Alone with Ted.

Alone.

Chapter Forty-Two

IVAN WIPED THE SWEAT FROM HIS head as he walked down the stairs and stepped over Barney's body. He swallowed the lump in his throat. Shame about what he'd had to do to Barney. But sometimes casualties were necessary to maintain the greater good. Sometimes, to keep order, you had to bypass order.

As he pushed through the double doors, he noticed a print of blood from his hand. Ted's blood. He'd slit his throat because he had to do that. Ted had destroyed the security of the barracks. He'd compromised everything they'd worked so hard for. Why couldn't anybody else see that Ivan had done what was necessary? Why did nobody else understand that?

When he stepped into the canteen area, lit up by a fluorescent light, he noticed five of his men were inside. Two of them — Gaz and Al — propped up against the door that led out into the courtyard. Stocky leaned against the back wall, exhaling rapidly as Pedro watched over him. Chef stood behind the canteen.

"What's going on here?" Ivan asked.

His voice seemed to catch their immediate attention. They all swung around with fearful eyes as he walked into the canteen. Pedro examined him from head to toe. Ivan looked down at his body. His hands were covered in blood. His uniform was similarly soaked. Blood of necessary casualties. Necessary sacrifices.

"They're getting too close," Gaz shouted. He pointed at the window with a shaky hand. "The zombies — there's too many of them. Way too many."

Ivan walked over to the window beside Gaz and Al and stared outside. Guns were firing sporadic bullets around the courtyard. The grass was covered with corpses. Some dead. Some not so dead. The path to the gateway was completely blocked. The fat fuck had succeeded. The barracks was invaded.

"Ivan, I'm sorry," Gaz said, "but we're going to have to get a move on out of here if we want to survive. We can take the underground route. At least then we'll have a shot at getting away. But we have to move. Quick."

Ivan's eyelids twitched. All the sacrifices he'd made just to secure this place. All the things he'd done — terrible things in the eyes of somebody from the old world. He hadn't done all those things just to give it all up. They could fight for this place. The battle wasn't lost, not yet.

He lifted his gun out of his pocket and moved over to the door.

"Ivan, what are you—"

"We're going to go out there and we're going to fight those things. We don't have to lose this place."

Al frowned and shook his head. "You're mad. Even if we clear the yard, there's the gates and the power. It's gone. It's all gone, and we—"

Ivan fired a bullet into Al's head.

The rest of the room jumped back in shock.

"We're going to defend this place," Ivan said nonchalantly.

He walked over to the canteen area and tapped his gun on the counter that Chef stood behind. "Where are the others?"

Chef straightened his back and raised his eyebrows. He stared directly into Ivan's eyes. "What others?"

Ivan's jaw tensed. The groans were drowning out the gunshots outside. Soon, they'd be the only ones left. They had to use what they could. Use bait. Human bait. "You know who I mean. Anna. Claudia. Chloë. Where are they?"

Chef gulped. His eyes watered. He kept focused on Ivan. Not many people could hold Ivan's stare for too long. Not many people dared. Wise of them. "I guess they must have slipped away," Chef said.

Heat worked its way into Ivan's cheeks. The fucker. The disloyal piece of shit. After all this time — all the things he'd done and kept secret. The bodies. The food he'd cooked. All this time, and Chef was nothing but a weak piece of shit after all.

But still, he stood his ground. Stared back at Ivan. Didn't budge, other than his twitching nostrils and quivering fingers.

Ivan stepped away from Chef and turned to the rest of the soldiers. They were still shell-shocked, staring down at Al's dead body. The creatures were so close to them now. Probably a matter of metres away from the door. They'd see the fluorescent light. They'd have heard the gunshots and the voices inside.

But it didn't matter anymore. Because Ivan had an idea.

"We—we need to go," Pedro called. "Whatever's happened is done. But we need to get out of here before they—"

A force rattled against the door. Gaz jumped back and ran over to the double doors of the canteen. He raised his gun and pointed it at the doorway, which continued to rattle as groans built up behind it. "Shit. Shit."

Ivan looked back at Chef. Held his stare. "You were a good man, Chef. You did good here. Made some good food. Somebody I trusted."

Chef didn't respond, but he held Ivan's stare. Ivan

wondered if Chef had an idea of what was going to happen to him. He must have done to stay here. Defy him like this.

But that just made it all the more exciting.

"You know, nobody will remember you as a hero," Ivan said. The door rattled on its hinges. The wood started to split.

"Guys, come on. Let's just go," Stocky shouted. "We need to get out of here some way."

Ivan moved in closer to Chef. He could feel him breathing against his skin. Quick, nervous breaths. He could smell the fear from a mile away, like a rabbit staring back at a wild dog.

"Ivan," Pedro called. "The door isn't going to hold much longer. We need to go."

"Oh, I'm coming," Ivan said. "I'm coming."

Then, he lifted his knife out of his pocket and stuffed it into Chef's flabby leg.

Chef collapsed to the floor and curled to his side. Blood sprayed out of his chubby leg as he wrapped his fingers around it and cried out.

Ivan crouched down beside him. The banging at the door was joined by rattling at the window. Ivan pushed Chef's bald head into the floor with as much force as he could. He smiled. "I'll remember you, though, don't you worry. I'll remember you for what you're about to do. The sacrifice you're about to make."

He lifted the knife and stabbed it into Chef's other leg.

Chef cried out and gripped both of his knees as Ivan rose to his feet. He walked past the door as pale hands started to reveal themselves. He walked past the window which cracked with the weight and number of creatures trying to push their way inside. He stopped at the double doorway leading out to the corridor and took one last look at Chef, who tried to struggle to his feet as blood oozed out of both legs.

"I'll remember you. Hero." He pulled the double door shut as the window finally gave way.

As Gaz, Pedro, Stocky, and Ivan walked down the corridor, Chef screamed out at the top of his lungs.

A necessary casualty. A worthy sacrifice. Hero.

Riley stared down at Ted's body. He tried to forget he was dead. Hoped that while he'd been preoccupied with fighting Ivan, he'd just come back to life.

But there was nothing left. Nothing.

He walked over to Ted and crouched down beside him. Ted's eyes stared up in fear, but they were devoid of life. Empty shells. His final act a courageous one. Something that benefited the group. Intercepting the generator put everybody at risk, but at the same time, it gave them a shot. Ted had made the tough decision. He knew he might be putting himself at risk in the process, but he'd made that call. He'd died with that call.

Riley reached for Ted's bloodshot eyes and closed the eyelids. He patted Ted's chest. Tried not to notice the deep gash on his neck or the growing pool of blood on the floor. "It's okay now," Riley said. He patted Ted on the chest again. "I'm sorry. I'm sorry."

Riley could hear voices downstairs. Shouting. Bickering. At least Anna, Claudia, and Chloë had a chance to get away. Perhaps Chef joined them. Although he couldn't condone Chef's actions, he'd helped them out. Hopefully. He couldn't overlook him for that.

Rising to his feet, Riley noticed something dripping down his face and onto Ted's white shirt. He was crying. A barrage of guilt crashed into him. If he'd told the group about what he'd seen in the freezer room earlier, then perhaps Ted would never have died. As it stood, Claudia knew about her daughter anyway. The other soldiers were seemingly manipulated into believing that the bodies in the freezer either weren't there, or they were killed for their curiosity. Poor Barney.

A gunshot rattled through the building. It came from the canteen. Ivan would be back for him soon. He'd come back for him and he'd finish him. He looked at his chest. A bandage covered the wound. He was fortunate that the cut hadn't been as deep as it could have been.

And then he saw Ted's static body on the floor opposite him and he realised nobody was fortunate. Not at all.

Riley placed his head into his hands. He wanted to break down and destroy Ivan for what he'd done. Tears were streaming from his eyes, but they seemed weak considering he'd just witnessed the death of his best friend. He felt nothing but anger. Guilt and anger. The same emotions he'd felt when he'd got into that car all those months ago and he'd driven it into that wall, hoping to take his own life. The same guilt and anger as when he found out he was a father.

No. Don't think about that. Not now.

Another gunshot sounded from the canteen. He could sense everything falling apart down there. Ivan turning against everybody, one by one.

Or maybe they were turning against him. He didn't know. He didn't particularly care. Not anymore.

He sniffed back his tears and took another glance at Ted's body. The candle on the wooden table started to reach its end. Soon, he'd be plunged into darkness. If he squinted enough, maybe it would just seem like he was back at the flat again. Back at the flat or the Chinese restaurant. Back in the living quarters of the barracks when everything seemed okay.

All of that was gone now. All of that was false. Things would never be the same again.

He looked around the room in the fading candlelight. A third shot sounded, followed by a loud scream. He could hear something else. A door creaking, or a window cracking. The gunshots outside had stopped now. The soldiers out there had either died fighting or ran away. Riley wasn't sure which fate was worse, after all.

He placed a hand on Ted's leg. Quite fitting that they were going to die in the same room. But there was no coming back to life in here. It wasn't a computer game. They didn't get a second chance.

As he looked back at Ted, Riley noticed something poking

out of his pocket. He reached over to it. It was the spanner he'd fought the creatures with back when they were defending the Chinese restaurant, before it burned down. Riley picked it up and turned it in his hand. Ted must have used it to interfere with the generator in some way. Riley avoided looking back at Ted's greying face. He couldn't see it again. Not now. The image would never leave him, anyway.

Footsteps echoed through the corridor downstairs. In the canteen, an even louder scream escaped the double doors. It sounded like Chef.

And it was soon drowned out by an army of groans.

"Out through the freezer."

The voice sent goose bumps down Riley's arms. Ivan. He was going through the underground route. From the sounds of things, he was trying to abandon his ship. He was going to get what he deserved. No — he didn't deserve a thing. He only deserved to be eaten a thousand times. He only deserved sharp, snapped off teeth to sink into his skin and tear every piece of flesh from his body. He only deserved the worst death imaginable.

The candlelight flickered out. A plume of smoke rose from it. The room was engulfed in total darkness.

Riley gripped the spanner to his chest and he waited. It would be over soon. It would all end soon. There was no other way about it, not anymore.

Ivan stormed down the corridor. Riley was upstairs, but he didn't matter right now. He'd go back to him later. He would find a new purpose for him. A greater purpose. He needed a change of plan. A change in his tactics. He'd been clumsy. Acting rashly and foolishly. He couldn't afford to do that anymore.

"So we're just going out of this place? Leaving through the passageway?" Gaz looked over his shoulder. The zombies were just behind the double doors. Soon, they would flood the corridor. Unless they got into the passageway fast, they'd be dead. And then undead.

Ivan stopped by the freezer room door. He stared inside. The bodies of his old colleagues stacked atop one another, legs and arms intertwined. He used to feel a sense of disgust for what he'd done. A sense of guilt and disbelief at his actions. But not anymore. He couldn't afford to. There was a switch inside everybody's heads — a switch monitoring how much a person can take. Ivan had switched that switch off.

If he flicked it on again, he'd die of grief.

Pedro looked inside the freezer room and turned away. His eyes watered. "They aren't gonna like this, Ivan. They aren't gonna—"

Ivan lifted his gun and fired at Gaz. He fired again at Stocky. Both of them were on the ground, clutching their chests as blood poured out of them and to the floor.

Pedro stared down at Stocky and Gaz. Fear drenched his face. He opened his mouth to speak, but no words came out. He looked at Ivan with uncertainty.

"What?" Ivan asked, reaching down and stuffing their guns into his pockets. Stocky and Gaz choked on their blood, struggling for their lives.

Pedro shook his head. Took a step back. "You… You just —"

"Killed them. Right." He turned to the freezer room door. The frozen corpses were starting to look less like humans every time he saw them. A good sign. A sign that his skin was thickening.

Pedro took another step back. "But… They were… They were…"

"They wouldn't have understood." Ivan walked into the freezer room. The bodies were beginning to thaw as the door stood ajar.

The life disappeared from Stocky and Gaz's faces. Gaz reached up his veiny hand towards Ivan, who stared down at it with pity.

The double doors swung open. A zombie stumbled

through. Loose greying flesh dangled from its arms. Its teeth were yellow and rotting.

Pedro stepped back over Stocky's body and stood just behind the freezer room door. He lifted his gun in the direction of the creature, which crouched down at Barney's body and started to investigate. Another creature followed behind. A piece of Chef's pale scalp dangled down its chin.

Ivan placed his hand on Pedro's gun and pushed it down. Pedro flinched with the contact, and stared on with wide eyes.

"What are you...? What are you doing, Ivan? What the fuck are you doing?"

Ivan turned to the pile of bodies. It was unfortunate that he had to make this decision, but it was a necessary one nonetheless.

"We're going to draw them in the freezer room with the bodies," Ivan said. "Lead them inside using Gaz and Stocky. We're going to feed them."

Pedro shook his head. More creatures pushed through the double doors. "You've lost it, bruv. Gone completely fucking crackers."

Ivan smiled. "Perhaps. But we're going to lure them into this freezer room. We're going to cut this wing off if we have to. We're going to go out of the passage and then we're going to bring Anna, Claudia, and her girl back."

"And why would they come back?"

Ivan thought of Riley. He knew there would be a greater purpose for him in the end. A way of utilizing him to his full potential. "We have something of theirs. Something I think they want very much."

"And when they get back here?" Pedro said. One of the creatures noticed him as he shivered beside the door.

Ivan puffed out a breath of cold air. "We're going to kill Riley. And then we're going to start from scratch here. We're going to start a new civilization. It'll take time, but—but it'll be worth it. It'll be ready for these creatures. We'll teach them that way. And Anna, Claudia, and Chloë are going to help us build this new civilization."

Chapter Forty-Three

RILEY WASN'T SURE HOW LONG HE had been bathed in darkness, but almost out of nowhere, a light emerged.

He opened his eyes. The light came from the doorway.

"Get up." It was Pedro. The light came from the tip of his gun. They'd come for him. Come to finish him off.

Riley gripped the spanner tightly and didn't move an inch. He could hear movement downstairs. Shuffling feet. Throaty groans. Pedro must have come through a ladder in the generator room. The corridor sounded inaccessible with groans. And yet they were still trying to keep hold of this place. Still holding on to the tiny hope that somehow, things were all going to be okay.

"I said, get up." Pedro grabbed Riley's upper arm and yanked him to his feet, sending a shooting pain through his chest.

Riley stared Pedro in the eyes. They were dark underneath. The white had turned a shade of grey, protruding blood vessels popping through his eyeballs. "Why are you doing this?" He pointed to Ted. "You know what he is now. You know what he's capable of."

Pedro's lip shook. He held his gun to Riley's chest and sighed. "I… There's no way out of here now. The courtyard's taken. Downstairs is almost beyond saving. But Ivan. He's…"

Riley grabbed Pedro's arm. "I didn't kill Barney. You know that." He kept his hand on his arm. It was a risk in doing so. He had no idea what Pedro was capable of. But he seemed like a man with morals. Fragments of the Pedro he thought he knew were beginning to surface again. He just had to hope that version of Pedro remained. He just had to pray.

Pedro gulped. He lowered his gun. The creatures banged against the walls of the corridor. "Ivan's luring the creatures into the freezer room. Luring them towards the—the bodies. And then he's going to go out there and… Your friends. They aren't safe. He'll find them. He always does."

"Wait — just slow down," Riley said. Confidence was returning to his body. The will to act. The will to survive. "What are you saying?"

"He's… He's going to use you as bait. He's going to use you to lure them back. And then he's going to kill you and he's going to… Anna, Claudia, Chloë. He's talking about starting up civilization again. He can't let go of this place. He's lost it. He's flipped."

A shiver ran through Riley's body. Ivan was going to kill him. And then he was going to use his friends to start his own messed up little civilization. He wasn't acting like a rational man, not anymore. Even the cannibalism had a sick, twisted sort of logic to it. It was within reason. But this was insane.

More banging came from downstairs. The wing must be filled with creatures now, like a shaken bottle of carbonated drink on the verge of bursting.

Riley inhaled deeply. "Then we need to leave him with no choice."

Pedro frowned. Shook his head. "There's nothing we can

do. Even if we... Even if we did something to him, he's drawing the creatures towards our only exit. He'd barricading this place. There's no other way out."

Riley looked at the burned out candle. The flame had long gone out. "How much access to fire do you have in this place?"

Pedro shrugged. "As much as every place. Not enough, if that's what you're wondering. And these walking corpses — they don't die in fire. Not at first, anyway."

Riley thought back to the Chinese restaurant. The way Trevor had lured the creatures in to the flaming building and the way they just kept on walking.

"We're screwed," Pedro said. The groans were deafeningly loud.

The smoke from the burnt out candle was still strong in his nostrils. Or maybe it was just the memory of the Chinese restaurant as it burned to the ground. "And what about explosives?"

Pedro opened his mouth as if to protest, and then he closed it. He knew what Riley was implying. It was written all over his face.

"Ivan's display cabinet. The C4. We're going to cause an explosion. It's going to be our route out and it's going to leave Ivan with nothing."

Riley rushed down the corridor in the opposite direction to the staircase.

"This idea," Pedro said. "It's mad. Almost as mad as Ivan's. It might not work."

"But we have to try something," Riley said. He stopped by the ladder down to the generator room that Pedro had propped up. Pedro's means of escape. His part of the plan. Shut the freezer room door when the bulk of the creatures were inside, finish off the lone stragglers in the corridor and the canteen one by one.

Pedro sighed. He followed Riley down the ladder into the darkness of the generator room. "There's no guarantee that this

C4 is even active. I know he claimed it was, but you know Ivan."

Riley stepped off the ladder. The chill of the silent, unheated generator room wrapped around him. The door was slammed shut, but there was movement behind it from the corridor. The creatures. They'd have to get past them if they wanted to get to Ivan's room. They'd have to handle them, somehow.

Pedro hopped from the ladder and shone the small light from his gun around the room. It was silent without the hum of the generator. But the second they opened the door, sound would radiate through it. They had to think about their next step. Carefully.

Riley stepped over to the door. He pressed his ear against it. The creatures were definitely just outside, which meant that they would be outside of Ivan's room too. They needed to clear them if they wanted to get to the C4. And then they needed to work out their next step from there.

Pedro lifted his gun and pointed it at the door.

"No," Riley said. He pulled the spanner out of his pocket. The top end of it was rusty and partly smeared with blood. "We need to take them out quietly. Ivan's plan to lure them into the freezer room is good for us. We want to keep them there. It'll give us more time. And the light. We can't risk keeping it on."

Pedro shrugged and lowered his gun, switching off the small torchlight above it. "I hope you're right about this, bruv. I really do."

Riley reached for the handle of the generator room door. His heartbeat raced. His chest tightened and tingled. Control it. Stay calm.

He lowered the handle and he peeked out into the corridor, breath still held. Pedro glanced over Riley's shoulder.

The creatures were lurching into the freezer room. There were six of them in the corridor. Loose flesh dangled from their arms as they feasted on Stocky and Gaz. The skin of the creatures was starting to smell even more putrid after two weeks dead. Flies hovered around them. In a few years, they'd be nothing but skeletons and muscle waste, gasping away as they reached out for an endless supply of food.

But the majority of the groans came from the freezer room. Ivan's plan was working for him. But it was working for Riley and Pedro, too. They needed to hurry, but they needed to be quiet.

"Come on," Riley whispered. He crept forward into the dimly lit corridor. A creature was crouched down on the floor, preoccupied with Stocky's body. Tendon and veins sprayed out of Stocky's neck like violent, deathly fireworks. Riley stepped past the creature. He thought about checking Stocky for spare guns or ammo, but it was too risky. Better to leave the creature to its food, if possible.

Pedro followed Riley. He tried not to look into the freezer room as he passed, where a mountain of creatures feasted on an even bigger mountain of bodies, bathing in their defrosting blood. Ivan must've been in the underground passage now. Making his way out. Waiting for Pedro to slam shut the door of the freezer room and pick off the remainder of the creatures in the corridor. Then fortify the main door somehow. Stop any more leaks of creatures.

Riley was going to create a leak. A great big foundation destroying leak.

Riley held his breath as he approached two creatures that were standing and wandering towards him. He rushed over to the first one and smashed the spanner into its skull with as much force as possible, knocking it to the ground. Pedro smacked the other creature down with the butt of his gun and stamped on its head for good measure.

The pair of them swung around. The two creatures that were feasting on Stocky's body hadn't noticed. The creatures in the corridor hadn't groaned. The creatures in the freezer room continued to squelch and slip on the frosty flesh. Worn-down teeth snapped through icy flesh. They couldn't close the freezer room door, not yet. It was a part of the plan.

Pedro nodded his head and puffed out his lips as they got to Ivan's room. The creatures were preoccupied. They'd dealt with the ones they had to deal with. Slipped by the ones they had to slip by. Now they just had to get into Ivan's room. Get to the C4. Plant it where the main wing entrance connected with the outer wall and send it crumbling to the ground. There would be no fortifying then. No hiding. Ivan could try to defend this place as much as he wanted, but it would be in vain.

Pedro pointed at the handle of Ivan's door. "Quick," he mouthed, as a creature at the end of the corridor rose its head from Barney's body and looked around in confusion.

Riley held his breath. Grabbed the handle. Started to turn it.

But something wasn't right. The door was locked.

His stomach sank. His skin began to crawl. He tried the handle again, and again, it didn't budge.

"Fuck," he muttered under his breath.

Pedro saw that Riley was struggling and threw himself over to the door handle. He, too, tried to move it out of place, but it was stuck.

Of course he'd locked his door. Of course they'd been so fucking foolish not to consider that.

A groan sounded at the end of the corridor by the double doors to the canteen. The dark silhouette of a creature started to stumble in their direction. More groans picked up at the other side of them. The creatures feasting on Stocky and Gaz's bodies.

And groans from the mass of creatures inside the freezer room.

"Fuck," Pedro said. He lifted his gun with his shaky hand and pointed at the creatures that were starting to stagger out of the freezer room door, frosty flesh covering their lips.

Riley looked back to the double doors. He could see four or five creatures honing in on him in the slight glow of the moon through the window. At the other side, the mass of creatures that Ivan had drawn to the bodies were blocking the route to the generator room.

"We have to go," Pedro shouted, backing up into Riley as more creatures groaned and spilled out of the freezer room. "Now!"

Chapter Forty-Four

"OUT THROUGH THE FRONT!"

RILEY HELD his breath as he charged towards the double doors. A few creatures were ahead of him, and he could just about make out their heads in the dimly lit corridor. But it wasn't enough. They could be on the floor. They could be waiting to nip at his heels and sink their teeth into his ankles.

Riley swung his spanner into the head of a creature. The creature flew to the floor. He felt cold blood splash onto the back of his hand. The creature was still groaning on the floor. "Your light, Pedro. Your light."

"But I thought you said—"

"That was when we were being stealthy!"

Pedro shuffled with the top of his gun and flicked on the small torchlight. He shone it ahead. Four creatures wandered through the double doors. They were still coming. So many had already made it in here and they were still coming.

Riley crashed his spanner into the head of another

creature. It fell to the floor and knocked back down the one that he'd unsuccessfully hit, which tried to pull itself back to its feet. He couldn't take all of them with the spanner. It wasn't enough.

A gunshot rattled in his eardrum. Another soon followed. In front of him, he saw the creatures falling to the floor as he approached them. He looked over his shoulder and saw Pedro with the gun raised. A swarm of groaning, unsatisfiable creatures marched out of the freezer room door, their appetite unending. "Guessing gunshots are okay now too, right?"

Riley nodded and made his way to the double doors as the creatures got closer behind them. "We need to be quick. We need to get outside. Is there any other way than the courtyard door? Anything that... that takes us around the side of the walls?"

Pedro panted as he caught up with Riley. "We can try a window. Maybe go through the kitchen and climb out into the side yard. But let's get out of this corridor first."

Riley and Pedro slowed down slightly as they pushed through the double doors. Pedro moved away from the doors as they swung backwards and forwards. The canteen was lit up by a fluorescent lamp and covered with blood. The window was cracked and the door had fallen to pieces. But it was empty. Quiet, except for the creatures behind them.

"Or we could try our luck?" Pedro said. "Looks pretty quiet here. We don't know how long that's..." Pedro's speech trailed off. He lowered his gun. "Oh shit. Oh shit."

Riley didn't see it at first, but when he looked over by the canteen counter where Pedro shone his light, he knew what it was.

Or more, who it was. Or who it once was.

Chef's chubby body dragged itself to its feet. His intestines spilled out of his opened up torso, which he partly feasted on. His eyes were glazed, his iris almost completely white. The blood on his face looked even more stark when contrasted with his pale skin. He stumbled over to Pedro and Riley, knocking cutlery to the floor.

Pedro raised his gun. His hand was shaking. Time seemed to stop. Tears ran down his face, illuminated by the fluorescent lamp. He looked as if he'd never had to shoot somebody he knew before. And yet, he'd been partly responsible for the storage of the human bodies. Partly responsible for the murder of his colleagues and friends. There was no getting away from that.

Riley stared at Chef. His footing was clumsy as he knocked a dish to the floor, smashing it into multiple pieces. The creatures from the freezer room would be in here any moment. He could hear them, getting closer and closer. They had to hurry. "Pedro, if you want, I can—"

A bullet from Pedro's gun fired through the air, once again sending ringing noises through Riley's head.

More blood trickled down Chef's forehead, and he fell to the floor, letting out a final blood curdling gasp.

Riley placed a hand on Pedro's shoulder. Pedro took in a few deep breaths. His bottom lip quivered and he wiped his eyes. "It's just... All the men I killed. All the men I... I thought I was doing the right thing."

Riley tensed his jaw. "We've all made some awful decisions in this world. But all we can do is choose to come back from them."

The double doors rattled open. A crowd of creatures pushed through, crushing one another up against the door frames and spilling out like ants from a nest.

"Come on," Riley said, starting to jog. "Let's try to get out of here."

Pedro took a final glance back at the creatures, nodded his head, and followed Riley behind the counter and through the kitchen door.

After smashing through the large kitchen window, the pair crept down the side alleyway towards the front of the barracks. They heard the creatures behind them as they kept low and moved further and further down the side of the wall and towards their exit. The light from Pedro's gun lit up the ground ahead, revealing any lone creatures that might have broken free of the pack, waiting to pounce.

"I don't know what your plan is here," Pedro whispered. His voice was still shaky. He was clearly still struggling with having to shoot down Chef. But perhaps it was more that he was struggling with all the bad things he'd had to do. All the atrocities he'd stood by and allowed Ivan to commit. Riley knew what it was like for something to eat at one's psyche. It wasn't easy.

"I mean, we get to the gates and maybe it will be clear. But then what? Where do we go from there?"

Riley crouched further down and moved through the grass at the very side of the barracks wall. The courtyard looked relatively empty apart from the occasional dark figure in the distance. He wondered whether the creatures saw in the dark, but there was no real logistical reason why their eyesight should be any better than those of humans. They were just dead humans, after all. Their sense of smell, too — they panicked about that on the television and in the movies, but was it really all that much better? From what they'd witnessed, it was nothing other than the groaning. The sound they emitted upon spotting live prey. One groaned, others followed. A perfect, relentless method of communication, and yet they didn't even realise they were doing it.

"Your friends. Anna, Claudia. Claudia's girl. I hope they're a long way away. I hope they're—"

Riley turned to Pedro and covered his lips with his finger. A lone creature wandered in circles a few metres from them.

Pedro stopped mid-speech and shrugged. "Sorry," he mouthed.

Riley nodded and pointed at Pedro's flashlight. Pedro sighed and switched the light off, and once again, they were engulfed in darkness.

Riley held his breath, and then he walked.

He stayed pressed up to the brick wall of the barracks as

well as he could as he rounded the directionless creature. He tried not to step on anything that might attract its attention. He could smell it from here. In fact, the stench had gotten so much worse recently. And it would only continue to get worse as the rot set in to the bodies. Wherever they went next — wherever *he* went next — he'd have to bear smell in mind somehow when defending the place.

After passing the lone creature, Pedro following, Riley saw the tall entrance to the barracks. The Great Britain flag that usually flew so proud at full mast was limp and low. There was no point to national pride anymore. They'd been stuck in this situation long enough now to realise the virus was global. Or that the rest of the world just didn't give a damn about Britain. Likely, in all honesty.

They turned with the wall and approached the gates, which were wide open. Their shoes squelched through watery puddles, which Riley safely assumed was blood. At the front of the gate, four corpses staggered in the direction of their peers. Riley stopped in his tracks and raised his arm to stop Pedro. They had to be quiet.

One of the creatures continued in the direction of the infested wing. It grumbled as it walked past. It hadn't seen them. If they just took this easy, they could get out of these gates and think about their next step.

"We sneak around these if possible," Riley whispered. "We make getting out of these gates our priority."

"And then what?" Pedro's attempt at a whisper wasn't quite as effective as Riley's.

Riley took a few more steps towards the main gate. "We find a car. Or shelter. We'll find another gun around here, surely. But we get away from here, one way or another."

Pedro didn't respond. Riley figured he didn't like the idea. What was there to like about it? He was basically telling Pedro that they were doing what all the foolish, stupid general population did. Run. Risk getting swarmed by creatures.

But what other choice did they have?

Riley edged closer to the front gate. He could almost feel the freedom now. It made him realise how long he'd been cooped up in these barracks. It was good, while it lasted. But he'd be on the road again soon. Anna, Claudia, Chloë — they'd be gone. But they'd be alive. Chef had given them their chance to get away. They'd be alive. They had to be. Somewhere.

As Riley moved around the gate, he heard a loud click above his head.

His eyes stung. He didn't understand it at first. He'd been squinting for the last however-long, and out of nowhere, he could see again. See the blood drenching the tarmac.

See the gates, wide-open.

See the courtyard lights shining at full beam.

"Oh fuck."

Riley turned around and looked at the courtyard. He could see the grass again, and his cold breath clouding up in front of him.

Pedro backed towards the gate. "The generator. The fucking generator."

A light humming noise kicked in, back in the main wing of the barracks.

Creatures turned around from their walk in the opposite direction and stared at Riley and Pedro, bathed in light.

Pedro looked outside the gates. "We're fucked. We're fucked."

The creatures began to groan and walk back out of the main wing of the barracks, towards their prey on display in the spotlight.

"We've got to go," Riley said. He turned away from the barracks and moved through the gates.

But through the gates, he saw what it was that Pedro was so fixated on.

Another horde of creatures were heading in their direction, wandering across the grass outside the barracks. Singing their deathly song at the top of their voices. Twenty. Thirty. Maybe more of them were invisible in the darkness.

"It's over," Pedro said, as he looked around at the oncoming hordes of creatures. "It's over."

Chapter Forty-Five

RILEY AND PEDRO BACKED IN TO one another. Creatures were approaching them from both directions. They were trapped. This was the end. There was no getting away.

Pedro raised his gun with his shaky hand and pointed at the creatures spilling out of the barracks.

"No," Riley said. He tilted his head at the creatures emerging from the darkness up ahead. "Save the bullets for our way out."

"Way out?" Pedro shouted. "We've got a better chance staying in here now we've seen what it's like out there. We... Out there, we don't know what to expect. And we can find a gun around the grounds. One of our soldiers — they must have dropped one. Or up on the wall. There must be something."

Riley squinted into the darkness. He tried to picture his surroundings as they had looked the many times Pedro and he sat atop that wall on watch. The tree-lined road. The terraced houses opposite. And the milk van.

"Riley, we need to make a decision."

"The milk van," Riley said.

"What?"

Riley pulled the spanner out of his pocket and approached the oncoming group of creatures. They were scattered around. Enough time to deal with them individually. For now.

"You *what?*"

"The milk van," Riley shouted. "Somebody... somebody told me something once. About drivers and their spare sets of keys." He thought back to Jordanna as she reversed the tanker. The delight on her face at helping Ted and him out. "If we can get to that van, we might have a chance of driving out of here."

Pedro shook his head and cursed as he looked back at the creatures approaching the spotlight. He stepped out of the light and joined Riley in the darkness, flicking on his torch. He was like a child taking their first leap into the swimming pool, submerging himself into the discomfort that was being underwater. Something Riley never liked.

"Come on," Riley said. He steadied himself as a creature stepped up to him. Then, he swung the spanner at its head and knocked it to the ground, cracking its skull in the process. He was getting better at this.

"I'm sick of bloody keys, bruv," Pedro grumbled, then raised his gun, aiming the light at the creatures in the distance. The pair of them jogged down the road away from the barracks, Pedro firing at creatures as they approached and Riley continuing to knock them down as they threw themselves at him. He was out of breath already. His knees were weak. They had to cross the road and get to the milk van. Fast.

They pushed past another few creatures. Fear gripped hold of Riley as he held his breath, sweat running down his forehead. He had to keep his cool. He had to stay focused.

He swung his spanner at another creature. He must have taken down about six or seven now. So this was what courage felt like. This was what feeling the fear and doing it anyway was about. Only the writers of all those self-help books probably weren't doing this sort of activity right now.

"There's too many," Pedro called. He fired at three of them as they sneaked up on him from both sides. Their path to the milk van was blocked. The terraced houses were on the left. "We need to get to shelter. Just anywhere that isn't the road."

"Let's—" Riley didn't finish his sentence because something smacked into his right hand side. He fell to the ground, smacking his head on the cold concrete as something pushed down on him from the side, dribbling into his ear.

The spanner fell from his grip.

He turned over and saw that a creature was on top of him. Everything seemed to move in slow motion. The creature pulled in to bite his neck. Riley's arm was too low down to stop it. He held his breath. Braced himself for the contact.

A gunshot cracked through the air. The weight of the creature fell on top of him. Pedro stood with his gun in his hand, pointed at the creature.

Pedro held his hand out and Riley grabbed it. As Pedro lifted him up, Riley felt a splitting sensation down his chest. He looked down at the bandage that covered the cut from Ivan's blade and saw that fresh blood was building up underneath.

"That doesn't look good," Pedro said. "But quick — we need to—"

"Riley!"

He knew the voice. He'd heard it so many times before. "Did you hear that?"

Pedro shot at another creature as it closed in on Riley. The pair of them stood in the middle of the road like animals waiting for the slaughter. "What? Jesus, Riley."

"Riley! Over here!"

He'd definitely heard it this time. It wasn't a trick of his imagination. "Shine your torch at the house."

Pedro shook his head and looked over his shoulder.

Creatures were stumbling out of the front gates of the barracks now, backing away from Ivan's safe haven.

"Just quick," Riley said.

Ivan shone his torch over at the terraced houses.

Tension built up in Riley's body.

Anna was at the window. Beside her, he saw Claudia. They'd made it out. They'd done it.

He waved back at them then nodded at Pedro. "Lower your light. The creatures — they can't see us."

Pedro sighed again then flicked off the torch. "Hope you're right about that."

Riley inhaled a deep breath. "Me too. Now come on — let's get to the house."

The pair of them ran around the remaining individual creatures, knocking them down where necessary, and up to the front door of the middle terraced house. The second they arrived, the door opened. Claudia stood there.

"Quick," she said, waving Riley in. She narrowed her eyes when Pedro approached the door.

"He's okay," Riley said. "He's with us."

Claudia tensed her jaw. Kept her focus on Pedro. "I sure as hell hope so."

Pedro nodded at Claudia and stepped through the front door of the terraced house.

The door slammed shut. The groans outside were drowned out.

For the first time all night, Riley felt a brief hint of safety again.

Ivan watched as they made their way into the terraced house. Riley and Pedro, the pair of them fighting side by side. Flames of anger burned in his stomach. He clamped his teeth together to resist shouting out at them. Because he wanted to lash out. And he could. He would. Just not yet.

The creatures stumbled past the gun-mounted vehicle without paying any attention. Ivan was completely still, and he kept the headlights off. He watched as the door of the terraced house closed, the grieving bitch of a mother welcoming Riley and Pedro into her home. Naive. Foolish of her to fall for the bait. Foolish of all of them, in fact.

He cracked open a can of Coca Cola that was wedged into the drinks holder beside the steering wheel. The drink fizzed and spilled all over Ivan's lap. He swore under his breath, being careful not to be too loud. He couldn't risk alerting the attention of the creatures, not now. Not after all this hard work. That would just be fucking foolish. Death by spilt drink. Just the luck he needed.

He looked around at the barracks. It was lit up again, the grey bricked walls bathing in the intense white spotlights. The courtyard was filled with creatures. They stumbled around aimlessly as they searched for movement, trying their hardest to hear something in the deadly silence of the night. The barracks didn't look good. But he could lead again. He hadn't lost everything, not yet. He could start again.

Only, with a few minor alterations to his leadership style.

"What's the plan, boss?"

Ivan had been concentrating so much that he barely remembered the two soldiers who were in the gun-mounted vehicle with him. He'd been fortunate to bump into them in the first place. But it hadn't been a night of good fortune, so these things had to even themselves out one way or another.

"Are we going in?" the other soldier asked. He shuffled his gun in his hands. Pedro and Riley must have just assumed everyone dead. Disappointing, really. He always expected better of them.

"Why can't we just—"

"We're going to make them wait," Ivan said. His throat was tender and the words felt forced. "We're going to make them wait and we're going to make them think they've got away. We're going to make them believe that they are safe. And then we're going to kill Riley in front of the women."

The soldiers were silent. More shuffling in the seats. Ivan

stared out at the terraced house. A small candlelight was visible behind the upstairs window.

"What—what about Pedro?"

Ivan smiled. "Like I said. We're going to kill Riley in front of the others. Pedro's a very big part of this plan. Now get some rest. You're going to need it."

"But I don't get why we can't just go in there. They killed Barney. Why doesn't Pedro just deal with them?"

Ivan took a final gulp from his can of Coke. "Sometimes, boys, the cruelest method of murder is tearing out the heart. Building up a bond then tearing it away." He pulled down the shutter on the front window.

Now, they just had to sit and wait. Wait for Pedro to carry out his part of the plan.

Wait for the screams.

Chapter Forty-Six

RILEY FOLLOWED CLAUDIA UPSTAIRS. PEDRO WAS close behind. The staircase was dark and dusty. There was a strong putrid smell in the air, like bananas that had been left to rot well past their ripest stage. But it was shelter nevertheless, and that's all they needed right now. His chest was beginning to sting again. Hopefully nothing too serious. They didn't need another setback, not now.

Claudia grabbed the handle at the top of the staircase. The door was painted with blood. Toys were scattered across the floor. Teddy bears cast aside, never again to be used. A ghostly reminder of what life was like when it was normal. A reminder of what was lost.

"Ted," Claudia said. Her eyes were watery as she stared back at Riley. "Is he—?"

"Yes," Riley said. "He's gone."

Claudia shook her head and sniffed back some tears before pushing open the door. "Make yourself comfortable. This place will have to suffice until it's safe to move on."

Riley stepped into the room. Pedro followed closely behind.

"I'm sorry," Pedro said. He couldn't quite look Claudia in the eye. "About your little girl. I'm sorry."

Claudia disregarded Pedro and held the door open. He joined Riley in the room.

Anna and Chloë were by the window peeking out of the hole-laden curtains. A candle burned on the circular dining table in the middle of the room. A bed was propped up beside the window. Cans of food were stacked atop a dressing table, mostly empty. It looked like this room had been a bedroom once upon a time. But things changed when the Dead Days arrived. Bedrooms, kitchens, sitting rooms — none of those were relevant anymore. It was all about what was the most suitable room for safety. The room with the best possible escape route. The room that was hardest for the creatures to invade.

"Glad to have you back," Anna said. She went to hug Riley but backed off and cleared her throat.

"Glad to be back, wherever back is."

"Is Ted okay?" Chloë asked.

Claudia stepped past Pedro. "Chloë, Riley's tired. You should let him rest."

Riley swallowed the lump in his throat as Anna and Chloë waited for him to give them the inevitable piece of news. "Ted... He's gone."

Anna lowered her head. Chloë's relieved smile at Riley's return dropped.

"I'm sorry," Anna said. "Did he—"

"Ivan murdered him. Slit his throat."

Anna's mouth dangled open. Chloë didn't even flinch. "That bastard," Anna said. "That fucking bastard." She peered over Riley's shoulder at Pedro, as if she noticed him for the first time since his entrance. "Do you have nothing to say about that? Nothing to say about your fucked up leader?"

Pedro stared at his feet. He didn't react to Anna's words. He took them, like he deserved them.

"Nothing at all to say about those—those bodies? About what you did to us in that canteen?" She stepped up to Pedro. "Nothing at all to say about—about how you held Riley back while Ivan sliced his chest?"

"Anna," Riley interrupted. "Pedro's okay. He's with us."

Anna shook her head. "No. I don't accept that. I don't—"

"I'm sorry." Pedro raised his head and stared Anna directly in her eyes. "That's all I can say. I'm sorry. I was doing what I thought I needed to do to survive."

Anna watched him intently, with the same level of intensity that she'd stared at everybody she'd had suspicions about. She pointed to his gun. "Then give us that. If you want to start proving your loyalty, you hand that gun over. It's our gun now."

Pedro looked down at his gun then back at Riley.

Riley shrugged. "Do as she says."

Pedro sighed and handed the rifle over to Anna. She grabbed it from him with a weighty tug and inspected it. "Good move. Now sit down. There's some canned shit over here." She reached for a tin of dusty, ancient looking soup and tossed it over to Pedro. "No can openers so you're just going to have to bite your way in or something."

Pedro examined the can in his hand. There was no way he was cutting through the solid metal lid any time soon. "Thank you. I appreciate it."

Correct answer, Riley thought.

"How did you end up here?" Riley asked.

"We had no choice, really," Claudia said. "When we got out of the... the underground passage, this area was swamped with those creatures. So we just had to go to the closest place we could. Figured we'd keep an eye out for you and Ted in case... Yeah."

Riley nodded. Every time somebody said Ted's name, he couldn't get that final image of him out of his head. The fear and sense of knowledge in his eyes as the blade sliced through his neck. Gargling blood on the floor. That wasn't the Ted he used to play Xbox with. The Ted who used to eat nachos and laze around.

"He did a good thing for us," Claudia said. "Ted did. He gave us a chance. I dread to think what might have happened if he hadn't interfered with that generator." Her gaze wandered over Riley's shoulder and at Pedro.

"Yeah," Anna said. "He was a good guy. I thought he was an absolute idiot at first, but he was good." She raised a half-open can of soup into the air. "To Ted."

Everybody else nodded in acknowledgement as Anna took a sip of the cold soup. She gasped as the thick tomato sauce made its way down her throat. "So I guess this is the point where we work out our next step."

"It has to be the MOD bunker," Claudia said. "The one we were heading to before…" Her vision diverted to Pedro again. "Before we found safety." It sounded like she had corrected herself out of politeness more than anything.

"Wait — you mean the bunker down in Goosnargh?" Pedro asked.

"What is it to you?" Anna said.

"It's no use. Passed by that way before we found your group. It might have been good before the countryside fell, but there's a horde of zombies over that way now. Drifting out of the cities, looking for food, y'know?"

Riley frowned. "So you're suggesting we head into the city?"

"Not into the city, necessarily. But I think there's better places to go than a rickety old bunker right now."

"Like?" Anna asked.

Pedro looked around at the group. His momentary pause said more than words could manage. He wasn't being totally open.

"Oh, come on," Riley said. "We're in this together now. Or you can go it alone. That's your call."

"Okay," Pedro said. "Okay. There's a place I know of. Down by the docks. And my... my gran kept an old canal narrowboat there."

Anna tutted and broke into a smile. "A narrowboat? Seriously? And you never thought to just float the fuck away on it?"

"Hey," Pedro said. He pointed at Riley. "You're in a room with a man who broke out of his high-rise flat in the middle of the zombie apocalypse. That place was perfect. No offence, Riley."

Riley shrugged. Funny thing for Pedro to make the 'no offence' remark about, especially after some of the more offensive things he'd revealed himself to be involved in within the last few hours.

"And what about this narrowboat?" Claudia asked. "What do you suggest?"

"Well, I... If we can get to it — which is a big 'if' — I'm pretty certain nobody will have found it. All the other boats at the docks, they'll be long gone. But not this. My grandma had it stashed away in a fuckin' dire old shed. Can't imagine anyone's gone in there."

"And say we get this narrowboat," Anna said. "What then? Where do we go on it?"

Pedro cleared his throat then crouched down onto the floor. The candlelight lit up his face. "I know how to sail this thing. And it held a fair load of fuel. And it can move manually too. So I say we float up the coast. Out of the docks, then down the Ribble and up the coast."

Anna glanced at Riley. She didn't respond straight away, which was a positive sign from her. If she didn't agree with something, she'd typically snap right away. But Pedro's idea wasn't so bad. They could go out to sea. Work their way up towards the Lake District, where it was nothing but countryside. Or head over to one of the small islands between them and Ireland. Not a bad idea at all.

"There's only one problem," Pedro said.

Riley held his breath. Braced himself for whatever disappointment Pedro was about to deliver. "Go on."

He nodded at the window. The groans had died down, but the staggering feet against the road were as loud as ever as the creatures shuffled from side to side.

"They'll move on," Anna said. "Besides, we've got enough soup in here to last us a few weeks."

"I'm not talking about the zombies," Pedro said.

Riley nodded. He knew what Pedro was talking about. "Ivan." The stinging on his chest flared up again. He'd have to take a look at it soon. He'd been delaying it as best as he could. Pretending not to notice it and trying to wish the pain away. But it was beginning to win the battle.

Pedro offered a single nod.

"He doesn't have to find us," Anna said. "We don't even know if he's dead or alive yet."

Pedro stared at the candle on the table. Wax dribbled and hardened down its side. "Maybe. Maybe not. But I don't like that we didn't see him out there. Or any of the other soldiers. Makes me wonder… what he might be telling them if they've managed to get together somehow."

Anna pulled the curtain so it was completely shut. "We'll cross that bridge when we come to it. We should get some rest. If we wake up early tomorrow, we can think about heading to that old narrowboat and getting it on the water. Riley?"

Visions of the knife moving across Ted's throat flicked through Riley's mind. Could he have saved him? Could he have done more to save him? Had he let somebody down again?

"Riley? What do you reckon?"

Riley snapped out of his day-dream and stood up. "Where's the bathroom?"

Anna rolled her eyes. "Bladder's still shit then?" She pointed to the door on the left. "Just don't stink it out too much."

Chloë sniggered as Riley walked towards the bathroom.

He needed a place to go. A place to be alone. He needed to think.

Riley wiped down the bathroom mirror, which was covered with grime. The bathroom had Velux skylight windows, which gave him just enough light to make out what he had to make out. He winced as he peeled his shirt away. The bandage that was wrapped around his chest was lined with blood. It couldn't be too serious. He couldn't allow it to be. The group — they didn't have the supplies they needed to look after him here. He just had to pray it wasn't infected.

He bit his lip as he pulled back the bandage. It felt like somebody was dragging razors down his body, nipping at the cut on his chest. When he'd fully removed the bandage, which was filled with a brown shade of dried blood, he stared at his reflection in the murky mirror. Fortunately, it did not look like the cut was bleeding anymore. He had been fortunate. Fortunate that Ivan hadn't cut any deeper. Fortunate that Pedro had made his way to that room and saved him.

Fortunate that Ted had sacrificed himself for him.

He shook his head. Tensed his fists. No. He couldn't view things that way. Ted would've died regardless of whether he'd interfered with that generator or not. They all would have died if he hadn't. But he'd given them a chance. He'd offered up his own life and given them a chance.

But Riley could've done more.

He smacked his fist into the mirror. He brought his hand back and smacked it into the mirror again. He could see his face crumbling away as the glass cut his knuckles. He punched it again and again and again as tears ran down his cheeks, and then he fell down and sobbed onto the cold, hard dusty bathroom floor.

His best friend was dead. Gone. And he wasn't coming back.

"You okay in there?"

Claudia. He thought about calling back and saying he was

okay. He thought about taking those deep breaths his therapist had taught him and responding in the calmest, most controlled of manners. He thought about the things the therapist said about riding out the tingling sensations; about accepting them for what they were — a figment of the imagination. He thought about it, but instead, he carried on sobbing.

The door clicked open. He felt hands on his back. He looked up. Claudia nodded her head at him. "I know," she said. "Come on. I know."

Riley lay down on the pillow that was propped up against the bedside cabinet. Claudia wrapped the blanket over him, like a mother looking out for her sick child. "You need to rest. We all do."

Riley turned over to his side. His bruised and cut knuckles masked the pain in his chest. Anna had seen to him after Claudia brought him out of the bathroom. Dabbed water on his chest and wrapped tissue paper around his knuckles. It was all she could do with the medical equipment she had on offer — very little.

"We rest," Anna said. "And then we wake up first thing tomorrow and we get ourselves out of here. Okay?"

Claudia, Chloë, and Pedro all nodded.

"Right." Anna lay down at the opposite side of the room by the door. She held Pedro's gun and pointed it in his direction so that he knew she was keeping an eye on him. "Sweet dreams. We've earned them, that's for sure."

Claudia blew out the candlelight and climbed under the covers next to Chloë. The room was silent.

Except for the feet outside. The creatures knocking into one another. They weren't groaning, but they were definitely out there. Riley could feel them, like that sensation when you knew somebody was staring at you. Just like that. Only they were the starers, and what they were staring at was completely terrifying.

He pressed his eyelids together.

Images of Ted, laughing and joking as he played his Xbox. Nachos spread across his face. Telling one of his awful jokes.

He'd made the choice to intercept the generator. He'd acted. And he'd saved their lives.

He took a deep breath in and let the images of Ted disappear from his mind.

Ted had given them a chance. Now they had to make damn sure they took it.

The room was silent but for Riley's light snores. The creatures that had been gathered outside were moving on, searching elsewhere for prey. There had been no more sounds from the barracks. No more sounds from anywhere, in fact.

But still, the creatures drifted on. On to their next location. Their next hope of a jackpot that was fresh meat. On to spread their death.

Pedro held the curtain with his shaking hand and stared out at the armoured vehicle down the road. He knew who was in there. He knew what he was planning. And he was supposed to be a part of this. He was supposed to be the one who dangled the hope in the group's face then took it away from them in the night.

Ivan's plan had changed. After all, catching Riley wouldn't guarantee the rest of the group would try to save him. The rules had changed.

He turned away from the curtain and looked over at Riley. He was fast asleep. All he had to do was kick the shit out of him while he slept. Leave his blood-splattered, caved-in head for the women to find tomorrow. His tensed his fists. Fuck.

He looked at Claudia and Chloë. Amazing how well a room could sleep no matter what shit had gone down. He wished he could just snap out of it right now and rest until the morning.

But that wasn't happening. Because he had work to do.

He crept over to Chloë and lowered his body. He was so

close to her now. All he had to do was wrap the cloth over her mouth, send her to sleep, then take her out to Ivan. The group would realise she was gone in the morning. Then they'd have their bargaining chip.

He heard a rustling over by the door. He looked up, holding his breath. It was Anna. She turned to one side and mumbled a few inaudible words in her sleep. He let go of his breath. It was okay. She was sleeping.

He looked back down at Chloë. All he had to do was take her. Take her, and Ivan and he could think about restarting that civilization of theirs again. If the rest of the world really was gone, then it was a viable enough plan. A sick fucking plan, but viable for sure.

But the group had been so good to him. They'd let him in. Riley — even after everything he'd done to him — had put his trust in him.

But that was Riley's problem. Too weak. Too naive.

He reached for the cloth in his pocket and brought it closer and closer to Chloë's face.

It would be over soon. Everything would be back to normal again, soon.

Chapter Forty-Seven

RILEY OPENED HIS EYES. THE GUILT that had been missing from his stomach the previous two weeks that they had been shacked up in the barracks had made a return. It was like a deep, throbbing sense of dread. A sense that something bad was going to happen. The same sense of dread he used to get even before these Dead Days. Only now, it was much more justified.

He rose from the pillow. His neck ached with the awkward position he had slept in. It was strange getting used to sleeping on the floor after the comfort of the army barracks beds just a matter of metres away, across the road. If only they could go back to that innocent, naive state they'd spent the last two weeks in. If only they could go back to pretending.

But the bodies. The frozen bodies. The things Ivan had done — the slice across his chest. Ted.

No. There was no going back. They had to pursue the new plan — this narrowboat Pedro knew of. They had to get away from here.

Riley looked around the room. It was dimly lit, and even though it was chilly, there was a heat about the place from the number of bodies that had slept inside. The number of sweaty, blood-drenched, fear-soaked bodies that had spent the night together. It was like staying in a cheap hostel somewhere overseas. They'd become too accustomed to the clean showers of the barracks. A luxury they'd taken for granted.

He looked over at Anna. She was still sleeping. Claudia was a little further over the other side of the room, her eyes also closed. He could just about make out Chloë beside her. They'd planned to leave as early as possible this morning. Riley wasn't even sure what time it was. But they'd survived the night. The creatures hadn't come storming in through the downstairs door. The shuffling outside seemed to have gone, in fact.

And Ivan. He hadn't found them.

Riley could hear the bathroom tap running. He saw Pedro's bed was vacant. Must have been what woke him up. Getting prepared for their new beginning. Their new start. Riley couldn't forgive Pedro for his part in Ivan's crimes, but he'd made his comeback from what he'd done. He'd seen wrong and right for what it was and stopped while he could. And he seemed serious about the plan to get away on the narrowboat. That was a start.

Rubbing his eyes, Riley rose to his feet and walked over to the curtains, which were filled with holes. Little beams of light shone through — a cold, crisp winter's day outside, waiting for them. He grabbed the curtain. Prepared to peek outside. He just had to pray it was clear. Pray it was empty.

He held his breath and opened the curtain.

The road was clear.

A smile twitched across Riley's face. The majority of the horde had vanished. The open-gated barracks grounds were still scattered with creatures and the spotlights still shone at full beam. But the road was relatively clear. Nothing they couldn't handle. They could get out of here. The milk van up the road — they could all get aboard that and try their luck.

But something else was different up ahead. Riley's semi-photographic memory from sitting atop that barracks wall and holding the gun beside Pedro meant that he'd seen the road a lot. The patterns of abandoned cars. A red car. A white car. A milk van.

But now, there was something different in the scene.

The gun-mounted, armoured vehicle that Lance and Stu had driven out of the barracks to distract the creatures. The same gun-mounted vehicle that Ivan, Pedro, and Stocky had saved Riley and the group and transported them to the barracks in.

It wasn't there yesterday. It definitely wasn't there yesterday.

Riley turned to the room. He needed to mention it to them. Ivan could be inside. He could be planning his escape in the vehicle. Or he could be intending to clear the barracks grounds with it. But they could use a vehicle like that. Even if it was only to get them to the location of the narrowboat, Riley couldn't think of many safer vehicles.

The bathroom tap continued to trickle. Pedro was taking a while in there. Riley knocked on the door, being cautious not to wake the others up. "Pedro?"

No response.

Riley knocked at the door again. He started to worry. Maybe something had happened to Pedro in there. Maybe he'd got bitten and not told anybody about it. He could be inside, waiting to sink his teeth into the rest of the group. He could be a creature.

Riley grabbed the handle. It might be locked, but he had to try.

To his surprise, the door opened.

He held his breath. "Pedro?"

When he'd opened it fully, he saw that the tap was running but nobody was in there.

His muscles tensed. He turned back to the room. Pedro

definitely wasn't in bed.

The armoured, gun-mounted vehicle outside the terraced houses. Something wasn't right. Something was desperately wrong.

Turning off the tap, Riley walked back into the room. He needed to tell Anna, Claudia, and Chloë. He didn't know what it was, but he had a bad feeling about what was going on. Why would Pedro have left the building? And why would the gun-mounted vehicle be outside all of a sudden? Unless Pedro had sneaked off to retrieve it for them. But that didn't make sense.

The more he considered it, the more Riley started to sense that perhaps Pedro hadn't been entirely honest with the group after all. Why had he gone back to the room for Riley when Ivan stayed downstairs? Why had he helped him? Really?

Riley stopped at the foot of Claudia's bed. He was about to call her name to wake her up, but he noticed something else. The mound beside her. The mound that he thought was Chloë when he'd woken up. It was nothing but a pillow. A large, plump pillow.

Chloë was gone.

A weight fell to the bottom of Riley's stomach. He didn't understand what was happening. But he could figure it out. He had a rough idea. If Pedro wasn't being completely honest with them, then there was a chance he'd taken Chloë. Taken her to Ivan. A bargaining chip. Or worse.

"Claudia," Riley said, his voice breaking. He needed to alert her. He didn't want to worry her, but she needed to know. They needed to work out their next step.

Claudia yawned and stretched out. "Ye—Yes?"

Riley's wide eyes stared at the pillow in Claudia's arms. His entire jaw quivered. "I don't know how to say this, but... but it's Chloë."

"What's going on?" A tired voice the other side of Claudia. Anna woke from her sleep. Her dark hair was fluffed up atop her head.

Riley's heart pounded. "It's... It's Chloë. She's gone. And

Pedro's gone. I think he's—"

"Everything okay in here?"

The voice froze Riley's speech right in its tracks. He turned around.

Pedro was at the door with a frown on his face. "Thought I heard some commotion?"

Riley walked over to Pedro. He couldn't believe he'd have the guts to come back in here. "What... What have you done with Chloë? Where is she?"

Pedro broke into a smile. He pushed the door open and tilted his head. "Little devil was just giving me a hand with breakfast. Beans and... beans. Hungry?"

Chloë stepped out from the side of Pedro. A strong smell of beans made its way into the room. Riley's muscles slackened and his heart returned to a normal pace.

She was okay. She was okay.

Pedro cleared his throat. The smile dropped from his face. "But there... there is something. I need to talk to you. All of you. Urgently."

Pedro took in a deep breath. The conversation had gone better than he'd expected. He'd dealt with them. Made them see sense. Now all he had to do was take Chloë to Ivan.

He looked down at Chloë. She was fast asleep in his blood-covered arms. The effect of the drugged cloth he'd stuffed in his pocket. It'd keep her out for as long as it needed to. That was Ivan's plan, anyway.

Opening the door, he let the early morning sunlight cover his skin. He was cautious not to attract the attention of any creatures as he stepped outside. He held his breath. Bit his lip. Ivan would be watching him. Waiting for the signs. Waiting for the clues that his plan was playing out perfectly.

Pedro lowered his head as he crept across the road. The road was covered in used bullets and broken glass — debris from the firefight last night. In the distance, inside the ground of the barracks, creatures wandered around aimlessly, puzzled by the lack of food.

But that wouldn't matter anymore. The fight was almost over. They'd be able to start again soon. Just one final act to do.

The closer he got to the gun-mounted vehicle, the more he started to consider whether he'd got things right. He'd take Chloë to the vehicle. Anna and Claudia would scream when they found what he'd done to Riley. And then Ivan and whoever was with him would move in.

The shutter of the vehicle raised. Ivan stared out at Pedro, bleary-eyed. He nodded at Pedro. Pedro nodded in return. He gripped tighter hold of Chloë's blanket-covered body. This had to work. It had to.

He stopped at the side of the vehicle. The side door swung open.

"Get in," Ivan said.

Pedro cleared his throat. Something he always did when he was fucking nervous. "Nice to see you too." He climbed into the vehicle, placing Chloë's flimsy sleeping body in the middle seat between them.

"Check him," Ivan said. He titled his head to the back of the van. Two soldiers were there. Dave and Adam. Always kept themselves to themselves. Barely made an effort to get to know the group. Which would make Ivan's plan all the more easy for them.

"Come on," Pedro said, as Adam reached forward and brushed his hands down Pedro's front. "No need for this."

Ivan narrowed his eyes and peered at Pedro. "Right. What took you so long? It's almost nine a.m."

Pedro pulled away from the soldiers behind him and shot a confrontational glance in their direction. "It's not easy doing what I had to do." He raised his blood-coated hands. "I'm not quite as comfortable making these decisions as you are."

"Evidently not," Ivan said. He lowered his head and rubbed his hand against the partly condensed glass of the front window. "So you've killed him?"

Pedro waved his hands. "Yes. I killed him."

"How?"

Pedro exhaled with disbelief. "Jesus, man. I've not been away that long."

"So if I went inside that house now, I'd find his body dead. Right?"

Pedro pointed at Chloë. "I've got the girl, for fuck's sake. What other proof do you need? But yes. You would. So now it's your call from here. Shall we go in there, or—"

"Wait." Ivan was short. Snappy. His face was grey and pale. The soldiers behind him didn't say a word. "We wait. Wait until they scream. I want them to feel that fear. I want them to realise what is happening. I want them to realise they can't trust anyone again." He tilted his head to the barracks. "And then we start from scratch."

Pedro gulped down the lump in his throat. He'd planned the timing in his head, but he wasn't entirely convinced by the reaction of the other troops. But he had to try to get this right. "Was it you? Who killed Barney?"

Ivan turned to face Pedro. "What did they say?"

"Hey," Pedro said. He raised his hands. "Just that it was you who killed him. Not them. Just like you killed…"

"Okay, okay," Ivan said. "Enough. How fucking long do these people sleep?"

Pedro noticed Adam and Dave exchange a wary glance when he mentioned Ivan killing Barney and the other soldiers. They were still completely silent. Hopefully he'd done enough. If not, he'd have to improvise. Work out how to handle them, too.

Pedro stared out of the window. His heart raced. He could see the following events playing out in his mind. He just had to say the words. The clue words. And then it could happen. The crazy, messed-up plan could begin.

"You know, we were so close," Pedro said.

Ivan frowned. "So close to what?"

"Normality. Even after they'd found the bodies we stored —oh, sorry." Pedro intentionally stopped himself as he noticed

Adam and Dave growing more fidgety and jittery in the back seat. "Sometimes difficult remembering who knows what around here."

Ivan peered at Pedro. His eyes scanned his face, like he was weighing him up. Working out what to do with him. Working out whether he had just slipped those words in there or whether it was all intentional.

"We could always move on," Pedro said. "Move on from this. Move on from the barracks and start again elsewhere. We shouldn't be fighting one another. We should be fighting the creatures."

Ivan shook his head. "This is moving on, Pedro. We don't just fucking walk away from something good. We've got a chance here. I'm thinking long-term. We can bring the women in. Start the… the cycle of life once again."

Pedro's stomach sank. Ivan's eyes were bloodshot, frenzied like an angry dog. He'd lost it. He'd completely lost it. So there was nothing else he could possibly do. "If that's what you really want. But I'm sorry."

Ivan paused for a moment. "Sorry for what?"

Pedro let go of his nervous breath. "Now, Chloë."

In what seemed like the space of a second, Chloë lunged from her blanket and pressed the drugged cloth into Ivan's face. Ivan was so caught off-guard by Chloë that he left his gun lying free in his pocket. Pedro grabbed it and pointed it at Al and Dave in the back, who raised their guns at Pedro.

But they were too slow. Pedro fired at one. Then he fired at the other. He'd won them over. Planted the seeds of doubt over Ivan. They were good men, but he had to do this.

Ivan's arms were flailing. He tugged at Chloë's hair, pulling out a chunk and sending her flying towards the window of the vehicle as his strength seeped away. The drugged cloth slid down his face. Pedro aimed the gun at his head as Chloë held her back that had cracked against the window. "You did good, Chloë," Pedro said. "You did so good."

Pedro pressed the gun against the side of Ivan's head. His

eyes rolled up into his skull. He tried to focus on Pedro as his pupils dilated. He tried to speak, but nothing but foamy saliva dribbled out of his mouth.

"I'm sorry, Ivan. But you did this. You fucking did this, not me. Not me."

Ivan's jaw began to tremble. He started fitting. Snot dribbled from his nostrils as Pedro kept the shaky gun pressed up to his temple. Tears started to fall down Pedro's cheeks. "You did this. I'm sorry. I'm sorry."

Ivan's fitting came to a sudden halt. His eyes closed. He was unconscious.

Pedro lowered the gun and wiped his eyes.

"We did it, Pedro. Why are you sad?"

Pedro looked up at Chloë. A chunk of her hair was missing and she gripped hold of her shoulder, which had collided with the window. He smiled and finished wiping away his tears. "Come on," he said. "Let's get this finished with and get you back to your mum. Good girl. Come on."

Pedro lifted Chloë out of the vehicle. He took a final glance at Ivan's unconscious body. He'd be out for a good three to four hours. Purer than chloroform, army-grade shit.

"Mum!" Chloë waved at the window, wincing and lowering her arm. She grabbed her shoulder, but the smile didn't disappear from her face. "I did it, Mum. I did it."

Pedro stared up at the group. They were all gathered around the window. Claudia had her hands in front of her mouth, and she was crying. Anna held her. And Riley stood behind them. He nodded at Pedro.

Pedro nodded back at him. "Let's get you back inside. Come on."

Chloë and he walked towards the door. There was just one thing left now. One thing he didn't want to do, but one thing that had to happen.

Riley appeared at the door to meet them. Chloë grabbed hold of him. He held her, then half-smiled at Pedro.

"Whatever you do next," Pedro said, "I don't want to be a

part of it. I've done my bit." He kept his head down, handed Ivan's gun to Riley, and pushed past him.

Riley stared at the gun-mounted vehicle. Ivan's static body sat in the driver's seat. Ted's killer. The killer of so many. He had one last thing to do. Something he just needed to do. And then they could go.

"You go inside to your mum, now," Riley said. "And get that arm seen to with Anna, too."

Chloë skipped past Riley and disappeared into the house.

Riley took a few deep breaths in. Gripped Ivan's gun.

Then, he walked towards the gun-mounted vehicle. One final thing to do.

Chapter Forty-Eight

A SHIVER RAN ACROSS IVAN'S SKIN. His head stung. At first, his breathing was calm. He was waking up in bed. Something had happened, he wasn't sure what. But he was okay. He was holding this group together. The bodies — the frozen bodies — none of that had happened. They were okay. Life was good. Supplies were good. They were okay.

But then a sense of dread and realization thumped him in the stomach. He pulled open his eyes. He was in a room he recognized. He was shivering. It was so cold. He just wanted to be enveloped in a warm, tight jumper. Something to keep him from this cold. His breath frosted in front of him. What was going on?

"Welcome back."

The voice came from the doorway. He looked ahead. He recognized the silhouette. Riley.

"Wondered when you'd be joining us again."

Ivan tried to step up but something was stopping him. He

looked down — his wrists were tied with plastic ties to the arms of a chair. His feet were also tied up. He was stuck. Trapped.

Riley stepped towards him. "A part of me didn't want you to wake up again. A part of me wanted you to rot on the side of the road for the things you've done. The people you've killed. The people close to me that you've hurt."

Ivan tried to reply to Riley as he crouched opposite him but he was just too cold. His army uniform had been torn away from his body. He was wearing nothing but his boxer shorts. No wonder he was freezing.

Riley tapped the gun against the floor. Ivan's gun. And he was avoiding looking behind Ivan.

Ivan knew exactly why.

"I wanted to kill you. Make no mistake about it. I think you're lucky to be here. To have another chance." Riley stepped up.

"Pl—please," Ivan said. "I—I… Please."

Riley turned away from Ivan and walked back towards the freezer room door. As he got about half way between Ivan and the door, he reached into his pocket and dropped a pair of scissors onto the floor. "The difference between me and you is that I'm willing to give people a chance. Even after all the horrible, horrible things I found in this freezer—" Riley gestured to the piled-up bodies behind Ivan without looking at them. "Even after all those things, I was willing to let you and your people stay here. But we didn't want to be a part of it."

"Please," Ivan begged. His lips were chapped and dry. He wasn't sure how long he'd been unconscious. Probably a few hours. "I can change. I can change."

Riley leaned against the door and smiled. "You, on the other hand, didn't give people a chance. You just wanted things your way. All your way. And look how it's ended up. Pedro's leaving with our group. Your men are all dead. But hey — you've still got your beloved barracks, right?"

A tear dripped down Ivan's cheek. Soon, it would freeze against his skin. He had to get to the scissors. He had to get out of here.

Riley kicked the scissors in Ivan's direction. "We're leaving. We're going to start again, from scratch. I suggest you do the same. If you can reach those scissors and get yourself out of that chair, of course. I've made sure the freezer is extra-frosty today."

Ivan shook his head from side to side. "I was only trying—trying to do the—the right thing."

Riley shrugged. "Well, you failed. You killed my friend. My best friend. And you would have killed us all. Pedro told me about your plans for the women. Ironic, really, how your patronising little view of how weak or strong they were was your downfall in the end. Chloë did good."

Ivan shook his head from side to side. "Please. Please."

Riley reached for the door handle. "Well, better leave you to it. We've got work to do, and so have you." He started to close the door. "Good luck, Ivan. Not many people would give you a chance after the things you've done. I hope you come back from them, I really do. But take one step at a time, huh?"

"Please!"

Riley slammed the door shut. The room descended into darkness.

Ivan's heart raced. He dragged the feet of the chair forward. He could only just see the scissors up ahead of him as a dim beam of daylight peeked in through a window. He just had to get to the scissors. He just had to get out.

His chair tumbled forward. His forehead smacked against the hard, frozen ground. He bit into his tongue and swore. He couldn't move. He'd fallen forward with the chair on his back so he couldn't break free, no matter how much he turned from side to side.

And staring down at him with frozen eyes and half-eaten torsos, the bodies that he'd kept in here. The ones that the creatures had been feasting on. Intestines spilling out. Chunks missing out of necks. Faces he recognized. Reminders of what he'd done.

"Please!" Ivan shouted, as he shuffled his chair from side to side, desperate to get the frozen bodies out of his eye-line.

He shuffled, and he shuffled, and he shuffled, as another intensely cold shiver ran through his body.

Then, he closed his eyes, the images of what he'd done flickering in his head like a montage, and he let out the largest, loudest scream he could.

Riley bit his lip as he walked down the corridor away from the freezer room, as Ivan let out a huge scream. He'd given him a chance. A chance to live. That was more than most would give him for the things he'd done. He'd given him a choice. That's what separated him from Ivan.

He took a look inside Ivan's room as he passed. They'd removed the weapons and ammo he had stashed in there. There should enough to get by on for now. Not for forever. Nothing was forever anymore.

But they'd cross that hurdle when they came to it. They couldn't make the mistake of over-preparation. That's what Ivan had done when he'd killed his soldiers. The fear of running out of food gripped a hold of him, driving him to obsession. They couldn't become another Ivan. That's where they were different.

Pedro was waiting by the cracked window and destroyed front door as Riley walked out. There were bodies scattered around the canteen. Bodies they'd had to deal with. Creatures, dead for a second time. For a final time.

"You done?" Pedro asked.

Riley knew he didn't need to answer as Ivan screamed again. "Yeah. We should go. Got everything we need?"

Pedro turned to the gun-mounted vehicle. Anna, Claudia, and Chloë were sat in the back. All of them were holding weapons. Armed and ready for the next step. "Ammo for the mounted gun should we run into any trouble. Weapons for everyone. Enough food to get us by for now."

"Which is all we need to worry about," Riley said.

Pedro hesitated for a moment and nodded. "Right."

The pair of them walked towards the vehicle.

"You made the right call, bruv," Pedro said. He didn't look Riley in the eye, but it was the first time he'd acknowledged Riley's decision to leave Ivan in the freezer room. Alive. "You were saying all those days ago about the guilt. About the things you've done. Well, you've done the right thing. The tough thing, but the right thing." Pedro walked past Riley and climbed atop the gun-mounted vehicle, back into the position he had been in when Riley and the group first saw him by the railway.

Riley looked back at the barracks. The foundations were destroyed. Ivan's screams had stopped. In the courtyard, a few creatures that they had missed out staggered in the direction of the vehicle, dried blood crusted around their teeth. It was a shame things couldn't work out here, it really was. But the only way was forward. Ted and he had done the right thing leaving the flat to find his Grandma. They'd done the right thing running out of that restaurant as it burned to the ground. And they were doing the right thing now.

"You coming?" Anna called. She was smiling as she sat in the vehicle.

Riley took in a deep breath of air. "Yeah. I'm coming."

He walked over to the gun-mounted vehicle and climbed in to the driver's seat.

"Sure you don't want me to drive?" Claudia asked.

Riley gripped the steering wheel. He examined his hands. They weren't tingling. His heart was beating fairly fast, but nothing like it used to. "I'm good."

"Well, let's get out of here!" Pedro called.

Riley reversed the gun-mounted vehicle and turned it around, then drove in the direction of the barracks gates, past the creatures in the yard, past the half-mast Great Britain flag, away from the terraced houses, the *'Please Save Us'* lettering

completely washed off.
   Away to somewhere new.

Chapter Forty-Nine

"CLEAR."

THEY CREPT AROUND THE DOOR of the old wooden cabin beside the docks. The journey down here had been difficult at times, but they'd made it. No losses. No hitches. They'd pulled together, like they were going to have to keep on doing from this point forward. There was no room for individuals in survival.

"Hell yes. You take the left, I'll take the right."

Riley nodded at Pedro and crept into the cabin. The narrowboat was intact, sat on a wheeled carrier, undiscovered.

Well, relatively undiscovered.

Riley closed in on the creature that wandered around, disgruntled by the light that now shone into the cabin.

"One, two, three…"

Riley sunk the knife into the creature's head. Its brains spilled out of its temple and it fell to the floor. Pedro did the same to the creature he closed in on, wiping his knife once he had finished.

Pedro inspected the boat for a few seconds then pumped his fist. "All looking good. Just got to get her on water now. Anna, Claudia — all good out there?"

Claudia and Anna poked their heads around the door as they held their guns. They both stuck their thumbs up in approval.

"Good," Pedro said. "Come on, Riley. Better move this thing."

They scanned the area once more then attached the narrowboat carrier to the back of the gun-mounted vehicle. Pedro jumped into the front seat. "I'll get her on the water."

Riley nodded. He could smell the burning behind them. It would be ready soon. He turned around and he saw the smoke was still rising, thick and black. His stomach sank slightly. But at least they'd finally given them a civilized way to go. Finally, Ted and Elizabeth had been given the exit they deserved. No secrets. No lies. No brutality, not anymore.

"You handling that okay, Chloë?" Riley asked.

Chloë turned around from the burning bodies and nodded her head, a smile on her face. He could tell that she had been crying as she bid her sister a final farewell, but she was a tough kid. She was a survivor. All of them were.

Claudia jogged over to Chloë with the two urns that Pedro had retrieved from the barracks and started to scrape some of the ashes inside. They couldn't take all of their ashes, of course. But as long as they gave them some sort of memorial. Some sort of send-off. Ted used to go on about how he never wanted any fuss when he died because the last thing he wanted to do was depress everybody. He wanted something quick. Something different. And to be buried with his Xbox. Unfortunately, the last part was going to be tough, but a spare copy of *Call of Duty* from the barracks would have to suffice.

A large splash crashed against the surface of the water. Riley turned and saw that the narrowboat was on the docks. Pedro rushed out of the vehicle and checked the boat. He'd warned the group that getting the boat onto the water might not be so easy.

"All good?" Riley called.

Pedro looked around. He had a frown on his forehead. He shook his head.

Riley's stomach sank. "Fuck. Fuck."

And Pedro burst into laughter. "It's perfect. Perfect. We're good to go, bruv."

Anna shook her head. "Don't do that. Just… don't."

Riley smiled at her. She smiled back. Well, as close as Anna got to a smile anyway. He took it as a smile, which was near enough.

"I'll start moving things onto the boat. You… Yeah." Pedro tilted his head over at Claudia and Chloë. "Take as much time as you need."

Riley and Anna took another look around the docklands. The place was usually filled with boats. It was a large, rectangular area, lined with restaurants and pubs. A cinema and a McDonalds. A nice, family place. Fitting conclusion to their time in Preston.

"Will you miss it?" Anna asked.

"Miss what?"

Anna raised her arms. "This. Preston. Best city in Europe. Oh no, wait. Best bus station in Europe. Only—"

"—A better bus station got built in Turkey. Yeah, I've told people the great myth of the Preston bus station many a time, don't you worry."

"So will you miss it?"

Riley looked around. Seagulls flew over by the high-rise office blocks of BetterLives. "I dunno. I've always liked Preston, I guess. But I always fancied myself as a traveler, too. Maybe it always was going to take an apocalypse to get me off my arse and seeing the world. You?"

Anna shrugged. "Been looking for an excuse to get away from here for years. Let's hope the world stays shit for a good while yet. What about friends? Family?"

Riley thought about his mum and dad. Wondered how they'd be getting on at the other side of the Atlantic ocean. Wondered whether the rest of the world was coping any better or any worse. And then he looked around at Claudia and Chloë as they walked away from the fire holding an urn each. Looked at Pedro as he threw tins and weapons from the army vehicle into the narrowboat. "I guess you…"

"Don't you fucking dare say something cheesy like, 'you're my family now.' Just don't. Or you're staying here."

Riley laughed. Anna laughed with him.

"You guys ready?" Pedro called. He revved up the engine and the boat coughed up water.

Riley held his hand out to Anna. "Shall we?"

Anna cringed at his hand then took hold of it. "Such a living cliché, Riley. Such a living cliché."

The pair of them walked over to the narrowboat. Claudia and Chloë followed.

"What about the vehicle?" Anna asked. "Could come in handy some stage."

Pedro puffed out his lips. "Ahh, I'll miss her. Served us well. But I guess we leave her for somebody else to find. Hope they treat her well. We've got a new ride now. A ride with beds and a little kitchen area. That's what you kids say, eh? 'Ride'?" He winked at Chloë. "Right, ready or not, here we go."

The engine of the boat kicked to life. For a few painful seconds, it did not seem like it was going to move. But then, as Riley stared at the water, he saw that they were getting further and further away from the docks. Further and further away from land.

All of the group cheered and high-fived one another as the narrowboat sailed down the docks, away from the high-rise city buildings and towards the river. They passed creatures. Most didn't even noticed their quiet vehicle. Some staggered into the water and fell into the unknown. Riley pictured Ted here with them, asking one of his inquisitive little questions. *Do those creatures drown?* I guess they'd find out.

Claudia and Chloë held the urns in their hands as they got further away from land and towards the river. "You ready, Riley? Go on, Chloë. You give Riley that urn."

Riley smiled at Chloë as he took the urn containing Ted's ashes from her. He held it in his hands. It was lighter than he expected. Especially for Ted. He giggled to himself. Ted wouldn't like that one.

"Three, two, one…"

Claudia threw Elizabeth's ashes out to sea. Riley followed, throwing Ted's out. He smiled as he watched the dust hit the water. Ted always loved the cinema at Preston docks. Fitting that he got his send-off here.

"Goodbye, Ted," Riley said, as the boat crept out of the mouth of the docks and into the River Ribble. "Goodbye."

He took a few calming breaths then turned around to Anna.

"So. Where next?"

What Next, Indeed?

It really sucks finishing a series, right? Fear not — Riley's journey has only just begun. If you want to be notified as soon as Season Two of *Dead Days* launches in 2014, sign up at the following website. You will receive new release updates, exclusive newsletters, special discounts and plenty more:

http://ryancaseybooks.com/fanclub

DEAD DAYS: SEASON TWO COMING SPRING 2014

About The Author

Ryan Casey is the author of several novels, novellas and short stories. He writes in various genres, with thrillers, horror and sci-fi to his name, but all of his works are bound by dark suspense. He revels in exploring complex, troubled characters in difficult moral situations, and is a sucker for a plot twist. His work includes Dying Eyes, Killing Freedom, What We Saw, Dead Days, The Watching, Something in the Cellar and Silhouette.

Casey lives in the United Kingdom and enjoys American serial television, is a slave to Pitchfork's Best New Music section, and wastes far too much of his life playing Football Manager games.

He posts a weekly blog at RyanCaseyBooks.com, discussing writing, publishing, and whatever the hell else he feels like.

Twitter: @RyanCaseyBooks

Printed in Great Britain
by Amazon.co.uk, Ltd.,
Marston Gate.